*Posy: Book Three*

# Pack

*By Mary Ann Weir*

# Table of Contents

## 1: The Truth About Mom

*Posy*

After the ceremony, I conked out and didn't stir until I woke up the next morning in our big bed all alone.

*No Wyatt?* I pouted. *Where's my fifth star?*

Looking at the clock, I saw it was almost ten and freaked out. Never in my life had I slept so late!

Yawning, I went to my bathroom, took care of business, got a shower, and blow dried my hair. After I was dressed, I grabbed my comb and my flower hairpins and went searching for Ash.

My nose led me to the home office, where I found my mates clustered behind Mason's desk as he showed them something on his laptop. When I stepped inside, their heads lifted in unison and their wide eyes made me suspicious.

"What are you guys doing?" I asked.

"Planning something, obviously." Closing the lid to the computer, Mason folded his hands on top of it and raised an eyebrow. "Yes, it's a surprise. No, we won't tell you."

My mouth dropped open, but Wyatt cut me off before I could speak.

"Hi, Posy. You look pretty today." He came over and took my empty hand in his.

"Mmm. I missed waking up with you," I murmured.

"I figured you needed the rest." He smiled and pecked my lips. "Princess, what's going on with your hair?"

Ash loomed over us with a scowl, and I smiled up at him.

"I washed and dried it." I held out the comb and the card of hairpins, then pooched out my bottom lip. "Fix it, waffle?"

Smirking, he put his hands on my waist, picked me up, and sat me on top of Mason's desk. As he worked, I yawned again and patted my hand in front of my mouth.

"So cute," Cole said, and my cheeks turned pink.

"How's it going with planning Ty's party?" Jay asked as he leaned one shoulder against the wall and looked at me.

"The queen and I have a list of decorations I need to buy," I told him. "After I get them, you guys can help me put them up. I described the cake I wanted and Tristan ordered it. Emerson and Angelo are going to pick it up Thursday morning on their way over here. Crew is getting the balloons, Matthew is in charge of setting the speakers up poolside, and everyone knows I told Tyler to be here at noon on the dot, so they need to arrive before that."

"Sounds like you've got it all under control," Mason said.

"Well, except for a present. What did you guys get him?"

"We're still deciding," Wyatt told me. "We were going to get him one big gift from all of us instead of a bunch of smaller, separate ones. Unless you'd rather get him something from just you?"

"No, I'm good with a big group gift, but we're running out of time. We only have two days. What about a place of his own so he can move out of the orphanage?"

"He'll receive the property of his choice when he finds his mate," Mason informed me, "just as we gifted the other betas."

"Okay, then what about a car?" I suggested. "He could really use it, and I bet he gets self-conscious about having to borrow one or ask for rides all the time."

Their faces were blank as they stared at me, and I began to fidget.

"I mean, it doesn't have to be some expensive luxury car or anything—"

"It's a great idea, honey."

"Cutie is so smart!"

"Why didn't we think of that?"

"We need to consult you more often, sweetness."

And Mason nodded.

"I'll talk to Dad," Wyatt said with a grin. "In fact, why don't we go over to the garage now?"

"Garage?" I tilted my head and blinked up at him.

"Dad owns the Busted Knuckle. He specializes in restoring classic and vintage cars. Ty worked for him until he became Ash's beta. Dad probably has a car in mind, or will at least have an idea of what Ty would like."

"Okay, great! So which of you are going to the garage and which of you are coming with me to visit my brothers?"

The game of Rock-Paper-Scissors that followed was intense, although I wasn't sure if they were playing to see who got to come with me or who got to avoid my brothers.

#

The twins' house was a mess.

James let us in when Jayden and I knocked on the door and warned us that the place was in an uproar.

"Hi, Posy!" the twins chanted when we walked in. "Hi, Alpha Jayden!"

"Hi, sisters-in-law!" I called back, which made them giggle.

They paused long enough to give me a hug, then went right back to flying around, their mouths moving as fast as their hands as they threw things in the boxes and bags that were scattered everywhere.

"Sweetheart, we'll pay for a crew to move your stuff," Aiden laughed as he caught Keeley around her waist and reeled her in. "You only need the essentials for now."

"And there's no rush." James took Callie's hands in his, then leaned down to peck her lips. "We can stay another day if we need to."

"No, it's not a good idea to leave the pack in your gamma and delta's hands longer than necessary." She shook her head. "It needs its alpha and beta right now."

"Okay, okay," James laughed, something I hadn't seen or heard in years. "But don't try to pack the whole house today, love. Like Aiden said, we'll hire movers, and we can buy you whatever you want once we're back at Green River."

"We don't need to waste the pack's money," she disagreed. "We have everything we need, right, Keeley?"

"Right," Keeley giggled.

*Wow. Callie's stepping into the luna role so naturally*, Jayden linked me with a smile.

*I see that. They all look so happy!* I turned to him. *And I'm happy that you came with me, even if it was because you lost at Rock-Paper-Scissors. You're much more open-minded about my brothers than the others. Except for maybe Ash. And possibly Mason.*

*I deliberately lost.*

*What?* My eyes widened as my mouth dropped open. My highly competitive mate lost at something *on purpose*?

*Yeah, so that I could come with you.*

*How do you deliberately lose Rock—*

*That's my secret.* He took my fingers in his hand and raised them to kiss my knuckles. *I wanted to escort you, my lady.*

"Aw! You two are so cute!" Aiden cooed as he released Keeley to let her go back to packing. "I'm so glad for you, Posy."

"I'm glad for both of you, too," I giggled. "I knew finding your mates would do you good."

"You were right, baby sister." James came closer. "Come with us to the kitchen for a minute. We have something for you."

"Oh?" Curious, I tilted my head.

"As we were tearing down the alpha house, we found some items Mom hid to save for us," he explained as Jayden and I followed him to the kitchen. "It's a miracle Father didn't find and destroy them."

"Whoa! What kinds of things?" I asked, threading my fingers through Jayden's.

"She made each of us a photo album," Aiden said as he came into the kitchen, too. "It has pictures of her, us as kids, and her family that we were never allowed to meet. Some other people, too."

"I always thought she didn't have any family." In my shock, I squeezed Jayden's hand and he gently squeezed back.

"That's what Father wanted us to think," James muttered darkly. "We're having a reunion with Mom's family in August. You should come with your mates."

"I'd like that. Is it at Green River?"

Now I was bursting with curiosity. Did I have aunts and uncles and cousins? Did I have grandparents?

"No, Mom's dad, our grandfather, was the alpha of the Crystal Caverns pack. His grandson, our cousin, is now the alpha, and Mom's family still lives there."

"Crystal Caverns?" Jayden eyebrows flew up in surprise. "Alpha Liam Swift?"

"Do you know him?" I asked right as James answered, "Yes."

"We helped him out with an issue three months ago," Jayden said.

His beautiful dragon eyes grew sad and his brow wrinkled up. At the same time, Quartz growled quietly, and I knew there was more to the story.

*Three months ago? Everett Breckenridge die three months ago,* Lark reminded me. *You think it happen at Crystal Caves?*

*Crystal* Caverns, I corrected. *I don't know, but we'll find out, just not when there's a risk of setting Quartz off.*

*Yes, yes, no ask when my Q around,* she agreed solemnly.

"Well, anyway," Aiden continued, "Mom left us a letter, too. After reading it, a lot of things make sense."

"Did you bring my letter? Or was it one letter to all of us?"

"One letter, and yes, we brought it." James handed me a white gift box. "This is your photo album. It's the exact same as ours. Somehow, she managed to go behind Father's back and get it professionally bound. The letter is in the box, too. Aiden and I made photocopies for our albums, so you can keep the original."

"Posy, be sure you want to know the truth," Aiden cautioned me. "You have every right to read that letter, but you might wish you didn't once you find out what really happened. You know the old saying that ignorance is bliss, right?"

Could the truth be that bad? Did I want to know? Or should I let it stay in the past?

I met Jayden's eyes as I thought about my brother's words.

*It's whatever you want, sweetness. I will support you in any decision you make.*

"James, Aiden, do you regret reading it?" I asked them.

"No, but it affects us differently than it does you," James said. "Just remember one thing, Posy. You have always been, and will always be, our baby sister."

I took the lid off the box to reveal lined paper resting on top of a hardcover book beautifully bound in celery green linen.

Picking it up with trembling fingers, my eyes ran over the letter, greedy to see what secrets my mother had to share, then pouted in disappointment.

"I can't read this kind of English." I dropped my hands to my lap, still clutching the paper.

"Baby sister, what do you mean?" Aiden laughed. "This kind of English?"

"Curved if. Or something like that. Emerson is going to teach Ty and me, but we haven't started lessons yet. He got busy with his mate and little brother."

"Ha ha ha, you mean *cursive*," Aiden laughed again and the other two chuckled.

"I'll read it to you if you'd like, sweetness," Jayden offered. "If you don't mind me knowing what it says."

"Of course I don't." I grinned at him and handed him the paper. "I'll tell all of you, anyway."

"Baby sister, we're going to give you some privacy while you read it," James told me. "And go help those two darling mates of ours not lose their minds. Is that okay?"

"Yes, thank you." I nodded.

He and Aiden hesitated for a second, then nodded back and left.

*They wanted you to hug them*, Quartz sneered.

*I know, my love.* I made sure the smile I gave him was full of dimples. *Q, when we get home, do you think you could convince your brothers to join us for a snuggle?*

*Convince them?* he smirked. *I'd have to fight them* not *to.*

"Ahem, now that you two have your date planned," Jayden interrupted with an eye roll, "do you still want me to read this letter now? We can always save it for later, sweetness."

"No, my dragon." I sobered up and lifted my chin. "I'm ready now. I want to know the truth."

#

*Jayden*

I cleared my throat before I began to read.
*Dear children,*

9

*If you are reading this, I died before I could explain anything to you, and for that I am sorry. A sad story poorly told on notebook paper will have to be explanation enough now.*

*Kendall Briggs was not my Goddess-given mate. We met at an alpha conference when I tagged along with my father, William Swift. At thirty, I was one of the oldest unmated females there, and Kendall the oldest unmated male at thirty-four. We chatted and found some common ground we thought we could build on, so we made an arrangement. We would be chosen mates with the understanding that we'd separate amicably if ever one of us found our true mate.*

"What's amicably mean?" Posy asked.

"Like friends."

"Since he wasn't her true mate, that's why he could hurt her, isn't it?" she whispered.

"Yes. I'm so sorry, Posy."

She sniffled a bit, but nodded her head for me to go on.

*Kendall did not stand by that agreement. When James was four and Aiden three, emissaries from the king arrived at Green River, and among them was my true mate. Logan Everleigh wasn't an alpha or a beta, not a gamma or even a delta. He was a regular wolf, as he liked to call himself, but to me, he was everything I ever wanted in a mate.*

"I bet Father wasn't pleased when she told him," Posy said. "What is an e-missionary?"

"An emissary is a representative," I explained. "Like we are when King Julian sends us somewhere."

"Thank you. Keep reading, please."

*When the emissaries left to return to the royal pack, I went with my mate and brought you boys along. I should have known then that Kendall was plotting something. If I hadn't been blinded by bliss, I would have realized that he'd never let his heirs leave Green River.*

*For three months, my mate and I lived in happiness and peace, visiting often with my family. Every day shone brighter, and I dared to dream we had the rest of our lives to spend together as a happy family. Logan loved you both, James and Aiden, as if you were his own sons. Posy, you would have been the apple of his eye, his little princess, if only he had lived to know you.*

"Oh!" she let out a hurt little sound. "I could have had a real father. I could have known what it's like to have a dad."

"Come here, baby."

Laying the letter on the counter, I wrapped my arms around her waist and cuddled her into me. She wiped her tears on my t-shirt and sniffed, then asked me to keep reading.

"Are you sure?" I whispered in her ear.

10

"I'm sure."

Against my better judgment, but knowing it was her right as Aiden had said, I picked up the letter and read, keeping her tucked into my side.

*Unfortunately, Kendall destroyed everything. Before I was even sure that Posy slept under my heart, Kendall found us and killed Logan. He killed my mate in front of my eyes while James and Aiden were at school. He reported to King Magnus that he'd found the man who'd 'kidnapped' us, but was too late to save me from Logan's 'madness.' He faked my death so that my family wouldn't know to save me, then spun a tale for his pack to think I'd been taken by rogues.*

*In his ignorance of the truth, the king praised Kendall for his unrelenting dedication to finding us and offered him compensation for the 'atrocious crimes' committed by a member of the royal pack.*

*How ironic that Kendall was paid handsomely for killing my innocent mate and dragging us all back to Green River - or should I say, dragging us back to hell?*

"What's atrocious mean?" Posy asked. "And ironic?"

"Atrocious means bad. Really bad. Like, *super* really bad. Ironic means the opposite of what you expect would happen."

"My mom knew some big words," she mumbled, fiddling with her fingers. "Even if this wasn't written in cursive, I would have struggled to read it."

"I can help you with improving your vocabulary, if you want. It wouldn't be a problem," I told her gently. "We can read together."

"And visit the alpha library!" Her eyes lit up, which I was happy to see because they looked so sad and dim just a second before.

"Yep. Did Tyler tell you about it? He's the only other one who really goes there."

"Yeah. At the ice pop party. Will you keep reading the letter now, please?"

"Of course."

Call me right or wrong, I refused to read the next few sentences to our girl. I'd tell her eventually, but for now, she didn't need to know some of this. It would only hurt her more and give her nightmares, so I skipped to the next paragraph.

*I don't know how much more my body can stand. I am only sorry to leave you behind, darlings. I'd stay and shield you until he beats the last breath from my body if I could, but I fear the sickness will end me before he can.*

*By now, I pray that you are free from the monster known as Kendall Briggs. If you are not, keep trying, my darlings. Try and try until you escape this wretched hell. If you cross the borders of his territory, head for my father's pack, Crystal Caverns. He and my family will protect you.*

"Ah!" Posy interrupted. "So *that's* how James knew who her family was."

I nodded, then finished reading the last bit of the letter.

*My loves, I am sorrier than words can say that I ruined your lives and caused you such suffering at the hands of that monster. I pray he meets an appropriate end for his atrocious crimes. Learn from your mother's mistakes, children, and wait for your true mate no matter how long it takes. It may be painful or embarrassing at times, but trust in the Goddess and await her gift.*

*I hope that all three of you know how very much I love you. May your futures be as bright or brighter than the one I dreamed for each of you.*

*Your loving mother*

"My brothers were right," Posy murmured. "This explains so much. I'm so sad for my mom. She didn't deserve what happened. What Father— No, I'm not going to call him that anymore. I'm going to just say Alpha Briggs. What *Alpha Briggs* did is truly atrocious, just as my mom said."

*At least Kendall Briggs met an appropriate end*, Quartz rumbled. *I find a lot of comfort in that.*

*An end* you *helped give him*, I snorted.

*Hence my comfort*, he said smugly.

"Oh! Do you think I might use my dad's last name instead of Briggs? It's my real last name, isn't it?"

"It is," I told her. "Posy Anne Everleigh. Beautiful, just like you, sweetness. I see no reason why you can't use it if you'd like to."

"Do you think there are any of my dad's family left in the royal pack?" Posy pressed tighter against me and squeezed my waist in a tight hug, and I squeezed her back.

If it pleased her, I'd go through the entire royal pack roster and interview every member of the older generation to find her father's family.

"We'll find out," I promised.

"Of course, they all think he was crazy and kidnapped and killed Alpha Briggs' mate. They don't even know I exist. Maybe I shouldn't try to find out."

"Baby, bringing the truth to light would clear the mud from your dad's name, and maybe bring closure to his family. It's your decision, as always, and nothing needs to be decided today. Take your time and think it over, all right, sweetness?"

"All right." She stretched up and kissed my chin. It was as high as she could reach. "I love you, my dragon. Thank you for coming with me today."

"Oh, Posy. My sweet girl." I kissed her forehead. "I'd lose Rock-Paper-Scissors for you anytime."

## 2: A Day in the Life

*Quartz*

"You guys are hot!" Posy giggled.

She'd finally managed to swim up from the bottom of the puppy pile, gasping for breath and sweating a little.

*Thanks, mate. You are, too. Very sexy,* Granite teased her, rubbing the top of his head on her knee.

"That's not what I meant and you know it," she scolded him with a grin. "Cuddling my wolves with all this fur is making me overheat. I mean, it's July! Didn't you guys shed any of this?"

*Of course we did. This is our summer coat.* Topaz rolled onto his back and squirmed around until she rubbed his chest. *We get fluffier in winter! Much, much fluffier!*

"I can't wait," she laughed.

*Mate like fluff?* Sid asked and shyly covered his eyes with one paw when she looked at him.

"Oh, yes." She gave him a gentle smile and booped his nose. "I love fluff."

*Our boys usually don't let us shift in the house because we shed everywhere,* Garnet told her. *They are being very generous tonight.*

"Aw, I'll vacuum it up later."

*Uh-oh,* Garnet and I said at once.

The three pups untangled themselves and sprang to their paws.

*Vacuum?!* they shouted in unison, their tails lashing back and forth in a frenzy and their tongues lolling.

Posy turned to Garnet and me where we lay at her back, then quirked an eyebrow in question.

*Go get it, if you want to know,* I suggested with a wink.

"Are you setting me up for something good or something bad?" she demanded as she got to her feet.

*Good,* Garnet said when I would have teased her a little bit.

Shrugging, she disappeared for a few minutes while the excited pups sat in a row in front of us. Garnet and I rolled our eyes. Sure, we liked the vacuum, too, but we weren't going to make fools of ourselves over it.

She came back with it and plugged it in, then stood there with her hands on her hips.

"Okay. Now what?"

*Suck me! Suck me!* Granite demanded.

Posy froze in shock, her eyes wide and her face as red as fire.

14

*Suck me! Suck me!* the other two pups joined the chant, and they all began to jump around.

Three werewolves of several hundred pounds each bouncing around a living room had a predictable outcome. Frames fell off the walls and a lamp tipped over before Posy got them to settle down.

"I think you mean you want me to run the vacuum cleaner over you?" she asked in a hesitant tone.

*Yes, yes, yes,* they yipped, looking like they wanted to start hopping around again, but her stern expression froze them in place.

*Put the black thingy on the scrunch-scrunch hose and suck us,* Topaz instructed.

Fortunately, our girl was smart and caught on quickly. In a minute, she had the pet grooming attachment hooked up and the vacuum turned on.

"Who's first?" she asked with a bright smile.

After Garnet and I got her back on her feet and scolded the pups for tackling her, Garnet told them that we'd go by age order, youngest to oldest this time.

Cackling, Granite laid down in front of her, and Posy began to run the 'black thingy' all over his fur. He sighed in pure bliss, making our girl giggle.

*We might have to set a time limit,* Garnet said. *Five minutes per wolf or you'll be here all night.*

*Five minutes!* Topaz and Sid whined.

"Ten minutes each sounds perfect to me," Posy said.

*That's almost an hour of vacuuming wolves,* I told her.

"I can do it. It's fun!"

*You're going to have to empty the canister after each of us then. It'll fill up fast.*

"Not a problem." She ran the groomer over Granite's cheek, making his eyes roll back in his head. "But I want one thing in return for this special treat, boys."

*Anything!* the pups promised in unison.

"Say, 'Groom me,' from now on, okay?" Her cheeks flushed cherry red again as she muttered, "I almost had a heart attack when you said to suck you."

In their innocence, the pups agreed readily, eager to please her, while Garnet and I shared a very adult snicker.

#

*Posy*

On Wednesday, the boys were off to work as soon as we finished breakfast. They wanted to take care of as much as they could today so that they'd be free all day for Tyler's birthday tomorrow.

After goodbye hugs and kisses, I decided to make sure I had all the food taken care of for the party. Mom and Dad were bringing hamburgers and hot dogs to grill, Mama and Papa were in charge of side dishes, and I was picking up buns and drinks. As soon as I wrote out my list, I'd find someone to run me into town and get this job done.

A knock at the door had me leaving the kitchen to look out the front window. Two filthy dirt bikes were parked at the end of the walk, and I could see muddy footprints coming all the way up onto the porch. *Argh! Not something else to clean!*

My mates did a great job of picking up after themselves and surface cleaning, for which I was grateful, but scrubbing was not on their radar. I found myself itching to do a deep clean of the whole house, but it was so large - and so many people came and went all the time - that I was really considering asking my mates if they'd hire a cleaning crew to come once a week and help me.

*They* are *billionaires, after all,* I muttered to myself, *and surely some wolf in the pack can use the extra bucks.*

Since I smelled familiar family wolves, I opened the front door to reveal Archer Barlow and Wayne Black standing on my porch, wearing nothing but swim trunks and covered in mud from their shoulders down.

"Hey, luna!" they said in unison and waved with the hands not holding mud-splattered helmets.

I had to look up to meet their eyes. Even at age fifteen, they towered over me, Wayne by six inches and Archer by eight, and I frowned.

Being a runt, I was used to always being the shortest person, but that didn't mean I had to like it.

"Hi, guys. I'm afraid your brothers aren't here right now."

"We know," Archer said.

"Mom sent us over to help you get ready for tomorrow," Wayne explained.

"I appreciate that," I said, "but why do you both look like mud puppies?"

"Ha ha ha!" Wayne giggled. "Hear that, bro? Mud *puppies!* Ha ha ha! You're funny, big sister!"

"We, uh, took a little detour on the way over," Archer snickered.

"Don't worry. We'll use the garden hose and wash the bikes and ourselves down." Smiling widely, Wayne reached out to pat my shoulder, but I pulled back before he could get mud on me. "Oops! Sorry. Anyway, you think of some jobs for us to do and we'll do them, okay?"

16

"Well, for starters, can you rinse the walk and porch off after you hose yourselves down?" I returned his smile with a dimpled one of my own.

"Sure thing! Playing with water is *fun!*"

"Although playing with fire is funner," Archer snickered again.

*Oh, Goddess, it mini Wyatt and mini Ash,* Lark marveled, *but no mini Jayden to balance out trouble!*

"Come around to the backyard when you're done," I said with a laugh, "and you can help me figure out what I need to do."

Leaving them to it, I went back inside the house to finish up my list. I'd picked up my pencil again when a brilliant idea struck me.

*A mini Jayden, huh? Hmm.*

I tapped my pencil on my chin a few times as I debated, then finally decided to just do it.

*Oh, Emerson,* I linked. *Are you busy today?*

#

*Angelo*

I was worried about Thoreau.

He'd been with us for seven days now and still could not sense his wolf. We fed him well and made sure he had proper sleep, I healed his bruises and wounds, and the *streghe* (witches) gave him antidotes to the wolfsbane, but the boy's wolf did not respond.

*I think we all know the truth, but don't want to admit it,* I thought to myself as I watched Emerson.

He was coaxing Reau to take a second drink of the potion my sister had brewed and sent over. The first dose should have neutralized the aconite he'd been shot full of, and it hadn't. Reau despised the taste and texture of the potion - not that I blamed him; it was nasty stuff - and was working himself into an epic meltdown.

"Em, if he drinks any more of that, it'll make him sick," I said in a gentle tone, not wanting to stress my mate out any more than he already was. "It's not doing anything, anyway."

Looking as helpless as I felt, my love set down the glass and pulled Reau in for a tight hug, holding him against his chest until the boy stopped crying.

"Sorry, Reau," he muttered into his baby brother's thick curls. "Why don't you go see what Leo's doing?"

Reau nodded and leaped to his feet after Emerson released him.

"Remember to knock first if his bedroom door's closed," I called as the boy raced out of the living room.

17

" 'kay, Gelo!" he shouted, making me shake my head with a smile.

The day we brought Reau home, Emerson had explained to both me and Leo how the boy was born with a condition that affected his social and emotional development. Reau could learn things in school as well as any kid, but he acted much younger than others his age.

He also said Reau hated loud noises, even fun ones like the fireworks we tried to watch on the Fourth, but he could get loud himself if he was happy or excited.

We also discovered that he got scared and panicked easily. Em said he hadn't been like that before, and we knew it was an effect of his parents' abuse. We hadn't been able to get many details out of Reau yet, but his physical condition told a lot of the story.

The poor kid's mental health was just as roached. He kept asking when we were going to make him go back in his cage, which broke our hearts. How often did they lock him in that dog crate?

Finally, two days ago, I took him outside and we set fire to the thing. He was more fascinated watching the flames than celebrating the destruction of his torture chamber.

I wasn't sure he fully understood the gesture, but he hadn't asked about his crate since then.

Now, with a heavy sigh, Em plunked down on the couch next to me, rested his elbows on his knees, and dropped his head in his hands.

"What do we do now?" he mumbled.

Clamping my hands on his shoulders, I kneaded the tense muscles.

"*Orsacchiotto* (teddy bear), do you remember the luna telling us she'd been given wolfsbane several times? Let's take Reau over for a visit. She's the resident expert in this, so maybe she knows or sees something we don't."

His head shot up and he looked at me with a hopeful smile.

"Okay. We—"

Then his eyes fogged over, and I figured he was about to be called out somewhere, which was fine. Our plan could get shelved until tomorrow, when we were going over to the alpha house anyway for Beta Tyler's birthday party.

"She's actually asking if we can come over. She wants Reau to meet the alphas' younger brothers, and needs one of us to take her into town for some supplies."

"See? The Goddess' hand at work." I grinned at him. "We'll take Leo, too. He needs to get out of the house a bit."

"Good idea."

*Thoreau Jones*

I jumped out of Bubba's big car and looked around. My little eye spied a pair of bikes parked at the top of the lot, and I ran to them.

"Reau! Don't touch!" Bubba called.

I just wanted to look. To show him that, I shoved my hands in my pockets as I walked around the two bikes.

They looked like fun! I wondered if they went fast.

"Hey, man. Who are you?"

I didn't know that voice, and I spun around to see who it was. We were here to see the pretty luna, not meet new people. My little eye spied two big boys. They were only wearing swim trunks and were all wet. For some reason, my insides fluttered as I watched the water run down the interesting bumps and lines of their chests and bellies.

*Why are there butterflies in my tummy? If I fart, will they go away?*

"You like our bikes?" asked Mr. Blond, walking up to me.

He was taller than me, which was scary, and I hunched my shoulders.

"I didn't touch!" I shouted.

"Okay?" Mr. Blond looked at Mr. Black-hair for a second, then back at me. "You want to go for a ride?"

With round eyes and a big grin, I forgot my fear and nodded my head really fast.

"I think that's a yes, Arch," laughed Mr. Blond. He came closer and held out his hand. "I'm Wayne Black."

"Can I take my hand out of my pocket?" I asked.

"Why do you need to ask?" Wayne Black tilted his head as he frowned at me.

"Bubba said not to touch. I put my hands in my pockets so he can see I'm not touching."

Frustration made me frown. Explaining took too much time, but Bubba said to be nice so people like me, and I wanted the boy to like me.

*If he likes me, he will take me for a ride. If I make him sad or mad, he will hurt me and not take me for a ride.*

"Oh. Yeah, sure." Wayne Black said. "That way, you can shake my hand."

I did, then looked at Mr. Black-hair. A giggle slipped out before I could stop it and I put my hand over my mouth.

"What's funny?" Wayne Black asked.

"You're Wayne *Black* and he's Mr. *Black*-hair." I giggled again behind my hand.

19

"I'm Archer Barlow." He held his hand out, too, and I shook it.

"What's your name?" Wayne Black asked.

"Thoreau Ezra Jones, but my nicky name is Reau."

"Sweet. Good to meet you, Reau." Wayne Black grinned. "I don't have a 'nicky name,' but you can call Archer Arch if you want."

"Arch." I stared at him as he stared back at me. "You are quiet, but you have pretty green eyes. I love them!"

He frowned, but Wayne Black laughed so hard that his face turned red.

"What is Wayne Black laughing at, Arch?" I asked with a tiny frown of concern.

"Just call him Wayne," Bubba said, coming up behind me. "You don't have to say his last name every time. He is one of Alpha Wyatt's younger brothers, and Arch is one of Alpha Cole's younger brothers. They're both your age."

"Wayne and Arch, I am Beta Emerson Jones' younger and only brother. Gelo is my brother-in-law, and Leo is our friend." I nodded my head, proud of myself for getting everything straight.

"Good job, Reau." Bubba patted the top of my head, and I looked up at him with a happy grin. "Are you okay hanging out with these guys for a while? Angelo, Leo and I want to talk to the luna for a bit."

"We got you, Beta," Wayne said. "He wants to go for a ride on the bike, anyway."

"He doesn't have any safety gear," Bubba started to say, but Gelo talked over him.

"He'll be fine, Em. Boys, don't take him far. Reau, have you ever been on a bike?"

"A bicycle!" I crowed. "Bubba taught me how!"

"A dirt bike is a little different, but we're experts, so you're in good hands," Wayne said.

I looked down at my hands, then his. Nobody's hands were on me.

Bubba leaned down and whispered in my ear.

"He means you'll be safe to learn with them because they know what they're doing."

I nodded, even though I thought it was a silly thing to say.

"All right, then." Wayne grinned, showing nice, white teeth. "We'll just go up and down the driveway. Nothing to jump, but you can really open 'er up since our brothers got it paved."

"Don't go too fast," Bubba told them. "And no wheelies!"

Leo laughed, but Gelo rolled his eyes and grabbed Bubba's elbow.

"Come on, worrywart," he said.

He pulled Bubba toward the front porch and had to put a lot of effort into it. Bubba was a big, big man.

"But they don't know how he is," I heard Bubba hiss.

"Then let them find out!" Gelo hissed back.

Leo followed them, shaking his head with a funny half-smile.

"Bye, Leo!" I called.

"Bye, Reau. Have fun."

My eyes lit up. I had been living with my brother for a week now and learned what 'fun' was.

I liked fun.

"All right, Reau." Arch handed me a helmet. "Put this on and I'll take you first."

"Hey!" Wayne frowned. "Why you first?"

"Because I'm older—"

"By seven weeks!"

"And more responsible."

"More responsible? You forgot to feed your goldfish and it died. How is that responsible?"

"Fish killer!" I yelled and pointed at Arch, shocked to my core. How could you starve an animal to death?

"I was *five*," Arch growled.

As he glared at Wayne, his wolf gleamed in his pretty green eyes, and I caught my breath. Tears made my throat close up, and I rammed the helmet on my head before they saw I was crying.

*Miss you, Tanner. Wish you would come back. Everything is scary without you here.*

21

## 3: Sad But True

*Emerson*

We ended up calling the king.

Well, little luna bunny did. She didn't even hesitate to disturb him, whereas I was freaking out.

While we waited for his arrival, she and Angelo traded looks, and I could see what they were thinking.

"Em, I know you don't want to hear it," she began, but I cut her off.

"Don't say it," I pleaded.

"You have to face the truth, *orsacchiotto* (teddy bear)," Angelo whispered in my ear, his arm around my waist. "The sooner you do, the sooner we can find ways to help Reau cope."

I nodded, my eyes stinging. I didn't want to accept it, but I had to.

Reau's wolf wasn't asleep.

He was dead.

My parents had killed him with an overdose of wolfsbane.

Luna bunny only called King Julian over here to officially confirm it.

He did, too. We managed to get Reau away from the dirt bikes long enough for the king to look inside him for any evidence that Tanner survived.

"Thanks, Reau." King Julian ran a hand through my baby brother's curls. "You can go back to playing now if you want."

*Say, Thank you, your majesty,* I coached Reau through the link.

"Thank you, your majesty." He gave the king an adorable smile that melted my heart, and I *dreaded* having to tell him the truth later.

"Leo, can you go out with him, please?" asked my luna bunny. "I'm not sure how much I trust three teens with two dirt bikes and a mile-long driveway."

"Sure thing." Leo smiled and draped an arm around Reau's shoulders.

As soon as they left, she broke down in tears, and I wasn't far behind. Angelo wrapped me up in a hug, and the king did the same with luna. The alphas and other betas picked up on her distress and linked me, frantic to know what was wrong. I told them about Reau's wolf before Angelo joined in and told them all to link him instead of me for the moment.

*By the moon, I don't know what I would do if he wasn't here right now!*

"I'm sorry," I muttered into his neck as I tried to stop the flood of tears staining his shirt.

"Oh, my darling, let out the pain," he whispered and hugged me tighter.

"That is freaking heartbreaking," I heard King Julian mutter over luna's sobbing. "I bet his wolf was one of the mature ones, too, and could balance Reau's child-like nature. "

"I don't know. I never met Tanner," I said. "My dad kicked me out before Reau's twelfth birthday."

A low rumble vibrated out of King Julian's chest as Onyx stirred.

"Yeah, I know, Nyx. Third time in less than a month I've gotten news of an alpha abusing a pack member, and this is the second case of it being family. I need to send out undercover investigators again."

I was suddenly glad Leo had left the room. The guilt he carried crippled him most days. Even something as small as the king's comment would have set back his recovery.

*Luna bunny knew Leo was uncomfy with the king,* Cove murmured. *She sent him away on purpose.*

*Sounds like our compassionate little sister,* I agreed with a halfhearted smile, too gutted at the moment for anything more.

Finally getting myself under control, I wiped my eyes with my t-shirt and looked around for a tissue. Angelo reached in his back pocket, pulled out a handkerchief, and handed it to me. I blew my nose and sent him a wave of love, which he immediately reciprocated.

I noticed luna was still huddled next to the king and felt guilty. It was my job as her beta to comfort and help her in any way I could.

*The mighty king of werewolves himself is comforting your luna,* Angelo linked me, picking up on my feelings through our mate bond. *She understands, orsacchiotto* (teddy bear). *Don't add the weight of unwarranted guilt to your grief.*

"I might have a suggestion to help Reau. I need to talk to some people first." King Julian kept his arm around luna's shoulders as her crying tapered off to a few sniffles. "In the meantime, Gelo, see if one of your witches will look into Reau's memories. I doubt he'll be able to articulate himself well enough for me to get a clear picture of what happened at Gray Shadows."

"I think Beatrix would be best for that," Angelo told him. "Sara can be obnoxiously blunt, and I don't think Reau would respond well to her. Ariel and Maria would do it with more kindness, but they get flighty and off-task so easily, and Reau might not have the patience for them."

"Let him enjoy the party tomorrow and see if Beatrix will do it on Friday. I want to know the details as soon as possible." King Julian let out a heavy sigh. "Depending on what she discovers, Gray Shadows also might be in need of a new alpha."

After the king departed, luna bunny asked Angelo if he'd take her into town for some things. I was surprised she asked him and not me - or even Leo, although he was still too fragile to trust in public with humans. She was afraid of Angelo, which is why we'd been keeping our distance, yet here she was asking to spend time alone with him.

*She misses us,* my smart wolf said. *She wants to get over her fear of him because she misses us.*

Thinking about it, I realized Cove was right.

*Such a brave luna we have,* I told him.

*Our brave little bunny luna,* he agreed.

#

*Angelo*

I didn't know what to do to make myself less scary to the luna, but I needed to figure it out.

My mate missed her and she missed him, and I couldn't be the reason why they kept their distance. Besides, out of all her betas, Luna Posy trusted Emerson and Tyler the most, and Emerson and Thoreau needed their luna right now.

*Emerson is so much scarier looking than I am, but she sees right past that to the orsacchiotto* (teddy bear) *inside.*

I was a little hurt that she couldn't do the same with me. I raised four little girls who never once looked at me with fear. Derision, anger, frustration, irritation in their rebellious teenage years, sure, but never fear.

*She's known him longer than me, that's all,* I tried to console myself. *She'll get used to me with enough time.*

Or maybe she heard too many grisly stories of everything I'd hunted down and killed, and that scared her so much that she wanted nothing to do with me.

*But Emerson's killed before, too. Hard to find a shifter, let alone a* beta, *who hasn't.*

Then again, he only ever killed in defense of his pack whereas I was paid to hunt my prey.

*She likes Leo well enough, even though she knows how much blood is on his hands!*

24

She was also quite able - more than any of us, even Julian - to separate Leo from the demon. I figured she had a lot of practice with that from dealing with Alpha Jayden and Quartz, who were the ultimate example of two opposite souls housed in one body.

*And this is how it goes when you don't have an animal spirit*, I sighed. *You argue with yourself and get nowhere.*

"You look a little like him," she whispered.

Whipping my eyes off the road, I stared at her profile as she looked at her knees. Her small body trembled a bit, and her fingers were tightly clasped in her lap.

"Alpha Briggs," she clarified. "You look enough like him to scare me. Exact same color of hair, same height, same build. Even your faces are similar. When you're not clean-shaven, I have to make myself look into your eyes to see that it's you and not *him*."

I'd learned a little about her past and all I could say was Kendall Briggs had been lucky to never cross my path. His end would have been much more tortuous than a quick and simple beheading. How could anyone do such things to someone so sweet and innocent?

It was a question I asked myself often when I hunted monsters, although I knew the answer. Such vulnerability drew them like moths to a flame and made them want to stamp it out instead of nurture and protect it.

That's what made them monsters.

"I'm sorry," she continued when I stayed silent. "I don't mean to hurt your feelings, and you can't help the way you look. Not that you should or would want to. You're very handsome, if you didn't know that. I mean, it's okay to say that, right? Even though I'm not a boy, can I still tell you that you're handsome, or is that not appropriate? Sorry, but I never knew anyone with the gay before Emerson and now you, and I don't want to offend you."

*What is she talking about?* I linked Emerson as she rambled on.

*The alphas were going to explain what gay means to her*, he sighed, *but it appears they haven't gotten around to it yet. Just go with it.*

"*Piccola coniglio* (little bunny)," I interrupted her, "anyone can tell anyone else that they're handsome or beautiful, and thank you. You're a cutie, too. I'm sorry I remind you of that *figlio di puttana* (son of a bitch). I can't do anything about my height or build, but I could change my hair. Um, maybe I could dye it? I can't cut it, though, because Emerson likes to play with it."

She giggled, and the knot of tension in my chest loosened.

"I can't leave my mates' hair alone, either," she admitted. "Especially Wyatt and Ash. I could spend hours petting them."

25

"It must be a wolf thing, yeah? Bird shifters don't really mess with each other's hair, at least not so much to be noticeable, whereas Em always has his fingers in my hair."

"I don't have much experience outside of a wolf pack, so maybe there are other shifters like that. Ha. Maybe even humans do it."

"Maybe." I patted myself on the back, happy that I'd made her relax enough to talk freely and easily with me. "So what color should I dye it?"

"Pink!"

"Pink? *Piccola coniglio* (little bunny), I would rock pink hair." She giggled again, which made me grin.

*Pink hair, here I come. Forgive me, orsacchiotto* (teddy bear), *but it's for your sake that I will do whatever it takes to get in her good graces.*

"I bet we'll find some dye at the grocery store," I told her. "Where else do you want to go? It's hot as blazes out today, so we'd better save that for last in case we get anything frozen."

She agreed, then rambled about everything she wanted to get. Every once in a while, I hummed to acknowledge I was listening and pulled into the store parking lot right as she finished reciting her list.

"Okay. Let's first go see if they have any of the giant pool floats left," I told her. "That way, we'll know if we need to go somewhere else. All that other stuff should be easy to find."

I turned off the engine and hopped out, then ran around to open her door before she roasted in there. Holding out my hand, I waited to see if she would take it, and she did. I wasn't sure that she wanted to, but she was so small, even for a runt, and it was a long jump to the ground for her.

As we turned toward the store entrance, I went to release her hand, but she held onto mine. I looked down and met anxious blue eyes.

"Don't leave me, okay?" she whispered.

"Never." I squeezed her tiny fingers very gently. "I'll be with you the whole time, I promise."

"Gelo?"

"Yes, luna?" I raised an eyebrow and never would have guessed how her next words would turn my heart to mush.

"You don't have to dye your hair. I can see *you* now."

#

*Posy*

As we ate dinner, I told the boys everything that had happened while they were at work. They were all happy and pleased that I was

26

okay with Angelo now, and told me how proud they were of me for facing my fear.

That made me blush, and I changed the subject to Thoreau's wolf. I could almost predict their reactions, and I was right. Ash and Jayden were sad, Cole and Wyatt furious, and Mason a mix of the two. They asked a few questions when I told them what the king had said, and they agreed with him about sending out investigators and replacing Emerson's dad as alpha of Gray Shadows.

To lighten the heavy tension in the room, I linked them the image of Archer and Wayne standing on our porch covered in mud. Mason rolled his eyes while the rest laughed, which is what I wanted.

"Um, I wanted to ask you something," I said slowly. "Do Archer and Wayne also have the gay?"

Stunned silence followed my question, and I cringed, afraid that they were upset with me. They still hadn't explained the gay to me like Jayden said they would. I only knew it had made Emerson - scary, monster-sized *Emerson* - too scared to meet his mate.

"What makes you ask that?" Ash frowned, but didn't seem angry.

"The way they looked at each other and Reau. And Reau looked at them that way, too. I was going to ask Emerson, but he was traumatized enough today, so I didn't."

"I don't think the way someone looks at another is a reliable indicator of him or her being gay," Jayden said.

"I get that, but still." I shrugged. "The way they interacted made me think they all three have it."

"All right. Stop." Mason pinched the bridge of his nose with his thumb and index finger. "You don't *have* the gay. You *are* gay. And it's not 'the gay.' It's just 'gay.' I'll explain it to you more after dinner, but I can't handle that conversation over pork chops and fried apples."

I giggled.

"But to answer your question, I never thought they were gay." Wyatt traded side-eye glances with Cole. "They grew up together as brothers, and I always believed their relationship was like ours."

"Whether they are or not, they're our little brothers and we love and accept them," Cole said firmly.

"Is there a problem if they are?" Ash asked me in a gentle tone.

"No. I'm just worried about them," I said and looked down at my plate. "Mom and Dad don't seem to supervise them too closely, not that I'm saying they're bad parents! I understand that they're wrapped up in the two little boys and the new one on the way. I worry that they'll take advantage of their parents' distraction to, um, get up to things they shouldn't."

Despite everything my mates and I - and their wolves and Lark - had done together in our bed, I still couldn't say 'sex' out loud.

"Get up to what things?" Ash asked, still frowning.

"She means have sex," Wyatt said bluntly. "She's concerned that they won't wait until they're eighteen."

"And Reau is super innocent." I bit my bottom lip before I continued. "Not that I think they would, or at least not purposely, but Archer and Wayne could very easily lead him somewhere he isn't ready to go or even understands."

"We don't even know if they *are* gay," Cole argued. "This is all speculation, and we can't ask them. We can't bring it up with the parents, either, because if they are, we'd out them before they're ready."

"True," Mason said, "but we *can* remind them that sex with *anyone* is off limits until they are legally adults. That's just werewolf law. What they choose to do after that is up to them."

"And we'll support them regardless of their sexual preferences," Jayden added, "even if they decide to reject their mates and choose each other."

"So you'll take care of it?" I asked, lifting my eyes to glance at each of their faces.

"Yeah, cutie, we got it," Wyatt assured me with a smile. "Don't you worry about it. Thank you for worrying about our brothers."

I nodded. Knowing they understood, I was content to leave it in their hands. I wanted no part of *that* talk with three teenage boys.

After dishes were done and the kitchen cleaned up for the night, Mason took me into his office and we had an interesting talk that made even my ears burn with embarrassment. I left feeling much more educated and also thankful that it was *him* who explained it.

*Imagine if it Wyatt!* Lark giggled.

*Yeah. He'd have made me squirm ten times worse and been proud of himself for it,* I grumbled.

Before we went to bed, we all cuddled together to watch the first in a series of dinosaur movies. It was just getting good when Cole sat up.

"Ty's at the door and wants to talk to us. He didn't want to knock in case Posy was sleeping."

"One of you let him in," I said. "*I'm* not getting up."

Snuggled into Jayden's side with Wyatt draped over my back, I was far too comfortable.

"He wants to talk to us, not *you*, anyway," Cole teased as he stood and went to the front door.

"Okay, but I'm not moving." I wiggled deeper into the couch and snagged one of the squishy pillows when Wyatt and Jayden got up. "I want to watch this."

28

"Sure, baby." Mason leaned down and kissed my cheek. "We'll take him to the man cave. Enjoy the movie."

"You want to pause it?" I asked, but my eyes didn't leave the screen. "I can wait."

The movie was really good, although I didn't like the part where the dinosaur killed the guy who hid in the toilet.

*He deserve it! Leaving pups to be eat!* Lark disagreed with a sneer.

"Nah, it's okay," Mason said. "We've seen this one a couple of times. It's about to get a little intense. Do you remember how to use the remote to turn it off if you get too scared?"

"I'm not a baby!" I pouted. "I won't get scared!"

I heard him chuckle as he walked away with the others, then Tyler's quiet voice as they greeted him.

*I wonder what he wants to talk about.*

*Maybe he want advice on mating,* Lark said. *You know his birthday tomorrow. Might find mate! I no think old lady at the O gave him The Talk.*

She giggled, and I nodded absently, my attention riveted to the movie as the kids and the archaeologist made it back to the visitor's center.

After a second, my ears sent her words to my brain and I tuned back into real life right quick.

*Hey!* I linked my boys. *Don't you dare embarrass Ty if he's here to talk about mates or mating!*

*Too late, sweetness.* Jayden sent me the image of Tyler's heavy blush as Wyatt smirked in the background.

*Fifth star, I'm warning you,* I snapped. *He trusted you to ask for your help and advice. Behave and stop humiliating him!*

*Aw, Posy!* Wyatt whined. *That takes all the fun out of it.*

*Well, I guess I'll give him The Talk then—*

*No!* they all said at once.

*We'll handle it tastefully, I promise,* Mason said, and I relaxed. If Mason Price said he was going to do something, he did it.

Satisfied, I snuggled into my fuzzy blanket with a happy smile on my face. Unfortunately, the dinosaurs were quick to wipe it off, and I ended up cowering under my blanket with my hands over my ears because I was, indeed, a baby.

*And* I forgot how to work the remote.

## 4: Happy Birthday, Tyler!

*Tyler*

"Thanks for the ride," I said as I climbed into Alpha Wyatt's gorgeous black Jaguar.

"Not a problem. I love any excuse to take my baby for a spin." He patted the steering wheel.

Today was my eighteenth birthday, and the luna had invited me over for lunch. Alpha Wyatt had been kind enough to offer me a lift, and I acknowledged that as the treat it was.

He didn't like sharing his toys with anyone, especially his prized Jag. He was famously precious with it. I remembered this one time, he made Alpha Ash walk home from school because he'd skipped a shower after football practice, and Alpha Wyatt didn't want his 'baby' tainted by Alpha Ash's stink.

His words, not mine!

"She is a beauty." Having never been in it before, I couldn't stop admiring the interior. "Bet it handles like a dream."

"Oh, man, you have no idea! And it rides as smooth as glass, no matter how fast you're flying."

"I can't wait until I save enough to get a decent vehicle," I admitted.

"That might be sooner than you think. Have you checked your investment portfolio lately?"

I hadn't. The truth was, I'd forgotten about it. As part of the beta compensation package, Alpha Mason invested half of our first month's paycheck for us. After that, we could decide if we wanted him to take any more out of our wages to continue to invest, or just let that small seed grow.

At the moment, I was letting the small seed grow, too nervous to risk anything until I had some more zeros in my bank account.

"It's only been a month," I reminded Alpha Wyatt.

"Yeah, I guess you're right. Let it ride for a year. Bet you'll have enough by then to get just about any car you want."

"I'm looking forward to that," I agreed with a grin.

*Find mate today*, River whispered, dancing excitedly on his tippy toes.

*Don't worry about that right now, Riv*, I told him, keeping my tone light. *We're going to have cake and ice cream with the luna and alphas. Won't that be fun?*

*Ice cream? Oh, boy, oh, boy!*

Distraction accomplished, I could tune back in to what Alpha Wyatt was saying.

30

We talked about cars for the rest of the drive, which was what we often chatted about. He was a motorhead like me, and that was thanks to Nathan Barlow. He gave me a job at his garage when I turned fourteen.

Once we reached the alpha house, Alpha Wyatt drove straight to the huge garage at the far end of the parking area and through the open door. On our way to an empty bay, we passed Mr. Barlow, who was crouched down next to a motorcycle.

"What's wrong with the Ducati?" I asked.

"I can't figure it out, so I asked Dad to have a look, but I didn't mean *right now*. Mom's going to kill us both if he comes in with greasy hands."

I snickered a little at that. Evie Black-Barlow was generally an easygoing woman, but she had strict views on some things and wouldn't budge.

After we parked and jumped out, Alpha Wyatt told me to grab Mr. Barlow and head in, and he'd join us in a moment. I wondered if he was going to wipe the Jag down and kiss the hood, and the mental image made me grin.

"Happy birthday, Tyler!" Mr. Barlow stood as I jogged over to him. "Haven't seen you at the Busted Knuckle for a while. How've you been?"

"Good, sir. Been busy with the beta duties."

"Yeah, I just get a grease monkey trained and he leaves to become alpha or beta," Mr. Barlow joked and clamped a hand on my shoulder.

"You have an entire succession of sons, Mr. Barlow," I deadpanned. "You're not going to run out of go-fers any time soon."

"How many times have I told you to call me Nathan?" He shook his head, then grinned. "Come on, son. My daughter-in-law is going to pee her pants if we're late."

"The luna didn't have to do this." Heat built in my cheeks, that stupid, splotchy blush I hated and couldn't help.

"Who's brave enough to stop her? Anyone who tries has five angry alphas to answer to."

That made me laugh.

"Truer words were never spoken," Alpha Wyatt said as he trotted up to walk with us. "Whatever our baby wants, she gets."

"She deserves a little spoiling," Mr. Barlow agreed.

"And it's easy to spoil someone as sweet as the luna," I added.

"Wait until you have your own sweet mate to spoil," Alpha Wyatt teased me.

And of course, that got the attention of you-know-who.

*Mate! Mate! Mate!* my wolf frolicked around in my head. *Find mate today!*

"Thanks, alpha," I muttered with an eye roll. "I just got Riv calmed down."

"Does he sense his mate? Is he acting crazy?" Mr. Barlow asked.

I opened my mouth to ask how I could tell when he amended his statement.

"I mean, crazier than his usual crazy," he chuckled.

"Who knows with him?" I shrugged. "He gets as excited over a shiny stone in the creek as he does ice cream."

*Ice cream! Me want ice cream! And mate. Me want ice cream and mate, Ty-Ty!* River shouted loud enough for all to hear, and I let out a long-suffering sigh.

"Well, then, *Ty-Ty*," Wyatt smirked and slung an arm around my neck, "let's go find some ice cream and your mate."

"Not funny, alpha," I grumbled as I tried to shove him off.

Laughing, he dug his knuckles into my head in a noogie before I managed to get free of him.

"Alpha!" I wailed and tried to finger-comb my hair back into place.

"Aw, you look good, kid," Mr. Barlow said with a laugh.

As we walked out of the garage and into the sunlight, my nose quivered as I caught the faintest whiff of butterscotch.

*Mate*, River breathed, understanding before I did.

*It can't be. It's probably something luna is making with lunch,* I told him. *Pudding or—*

*No, Ty-Ty. Me smell mate.*

Then the breeze shifted and slapped me full-force in the face with the scent, confirming River's words. I staggered and almost fell on my butt, and Alpha Wyatt grabbed my arm to keep me on my feet.

"Whoa! Okay there, buddy?"

Words dried up and died in my throat at the wondrous realization that I had a mate.

"Go around to the pool, Ty," said a voice from far away. "She's waiting for you."

My feet taking over, I raced across the yard and around the house and skidded to a stop because there she was.

My brown-eyed goddess haloed in sunshine.

My beautiful mate.

My Peri.

In the background, I heard voices shout, "Happy birthday!" but all my focus had narrowed to the girl standing before me.

I held out my arms and she fell in them and nothing could have been more perfect than that one crystalline moment.

"I'm so, so happy it's you," I breathed as I held her tight against me and savored the sparks dancing between us.

"Me, too!" she whispered. "I didn't dare to even *wish* for this in case I jinxed it."

"Same." I nuzzled my nose into her hair, smelling Miss Dior mixed with butterscotch and falling more and more in love with each inhale.

"Tyler?" The luna's voice brought me back to reality. "Why don't you take Peri for a walk while we finish up with the grilling?"

I tore my eyes away from my mate to look at the luna and saw nothing but kindness in her eyes. I gulped and nodded, then looked down at my mate - *my mate!* - and her sunshine smile made my heart stall in my chest.

As I led Peri away, we heard the luna tell her mates, "And by *we,* I mean, *you.*"

My mate and I looked at each other and traded grins.

We were about halfway down the driveway before I could speak again.

"Sorry," I murmured. "I'm still in shock."

"Trust me, I am, too," she giggled. "I wish I would have talked to you more at school. I wanted to, but I had to appease the mean girls."

"Wait. What? You *wanted* to talk to me at school?"

"Of course, but if I did, the mean girls would target me." She must have seen my confusion because she went on to explain. "You're gorgeous and mysterious, and they've marked you as off limits to the rest of us peasants. Haven't you noticed how no girls approach you other than Korine, Heidia, and Olivia?"

I blinked. Those three were absolute pests. I was always dodging them and going out of my way to avoid them. Then my brain processed more of her words.

"What do you mean gorgeous and mysterious? Are you sure they're talking about *me*?"

"Um, one-hundred percent. And you are both of those things." Now *her* face turned red. "Gorgeous speaks for itself, and you're mysterious because you don't interact with girls or let them get close to you."

She tilted her head as she stared up at me.

"You didn't realize any of this, did you? Why did you think girls avoided you?"

"I live in a freaking orphanage, Per." I rolled my eyes. "I don't have the money to buy the right clothes or shoes, and I'm—"

*Broken*, is what I was going to say before my brain caught up to my mouth. I didn't want her to know that yet, would have done anything to keep her from *ever* knowing that, so I improvised.

"Not 'gorgeous' or whatever." I put air quotes around the word.

"If you don't know how good-looking you are, I can't explain it to you. And clothes and shoes don't make a difference. At least not to me."

Once again, her sunshine smile stole my breath.

"Ty?"

"Yeah?"

"What do I smell like to you? You smell like lilacs to me." She giggled and covered her mouth with one hand.

I gently took her wrist in my hand and pulled it away, then linked our fingers together.

"Don't cover your smile, sunshine," I whispered. "It's so beautiful."

"Oh!" Her cheeks glowed dull pink. "Thank you. I've always been self-conscious ever since Cole teased me when I was ten or eleven. He said my cheeks puff out like a chipmunk's when I smile. I mean, my face is naturally round, and I've struggled with a few extra pounds ever since puberty hit, so yeah, my cheeks *are* chubby and smiling makes them—"

Shaking my head, I laid the fingers of my free hand over her lips.

"Don't worry about what your dumb brother said when you were a kid," I told her. "And round and chubby cheeks are sexy as hell."

Her lovely brown eyes widened and red flared across those cheeks, and I realized she had no idea - no idea at all - of how beautiful she was to me.

"Peri, you are adorable." Dropping my fingers from her lips, I grabbed her other hand and held it, too. "And to answer your question, butterscotch."

"Okay." She took a deep breath, then said, "Ty, I'm afraid I'm going to wake up and this will all have been a dream."

"Me, too," I murmured, "but maybe this will make it seem more real for both of us."

Leaning down, I touched my lips to hers and delighted in the mate sparks that erupted between us.

"Oh, my," she breathed when I lifted my head.

"Yeah." I gently squeezed our interlaced fingers. "Listen, Peri, I don't have a big bank account, and I'm still dealing with some issues from my childhood, but I have a good-paying job and I swear I will work hard to provide you with the life you deserve."

"I don't even have a bank account or a job, but I know we're going to be fine." Her eyes grew wet as they locked with mine. "You know how I know that? Because we'll be together. So long as we're together, we can face anything, right?"

"Right. And we'll be together forever, sunshine, because I ain't letting you go any sooner than that."

She loosened her hands from mine so she could wrap her arms around my waist, then she squeezed me hard enough to make the breath huff out of me. Folding my arms around her shoulders, I held her just as tight.

"I love you, Ty," she whispered into my chest.

"I love you, too, so much." I kissed the top of her head. "My beautiful mate. My sunshine. My Peri."

#

We came back from our walk just in time to dig into hamburgers and hot dogs with everyone, then the alphas carried out an enormous cake and buckets of ice cream.

River was in heaven and made me look like a pig, but Peri laughed and said to let him have his fill as it was his birthday, too.

"Time for your present!" Luna Posy sang out.

My eyebrows shot up. I certainly wasn't expecting a present. Finding Peri for my mate was like a hundred years' worth of birthday and Christmas presents combined; I didn't need anything else.

"You didn't have to get me anything, luna," I told her, knowing that hated blush was stealing over my face again.

"She didn't. We *all* went together and got you one big gift." Alpha Ash handed me a small gift box wrapped in blue paper with a white bow.

"Open it, Ty!" luna squealed as she bounced up and down on her toes. "It's a new—"

Alpha Mason got his hand over her mouth before she could say what it was, and we all laughed. Her face turned red with embarrassment, so I made a fuss about unwrapping the box to draw the attention away from her.

Taking the lid off, I frowned when I saw what was lying on the white satin. I tipped the box so it fell into my hand and checked it out.

*A BMW key fob. A real one, too. Wait a minute—*

"No, you didn't," I whispered.

"Yes, we did!" the luna squealed. "It was my idea, Ty! Wyatt and Dad picked what kind of car, but it was *my* idea!"

She squirmed out of Alpha Mason's hold and jumped on me, and I fumbled the box to catch her, but managed to hold onto the key fob. No way was that leaving my hand any time soon. Laughing, Peri picked up the box and set it on a nearby table, then joined our group hug.

*Luna so excited!* River skipped about in my head, feeding off the energy around him. *Mate happy, Ty-Ty happy, and me happy! Me happy boy, Ty-Ty!*

Oh, Goddess. I still needed to introduce Peri to River. Well, she knew the alphas' wolves, and Sid was almost as much of a baby as River, so maybe she would be okay with him.

"Ty?"

I blinked and looked at Alpha Cole.

"Want to go see your new Beemer now?" he asked again.

"Sure, but, um, first, I can't thank you all enough." I knew that damned blush was spreading over my cheeks and probably down my throat, but couldn't do anything about it. "You didn't have to do any of this, and you certainly didn't have to get me a *car*."

"No, we didn't have to," Alpha Jayden grinned, "but we *wanted* to. You deserve it, Tyler. We're all very happy to be here with you to celebrate both your birthday and finding your mate."

Alpha Wyatt handed me a second key fob.

"I had the pleasure of driving it down from the dealership yesterday," he said. "Purrs like a kitten and you'll think you're floating, it drives so smooth."

"As smooth as the Jag?" I asked with a grin.

"Not quite," he laughed. "I just parked it in the driveway. Come see."

He led the way and, when I rounded the corner of the house, I came to a shocked standstill. It was a beautiful dark blue Alpina XB7, worth well over a hundred thousand dollars.

I raised my trembling hands to cover my face, blinking against the sting in my eyes. I felt Peri's arms wrap around my waist, and I dropped my arms to her shoulders, squeezing her tight as I buried my burning face in her hair.

"While we're overwhelming you, we might as well tell you about your new living arrangements," Alpha Mason said.

"As you know, part of the beta compensation package is your choice of available properties in pack territory once you find a mate." Alpha Ash's dark eyes glittered, and he looked like he was holding back a grin. "However, we can't let you pick one, Ty."

"Oh, no worries." I was already flustered from the car. I couldn't even entertain the idea of being given a *house*. "I was thinking maybe an apartment—"

My sunshine giggled, covering her mouth with her hand. I really needed to break her of that habit.

"You misunderstand," Alpha Cole said. "We can't let you pick because Peri already has."

"She's dreamed of living in this certain house for years," Alpha Wyatt chimed in, "so you can't disappoint her and pick somewhere else."

When they got me to understand which house Peri wanted, my mouth fell open.

"But, alphas, that place is worth hundreds and hundreds of thousands of dollars!" I protested.

"Sorry, dude." Alpha Ash shrugged. "You'll have to suck it up and accept it. It's what your mate wants."

*And mate gets what mate wants!* River decreed, and I held up both hands in surrender.

"I don't know what to say." My voice came out husky with emotion. "I wasn't expecting any of this, so I'm not prepared with a thank you speech. I'm grateful beyond words for the car and the house, but what really means the world to me is each of you. You're the family I never had and always wanted."

My throat clogged up so I couldn't say anything else, and I quickly swiped my eyes with the heels of my hands before the tears could fall.

Tiny arms snaked around my waist and the gentle aura of my luna calmed me right down.

"And you mean the world to us, Tyler," she said as she hugged me. "We are your family now and forever."

I smiled down at the top of her head, then glanced over at my mate, whose eyes were filled with nothing but love.

*Best. Day. Ever!* River howled in my head.

*Absolutely, Riv. Best day ever.*

## 5: Pool Party

*Posy*

After Tyler had a chance to admire his new car, we all returned to the pool area, and I asked Wyatt to start some music so people could dance if they didn't want to swim.

"We have live entertainment first," he said with a grin, and pointed over my shoulder.

Whirling, I saw Jayden carrying his guitar and a stool over to the microphone, and excitement filled me. Grabbing Wyatt's arm, I tugged it so he would look down at me.

"Is he *really* going to sing and play for us?" I squeaked with sparkling blue eyes.

"Yeah, and I'm sure he has a special song planned just for you, cutie."

I clasped my hands under my chin and started jumping up and down. He laughed at my excitement, but I didn't care.

"So I have a few songs I want to sing for you today," Jayden said into the microphone as he sat on the stool and messed with the top of his guitar. "First one, of course, is for our girl. Ty, you don't mind if I serenade your big sister first, do you?"

"Of course not, alpha!" Tyler called back, his grin huge and his arm around Peri's waist.

"You might as well start calling us brothers-in-law," Jayden smirked as he looked up from his guitar, and everyone laughed. Then his eyes found mine. "Posy, every word of this song is yours."

He strummed the guitar in a soft, sweet melody, then his amazing voice sang words of love, calling me darling and his everything and his lifetime. In every note, he poured out his heart and soul. Tears overflowed my eyes, and I had to cover my mouth with my hand to muffle the sob that slipped out. It was a good thing Wyatt was holding me in his arms. Otherwise, I would have gone to my knees.

As the last word echoed around us, I ran to my dragon-eyed mate. He took his guitar off and held it to the side as I slammed into him and threw my arms around his neck. Laughing softly, he curled one arm around my shoulders and kissed the top of my head.

"I love you, Jayden," I wept into his throat and ignored how the applause around us turned into a chorus of *awws*.

"I love you, too, precious girl." He ducked his head down to kiss my wet cheek.

"You will play the guitar and sing for me again," I demanded as I pulled back to meet his eyes. "And often."

"Your word is our law," he whispered. After pecking my lips, he asked, "Want to hear the rest of my little concert?"

"Yes, please. And thank you, Jayden. You are an amazing musician and singer."

"Thank you, sweetness." Dull pink skimmed over his cheekbones.

"All right, princess." Ash came up behind me and cupped my shoulders with his huge hands. "Can I have a turn hugging you while Jay does his pop star impersonation?"

Tilting my head back far enough to bump his chest, I met his upside-down chocolate eyes and gave him a big, toothy grin. Taking that as a yes, he gathered me up in his arms and sat me on his hip. It seemed to be his favorite way to hold me because he did it almost every time he carried me.

"All right, Tyler," Jayden said into the microphone. "I picked this song because I think it captures today perfectly. I hope you like it."

His guitar exploded into a fast-paced song that took me by surprise, and I had to listen hard to make out the words because he sang them so fast.

"By the moon, he's good," Ash laughed as he bounced me around to the rhythm. "I always get my tongue tangled when I sing those lyrics."

I grinned and petted his curls, then the song slowed down and I could understand the chorus.

"What is this song called?" I asked Ash.

"*Good to be Alive* by Andy Grammer."

"And the one he sang for me?"

"*Lifetime* by Justin Bieber."

I nodded and stored the information away for later, then re-focused on my amazing mate. Everyone around us was dancing and singing along with the song, and I was glad Matthew had set up quality speakers. Jayden's voice was too good to be lost in the noisy crowd.

When he finished, he stood and took a bow and everyone applauded or screamed appreciation.

"I'm slowing it down now for our newest couple," he said as he perched on his stool again. "When this song was released, Peri fell in love with it and begged me to sing it for her and her mate if she ever found him. Well, Per, today is that day."

This song was a lot slower, but not as much as mine had been. It was about falling in love over and over again, and it suited Jayden's voice perfectly.

*I wonder which professional artist made this song famous. I bet my boy could give him a run for his money!*

39

"*Fall into Me* by Forest Blakk," Ash told me as if he read my mind.

Jayden slowed things down even more with the next song, which he dedicated to all the newly mated couples. It repeated the line, "I was made to love you." It was the perfect sentiment for any shifter since we truly were built to be with our Goddess-given mates.

"I didn't know this one," Ash admitted, "so I had to ask him. It's called *Made to Love You* by Drew Angus."

"It's beautiful," I said and he agreed.

The last song, Jayden said, was to celebrate "all the oldies."

"Looking at you Mom and Dad and Mama and Papa," he said, getting a laugh from most of us and raised eyebrows from Dad and Papa. "Everyone, grab a partner and get ready to dance!"

"You're going to like this one. It's by Walk the Moon." Making sure my legs were secure around his waist, Ash took one of my hands in his, held it against his heart, then supported my bum with his other arm. "Shut up and dance with me."

"Okaaaay," I said hesitantly. "I thought I was. You didn't need to tell me to shut up, though."

"No, baby," he laughed. "That's the title of the song. I'd never tell you to shut up!"

Giggling at my mistake, I locked my free hand around his neck just in time for him to start dancing to the music. He spun me around with a giant grin, his eyes alight with energy and excitement, and I loved seeing him this way.

As he whirled me around the backyard, I looked at my family with a happy heart. Wyatt was dancing with William in his arms much like Ash held me, and Cole had Winnie up on his shoulders, making the little guy giggle as he moved his arms up and down.

The betas, their mates, Luke, and Gisela were jumping up and down with their arms in the air, having fun and not caring what they looked like. Each time Jayden sang, "Shut up and dance with me," they all joined in, which made me giggle.

Mama and Papa moved in an old-fashioned dance with lots of swirls and dips, Mom and Dad were welded together and swaying from side to side, and the king and queen slow-danced while staring into each other's eyes.

Leo stood off to the side alone, a drink in his hand as he watched everyone with a blank face. I understood what he was thinking; he didn't feel he had any right to enjoy himself, even with something so simple as dancing and singing at a birthday party. That made me frown, but then Mason, who was *never* going to dance in front of anyone, walked over and began talking to him. Whatever my mate said made Leo bark out a laugh, and I supposed that was good enough.

As for Wesley and Wade, they took advantage of the empty pool to round up all the floats and pool noodles and seemed to be building some kind of fortress.

*Wait a minute. Where's Reau?* My eyes ran around the backyard again. *And I don't see Archer and Wayne, either.*

"Ash, where are Archer, Wayne, and Reau?" I asked.

"I'm not sure. Do you want to link them or shall I?"

"I just want to make sure Reau didn't wander off alone."

When Ash didn't respond, I glanced at him and knew from his hazy eyes that he was linking the boys. After a few seconds, he blinked and focused on me.

"Arch and Wayne said the loud music upset Reau. They're with him in the man cave, teaching him to play Minecraft."

"Oh, good." I let out a relieved sigh.

"We had that talk with them, by the way," he told me. "They were shocked that we thought they needed the reminder, but were chill about it."

"I was surprised that Wayne and Archer welcomed Reau so easily. The two of them have been friends almost all of their lives, yet they let this newcomer into their circle almost instantly."

"That's good, right?" He grinned at me, his teeth blazingly white against his brown skin. "Listen, Wayne and Arch get a little wild, but they're good kids. Wayne's funny and easygoing, Arch is smart and mature, and Reau, well, I think Reau is in his own little world most of the time. He's kind of like a leaf floating on the water, letting the ripples take him where they may."

"True. I'm glad Wayne and Archer seem fine with that. He needs a friend his age, especially with school starting in two months." With a content sigh, I rested my head on his shoulder and rubbed my nose against his throat. "I love you, waffle."

"And I love you, my little cupcake. Our sweet Posy."

## 6: Memories

*Posy*

The day after Tyler's birthday party, the king decided to cut his vacation short. He wanted to introduce Queen Lilah to his family and the royal pack as well as set the wheels in motion for her coronation. He also wanted to research a couple things, such as my biological father's family and the idea he'd had on how to help Thoreau.

While Wyatt made a copy of my mother's letter in the home office, I hugged Queen Lilah and Gisela goodbye, and we exchanged phone numbers to keep in touch.

"And you'll come to the coronation, too, right?" the queen asked, her eyes glittering with tears. "I'm going to be scared to death, and it would mean so much to know you're there to support me."

"Of course, I'll be there," I assured her and squeezed her in another tight hug. "If my mates can't come, I'll make my betas bring me."

"Your mates will be there. The five alphas have a VIP place at all court functions," King Julian said. "I told you, they're my best friends and closest advisors. They don't have a choice about coming."

He smirked at my boys, and Cole and Jayden chuckled.

"Here you go, your majesty." Wyatt came down the porch steps and handed the king the copy of the letter. "Let us know what you find out."

"I will." King Julian took the paper and looked at me. "I'll get to the bottom of this, Posy."

"Thank you, sire." I dipped my head. "I'd like to meet his relatives, if there are any."

"I'll arrange that in time for the coronation," he promised, then turned to Mason. "Keep me informed about the Gray Shadows situation. I want to render a judgment ASAP based on what you find out."

I had forgotten that Beatrix was going to look at Thoreau's memories today. I wanted to be there for that. I had a gift for him. It wouldn't replace his wolf, Tanner, but might comfort him. Plus, my mates said just my presence as his luna would help him.

The boys all did that bro hug, I squeezed the queen and Gisela one last time, and shook the king's and Luke's hands, and then they were gone.

"Well, that wasn't much of a vacation for him," I said as Ash took one of my hands and Cole took the other.

42

"The fact that he found his mate more than made up for it," Jayden said with a laugh. "And Onyx got to kill some bad wolves and wrangle with Quartz, so it's all good."

Not an hour later, James and Callie drove up in his truck, followed by Aiden and Keeley in Gretchen, the twins' pink VW Bug.

"You're leaving, too?" I pouted.

"We want to meet our new pack and get settled in our new home as soon as possible," Callie said with a bright smile.

"Spoken like a true luna," Cole told her.

"Another thing to get used to," she replied with a giggle.

"Take care of yourselves and keep in touch." I hugged the twinnies. "Peri still has our group chat going, so use it."

"Of course!" they said together.

"And we'll see you at the Swift reunion in August, right?" Aiden asked as he laid his hand on top of my head.

"Yes, my mates said we can go!" I grinned up at him. "And they know Alpha Liam."

"We have an alliance with Crystal Caverns," Mason explained. "Jay was over there three months ago to help with an issue."

As the guys chatted and the twins asked me about Green River, I kept my eye on Jayden to make sure he was okay and eventually blew out a sigh of relief to see that he appeared to be.

*Maybe what happened at Crystal Caverns isn't how Everett Breckenridge got killed,* I thought to myself, *although the timeline fits.*

Not that I would bring it up *now*. The twins were Everett's little sisters and didn't need to go into their new life with that sad reminder, and if Jayden - well, *Quartz* - was chill, I wasn't going to do anything to upset him.

After a round of hugs and handshakes, we waved goodbye to them, and I turned to my mates.

"When is Beatrix going over to Emerson and Angelo's? I want to be there to hear everything and give Reau his gift."

"The twins have been meeting with Gelo at ten every morning to work out the details of their apprenticeship," Cole said, looking at his watch. "They're going to bring Beatrix along today, so we need to get our butts in gear."

"So," Wyatt drew the word out, "let's divide the jobs. On the docket, we have going with Posy, meeting with the representative from Cold Moon, supervising fighter practice, and the ever-loving paperwork."

"I can go by myself if it's a bother and you're busy," I tried to say, but they all shot me down.

"You will always have an escort, whether it's us or the betas," Jayden said. "In this case, one of us needs to witness Beatrix's findings as the king's official representative, anyway, so that's that."

"Well, boys, you know there's only one fair way to assign jobs for today," Ash said, and I giggled as they all put a hand behind their back. "First winner gets to go with Posy. Ready? Set? 1, 2, 3!"

\#

On the way over to Emerson and Angelo's, Cole explained what Victorian style was and that their house was a classic example of it. When we pulled up, my jaw dropped at how gorgeous the place was. A big, beautiful porch, fancy woodwork, and a tower on one side with a cone roof all added up to something out of a fairy tale.

"Wow!" I breathed. "I never saw a house like this!"

"Ostentatious, isn't it?" Cole muttered with a snort.

"What's that word mean?"

"*Extra* extra. Over the top showy."

"Oh. But it's super pretty!" I grinned at him, flashing my dimples, and he chuckled.

"If you say so, honey."

I knew Cole was a simple kind of guy, and 'fancy pants' would never be his style.

After we parked, I unbuckled, reached into the back seat for Thoreau's present, and turned to open my door only to find Cole already opening it.

"You sure move fast." I smiled up at him.

Smirking, he leaned forward and tucked my hair behind my ear.

"Fast, slow," he whispered in my ear, "soft, hard. I can move any way you want me to move."

Fire scorched my face as I shoved his chest to push him back. "Cole!"

Laughing, he put his hands on my waist, lifted me out of the SUV, and put me on my feet. I grabbed his hand and tugged him toward the front door, eager to see inside this beautiful house.

"The twins and Beatrix beat us here," he noted, pointing to a truck with his free hand, and I nodded to acknowledge him.

The front door opened before we could knock, and Emerson welcomed us inside his home. He gave us a little tour, which made my jaw drop again. I would have to come over sometime when I could look around to my heart's content. There were so many little nooks and corners to explore, not to mention random stained glass windows, spiral staircases, and hidden spaces.

We ended up in the large living room, where Beatrix, her mates, Angelo, Leo, and Thoreau were seated and chatting. After greeting everyone, I sat down next to Thoreau on the love seat.

"I got you a present, Reau!" I handed him the big gift bag.

"For me?" His eyes widened and he took the bag carefully with both hands. "Thank you, luna!"

"You're welcome. Open it up!" I clapped my hands with excitement.

He slowly took out the tissue paper, then squealed and lifted the wolf stuffy out of the bag. He stared at it for a few seconds, then smashed his face into its belly and squeezed it tight.

"It's the same colors as Tanner," he whispered. "How did you know, luna?"

"Oh, I didn't. I picked the one I thought you'd like the best. Do you want me to get you a different one?"

"NO!" he screeched. "It's Baby Tanner. I love him! He's mine forever."

"That's right," I soothed and rubbed circles on the boy's back. "He'll be with you for as long as you want him to be."

While I was talking with Thoreau, I listened with half an ear as Beatrix talked with Leo.

"I have something for you." She handed him a small white jewelry box. "We destroyed everything else that was in the trunk you found in the bayou, as it was all black magic or tainted by black magic, but there was nothing wrong with the ruby pendant. We purified it just to be safe, and now it's clean to do whatever you want with it."

Leo made a face as he opened the box and stared at the gem that had cost him so much.

"We know you might not want it, but no one else has the right to it," she said with a shrug and gentle smile.

He sighed, but didn't say anything and slipped the jewelry box into his pocket.

"All right, Reau," Beatrix chirped as she turned to him, "you ready to do this?"

"No," he said with a pout.

"It won't hurt, I promise. And you can hold your wolf stuffy the whole time."

"No."

Beatrix cut her eyes to Emerson, then me, then back to Thoreau.

"This has to happen," Emerson explained to him. "The king ordered it. We can make you more comfortable, though. What would help, Reau?"

"Will luna hold me?" he asked in a small voice, and my heart leapt into my throat.

"Of course I will," I said without hesitation. "You want to sit on my lap?"

"Little luna bunny, he's bigger than you are," Emerson pointed out with a frown. "How about you sit next to her, Reau? Then you can cuddle her."

"That works, too," Thoreau agreed.

He still ended up half on my lap, like he did when I met him, his head on my thighs, his thumb in his mouth, and his unique eyes fixed on mine.

"Does it matter if he goes to sleep?" I asked Beatrix.

When she shook her head, I began to pet his curls. They were so clean and well cared for now, such a stark contrast to that first day. His bruises were gone, although he was still awfully skinny, but I knew Emerson and Angelo were doing the same as my mates were with me: gradually increasing his food intake so he gained weight slowly but surely.

Beatrix settled herself on the floor next to our love seat, and lifted her hands to hover over the boy, but not touch him. A shimmery haze built in the air, and I thought it best to keep Thoreau distracted while she worked.

"Here's Thoreau," I crooned, making a song of it, "with his pretty eyes and curly hair. He lives with his Bubba, who's a real teddy bear."

"Hey, now, luna," Emerson growled playfully, which made Thoreau giggle around his thumb.

"More!" Thoreau demanded.

"Be polite, Reau," Angelo reminded him.

"More, please, luna," the boy said in a softer voice.

A little flustered, I hurried to make up more verses in the song I was inventing on the spot.

"And there's Gelo who shares his great big house," I sang, "and Leo who can be as quiet as a mouse."

Thoreau's eyelids were starting to droop, so I sang on.

"They live in the forest with the trees, and all around are birds and deer and bees. There's lots of room to run and jump and play, and that is how Thoreau spends every day."

I was out of ideas and looked at the others with pleading eyes, but they only chuckled. Making a face at them, I cobbled together another verse.

"From their yard, they watch the moon rise at night. Reau likes it when it's big and round and white."

46

"Okay, I'm done," Beatrix whispered as she lowered her hands and the shimmer faded.

Instantly, her mates surrounded her and picked her up off the floor, then carried her over to the couch.

"And Reau's asleep." I let out a deep breath. "Whew. I didn't realize how stressful it is to rhyme on demand. I think I'd better memorize some little songs so I don't have to make up any more."

"You did fine, baby," Cole said with a soft smile. "You kept him calm, which was all we needed."

He turned to Beatrix, who met his eyes and shook her head. Considering how her mates were practically cocooning themselves around her, she was shaken and upset by what she saw.

*I don't think any of us are surprised,* I muttered to Cole. *They transported him in a **dog crate** and told him that Em would kill him or keep him - and he was okay with that. I think that speaks to the kind of environment he was in just as much as any memory reading.*

*You're right, baby, but it's a formality. The king can't issue verdicts without evidence.*

I nodded. Knowing he needed to talk with Beatrix, I told him I'd stay with Thoreau while he slept and they could take their conversation elsewhere. I knew the boy had been starved and abused; I didn't need to know the details right now or be a part of whatever King Julian decided.

All I needed to do was help this boy heal, and that's what I was going to do.

Even if it meant making up silly songs and holding his head as he slept so he wouldn't wake up alone.

## 7: *Photo Albums*

*Ash*

Paperwork sucked.

It sucked *a lot*.

In fact, paperwork sucked the suckiest of all the suckness in suckdom.

That made Sid giggle, which brought a smile to my lips, too.

Then the door flew open, and Cole threw himself into the chair in front of my desk.

"Was it as bad as we thought?" I asked, putting my pen down with relief.

"Yeah." He ground the heels of his hands into his eyes with a groan. "Beat him. Starved him. Convinced him he was 'retarded.' By the moon, I *hate* that word. Tortured him by telling him that's why Em left. Did nothing to grow his brain. Kept him locked in that dog crate ten to twelve hours a day. Isolated him from his pack. Killed his wolf, but you knew that."

"Yeah." I hung my head and tried to calm Sid, who was out for blood now.

"Every kind of abuse but sexual. Thank the Goddess for that at least." Cole blew out a heavy breath. "You know the king is going to strip Alpha Bellamy and Luna Ivana of their status, if not order their execution. If we're asked to do it, Ash, I don't think I can without ripping the pair of them to shreds."

"The luna participated?" I asked, aghast.

Sid howled his rage, and I knew Cole could see him glittering in my eyes. Anything involving an injury or outrage to a pup roused Sid's fury like nothing else.

"She did," he confirmed. "Worse than the alpha with some of it."

"I can't imagine parents of either gender hurting their own pup," I ground out as I struggled to hold Sid back.

"Me, either."

*Let me out!* Sid growled.

*No. You'll run all the way to Gray Shadows and kill them both.*

*They not deserve to live,* he hissed with unusual venom.

*The king has not authorized either their capture or their executions yet,* I reminded him. *You can't touch an alpha on his territory without the king's order unless you want to start a war.*

*Then I start a war!* he howled loud enough for Cole to hear.

"Sorry for getting Sid stirred up," my brother sighed. "Sid, we have to wait until the king reviews the evidence and makes a decision. No pups are being harmed right now—"

"So far as we're aware," I muttered.

"So far as we're aware," Cole agreed, "and you know very well that the king will not allow Reau's abusers to go unpunished."

*He better punish them or I will,* Sid declared, and settled into a sullen silence.

"Listen," Cole said as he stood, "I need something mindless to do for a while and you need to get Sid settled. How about I take over the paperwork and you go be with Posy for a bit?"

"Where is she?"

"She was going to get a head-start on dinner, then said she was going to chill for a bit."

Happily yielding my seat and handing him my pen, I went looking for our girl and found her curled up on the sofa in the living room. She had Mr. Nibbles cuddled in her lap as she looked through the photo album that her brothers had given her.

"Princess? Can I join you?" I asked in a soft tone to keep from startling her.

"Oh, sure. You want to see a picture of my parents?"

"I'd love to."

She moved so I could sit next to her and hold half of the album on my lap.

"Look at them." She tapped a photo of a man kissing the side of a laughing woman's face. "How could anyone look at these photos and think he kidnapped and killed her?"

"I think Kendall Briggs was a master manipulator," I said. "He even convinced King Magnus."

She turned the page to display a group shot of five or six people.

"This is her family. The Swifts of the Crystal Caverns pack. I don't know any of them. I wish she would have labeled them."

"That's Liam Swift, the current alpha," I pointed to the guy on the left side of the photo. "Obviously this was taken well before he was alpha, but I can still recognize him from what Jay linked us."

"Ash," she said in a slow, careful tone that put me on guard, "Jayden helped Alpha Liam with something three months ago. Is that when and where your beta died?"

I sighed. I should have - we *all* should have - known she'd put the pieces together correctly. Our girl was smart.

"Yeah. Mase was helping the king with an issue at the royal pack. Cole was in Texas acting as a mediator between two packs, and Wyatt and I were still in school. So Jay took Ev Breckenridge with him and left the other betas in charge of the pack until he, Cole, or Mase got back."

"Did Ev die because of something Quartz did, or in Quartz's place?"

I blinked.

"How did you—"

"Based on Quartz's reaction at dinner when it was brought up," she said with a little shrug. "Why else would he be so upset? Either Quartz caused his death, or he died saving Quartz."

*Forget smart*, I marveled. *Our girl is a genius.*

*Yep!* Sid was much happier with our mate distracting him from his anger. *Smartie smart mate!*

"He took a hit meant for Quartz," I admitted. Debating whether or not to tell her the whole truth, I decided it would do no harm for her to know. "It was the damndest thing, too. Ev was shifting into his wolf and the attack hit him just at the right second to kill Ev, but miss Spring. Never heard of anything like it."

"Wait. What? The man died, but the wolf survived?"

"Yeah. Jay brought Ev's body back, along with a whole and functional wolf." I paused, then reframed my answer. "Well, for a given value of functional. Spring wasn't doing too great without his other half."

"So what happened to him? Is he still alive?"

"He is. He needed more help than we could give him here, so King Julian took him to the royal pack, where some healers and elders are working with him." I tilted my head as a thought crossed my mind. "I wonder—"

"What? You wonder what?"

"Hmm? Oh. Just something the king said this morning. Do you think he might try to introduce Spring to Reau?"

"Like, a wolf who lost his shifter becomes friends with a shifter who lost his wolf?" She frowned, then nodded. "It might work. For comfort, if nothing else."

"Hmm. I think it will all depend on how stable the king decides Spring is right now. The last thing we want to do is make Reau's situation worse by introducing him to a nutso wolf," I said dryly.

"True enough." She set her photo album on the coffee table. "There are some more pages of people I don't know at the end that I think might be my father's people. I hope the king finds at least one relative still alive in the royal pack. I'd like to know more about him."

"I would, too. He created a great daughter, after all." I grinned down at her, and she blushed. "Mom and Mama made a book for us as well. It's a family photo album, but also tells the story of how Five Fangs came into being. Want to see it?"

"Of course!"

I got up and grabbed the book from the shelf in the corner. It was a lot like hers, professionally bound in hardcover, but in black leather, not green linen. Sitting down next to her again, I took a big breath, then opened the cover to a picture of my parents.

"So it starts with these people. Gabriel and Kristy Mitchell. I told you they died when Dark Woods was attacked by hunters when I was two, right?"

"Yes. I'm so sorry." She laid a hand on my arm.

"I don't really remember them, but it's so damn sad. Look how young they are. They never really got to grow up, you know? Dad was only twenty-one, and Mom was twenty. I don't know much about his family, other than that his mom, my grandma, came from Samoa. Her family moved here when she was in high school and that's where she met my granddad, who was the alpha of Dark Woods, and it turned out that they were mates."

"Wow. Samoa. That's in the Pacific Ocean, right?"

"Mm-hmm." I nodded. "Closer to Australia than the US."

"I wonder how far away it is from Bora Bora."

"I don't know, but we can look it up later if you want. Why?"

"Because Mason said we could go to Bora Bora sometime and if it's close enough to Samoa, why not stop there, too?" She bounced in her seat as her thoughts whirled. "Do you think any of her family still lives there?"

"Again, I don't know, and I wouldn't even know how to find out. A lot of that information was lost when Dark Woods fell."

"That's when you went to live with Jayden, right?"

"Yeah. His dad, Jay, was my mom's brother."

"That's right!" she chirped. "Peri told me and Ariel that you and Jayden are cousins!"

"Mm-hmm. Uncle Jay and another one of my dad's allies, Shawn Black of River Rapids, got the call when the hunters attacked, but by the time they got there, nearly all of my pack was dead. Of course, they had slaughtered a lot of the hunters, too, so it was kind of a clean up and salvage mission from that point on."

"Shawn Black was Wyatt's dad."

"Yep. We'll get to that part of the story in a minute." I flipped the page to show the photo of Jay and Denise Carson. "So Uncle Jay and Aunt Denise adopted me and folded the survivors of Dark Woods into their pack, Moonset. Since the two packs share a border, it was easy to do. They buried the dead and life went on."

"Do you know how your mom died?"

51

I knew why she was asking. It was unusual for a luna to be on the front lines and not in the safe room with the pups and other vulnerable pack members.

"Uncle Jay found her a few feet from my dad. She was quite a warrior, one of the best in Dark Woods, actually." I chuckled. "Uncle Jay used to take credit for that, saying he was the one who taught her everything she knew about fighting."

"Wyatt said he'd teach me some self-defense. I haven't brought it up again because you seemed against it, but I would like to be able to take care of myself."

"I know, and I thought about it since we had that conversation, and he's right. You never know what situation might crop up, and you should have *options*, as Peri likes to say." I pecked her forehead. "And it's just smart."

"Thank you. I have no desire to be a warrior, if that eases your mind. In fact, I'm not even sure I'd make it through a single session of fighter practice. But yes, I'd like options in case I ever find myself alone in a bad situation."

"Then we'll make that happen." Looking back at the photo album, I turned the page to show five boys and one girl climbing a tree. "Here's all of us with Mason's twin, Willow. He told you about her, didn't he?"

She nodded as she studied the picture, and I continued telling the story.

"Uncle Jay was best friends with the three alphas whose territory bordered Moonset. Royal Price, Mason's dad, Shawn Black, Wyatt's dad, and Nathan Barlow, Cole's dad. After I went to live with Uncle Jay and Aunt Denise, we always were at one of their places or they were over at ours. That's how we boys became such close friends, along with Willow, and our dads encouraged it."

"Did they know then?" She looked up at me with curious blue eyes. "Did they know that their packs would one day merge into one?"

"No. Not then." I turned the page to show her Royal and Julia Price with Mason and Willow the year before the sickness hit. "Poor Willow died in the first wave of the sickness, then Nathan's wife, Kelly."

"She's Cole, Peri, and Archer's mom?"

"Yeah." Going to the next page, I showed her the Barlow family. "She was a great lady. Very independent. Very strong. Of course, that's the memory of a twelve-year-old Ash."

"Ah. I see she's the one who Cole gets his darker skin tone from."

"Her dad was Maori, one the aboriginal peoples of New Zealand, and her mom was from the Haida tribe in Alaska," I explained. "Cole and Archer got Nathan's green eyes, but all three of them got their mom's dark hair and brown skin, and Peri got her brown eyes."

"Wait. Peri has blonde hair." Posy tilted her head as she looked at me.

"She dyes it, baby."

"Oh!" She blinked, then looked back at the photos. "It's so sad to see their smiling faces in these photos and know that they were gone less than a year later."

"I know." Draping my arm around her shoulders, I pulled her into my side. "You want to keep looking or stop here for now?"

"I'd like to go on. Is it too hard and sad for you?" She turned her earnest face up to me, and I smiled down at her.

"You're such a kind, considerate girl. It *is* hard and sad, but I have many, many happy memories that help."

She turned the page for us and saw the Carsons with Jay and me on either side of them.

"I just realized that Jayden's name is made up from his parents' names," she said with a smile. "Jay and Denise."

"Yeah. They thought Jay Junior would get too confusing, but we call him Jay most of the time anyway. They were great people, Posy. I wish you could have met them. Aunt Denise would have loved you so much and Uncle Jay would have teased you about your height mercilessly. I can almost hear his voice calling you Minnie Mouse."

She laughed, but it was true.

"I'm glad you had them to love you after your parents died."

"Me, too. They died within three weeks of each other." I looked up at the ceiling and blinked until the stinging in my eyes passed. "After losing his luna, Nathan was struggling to keep his family together while running Great Rocks. Royal was in slightly better shape over at Earthshine, so he and Shawn pitched in to help with Moonset, but I think they were all wondering what they were going to do. Thankfully, the sickness had nearly run its course and our doctors were administering vaccines and cures."

Taking a deep breath, I turned to the next page in the album. The hardest page to look at, even harder than my own parents and my adopted ones. In the photo, Shawn Black stood with his arm around Evie's waist. Wyatt was on their left and Wayne on their right. Wade stood in front of Wyatt and Wesley in front of Wayne.

"Then, right when we thought we were safe, we lost Shawn Black."

I couldn't talk for a minute. Couldn't even look at the man's picture. I wasn't ashamed of the tears that ran down my cheeks, but I didn't want to upset our girl.

"Ash," she whispered.

Picking up the photo album, she moved it to the coffee table, then took its place on my lap. I hugged her as close as I could and buried my face in the crook of her neck and tried not to sob.

"It's okay, Ash. You can cry. It's okay to grieve when we lose someone we love."

"He was a great man," I choked out. "I mean, you hear that all the time about people who've died, but Shawn Black truly was. He was kind and funny and smart and compassionate. He always knew what to say and do. He stuck up for Mase against Royal all the time. He wasn't afraid of anything. He loved his mate and kids. He was fair and brave and charismatic. All of us boys idolized him."

I released her to grab the neck of my t-shirt and wipe my eyes, then cupped her face in my hands.

"When he died, it hurt everyone who knew him." My voice came out as a husky croak, and I cleared my throat. "But Wyatt? Goddess, Posy. It *shattered* Wyatt. That's his story to tell when he's ready for you to know, but I was so scared. All of us were. We thought— We thought he might try to—"

I couldn't even think it, let alone say it.

"Shh." She ran her hands through my curls and kissed my forehead as tears filled her own eyes. "Thank the Goddess he didn't. I don't even want to think what life would be like without Wyatt."

Right as I felt her body tremble, the alpha link was slammed with my four brothers demanding to know why our girl was upset. Rolling my eyes, I didn't go into more detail than to say that she wanted to look through the photo album her brothers gave her and that led to looking through *our* photo album.

*Do something to make her happy!* Wyatt insisted.

*Don't dwell on the morbid past that nobody can change!* Cole snapped.

*See if she wants to make brownies,* Jay suggested. *That will cheer her up.*

Mase remained silent. In the past, that wouldn't have been unusual; however, since Posy came into our lives, he'd become more vocal, and I wondered if he was thinking, or if he'd run into trouble with the Cold Moon representative.

*Mase?* I asked.

*She has a right to know,* he said begrudgingly, *but take a break if she gets too overwhelmed.*

"Is that when your surviving parents decided to combine packs?" Posy asked, drawing my attention away from my brothers.

"Yeah. We started hearing stories of rogues raiding decimated packs and other alphas taking advantage of the situation to claim

54

territories that weren't theirs, although King Magnus put a stop to that. It was one of his last decrees before he abdicated the throne to King Julian."

I shifted her to lay in my arms before I continued.

"Nathan couldn't hold Great Rocks together without a luna to hold him together, and Evie was, well, she was in no condition to hold her family together, let alone River Rapids. Royal and Julia had completely taken over running Moonset after Shawn's death while still trying to run Earthshine. With Dark Woods folded into Moonset, they were running three packs. It was insane. So the four of them got together and made the only decision that made sense."

"And the Moon Goddess approved?" Posy snuggled closer, and I ran my hands down her long hair.

"Yeah. At the next full moon, they made the announcement about the packs and that Nathan and Evie were choosing each other as mates, and the Goddess blessed their union as well as the merging of the packs."

"That must have been something to see." She raised her head to meet my eyes.

"It was dazzling. Like being in the center of a meteor shower. We all felt a sense of rightness and relief." I grinned down at her. "That night, she visited me and my four brothers in a dream and told us we'd find you."

"So that's how you knew." Her big blue eyes stared up at me with pure love, and my heart squeezed.

"So that's how we knew." I kissed the tip of her nose. "Now, how about we take a break from the past and make some brownies?"

"Brownies? Yes, yes, yes!"

And to the kitchen we went.

## 8: Tag!

*Lark*

Someone tickled my mate link and woke me up.

*Psst! Lark!*

*Granite?* I muttered. *What's wrong?*

*Nothing. Wake up and come play with us!*

Blinking my eyes open, I realized Posy was still asleep, and it seemed like the boys were, too, judging by all the wolf-lit eyes that peered down at me.

*What time is it?* I asked when I saw no light coming from the windows.

*Who cares?* Topaz bounced off the bed with a giggle. *We want to play, dearest!*

Blinking, I looked at Quartz, who wore a tiny smile.

*Only if you want to, little mate,* he said with a shrug.

*We shift when we get outside,* Granite said. *Hurry, my love! Before boys stop us!*

*Okay, okay.* I slid off the edge of the bed and almost stumbled to my knees.

Thankfully, Garnet caught me before I hit the floor.

*Sorry. I still not used to our human body,* I apologized with a blush.

*It's okay, sweetheart.* He smiled and leaned down to boop my nose with his. *You'll feel steadier once you walk around a bit.*

I nodded and let him lead me to the stairs.

*Um, I think I better carry you down, sweetheart,* he said, and I agreed wholeheartedly.

Falling down the stairs would put an end to our adventure real quick, although some of my mates were far from stealthy. Topaz, Gran and Sid had their hands over their mouths to muffle their giggles, but were still obnoxiously loud.

Sure, Posy was dead to the world, but if at least two of the boys weren't awake by now, I'd never chase another chipmunk.

For whatever reason, their human halves were letting us 'get away' with sneaking out, and I guessed they were either too amused - Cole and Jayden - or sleepy - Wyatt and Ash - to object. Or maybe they just wanted to give us bonding time.

*It hard to tell what humans thinking unless they tell you,* I admitted to myself.

As soon as we were downstairs, my wolves hustled us to the front door and opened it, dropping their t-shirts and boxers in a pile on the porch before shifting into their wolf forms. Going with the flow, I pulled off Mason's big t-shirt and skinned my panties down and shifted, too.

*Run or play in the yard?* Sid pranced in a circle with excitement.

*We'll stay in the yard since it's dark,* Quartz decreed, and no one argued with him.

Granite sidled up next to me and put his snout in my ear.

*My love, you know how play tag?* he whispered.

*Yes,* I whispered back.

*Good. You it!* he shrieked, then took off.

*That not fair!* I pouted. *I too slow. I never catch any of you.*

*You can do it, my darling,* my shy Sid encouraged me. *Just try.*

Stirred by mischief, I sprung forward and surprised him. I *almost* caught his tail before he dodged away with a joyful yip.

That started a chase that led all over the yard and to the treeline and back to the porch. The other wolves joined in, and I finally managed to tag Garnet. I knew he let me, and I was fine with that. I couldn't compete with any of them physically, and Garnet could only stand to watch them tease me so long before he intervened.

*Just like Mason with Posy,* I thought to myself with a secret smile.

The game grew more intense now that I wasn't it, and I laughed and howled as my wolves contorted and dodged and leaped over each other. When Granite was tagged, he came for me, but I dove between Sid's front legs and kept going, emerging from under his tail, and ran for the driveway.

Ash had left his SUV parked there instead of in the garage, and I knew I could fit under it. I was *almost* positive that Granite, who was nearly four times my size, couldn't - and I was right.

While I snickered at him from under the vehicle, he ran around and around it while whining that I was cheating.

*I am not,* I told him. *I take advantage of my size and outwit you.*

*I could tip this over if I want to,* he taunted. *Come out or I will!*

*Don't hurt Ashy's toy!* Sid called, making me grin.

*Yeah, don't hurt Ashy's toy!* I told Granite. *Better hope you no get a scratch on it already!*

*Aw, you no fun, Lark.*

From my spot on the ground, I saw Topaz's paws sneaking up behind Granite and had to hold back my giggles so he wouldn't suspect anything. Right as Granite dropped his front half down and stuck his head under the bumper, Topaz grabbed his tail and tugged it.

As Granite yelped and whirled on his brother, I slipped out the other side and ran to find another hiding spot.

*Here, little mate*, Quartz murmured.

I raced up to where he sat on the grass, and he raised one paw. I slipped in under him and squiggled around to face forward as he lowered his foot. Careful to keep my nose down, I peered through his chest hair to watch Granite chase Topaz. He managed to tackle him when Topaz began to wheeze with laughter.

*You it!* Granite shouted, then went back to Ash's SUV. *It okay, Lark. Paz it now. Come out, my love.*

When I didn't respond, he dropped down to check under the vehicle.

*Hey! She gone!* he shouted.

*See if you can find her, Gran*, Garnet told him, then linked me to stay still. *None of the pups saw where you went. See how long you can fool them.*

*Hide and Seek!* Sid screeched, and Topaz spun in frenzied circles.

That wasn't an easy game for wolves to play since we couldn't turn our keen noses off. Right now, though, Quartz's scent was covering my own; as long as we didn't move, none of them could sniff me out.

The three pups put their noses to the ground, but I'd run all over the place in the last hour. My scent was everywhere, from the yard to the treeline to the driveway.

*You have to try harder than that, my loves*, I crowed.

Quartz's chest vibrated above me with silent chuckles, and I wagged my tail, pleased with myself for amusing him.

*Where is she?* Topaz demanded after a few minutes. *Did she go back in the house?*

*No*, Garnet assured him. *She's out here somewhere.*

*You know!* Sid accused and tackled him.

Topaz and Granite joined in, and Garnet huffed with laughter as the three pups rolled him around and jumped on him.

*I don't have her*, he managed to get out.

That's when their beady eyes turned to Quartz, and I slowly and silently withdrew even further under him.

*Q!* they whined in unison and came over to stand in front of him in a half circle. *Where is she?*

*Here I is!*

I burst out from under Quartz with a big grin, making them jump back with a start.

*My darling!* Sid poked his nose in my left ear.

*My love!* Granite licked my right cheek.

*Dearest!* Topaz rolled me onto my back with his paw and snuffled my belly.

Giggling, I let them fawn all over me for a few minutes. By then, the sun had come up and we all knew the boys would have to get their day started soon.

*I have so much fun, my loves,* I said as Quartz shooed the pups back and Garnet helped me stand up. *We do that again sometime!*

*Maybe we can go swimming together!* Topaz suggested. *I love swimming!*

*Yes, yes! We have great big pool in backyard,* I chirped.

*We're forbidden to go in it, sweetheart,* Garnet informed me. *We shed too much hair and it clogs things up. I don't understand all the workings of it, but we did it once, and our boys had to spend a lot of money to fix it.*

*Oh,* I pouted.

*But we can swim at lake,* Granite said. *We swim there lots in hot weather.*

*Oh, boy! I like that. It sound like lot of—*

Ash's alpha tone interrupted me.

*Rogues in Dark Woods!*

And just that quick, our fun morning turned into an emergency.

#

*Ash*

We let the pups have fun under Quartz and Garnet's watch, not too worried about it and happy to see them happy.

Then I felt the border of Dark Woods quiver as rogues crossed it.

*Rogues in Dark Woods!* I shouted, then closed my eyes to concentrate on what the territory was telling me. *They're chasing something, another shifter. I can't tell what kind, but they're heading toward the Moonset border. It's like they're on a straight path to Emerson's.*

*How many?* Cole asked.

*Feels like twenty, but my gut says more. I can't explain it.*

*Twenty!* Wyatt growled. *That's a big pack for rogues.*

It was. Most banded together in small groups of four or five, maybe ten at the outside. Twenty made us all wonder if something bigger was happening.

*Might be some kind of magic at play,* Jay suggested.

*Lark, go to the safe room and give Posy back control,* Mase commanded. *Posy, keep the mate link open. We'll send the betas to you.*

*Don't let anyone except their mates in the safe room. Then you stay there until you hear from one of us. Clear?*

*Clear.* Our girl didn't hesitate. Her furry little butt flew toward the porch and through the open front door.

Seeing that, we took off, giving our wolves free rein to run, and issued orders as we went.

*Rogues in Dark Woods*, I linked the pack. *Border patrols, maintain your routine. All available warriors, to the border near Emerson's. Do not let them cross into Moonset.*

*Emerson, they're headed your way,* Wyatt linked all the betas and Angelo. *Get Reau into your safe room, then try to get us a visual. Take Gelo and Leo with you. Hold the line if you can. Rest of the betas, to the alpha house now. Your luna is in the safe room. Your mates can join her if they want.*

*My flock will fight with me,* Gelo linked back.

*This could be chaos,* I said to my brothers only. *We haven't had a chance to work out any kind of strategy for using him and the witches in a fight.*

*Gelo, until we make a plan, don't get in our way and we won't get in yours,* Mason linked him, the witches, and us.

*Understood,* was his response.

*Sons, where do you want me?* Dad asked. *Evie and the kids are in the safe room, and Arch and Wayne are on guard outside.*

I felt Cole's hesitation, not because he doubted his father's ability and strength, but because he didn't want to lose him. It was a fear we all had after the sickness. None of us wanted to bury any more loved ones, especially parents.

But when the pack was in danger, sentiment had to take second place to practicality.

*To the border,* Cole told him.

*And me?* Papa asked.

*Also to the border,* I said when Mase remained silent. *I think we'll need as many fangs as we can get for this one.*

*Did you sense something else about the rogues?* Wyatt asked through the alpha link.

*No.* I shrugged. *Like I said, just a gut feeling.*

*Well, for once, I hope your gut is wrong.*

*Me, too, brother. Me, too.*

## 9: Invaders

*Emerson*

Having the Angel of Death as your mate had a lot of benefits, including an instant understanding of danger.

Angelo sent Leo to get Thoreau to the safe room and had his gun belt on before I was done shifting. He shrugged on his weapons harness, complete with a sword hilt poking up over each shoulder, as we ran down the stairs.

"Leo?" he shouted.

"He's in the safe room with his wolf stuffy," Leo hollered as he came pelting up the basement stairs. "Scared but promised to stay there until he hears from one of us."

*Best we can hope for*, I linked them.

I was angry at myself for not practicing the safe room with my baby brother before now. It was going at the top of my priority list after today.

"Shift while I talk," Angelo told Leo. "We'll jog a line twenty feet apart. Don't lose sight of each other and link the alphas directly as soon as you see something. Alpha Ash said they're still heading our way, but he'll let us know if they change course."

*Got it*, Leo and I linked at the same time.

"Move out."

I should have been with my luna, guarding her with my life, but I understood the alphas' orders. The enemy was in my backyard, so to speak. Still, I couldn't stop myself from linking Tyler as we trotted along.

*Is my little luna bunny in the safe room?*

*Of course.*

That made me breathe easier. The alphas had spared no expense when they built their safe room. It was impregnable and had independent water and air systems. It could only be locked and unlocked from the inside, and there was an emergency exit tunnel that led to a location only the alphas knew. They had dug it themselves to keep it secret.

At the time, I'd thought Alpha Mason had invented the job to keep alphas Ash and Wyatt out of trouble for the summer, but now I could definitely see the value of it. I needed to do something like that for our safe room.

*Peri's with her,* Tyler continued, *and the rest of us are on guard outside. What's happening there?*

*Nothing yet— Wait.*

Cove's ears pricked up right as Leo linked me that Ruby heard something. Knowing Angelo's senses were sharper than a human's but nowhere near our level, I alerted him. He immediately froze and linked us to hold our positions and listen.

Something was moving through the forest about fifty feet in front of us, last autumn's leaf and needle fall crunching softly under irregular, quick footsteps. Whatever it was, it was lighter than a wolf. I let my mate know, and Angelo drew the two handguns from his hip holsters.

*Shifter*, Cove told us all, *but I not smell this before.*

"I smell a witch," Angelo said, drawing in a deep breath through his nose.

*I smell mate!* Ruby yelped, and Angelo and I both felt Leo's shock.

Before we could blink, a red fox staggered out of the undergrowth, her tongue hanging out and her sides heaving. She had her front left paw tucked up beneath her and limped along. Her beautiful amber eyes suddenly fixed on Ruby, and she ran as fast as she could on three legs, dove under Ruby, and laid there panting. Ruby sniffed all over her, pausing on her injured paw, then began licking it.

"Can she tell you anything?" Angelo asked as he scanned the forest.

*Dire wolves*, Ruby linked us and the alphas.

*Do what you can*, Alpha Jayden responded right away, *but retreat rather than die.*

*Em's a beta, Leo's a former alpha, and I'm me.* Angelo shot me a cocky wink. *We'll hold the line, alpha, **and** give them hell.*

Meeting his eyes, I smirked and nodded.

*Leo*, I said, *send her to our house. I'll tell Reau to meet her on the porch and take her back to the safe room with him.*

As Leo sent his little mate off, I linked Thoreau and caught him up to speed. The fact that she was Leo's mate didn't faze him, but meeting a real, live fox shifter had him jumping with excitement.

I rolled my eyes.

*Get back to the safe room with her as soon as you can*, I told him. *And she's hurt, so be careful.*

*I will, Bubba. Promise!*

*Here they come*, Cove rumbled to us and the alphas.

I closed the link with Thoreau to focus and heard twigs snap and the rhythmic thud of running paws.

Shrieking yips broke the early morning silence, and the rising sun glinted off the mass of dark fur coming toward us in an unfurling carpet. Angelo cocked his guns, Cove crouched into attack position, and Ruby bared his fangs.

*What's your ETA?* Angelo linked the alphas.

*Seven or eight minutes,* Alpha Cole said.

*But we're here,* someone linked us.

Delta and Lake, Zayne and Zayden Maxwell's wolves, filled the gap between me and Leo. I glanced at my mate to see Beatrix standing on his far side, strands of her hair rising as a fiery halo built around her.

Angelo stepped forward, his guns up and trained on the lead wolf.

"You've crossed into Five Fangs territory!" he bellowed. "Stop where you are!"

The dire wolves slid to a stop, leaf litter kicking up from their paws, and I did a quick head count as they focused their burning red eyes on my mate.

*Twenty of them,* I linked the alphas. *Near as I can count.*

*Leave at least one alive to question,* Alpha Mason commanded.

*Confident in us, isn't he?* Zayne smirked, making me, Leo, and Zayden chuckle.

The lead dire stepped forward, and a sound like breaking glass filled the air.

*That fox is ours. Give it back.*

"She is the mate of one of our wolves," Angelo called out. "Whatever claim you have on her is gone. Now, leave in peace or die in pieces."

*A man, a witch, and four little wolves.* The dire scoffed. *Who are you to threaten us? Stand aside or die yourselves.*

"Bring it if you're hard enough, pup." Angelo grinned. "You'll be my first kill of the day."

The dire laughed, a piercing screech that made Cove's ears hurt, then surged forward.

Angelo's guns barked, then barked again, and the dire dropped, his body soon lost in the trampling paws of his pack mates as they swarmed toward us.

*Guess they think they hard enough,* Cove murmured with a smirk.

*Guess so,* I snorted. *Let's find out.*

\#

*Quartz*

Jayden kept me in check until we heard the sounds of fighting, then gave in to the inevitable.

*Permission?* I growled.

*Granted, but leave one alive,* he reminded me.

*No promises*, I growled, and he rolled his eyes.

Leaping over a fallen tree, I landed in the midst of the battle. Not wasting time, I attacked the first dire wolf I saw. Dropping low, I sank my fangs into his belly, dug my paws into the dirt, and yanked hard. Blood burst in my mouth as his guts spilled out, and I danced back as he whirled and snapped at me.

Even if dires had accelerated healing, which they *didn't*, he couldn't retract his intestines back into his body faster than I could lunge, and I clamped my jaws around his throat and shook my head like a dog does with a squirrel. He pawed at me, and one of his wickedly sharp front claws caught my left ear.

That pissed me off good and proper.

I liked when Posy played with my ears.

Keeping my hold tight on the dire's throat, I pushed him up onto his back paws and rose with him, then jerked down with all my strength. My jaws ripped out his trachea, and red sprayed me like a shower from the new hole under his chin.

He swayed for a second and his crimson eyes glared at me, but he was dead. His brain just hadn't caught up with that fact yet.

Already forgetting him, I whirled back into the fight, one ear flapping by a thread, my white fur drenched in the blood of my enemy, and a windpipe dangling from my grinning maw.

*And you wonder why everyone is scared of you*, Jayden sighed.

*I don't wonder at all,* I sneered and leaped at my next victim.

#

*Wyatt*

Running at full speed, my brothers and I tore into those dire wolves like the wrath of the Goddess.

Quartz killed one within seconds of our arrival and already had another by the balls.

Yes, literally.

Garnet and Topaz each battled a dire, and Sid and Granite paired up to take on one. Cove and Ruby were also partnered, as were Delta and Lake, who probably didn't know how *not* to fight as a team.

Beatrix was already there, and her sisters arrived soon after we did. Blue and green hexes and fireballs hissed through the air and slowed the dires that they hit, which is when Angelo danced in. He'd ditched his pistols at some point and now swung a razor-edged sword that cleaved off the dires' heads like their necks were nothing more than silk scarves.

Dad and Papa got there almost at the same time and dove right into the fight, each one targeting a dire, and our warriors soon followed in twos and threes until we had thirty wolves on our side.

The battle was won at that point and, minutes later, there was only one dire still breathing. Garnet had it pinned down with his jaws clamped on the back of its neck. The witches bound it with magic, and four of our warriors carried it back to Emerson's, where they'd borrow some clothes and a vehicle to drive it to our cells.

While Sid, Topaz, Dad, and Papa tried to convince Quartz it was safe to give control back to Jay, Garnet linked with our girl and the betas to let them know it was okay for Posy and Peri to come out of the safe room, but we wanted them to stick around until we got home. Posy, of course, volunteered to make a big breakfast for them.

Meanwhile, Granite accompanied Angelo as he checked each dire to make sure it was dead. No one wanted a surprise later.

*They were chasing a fox shifter?* I asked him as we went.

"Yeah. She's Leo's mate *and* a witch. Pretty sure an earth one, since I didn't recognize the scent of her magic."

*Jackpot!* Granite crowed. *Full coven in the pack!*

*And a fox shifter,* I added. *The sickness wiped them out by the skulk, you know, and now they're the rarest of us all.*

"I can't wait to see what kind of offspring we get from these blends of shifters," Angelo said with a laugh.

I thought of the donkey dragon babies from the movie *Shrek* and giggled.

*Five Fangs is already a haven for waifs and strays*, I joked. *Might as well add in a few mutant babies to keep it interesting.*

"Interesting?" Angelo shook his head. "I don't think 'interesting' is the right word to describe a nest of feathery pups with beaks and furry chicks with fangs."

That image made Granite laugh so hard, he snorted snot bubbles out of his nose.

#

*Thoreau*

Sitting on the couch in the safe room, I petted the ball of soft red fluff curled up beside me and hummed happily. She was so pretty and soft!

*Reau, let us in, please*, Bubba linked me. *The danger is gone now.*

*The fox said not to let anyone in while she was sleeping,* I told him, *and she's still sleeping.*

*Well, I am your bubba, and I'm telling you to let us in.* Bubba sounded like he was trying not to laugh. *The alphas want to talk to her, and Leo needs to make sure his mate is okay.*

*All right, but if she gets mad and buries me in an earthquake, it's your fault!* I warned him and carefully stood up so I didn't wake the fox.

*What makes you think she'd do that?* he asked as I unlocked the door and opened it.

"She said she would bury anyone in an earthquake who woke her up." I blinked up at him.

"Did she say anything else, Reau?" Leo pushed past me into the room and dropped to his knees in front of the fox.

"Just her name," I said with a shrug. "Bubba, can we have breakfast now? I'm starving."

"Sure." Bubba scrubbed his big hand through my curls. "The alphas, the witches, Mr. Barlow, and Mr. Price are joining us. Angelo's making a feast of pancakes and bacon."

"Pancakes?" I squealed and clapped my hands. "Oh, boy!"

I moved to race up the stairs, but Leo called me back.

"Reau!" he whined. "What is it?"

"What's what?" I scowled, cranky to be held up when pancakes were in my future.

"Her *name*," Leo sighed. "What is it?"

"Poppy Torres." I grinned as I looked at him and remembered the rest of what she'd told me. "Oh, and she said to tell you that if you try to run away or reject her, she'll hunt you down and gut you like a fish."

Laughing at Leo's big eyes, I ran up the stairs, hoping Gelo didn't forget to put chocolate chips in my pancakes.

## 10: Foxy Lady

*Leo*

I looked down at the gorgeous creature curled up beside me on the couch and felt my heart stutter.

I hadn't seen her human form yet, and I didn't need to. I loved her already.

And I didn't deserve her.

There was no way to know how many shifters had died before they ever found their mates, but I knew *exactly* how many my hands or my orders had killed in the last year. How many people I'd condemned to live without their Goddess-given mates.

So how in the name of the moon did I deserve a mate? *Me*. A demon-tainted shell of a man whose existence was dependent on a luna's pity and her alphas' charity?

I knew why I was living where I was. The alphas wanted to make sure I didn't have any lingering diabolical influences, hence the Angel of Death as a housemate. The luna, Goddess love her kind heart, wanted to make sure I didn't have any suicidal tendencies, hence the mother hen known as Beta Emerson Jones as a housemate.

And as for our third housemate, Thoreau considered anyone a friend who treated him with the least bit of kindness, whether it was letting him ride a dirt bike or helping him get his shirt buttoned right or just making him a 'peabutter sammich.'

*I swear, that kid would live on those if you let him,* I chuckled to myself.

A flicker of electricity stirred the hair on my arms as my mate began to shift, and I realized I knew nothing about fox shifters. I didn't even know if the fox was a separate spirit, like it is for us wolves, or only a form, like it is for bird shifters.

*I do know I should have gotten her some clothes*, I growled at myself as I stood up.

Stripping off my t-shirt, I held it out in one hand while keeping my back to her.

"Sorry," I muttered. "I can get you something better to wear in a minute."

I felt her take it from my hand and let my arm drop back to my side.

"This is fine," she murmured, and I could hear a smile in her voice. "It smells like you. Like peaches. Mmm. Yum."

*Peaches! Mate says we smell like peaches!* Ruby yipped gleefully, and a little heat flared across my cheeks.

"You smell like lemons. Fresh. Clean. Pure." *Everything I'm not.* "Are you okay? I saw your one paw was hurt. Do you need healing?"

"No, just needed enough sleep to heal myself. I've been running for three days. You can turn around, by the way."

Lifting my eyes to the ceiling, I took a deep breath and let it out slowly.

*One look,* I told Ruby. *One look to hold onto after she rejects us.*

*She won't,* he smirked.

*Don't make it more painful than it has to be,* I growled at him. "Mate? Are you okay?"

A small hand touched my bare shoulder, and I shivered as sparks flared where our skin connected. I heard her sharp inhale and knew she felt them, too.

I still didn't turn to face her. I knew that if I saw her, I'd lose all the strength it was taking me to do the right thing.

"Listen," I muttered, my voice low and rough, "Reau told me what you said, and I won't, but I suggest you reject me."

"What makes you say that before I even know your name?" she asked.

*Because I am going to wreck this,* I told her silently. *I am going to smash this so bad, you won't feel guilty when you leave me. I want you to hate me so your precious heart can be free to find a better life.*

"Leo Espen Halder," I bit out coldly and turned my head just enough to see the hand still on my shoulder, "so you can say it correctly when you reject me."

"Well, Leo, I'm Poppy, and I think the first thing you should know about me is that I do a thing called what I want." Now she sounded like she was laughing. "And rejecting you is not something I want. Why do you want me to?"

"If you knew the things I've done, you wouldn't ask. You'd just run." I barked out a harsh laugh. "I cannot and will not ask you to sacrifice your future. Reject me now and be free to seek your happiness wherever you want."

Her hand left my shoulder, and my heart constricted at the loss of her touch. Ruby whimpered as the sparks fizzed out, but then wiggled with excitement when a flurry of movement brought her around in front of me. My eyes drank in her beauty; I could not have imagined a more perfect woman.

Her hair was stick-straight, black as a raven's wing, and flowed down her back in a dark river. My shirt was huge on her, but

68

couldn't hide her round curves. Her liquid black eyes locked on my face as she studied it as thoroughly as I was studying hers.

Perfect cupid's bow lips, high cheekbones, and toast-brown skin, taut and smooth like a plum.

The smell of lemons intensified as she doused me with her magic. Her eyes grew sharp and her face turned stern, and I shuddered because I knew what she saw inside me.

"You *will* tell me everything that hurt you," she commanded, "so I can understand how you need to be loved."

"Poppy." I blinked at the sudden sting in my eyes. "I'm not good for you and have nothing to give you. Not even a home or an income. I'd only disappoint you."

"*I* am good for *you*, and the only thing I need you to give me is yourself. Your love and your loyalty. And I don't have a home or income, either." She rolled her eyes. "Obviously, I don't even own a pair of shoes right now, but you know what? We'll figure it out together."

I raised one shaking hand and cupped her face with it. Stroking my thumb over her full cheek, I savored the mate sparks. She smiled and leaned into my hand.

*I don't know how much longer I can hold out and be noble here.*

"Leo, the Goddess led me here to you *and* to this pack for a reason, and I think some of it might have to do with the sister witches I sense in this house."

*Oh, yeah,* I thought. *Forgot about them.*

*See?* Ruby yipped. *The Goddess' hand at work.*

"My alphas are here, too," I told her. "They're going to want to ask you a lot of questions. Let me get you a pair of pants, then we'll meet everyone. Sorry I don't have any, um, underthings for you."

"It's fine. I'll appreciate anything."

*Reau, buddy, bring me a pair of your sleep pants for Poppy, please*, I linked him.

*She's not a fox anymore?* he pouted.

*She can't stay a fox all the time.* I rolled my eyes. *Don't you want to meet her?*

*Is she pretty?*

*Very.*

*On my way!*

*And she's mine, Reau,* I growled. When he didn't answer, I repeated, *Reau?*

"We'll go shopping later. The pack has emergency funds for situations like this," I explained to her.

Then Thoreau was thundering down the basement stairs.

69

"Here, Poppy! Pants!" Yelling that, he flung them at her in his enthusiasm.

She caught them before they could hit her in the face, and fury almost blinded me when I saw the raw skin of her left hand. Carefully, I caught her arm and held it still so I could examine the injury.

"Did those mutts do this?" I asked through clenched teeth.

"No. It's a long story that I'll have to tell your alphas anyway." She smiled at me. "It'll be back to normal by tomorrow, Leo. I promise."

"I got you my favorite pair, Poppy!" Thoreau interrupted, still yelling. "They're super soft!"

"That's too loud, Reau," I grumbled.

"Sorry," he whispered.

"Thank you." She flashed her strong, white teeth at him in a wide grin. "It's very kind of you to loan me your favorite."

"Can you be the fox sometimes just so I can pet you?" Dismissing her gratitude, he tilted his head and his stone-colored eyes stared at her innocently.

"Sure!"

"Reau, meet us upstairs, okay?" I said. "Poppy needs to get dressed now."

He nodded, then was gone as quickly as he came.

"He's a very sweet boy," she murmured as she stepped into the sleep pants and pulled them up.

"Yeah, he is. He's got some issues—"

"I know, and he has a hole inside him, too. Don't worry. I'm here now to help you both heal."

"Poppy?" I couldn't help but give her one last out. "If you choose to stay, if you accept me as your mate, my life is yours. My love is yours. My loyalty is yours. Until I take my last breath, all that I am and ever hope to be is yours."

I laid my finger over her lips when she opened her mouth to reply.

"But don't stick around and make me believe you'll keep me if you're only going to reject me later. I'm already so broken, I don't even know where all the pieces are, never mind how to put them back together again. Just do it now and get it over with so I don't have to be tortured by false hope, too."

My speech finished, I dropped my hand and waited for her to finish crushing the last bits of me that weren't already shattered. Despite her earlier words, I couldn't believe that she'd choose me. That she would find me worthy enough to be her mate.

"I, Poppy Steep Rock Torres—"

*Well, hell.* I closed my eyes. *Here it comes.*

*No!* Ruby howled.

"Will love you my whole life, Leo Espen Halder. You and no other. You are mine, and I am yours."

And two arms went around my waist and squeezed me tightly. Heart thudding, I folded my arms around her shoulders and hugged her back.

"Poppy," I whispered into her hair and my voice cracked. "Please don't leave me."

"Never. I can't force you to believe me, Leo, but you will eventually." Her shoulders shrugged against my chest. "Then I can say I told you so. Win-win for me."

"I don't know." From somewhere, I found enough mischief to tease her. "It's kind of unfair to make announcements like that when you can see the future and I can't."

"Is it my fault that I'm perfect?" She pulled her head back enough to look at me, her liquid black eyes snapping.

"No, it's not and, yes, you are," I grinned down at her, feeling lighter than I had in a long, long time.

"Good boy!" She reached up and patted the top of my head with her uninjured hand.

With a playful growl, I picked her up by her waist so we were nose to nose.

"Oh, am I going to have fun kissing that sass out of you, little vixen," I murmured and stared into her dark eyes.

"Since I'm ninety percent sass, I think that will take a lot of kissing." Her lips curled into a smirk. "Decades and decades and decades."

"Oh, a hundred years at least," I whispered as I pressed my lips to hers.

## 11: Lost and Found and Lost

*Cole*

While we waited for Leo's new mate to wake up, we borrowed some clothes and shifted. Thank the Goddess Emerson was a big guy like me and Mase! Thoreau was tickled pink to loan his t-shirts and shorts to the witches, who had flown to the fight, and Angelo kitted out Wyatt, Jay, and Ash. We all held back our laughter when Ash sighed and looked down at where Angelo's pants ended just below his knees.

"Think of them as long shorts," I suggested with a snort.

He sneered and flipped me off.

Then we chowed down on pancakes, linked Posy, and caught up with everyone. We were all happy to see Thoreau adjusting well, even though there were several signs that he needed help beyond the love and care of his new family.

While I watched the boy chat excitedly with Wyatt about Arch and Wayne and dirt bikes, I linked Emerson and Angelo, telling them that we could look into a counselor or therapist for him. They said they already had a meeting set up with a shifter from the royal pack that owed Angelo a favor. I was glad, and I knew Posy also would be when I told her.

"We wanted to set Leo up to see him, too," Emerson said, then bit his lip as he looked at his mate.

"He's refusing so far." Angelo sighed and squeezed Emerson's shoulder. "He needs time. We'll keep our eye on him until we can convince him."

"Posy will talk to him, too," Jay said with a nod.

"She certainly has a weakness for the underdog, doesn't she?" Ariel murmured with a gentle smile. "It's admirable how she can be so caring after what she's endured."

"She's a badass bitch, all right." Ash puffed out his chest and beamed proudly.

"That's not the nicest way to say that your mate is a strong woman, Ash." Papa rolled his eyes at him.

"It shocked her the first time I said it," he admitted, "but I think she kind of likes it now, not that *she* would ever say a swear word."

After our late breakfast, we sent Zayden and Zayne to trace the dire wolves' trail back to where they crossed into Dark Woods and make sure there weren't any more surprises waiting across the border. Beatrix insisted on going along; since her mates and Angelo were fine with that, who were we to say no?

Then Sara and Ariel volunteered to fly back to the alpha house and bring some vehicles over for us to drive home. Maria, on the other hand, decided to stay in case Poppy woke up before they came back.

Once we were settled in the living room with cups of coffee, Mase asked if anyone had ever visited the Cold Moon pack.

"Yeah, I have," Emerson volunteered. "A couple of months before I found Five Fangs, I met with the alpha to see if it might work out for me to join the pack. Why?"

"Did you meet his luna?" Mase asked.

"Craziest woman I have *ever* had the misfortune to meet," Emerson grouched, then turned to Angelo. "Babe, I'm telling you now, if I lose my mind, put me down. Do not let me hurt people and linger for years in madness and misery."

"*Orsacchiotto* (teddy bear), you forget I have healing in these hands." Angelo smirked and wiggled his fingers at him. "I'll keep your mind straight."

"The only straight thing about you, Em," Wyatt snickered, unable to help himself. "It's good that you have Gelo's magic hands to keep you from losing your nuts."

"Wyatt!" Jay hissed. "There's a lady present! And the expression is losing your marbles, not your nuts."

"Eh, marbles, nuts, same thing. And if he's going to pitch me balls, I have to swing at them."

"Stop thinking with *your* balls for five minutes!"

"Why are you thinking about my balls?"

"I didn't say I was! I said *you* were."

"But you had to be thinking about them to think *I* was thinking with them. I mean, I know they're tremendous, interesting, and amazing, but, dude, you're my *brother*. It's wrong for you to obsess over them like this."

"Wyatt, I am going to cut your balls off and shove them down your throat if you don't shut the hell up!" Jay gritted through his teeth.

Papa's head swiveled from Wyatt to Jay and back like he was watching a tennis match, an impassive look on his face, but his eyes glinted with laughter. Em's face turned beet red, Dad choked on a laugh, and Angelo hid a grin behind his hand. Thoreau looked clueless, Maria and Ash were giggling messes, and Mase looked done.

I mean, he looked *DONE*.

Being around Papa always put his hackles up and made his icy front downright arctic. Add in this morning's surprise fight and now Wyatt's antics when he was trying to have a serious conversation, and he was about to erupt.

With a sigh, I reached around Maria and slapped Wyatt upside the head.

The little cunt had the audacity to scowl at me.

*Bro, I just saved your life*, I linked him with an eye roll. *You should say thanks.*

*Jay wouldn't cut—*

*Not Jay. Mase,* I hissed. *Be quiet for a bit, Wy. He's on edge.*

Wyatt's eyes cut over at our eldest brother, who'd turned to face Emerson and resume his questions while ignoring the rest of us.

"What did the luna do that made you think she was crazy?"

"For one," Emerson began, "she carried around a doll and called it her pup. For another, the way she dressed and her make up, I can't even describe it. Like a little girl who had gotten into her mother's closet or something. And then, the thing that made me light out of there—"

He swallowed hard and glanced at Angelo before looking back at Mase.

"She, uh, she assaulted me."

"You know I need more details, Em."

"She tried to—" His face paled and two bright spots of red bloomed on his cheeks.

"Oh, *orsacchiotto* (teddy bear)," Angelo crooned and pulled him into a hug, tucking his mate's face into his neck. "I'm here. You're safe."

"She tried to touch me," Emerson muttered against Angelo's throat. "You know what I mean. She said I had to prove I was gay. I wanted to break her neck, but the alpha was there with his beta and gamma. I was a big, strong kid, but I wouldn't have stood a chance against all three of them."

"What did the alpha do during all this? *Watch?*" I asked, feeling as disgusted as Emerson must have.

"Yeah. It was surreal. They all stood there and watched." Emerson leaned more into Angelo's embrace and put his arms around his mate's waist. "I grabbed my backpack and ran out of there as fast as my legs could take me. I ran all day and into the night and didn't stop until I couldn't run anymore."

"How old were you?" Angelo asked with gritted teeth.

"Seventeen. I'd been on my own for about a year and a half, and I'd seen some strange and scary stuff, but nothing like that."

As Angelo rubbed Emerson's back and murmured sweet reassurances in his ear, we all saw the homicidal glint in the eyes of the Angel of Death. The Cold Moon luna was as good as dead.

"I need to report to the king first," Mase said as he met Angelo's glare. "He needs to know what else has happened in the past three years. Once King Julian gives his orders, I'll go with you."

74

And that was good enough for Angelo, apparently, because he gave Mase a curt nod.

"We need to call him anyway about the other alpha and luna issue we have," Jay reminded us, jerking his chin at Thoreau, whose eyes were fogged over as he linked someone.

*Most likely Arch and Wayne*, I thought and wondered what he had in common with them other than a love of dirt bikes.

"And he might want to know we found a fox shifter," Ash added, drawing my attention away from Thoreau.

Speaking of, we heard murmurs and footsteps coming up the basement stairs, and Maria bounced in her seat, clapping her hands with excitement.

*So much like Posy*, I linked my brothers, who hummed or smiled in agreement.

"Poppy!" Thoreau shouted and ran to the door.

Before the rest of us could even see her, he had her engulfed in a bear hug.

"Reau, come sit down and mind your manners," Angelo told him in a soft tone. "You've already met her and none of us have."

"But I just like her so much," he whined, but did as Angelo said.

"Everyone, this is my mate, Poppy Torres," Leo introduced the dark-haired beauty, then went around the room and told her all of our names.

"It's a pleasure," she nodded her head with a little smile. "Thank you for saving my life."

"You're welcome," I spoke on behalf of my brothers. "Would you mind telling us how you ended up being chased by a pack of dire wolves?"

"Well, I am a foxy lady, you know," she said with a flippant grin.

"Oh, my Goddess, another Wyatt," Mase muttered and covered half his face with one hand.

"Watch out, alphas," Leo said with a smirk. "She's got her sassy pants on."

"Oh, honey, all my pants are sassy," she shot back.

"Nuh-uh," Thoreau protested. "Those are *my* pants and they're not sassy. They're plaid. I wouldn't wear *sassy* pants!"

Maria, Dad, Ash and Wyatt burst out laughing while the rest of us chuckled. The kid looked around in confusion, and I leaned over and ruffled his curls.

"Reau, do you know what sassy means?" I asked with a tiny smile.

"No."

"Good," Emerson told him. "You don't need any sass."

"The wound on your paw— Well, I guess your hand," Angelo said. "Is it healed?"

"It will be by tomorrow." Poppy held up her arm to show the angry-looking red skin covering her left hand up to her wrist.

"Let me do it now, please," he said and went to her. "No reason to be in pain that long."

When she nodded, he touched his fingers to hers and a golden halo surrounded her hand for several seconds. After it faded, it looked normal. She flexed her fingers, then grinned at him.

"Thank you!" she chirped.

Angelo nodded and sat back down next to Emerson.

"You said those mutts didn't do it?" Leo prompted her to begin her story.

"I chewed my paw off to escape a prison."

All of us stared at her dumbly as we unpacked that sentence. Papa was the first to open his mouth to begin the questions, but she held up one hand.

"About two weeks ago, I was minding my own business, just trotting through the forest, when I was shot with a tranquilizer dart," she said. "I woke up in a concrete and brick room with one leg in a shackle that was anchored to the wall. Several other shifters and creatures were in the same situation."

She went on to explain that men fed and watered them and cleaned up the room once a day, but did not communicate with her or any of the other prisoners. They didn't even talk among themselves. She was fairly sure they were human, as she did not sense them being shifters nor having magic ability.

"Four days ago, two new men came to "inspect" us," she continued, "and it was easy to tell that the one man was in charge of whatever was happening there. The other seemed to be a personal assistant. As they walked past me, Richard - what I called the head honcho in my mind - asked his assistant how soon the lab would be ready because he wanted these abominations eradicated as soon as possible."

Instead of breaking down in tears as some would, Poppy lifted her chin and her eyes were fierce.

"I don't know how it is with any other witch, as I've never met any before you, Maria, but I can't use my magic in fox form. That night, I chewed my paw off enough to slip out of the shackle, snuck out of the window, and ran. I ran for three days. I don't know if the dire wolves were sent by Richard, or if they picked up my trail on their own. However, I do know the Goddess was guiding my steps: as soon as I crossed into your territory, I sensed my mate."

Here she stopped and smiled up at Leo, whose eyes burned with rage. When he noticed her looking at him, though, he bent down and kissed her forehead.

"The rest you know," she finished and snuggled into Leo's chest as his arms went around her shoulders.

As usual, Mase took charge. Not that I was complaining. I was still digesting her story.

"Dad, will you and Papa go with Wyatt and Ash to interrogate our prisoner?" Mase asked, and I think we were all surprised he'd included Papa. "Cole and I need to call King Julian about Cold Moon and Gray Shadows and can inform him about this at the same time, but I would like to know if those dires were from the prison or a stray pack."

"I think we all know the answer," Wyatt said with a frown, "but we'll find out for sure."

"What do you want me to do, Mase?" Jay asked.

"Poppy, can you give us a general sense of where this prison was?"

"If you have a map, I can mark what I remember," she offered.

"Jay, work with her on that, please," Mase directed, "then go home to Posy so the betas can collect their mates."

"I would like a hand in cleaning out this prison," Angelo growled, "but I also need to take care of the Cold Moon luna."

"We'll sort out who goes where and when after we talk to the king," I told him, and he nodded.

*Sorry to interrupt, alphas,* Matthew linked us out of the blue. *I know you're busy, but we have a problem.*

*Is Posy okay?* my brothers and I linked back at once.

*Did something happen to my little luna bunny?* Emerson demanded.

*What's going on, puppy?* Maria asked.

I sank into the mate bond, going deeper and deeper until I felt the distress Posy was trying to hide from us. I bumped the mate link, but she wouldn't open hers. Glancing at my brothers, I saw they'd tried, too, and gotten the same response.

*What's wrong, Matthew?* I barked as fear gripped my heart in an iron fist.

*Mr. Nibbles is missing.*

## 12: Solving Mysteries

*Jayden*

As soon as Sara and Ariel showed up with mine and Ash's SUVs, we gave Ash's to Dad and Papa and sent them to the prison to interrogate the dire wolf.

Then I turned my SUV around, my brothers and the witches piled in, and we headed home.

Emerson wanted to come along, but we needed him to stay and help Poppy make a map and sketch the prison with guard placements. Angelo convinced him, saying we needed the information she had before we could tear the place down.

On the drive home, Mase called the king to give him a short summary of everything with the promise of a detailed report later after we resolved a "small domestic crisis."

And it *was* a crisis, even if not everyone would recognize that as such.

Mr. Nibbles was Posy's one and only friend for a long time. When her mom died, he was there. When her 'father' beat her bloody and broke her bones, he was there. When she was abandoned by her brothers, he was there. Even if he was only faux fur and stuffing, Posy loved him and depended on him for comfort, and he'd always been there to provide it.

And now he wasn't.

"Can you drive faster?" Wyatt hissed from the passenger seat.

*Apparently, you're not the only one who's worried*, Quartz snorted.

*You should be, too,* I rebuked him. *Posy is upset.*

*I never said I wasn't worried. I'm just better at hiding it than all of you.*

Arriving at our house, we found an overturned ant hill. Tristan searched the flowerbeds in the front yard. Crew walked along the treeline and peered into the underbrush. Going inside, we found Tyler opening every cupboard in the kitchen, Peri turning the dining room upside down, and Matthew on his hands and knees looking under the living room furniture.

"Where is she?" Mase growled, startling his beta.

Matthew shot up and whacked his head on the coffee table with a little wince.

"In her special room," he said. "She's checking it for the fourth time. Alpha, we've looked *everywhere!* In the cabana, in the pool itself, all over the backyard, every room in the house. What are we going to do?"

"I'll go talk to her and see the last time and place she saw it," Cole said, already trotting toward the stairs. "Keep looking!"

Wyatt volunteered to double-check our bedroom and bathrooms, Mase took the guest rooms, Ash headed for the home office, and I went to search the laundry room and basement, even though Posy had *never* gone down there.

The basement wasn't creepy or covered in spider webs or anything like that. It was finished with flooring and walls and lighting. We'd never decided what we wanted to do with the space, though, so it was empty. Of course, Mr. Nibbles wasn't down there, and I headed back upstairs.

*Something's wrong with Sid,* Quartz said out of the blue.

*Great. That's what we need right now,* I mumbled to myself, then asked Quartz what he thought was wrong.

*He hasn't said a word, not a peep to any of us or Ash, since Matthew linked us.* Quartz shrugged. *And he's ... squirmy.*

*Squirmy,* I repeated slowly.

*Remember that time he ate all the ice cream that Mom got for Wade after he had his tonsils out? And Wade cried because his throat hurt? And Mom had to go back to the store after dark? And she was pregnant with William and tired and upset because Dad had to go out of town unexpectedly?*

*Yeah, I remember.*

*He's the same as then. Squirmy.*

I blinked rapidly a few times.

*Oh. Oh, no.*

Linking my brothers and the betas, I told them to bring Posy to the living room.

*You found him?* Mase asked hopefully.

*I think a certain someone knows* exactly *where he's at,* was all I said.

#

*Posy*


"Okay, this is going to be difficult," Jayden told me as he sat me down on the couch.

Oh, no. Had he found Mr. Nibbles in bad shape? Had something destroyed him?

My heart raced and my lungs went into overdrive.

"Don't panic, sweetness. Everything's going to be okay." He smiled at me. After I nodded, he turned to Ash, who leaned against the wall near the fireplace. "Ash, let Sid ascend. I need to ask him some questions."

Ash's eyebrows flew up in surprise.

"You think he knows something?"

Sid knew where Mr. Nibbles was? Then why didn't he tell me? I was confused.

"Mm-hmm." Jayden sat next to me and held my hand.

"Oh. Is *that* why he's been so quiet? Sure. Mase?"

With a frown, Ash looked at Mason, who nodded and moved closer to him. I didn't understand what was going on, but Jayden gave me a kiss on my cheek. Wyatt came over and sat on my other side and held my free hand. Cole stood behind the couch and squeezed my shoulder. The betas, the witches, and Peri watched in silence.

"Posy," Jayden whispered in my ear, "don't be surprised if he regresses."

"What does regress mean?" I whispered back.

"It means to move backward. Sid will act younger and younger the more upset he gets."

"I don't want him to get upset at all!" I protested.

"Sometimes, we *have* to get upset, sweetness. It's life. Trust me?" He brought my fingers up to his lips and kissed them.

"I do. Just don't—" I swallowed. "Even if he knows something about Mr. Nibbles, don't upset him too much, okay?"

"I'll be gentle. We all will. Otherwise, he'll go into baby mode and endless sobbing won't help anything."

I grimaced, but nodded, then looked back at Ash.

As soon as his eyes flared neon green, his whole posture changed. His wide shoulders hunched in, his front teeth sank into his bottom lip, and his fingers tangled together like mine did when I was nervous or afraid or both.

I didn't want him to feel like that, but I also wanted my bunny.

"Sid," Jayden said quietly, "where's Mr. Nibbles?"

Sid-in-Ash's-body shook his head, sending his curls dancing wildly, and his eyes darted around the room before settling on the floor near my feet.

"I no know," Sid muttered.

"You *do* know." Jayden's voice stayed calm and quiet. "Tell me, buddy. What happened to Mr. Nibbles? No one's going to be mad, right, Posy?"

"Oh, no, I won't be mad," I told Sid. "I promise."

Tears formed in his eyes and slid down his cheeks, and I stopped caring about Mr. Nibbles. I wanted to go to my wolf and comfort him. My other mates realized that, and Cole's hand tightened on my shoulder while Wyatt and Jayden gripped my hands.

"Me no mean to," Sid muttered.

*Oh, Sid,* I thought.

"Whatever happened, I know you didn't mean to," I told him, and he raised his wet, red eyes to mine.

"Me sowwy. Me so sowwy," he choked.

This was breaking my heart. Yanking out of my mates' hold, I went over to him and motioned for him to come down to my level. I knew he was miserable, but I didn't expect him to drop on me so heavily, and my knees buckled. Mason caught me - us - and basically controlled our fall to the floor, then helped me out from under Ash's ginormous body.

Sid didn't want to let me go, which I understood, so we ended up with me in his lap and his face in my throat. He tightened his arms around me so hard, it hurt my ribs, though, and tears spurted to my eyes.

*Mason,* I linked, panicking just a little. *He's squeezing me too tight!*

Instantly, Mason grabbed Sid's wrists and pulled his arms away.

"You're hurting her, Sid," he murmured. "You can't hug her that hard."

"Me sowwy." Sid slumped limply. "Me no hurt mate."

"Shh. It's all right. It was an accident," I whispered and petted his curls.

Mason cautiously released his wrists, but stayed crouched next to us.

"What happened with Mr. Nibbles, my heart?" I asked. "You can tell me. I won't hate you. Not ever. And I won't be mad."

Sid nodded, but didn't take his face out of my throat.

"Last night, we went in woods, 'member?"

"I do." I kissed his forehead. "Ash ate too many brownies and was on a sugar high, so you two went on a run to burn off some energy before bedtime."

I heard one of the betas snort and had to hide my own smile. Brownies before bed weren't going to happen ever again in this house. Ash had been bouncing off the walls.

Of course, it didn't help that he ate one whole pan all by himself.

"When me come back," Sid continued, "me see Mr. Nibbles by couch. Me say, 'Mr. Nibbles, this not you bed. Me take you to you bed.' And me take him to mate's special woom."

"Oh. Thank you. That was very sweet of you. Was that while I was in the shower?"

81

" 'Es, 'es, but den—" He swallowed hard and knotted his fingers together again. "Sid pway wif Mr. Nibbles a widdle bit and Mr. Nibbles— Mr. Nibbles get huwt."

*He slipped into third person*, I linked my mates. *Does that mean he's getting more upset? Should I stop asking him questions?*

*He needs to admit his mistakes, princess, not hide from them*, Ash told me, his tone firm. *Tell him to bring you Mr. Nibbles.*

"Sid, did you, um, hide Mr. Nibbles?" I took his hands in mine and untangled his fingers.

" 'Es. No want mate to see. Sid sad and 'shamed."

"Sid." I held his face in my hands and looked into his eyes. "You are worth a thousand Mr. Nibbles."

"Sid is?" he whispered.

"Yes, you are. I know you didn't mean to hurt him. Can you please go get him for me?"

"Mate no mad? Mate no hate Sid?" His eyes looked so sad, I couldn't stand it.

"No, my heart." I pecked his nose, then either cheeks, then his lips. "I love you. Forever and ever."

"Sid get Mr. Nibbles." Sitting me on the floor, he left the room.

"This is much more emotional than I imagined it would be," Ariel sighed, leaning against Tristan. "I mean, I know it's stressful for you, luna, but I didn't think Sid would be so upset that he'd regress."

"He cannot handle someone being mad at him," Jayden explained. "Since it's Posy, that makes it ten times worse. Plus, like he said, he's ashamed of himself."

"He's already the baby-est of the babies," Mason muttered as he draped an arm around my shoulders. "He doesn't have that far to regress to reach a toddler stage."

"You know," Peri said, "so long as Sid didn't rip him into pieces, I can probably fix Mr. Nibbles."

"Oh, that would be great." I clasped my hands under my chin and smiled at her.

"I don't think he would have done that." Wyatt shook his head. "As soon as he realized he'd 'huwt' Mr. Nibbles, he would have been too devastated to do more damage. The fun would have been over."

"Good point," I agreed.

Sid came back into the room. He had a white grocery bag in his hands. After he sat down, he held it out for me to take.

*Please don't be in pieces*, I chanted. *Please don't be in pieces.*

Opening the bag, I looked inside, then fell flat on my back and laughed with relief. Mason took my face in his hands and hovered over me, and my other mates panicked and rushed over to surround me, but I waved them back.

"Peri, one ear came off." I held up the bag. "Come see."

She walked over and took Mr. Nibbles out of the bag and examined him while I stared up into Mason's worried eyes.

"I love you," I told him, then looked at the others. "I love all of you so much."

They all let out a deep breath and sank back to sit around me.

"Oh! This will take ten minutes to fix," Peri said, and everyone let out a breath of relief. "I just need a needle, a pair of scissors, and some brown thread."

She went over and rubbed her knuckles in Sid's curls until he whined and pulled away.

"It's an easy repair, Sid," she told him as she dropped down to hug him, "but don't do it again. Mr. Nibbles isn't your toy to play with. Stuffed animals can't hold up to rough play like plushies made especially for dogs. Understand, pup?"

" 'Es. Sid no huwt Mr. Nibbles again."

At her words, a brainstorm hit me. I sat up and clapped my hands with excitement.

"You know what we're going to do? We're going to buy my wolves some toys! Cole, Wyatt, Ash, please go shift." They hustled out of the room and I turned to Mason. "Could you wait to shift until we get to the toy shop, please? That way, you can drive us in your truck and the wolves can ride in the back. Will they all fit?"

"Yeah. We've done it before," he told me, "but I don't know where I can shift in a parking lot in front of a human store."

"In your truck. All the windows are blacked out, right?"

"*And get all that hair on my seats?!*" He crossed his arms over his chest and narrowed his eyes at me. "I think not."

"It's not like I can't vacuum it out when we get home." I narrowed mine back at him.

We had a stare off for a few seconds, then he rolled his eyes.

"Fine," he muttered, then pulled me against his chest and hugged me. "I don't know why I bother to fight it. We both know I'm always going to give you your way."

My lips curled into a satisfied smile as I snuggled into him, but I made sure it was gone before I turned my head and looked at Jayden. I chose my next words with great care. Quartz needed a different approach.

"You don't have to shift if you don't want to, Jayden. Quartz would be a party pooper, anyway."

Of course, Granite, Topaz, and Sid came running back in the room right as I said that and snickered.

*I would not*, Quartz declared, sounding outraged.

"But you probably won't even pick a toy." I pooched out my bottom lip.

*I neither need nor want a toy,* he sneered the last word.

"Would you rather stay here?" I sighed and dropped my eyes. "I guess I can take the pups by myself—"

*No, I'm coming along! Jayden, I will shift now and ride in the back with the pups.* Someone *has to keep them from jumping out and chasing the first cat they see.*

*Hey!* Granite yelped. *I only did that once!*

*Once was enough!* Quartz snapped and turned to me. *Little mate, I will pick a toy because you desire it, but don't expect me to ever **play** with it.*

I nodded and turned my face back into Mason's chest because I couldn't hide my satisfied grin.

*You're amazing,* Peri linked. *You know how to handle each one of them.*

*I'm learning,* I told her. *You seem to be just as amazing at managing Ty and River.*

*I'm learning,* she echoed with a chuckle.

"Luna," Tristan said, "I don't think they're going to let you in the toy shop with a wolf, let alone five of them."

"*Six,*" Tyler corrected. "Riv's demanding a toy now, too. Per, let's go along and you can help the luna wrangle her sled dog team."

"And we'll go to the pet store, not the toy shop. Crew," Mason looked at the beta, "link Bel Aire and let him know we're coming in wolf form with our luna."

"Then we're coming, too," Matthew and Sara said in unison, then looked at each other and scowled.

"The more, the merrier," I giggled.

Crawling over to Sid, I wrapped my arms around my fluffy baby.

"If something bad ever happens again, don't hide it from me, okay?" I kissed the top of his head. "I won't be mad, and there's nothing you could ever do to make me hate you."

*Sid pwomise. Sid will be good boy. Sid will be mate's good boy always and always.*

"Oh, my heart, you already are."

## 13: Toys!

*Quartz*

Wonder of wonders, no one jumped, fell, or was pushed out of the truck bed on our way to the pet store.

*Seems like a good omen, but only time will tell.*

After Mason shifted and we gathered around her, Posy said we could have twenty minutes to look around the store before meeting up in the toy section. Then she handed Topaz over to Sara and Crew, most likely hoping the beta's calm nature would help with Paz's hyper one.

Sid and River wouldn't be separated, so Peri was stuck with both babies. I didn't think they'd be much of a problem, though. They'd be on the hunt for someone to pet them, and the parking lot was half full of cars, so there should be plenty of opportunities for that. Just in case no human customers obliged, however, the young shifters employed here would be delighted to play with them.

Posy asked Granite to go with Tristan and Ariel, recognizing that they were more mature than Matthew and Maria, whom everyone now referred to as M&M. Gran was probably going to be the hardest manage, so he needed a firm hand, which Tristan and Ariel could provide without becoming sarcastic, like Sara would, or a puddle of giggles, like M&M would. Personally, I believed she was sending Garnet with M&M to supervise *them*.

As for me, I would go with our mate.

*Thank the Goddess for that.*

Things got a little sticky when she passed around collars and leashes. With a sour frown, I put a paw up and slowly shook my head as she knelt in front of me with a blue collar in her hand.

"You won't be able to go in without it." She pointed to the sign on the door. "What if you carry your own leash? Will that make it tolerable?"

I blew a heavy breath out of my nose, but dipped my head in a nod. Bending down to snap the collar on, she kissed the top of my head.

"I'm sorry. I know this hurts your dignity," she whispered in my ear. "Thank you for being such a good sport and helping me with these crazy pups."

*Garnet would have been fine supervising them,* I admitted, *especially since the betas came, too. You didn't really need me.*

"Oh, my dear, dear wolf. I will *always* need you."

Pleased with her words, affection, and attention, I smiled a little and took the handle of the leash in my mouth when she held it out.

A few months ago, I would have either laughed myself sick or ripped out the throat of anyone who suggested I would be shopping for dog toys in a pet store, yet here I was.

Wearing a damn collar, no less.

*You're as whipped as the rest of us,* Jayden teased.

*Only for our mate,* I huffed.

"Please stay by my side, Quartz," Posy requested. "I'm so nervous around strangers, and the store looks busy."

*I won't leave you, little mate,* I promised. *If it helps, the owner, Spero Bel Aire, is one of our pack members. So are about half the employees.*

"Thanks, but pack or not, they're still strangers."

*I will let no human harm you,* I vowed, *and the shifters don't dare touch you. They know I'd kill them if they did.*

Acknowledging my words with a nod, she checked to make sure my brothers and River were collared and leashed and received thumbs up from everyone. Her trembling hand clenched in my ruff, but she led the way through the automatic doors with her chin up and her shoulders back.

*Our badass bitch, indeed.*

Of course, six big wolves coming into a pet store drew a lot of attention. With busy noses, Topaz and Granite dragged their handlers past us in a rush, and Garnet trotted behind to help keep an eye on them.

Sid and River, on the other hand, stopped and sat like good boys while looking at the humans in the checkout line with big eyes in hopes of pets.

*Attention whores,* I sneered. *You'll do anything for a belly rub, won't you?*

*Belly rubs!* they shouted in unison, which made me roll my eyes.

"We'd better stay with them in case they get too much for Peri to handle alone," Posy murmured in my ear, and I agreed.

Drawn like a magnet by the babies' puppy eyes, a little human girl came running up to us.

"Hi! Can I pet your doggies?" she asked politely, her hands behind her back as she waited for a response.

"Sure," Peri told her with a smile. "They're very good boys!"

"This one walk himself!" the kid squealed and pointed at the leash in my mouth.

"He thinks he's human," Posy pretend-whispered to her, making the girl giggle, then gestured toward the others. "The one with the black stripe down his nose is Sid, and the light gray one is River. They both love cuddles."

When the girl looked at them, immediately Sid wagged his tail and River lolled his tongue.

*Shameless gluttons,* I scoffed at him.

*Party pooper,* Sid shot back, then tilted his head and asked, *What glutton means, Q?*

Rolling my eyes at him, I watched to see what the kid would do. Of course, she ignored them and stretched her fist out to *me.* I stiffened and folded my ears back, but knew I'd have to tolerate it. Posy would be upset if I so much as raised my lip at the child.

"Oh, no. Not this one." Posy turned so her body was in between the little girl and me. "You can pet any of the others, okay?"

"Aw!" the child whined and pooched out her bottom lip. "But he looks like he needs cuddles!"

I expected my mate to explain that I wasn't good with people or even warn her that I was 'aggressive.' Both of those things were true, of course, but I wouldn't have hurt the little girl even if Posy wasn't there.

I wasn't that much of a monster.

*Does she think I am?* Sudden doubt struck me. *Is that why she's keeping the kid away from me?*

"Sorry, sweetie, but this one's special. He's so precious to me, I get jelly if others touch him."

Laying her hand on top of my head, Posy smiled at the little girl, and I scolded myself for being silly enough to doubt her.

\#

*Sid*

"Here, honey." Peri distracted the human pup pestering Quartz and motioned her over to me and Riv. "These boys here are a bit extra, but friendly and playful."

The little pup giggled and held out a teeny fist for us to smell. Obediently, we did, then danced around a bit because we were so excited to play with her. She threw her head back and laughed, then ran her tiny hands all over my face. After booping my nose with hers, she turned to River and did the same thing.

*By the moon, I love pups!*

*Me, too,* River yipped. *Ty-Ty, make pup with mate! Me want pup!*

*Eventually, Riv. We want to practice making them for a while first,* Beta Tyler smirked. *Maybe in a few years.*

*Too long, Ty-Ty!* River whined.

*Mate said we might have pups in a few years, too,* I told him. *Whoever has pups first, promise to let the other play with them, 'kay?*

*Yep-yep, Siddy! Me promise!*

I was so happy, I bounced around a bit until Peri shushed me and said I could accidentally hurt the little human. That got me to stop real quick. *No way* would I ever hurt a pup.

An adult came over and chatted with Peri while me and River sniffed and snuffed all over the pup. She giggled and cooed and her tiny hands rubbed all over our fur. Every few strokes, she went against the grain, which made us shiver.

"Mommy, look!" she called to the adult when she did it again to River. "Why he does shaky-shaky?"

"Go with their fur, Natalie, not against it," the adult corrected the pup, then looked at Peri. "May I show her?"

"Yeah, of course. This is River and this is Sid." Peri pointed to each of us when she said our names. "They're big babies."

The mommy set her bags on the floor, then ran a hand down each of our backs and stopped to scratch the Good Spot right above our tails. Me and River sighed in bliss.

"Thank you for letting us pet your dogs," the mommy said as she gathered her things and took the pup's hand.

"You're welcome." Peri smiled at her and waved them goodbye.

I whimpered, not wanting them to go, and River did, too.

"Come on, babies." Rolling her eyes, Peri tugged our leashes, not that it did anything. She couldn't move us unless we wanted to. "Let's find others who will love on you."

Okay, that made us want to.

We were walking down an aisle full of tweety birdies when a rough-looking, tattooed guy the size of Cole came around the corner and stopped dead.

River eyed him, his ruff a little standy-up, wanting to make sure the dude wasn't a threat to his mate, but the man only grinned and hunkered down in front of us.

"Doggos!" he crowed. "You want pets? Come here and get pets, doggos!"

*Yes!* we screamed.

Jerking the leashes out of Peri's hand, we ran ahead and tackled him to the floor and licked all over his face.

Ashy and Ty-Ty yelled at us, but the guy was laughing so hard that tears rolled down his cheeks, so we ignored our boys.

"Jason!" the human hollered. "Come meet these doggos, Jason! They're awesome!"

Before we knew it, another escaped prisoner-looking dude came over and sat right down to join in our pet fest. Peri told them our names, then covered her mouth and giggled as she watched us play.

*This place is heaven!* I told River as the new dude gave me belly rubs.

*Let's stay forever, Siddy!*

#

*Granite*

Sometimes, Jay listened to old-days music. Once, he played this song that went, "Hallelujah! Hallelujah!" and I asked him what that word meant. He explained it and, ever since then, the song played in my mind when something awesomely super-duper amazing happened.

It was playing loud and clear right now.

Everywhere I looked, I saw something tasty to eat!

Biscuits in bins, cookies in crates, pig ears by the pile, kibbly-bits in buckets, and bully sticks in baskets... It was like the all-you-can-eat buffet that Roger had at the diner on Sundays.

Topaz pulled a huge bone off a shelf and trotted away with it, Sara chasing after him and Crew moseying behind them. Grazing at the cookie bar, I scarfed down about a pound before my ear heard something going squeakity-squeak, and I *had* to find out what it was.

Dragging Tristan along and leaving Ariel's slow self behind, I quickly found an aisle full of little white cages and watched with extreme interest as a couple of fluff balls ran their stubby little legs off on a tiny treadmill.

*No, fluffs! Stop that! Fat makes you tasty!*

As soon as we came into the store, the cats had huddled in the far corners of their glass boxes, smart enough to know that I wanted to eat them. These little dummies didn't stand a chance.

If Posy wasn't here, the cats wouldn't, either, but something in my gut - and Wyatt's nagging voice in my ear - told me she would be upset if I ate one.

Plus, the last time I did, I pooped hairballs for two days. That was not fun. Still, cats were tasty enough to make up for that...

*No, Gran,* Wyatt groaned. *No cats! We do not eat cats. Now, be a good boy.*

*What these, Wy?*

*Hamsters.*

*They cute!* I squealed, watching them tumble all over each other and fight for a turn on the treadmill.

*Sure, sure,* Wyatt sighed, *but we're here to buy toys, not hamsters.*

Tristan went to the end of the aisle to flag Ariel down, and I took my chance. Standing up on my hind legs, I grabbed one of the white cages in my teeth and carefully set it on the floor. The hammies started scurrying around, making me even more excited to chase them. I pawed the top off the cage, shoved my snout in, and snapped one up.

*No, Granite! Bad boy!* Wyatt bellowed. *Don't eat the hamsters!*

*You said no eat cats!* I argued, gulping down another one. Goddess, they were good! *These not cats. These hammies!*

"Oh, shit!" Tristan finally noticed what I was doing and yanked my leash, trying to get my head out of the cage.

*Good luck with that,* I snickered and swallowed a third one.

Ariel!" Tristan yelped. "I need help!"

I managed to snag two more before he grabbed my collar and heaved so hard that he hauled me halfway down the aisle before I finished swallowing. When did he get so strong? Then I realized his wolf was helping him.

*Back off, Creek, you traitor!* I snarled.

*Sorry, Gran,* Creek smirked. *Alpha Wyatt commanded me.*

"Hope the luna brought her credit card," Tristan muttered.

He dragged me along to a bunch of big glass boxes full of water. Small, shiny things zipped around inside them, and I forgot all about the hammies.

*Hallelujah! Hallelujah!* I danced around on my tippy toes. *Whatever these are, I bet they tasty, too!*

\#

*Topaz*

"What a good boy you're being," Sara cooed.

Raising my eyes, I looked up at her, but didn't stop gnawing on the bone I'd found.

"How about we make you pretty for Posy? Hmm? Would you like that?" she crooned.

I blinked twice, then nodded, and she skipped off with a funny grin. She could do whatever she wanted to me so long as I could lay here on this soft bed and eat my treat.

With my leash looped around his wrist, Crew dragged another cushy bed off the shelf and next to mine, then curled up on it with a happy ahh.

"Good call, Paz," he murmured and patted my head.

*Why don't we have beds like this at home?* I asked Cole.

*You don't need them.* He rolled his eyes.

*And bones for nibbles?*

*You don't need them, either. And it's not a bone. It's rawhide shaped like a bone. I'm not sure rawhide is healthy for you.*

*Tastes good.*

*You think everything tastes good,* he scowled.

90

By then, Sara was back with a basket of stuff.

"What's all that?" Crew asked her.

"Stuff to make you good boys pretty!" she giggled.

Crew and I traded side-eye glances, then both of us shrugged and I went back to gnawing.

"But Paz has a chewie and I don't," Crew pouted.

"If I give you a chewie, I can pretty you up?" She tilted her head to the left a little.

"Sure thing, dewdrop."

"Ha!" Rooting around in her shopping basket, she pulled out a bag and handed it to him. "Human-grade venison jerky. Chew away, babe."

"Thanks." Ripping the bag open, Crew popped a square of the jerky in his mouth. "Have fun, sweetheart."

"I intend to," she smirked.

And that's how we ended up with red bows in our hair, plaid bandanas around our necks, and white tutus around our waists.

#

*Garnet*

Okay. Not too bad. The store wasn't destroyed, there was no blood or fire, and no one died.

*Unless you count the hamsters Granite ate,* Mason grumbled.

*Aw, who could blame him for that?* I chortled. *The little fuzz balls going around and around on that exercise wheel were just taunting him, really.*

Sure, our bill came to nearly $2,000, but what was money for if you couldn't spend it? Besides, we'd all had a great time. Even Quartz laughed when he saw Topaz and Crew's matching outfits.

And now we were trotting out to Mase's truck with our toys dangling from our mouths, all except for Quartz, who couldn't be bothered to get his from Posy.

*They're for **dogs**,* he sneered when Sid asked him where his 'stuffy' was. *We are not **dogs**. We are wolves. Alpha wolves.*

*But you pick one,* Sid said, confused.

*It's for Lark. I told her to choose what she wanted and I'd get it for her.*

*But what will* you *play with?*

*Not a **dog** toy, I assure you.*

While Sid pouted at Q's hardheadedness, Topaz and Gran giggled together and shouted, *Party pooper!*

Moving fast, I blocked Quartz as he lunged at them and he plowed into my shoulder. I had my feet firmly planted, though, and he

91

didn't budge me. With a low growl, he raised his upper lip at me, his nose wrinkling, and I nipped his ear in warning.

*Stop before Posy sees you,* I snapped. *She's happy and laughing right now. Don't ruin it. And ignore the pups; you know they live to get a rise out of you.*

*Hmphf,* he grumped.

Tipping his nose up, he turned away and made sure his tail swished me in the face before he trotted off.

I rolled my eyes.

*Party pooper? More like drama king.*

#

*Posy*

After our ... eventful trip to the pet store, Mason and Cole disappeared into the home office to call the king, and Jayden linked Emerson and Angelo to see what further information they'd dug up. Meanwhile, Wyatt and Ash helped me put a meal together, although it was more work watching to make sure they didn't screw up than if I'd just done it all myself. Still, the time spent together was what mattered.

As we all sat down for dinner, Mason, Cole, and Jayden shared what they'd learned, then my mates discussed how they were going to divide up the tasks the king had given them.

"He *does* know you have your own pack to run, right?" I grumbled.

They all laughed, but I didn't want to be separated from them again.

"Except for whoever goes to the prison, it'll only be for one day," Cole assured me, "and two of us aren't leaving pack territory at all."

"You won't have to sleep a single night alone," Mason added with a smile.

"Good." I liked hearing that.

After a lot of back and forth, they decided that Jayden, Angelo, Zayden, Zayne, Beatrix, and Sara would go check out the prison. They would scope it out and decide if they needed reinforcements or could handle it themselves.

Quartz snorted, insulted that anyone would think *he* needed back-up.

Although both Mason and Angelo wanted to deal with the Cold Moon luna, my mates felt it would be better to send Cole, Maria, and Ariel. They knew Angelo would flat out kill the luna with or without the evidence King Julian requested.

Also, Cole didn't think he could hold his temper if he went to Gray Shadows. Not after what Beatrix had shown him of Thoreau's

92

memories. Same with Ash. Knowing the alpha and luna had abused their own pup, Sid would not be able to restrain himself.

So Mason said he would go to Gray Shadows and deal with Emerson and Thoreau's parents.

"I'll take Leo and Poppy along," he decided.

"Why Poppy?" I asked.

"A witch can make sure we don't miss anything." Mason shrugged. "It's just smart, plus neither of them will want to be separated."

"Which leaves Wyatt to do paperwork and Ash to take care of a couple of visitors from the royal pack," Cole finished up.

"Wait. What?" Ash said.

"Visitors?" Wyatt raised his eyebrows. "And why do *I* get stuck with the paperwork?"

"Reau's new therapist," Mason explained. "One of Angelo's buddies who owes him a favor."

"And Spring," Cole said with a grin, and it took me a second to remember that Spring was Everett Breckenridge's wolf. "King Julian thinks he and Reau would be great companions."

"Dude!" Ash jogged his leg up and down as his eyes lit with happiness. "I'm so excited to see Spring and welcome him back in the pack!"

"That's wonderful!" I clapped my hands.

"You need to be there when they meet, Posy," Jayden said. "Your presence alone will keep them calm and comforted, and you always know the right thing to say."

I blushed, still not used to any sort of praise.

"Staying at Emerson's with your betas is a win-win for everyone, sweetness. Your betas will be missing their mates, and you can occupy them with running in circles for you."

I laughed, remembering the day they kept bringing me and Queen Lilah ice pops.

"It's a good call to have Ash with Spring," Wyatt was big enough to admit, "even if I have to man the office."

"Ash sucks at paperwork and you're really good at it." Mason shrugged. "I like knowing it will be in your hands."

Wyatt ducked his head, but I still saw his smile at Mason's compliments.

*My boys,* I thought, my heart full of love and happiness.

## 14: Cold Moon

*Cole*

I hated to leave Posy the next morning, even knowing that two of my brothers would be there, as well as all her betas.

If I had my way, I'd never leave her side.

*Me, either, boss,* Topaz sighed.

*Still, it's only for today,* I reminded us both.

*True,* he agreed.

Tristan and Matthew dropped Ariel and Maria off right on time, and we set out on our four-hour drive. They were good company, so the miles flew by and we were pulling up to the alpha house of Cold Moon before we knew it.

Alpha Thaddeus Quake stood on the front porch waiting for us. He was about Jay's height and size and had rich, dark skin and a soft-looking halo of black hair. I guessed his age to be close to fifty, a little older than most alphas, who usually handed the job off to their sons as soon as they reached eighteen or so.

King Julian said their son, Kayvon, was twenty and more than capable of taking over the pack. Unless I found something to the contrary, he was to be installed as the next alpha.

Mase told me that Alpha Quake was unaware that his beta had asked for our help, but he *did* know we were coming. In true Mase style, he'd called and made an appointment.

"Alpha Barlow." Alpha Quake held out a hand and I shook it. "It's a pleasure to finally meet one of the famous alphas of Five Fangs, but I don't know why you requested this meeting."

"Alpha Quake." I inclined my head. "Beta Napoleon Brooks contacted us to see if we might know of a way to help his luna."

*Way to throw his beta under the bus, boss,* Topaz groaned.

*Oh. Yeah. Did not think of that.*

Alpha Quake's thick black eyebrows flew up.

"He did?"

"Yes, sir. My condolences on your mate's ongoing illness."

"Thank you. I appreciate it. What help do you think you can provide? I've had every shifter doctor I know or could hire, including the royal one, look at Norah to see if they knew of a cure."

"These are Maria Rose and Ariel Harrington, mates to two of our betas." I waved my hand at the girls standing behind me. "They're healers and powerful witches. We think magic may be at play since no shifter doctor can identify what's wrong."

"Oh! I never considered that!" His eyes lit up with hope. "Come on in and meet my Norah."

The alpha led us through the front door and into a spacious living room, where a young man sat on one of the couches and stared at a woman huddled in a recliner in the corner.

"This is our son, Kayvon. He'll be the next alpha as soon as he finds his mate," Alpha Quake told me what I already knew.

I studied Kayvon as he stood. It was easy to see his father in his face, although he was a lot taller, about my height, but lean as a whip. His eyes were honest and his demeanor serious, but not aggressive.

"Alpha Cole Barlow of Five Fangs," I introduced myself as we shook hands. "Just out of curiosity, is that a personal preference or a Cold Moon tradition?"

"Tradition." Kayvon shrugged. "Although I see the wisdom of it. An alpha needs a luna to hold him together, right?"

"He surely does," I agreed. "Without a luna, an alpha falters and so does his pack."

"Exactly." Kayvon's black eyes bore into me.

*He knows something*, I linked the witches. *I'll try to get him alone and ask.*

*Okay, alpha,* they said in sync.

"And this is my Norah." Alpha Quake went over to the recliner and crouched in front of it. "Dear, can you say hello to our guests?"

"Pops, she hasn't spoken for two years." Kayvon ran a hand down his face. "What makes you think she's going to say hello now?"

"Hush, Von." Alpha Quake waved a hand at him. "She'll hear you. Don't hurt her feelings."

As they muttered at each other, my eyes swept over Luna Norah Quake and I knew we were too late. Whatever was wrong with her, she was gone. Her lungs might still be breathing and her heart beating, but nobody was home in those brown eyes.

She sat limply on the chair, not moving. A cloth doll sat on the chair next to her, but she didn't pay any attention to it. Her hands rested on the chair arms as if *she* were the doll and someone had posed her that way.

The witches went right over to her. Ariel stood next to her and held a hand over her head while Maria crouched in front of her and lifted up both hands. The air shimmered with magic.

"It's not hurting her, is it?" Alpha Quake asked as he and his son sat on the closest couch.

"No, sir," I assured him.

It didn't take the witches long to find something.

*Alpha Cole, this is not good,* Ariel warned me. *Her wolf is dead and, for all intents and purposes, so is she. Alpha Quake is not going to take this well.*

*That's what I thought,* I said.

*Will Kayvon be able to step up as alpha without a luna, even if it is their tradition here?* Maria asked. *Or did King Julian leave other orders for the leadership here?*

*Kayvon will lead, regardless of his mate status. The king ordered it so.*

"Hey, Kayvon, while they work, could you show me where the bathroom is?" I asked.

Fortunately, he was smart enough to take the hint.

"Of course."

*Wait until I get back to tell him anything,* I told the witches.

As soon as we were down the hall, Kayvon stopped me and gave me a hard look.

"She's gone," I told him.

"I know. I've known for a while. Now what? Pops can't end her, and I don't think I can, either, but it's not right to let her continue suffering."

"I'll take care of it," I muttered. "Are you prepared to step up as alpha? I understand your tradition here, but, even if your father wants to live afterwards, he's not going to be able to run the pack anymore."

"I know that, too. I've been to every pack in North America except for yours and Black Night. I'll visit those two and pray my mate is in one of them. But even if she's not, I can lead without a luna. At least for a while."

He took a deep breath and his eyes flicked to the floor before meeting mine again.

"But what happens if I don't ever find her?"

"You've got a few years before it becomes an issue," I told him. "You'll find her before it does."

"I pray to the Goddess you're right."

*Me, too, friend.*

"Well, you're welcome to visit Five Fangs any time to look for her," I told him. "Uh, before we go back to your parents, I really do have to use the bathroom."

"Sure, man." He pointed to a door on the left. "I'll be in the living room."

"Yeah. Thanks."

He nodded, turned, and left.

I did my business, washed my hands, and headed back, reminding myself to ask the witches if they needed to go before we left here.

When I entered the room, Maria and Ariel stood up and stepped away from the luna. They clasped their hands in front of them and looked at me.

"Let's hear it," I said.

"Alpha Quake." Maria drew a deep breath and looked at him. "Your mate is infected by a parasite. It ate her wolf first. Maybe four or five years ago now. Probably so her wolf couldn't fight it or heal Luna Norah."

"Then it began to eat her," Ariel picked up. "Alpha, I'm so sorry, but there is nothing of your luna left inside this body."

"She is not gone!" he blustered at the witches and looked at his son. "They're lying! They're making it up because they don't know what's wrong with Norah, either!"

"Pops, they're not lying." Kayvon laid a hand on his shoulder. "Mom is gone and has been for a long time. I know it, Beta Brooks knows it, and I think you do, too, somewhere deep inside."

"She's your *mother!*" Alpha Quake growled.

"She *was* my mother," Kayvon corrected, keeping his voice even and calm, "and a great one. Look at her, Pops, and remember your mate. Does this look like your luna? Does this look like my mom?"

"She's sick! That's what's wrong. She isn't— She isn't *gone!*"

"Alpha," Ariel intervened, "we know this isn't what you want to hear, but your denial is only making things worse."

"Could you do it?" Alpha Quake looked at her, then Maria, then me. "Could any of you end your mate?"

The thought of Posy even being sick or hurt speared my heart like an arrow. To think of her dying or needing mercy from one of my brothers or myself? I shook my head. The kind of agony Alpha Quake was in couldn't be imagined, only experienced, and I prayed to the Moon Goddess that I never, ever had to.

"I didn't contact the king because I knew he'd send investigators and that would lead to her death." Alpha Quake glared at his son. "And see? I was right. That is exactly what happened."

I believed the witches when they said the luna was no more, but that wasn't what was going to sell my argument to the alpha. Playing on his heart disgusted me, but if I could avoid a fight or burning a bridge, I would.

"Will you allow me to show mercy to your luna, Alpha Quake?" I asked. "She will feel no pain, I promise you. Only relief from this unending torment."

He dropped his head in his hands and his shoulders shook. Kayvon laid his hand on his father's back and patted it.

*How do we do this?* I asked the witches as the two men grieved. *I mean, I know how to kill her quickly and painlessly, but what about this parasite?*

*We have a container to trap it in,* Maria explained. *We'll pull it out and secure it. When we get home, Gelo will kill it.*

*Do we* have *to transport it?* I was worried about it escaping. *You two can't kill it? Can I kill it?*

*It would latch onto you the second you touched it. Can you kill it without touching it?* Ariel asked.

*No,* I admitted begrudgingly.

*And we're not strong enough with just the two of us. If we had even one more witch here, sure. Gelo can take care of it with one shot.*

*Don't worry, alpha,* Maria added. *Once it's in the container, it can't get out on its own.*

*All right,* I agreed, convinced it was all we could do.

Finally, the father and son raised their heads, and Alpha Quake met my eyes.

"Make it as painless as possible," he requested in an emotion-clogged voice. "Even if she can't feel it."

"I will," I promised, "and with utmost respect."

Moving to stand next to the luna, I slid my hand under her black dreads and gripped the back of her neck. The sharp metal zipper at the top of her dress bit into my palm and I hissed. It was cold enough to send a shiver through me, but it wasn't as cold as her skin.

*Like she's already dead,* was all I could think.

*Poor thing is, boss,* Topaz said.

"Wait, alpha!" Maria squealed loudly. "Let us get the parasite out first!"

"Oh." I jerked my hand away.

"That way we can be sure we got it and it doesn't escape its host," Ariel explained.

"Makes sense," I murmured, distracted.

My palm stung. Glancing at it, I saw a tiny dot of blood by my life line.

*Why do women wear such things?* I grumbled to myself. *Regardless of what the industry says, fashion shouldn't be painful.*

*I'll heal it, boss!* Topaz chirped, and the teeny cut zipped closed with a zap of moon magic.

*Thanks, buddy.*

He wiggled at the praise and I rolled my eyes.

Turning my attention to the witches, I watched as Maria opened her bag and took out a glass jar with a rubber seal and hermetic metal latch lid.

"Ready, Ariel?" she murmured.

"Ready."

The air once again shimmered around the luna. Maria opened the lid on her glass jar and stood by as Ariel moved her hands in a pulling gesture. After a few seconds, a reddish black mass crawled out of the luna's mouth, and I had to force myself not to throw up. It looked like a giant leech, but had an evil aura.

*That's so disgusting,* I couldn't help thinking.

As soon as the fat creature appeared on the luna's lips, Maria swept in. It plopped wetly to the bottom of the jar, and she slapped the lid down and flipped the latch closed.

"Got it!" She held up the jar. "One parasite, secure and contained."

"Do you want to say goodbye?" Ariel asked the Quakes in a gentle tone. "It's safe to touch her now."

"I made my peace with this two years ago," Kayvon said, shaking his head.

Alpha Quake stood and went to his mate, and the rest of us moved to the other side of the room to give him privacy.

"What will you do with that?" Kayvon pointed to the jar in Maria's hands.

"Our cousin, Gelo, will kill it when we get home."

"Your cousin Gelo." Kayvon's flat tone said he was unimpressed.

"He's also known as Angelo della Morte," I said with a little smirk.

"The Angel of Death?" His eyebrows shot up.

"The one and only."

"Naw, bro." For the first time since we met, a little smile curled his lips up. "I can't think of the Angel of Death as Cousin Gelo, man."

"I hear you." I grinned. "You should see him all soft with his mate one minute, then slaughtering his way through a pack of dire wolves the next."

"I'd like to meet this dude sometime," he said.

"Like I said, you're welcome at Five Fangs anytime. In fact, I'd like to offer an alliance if you're interested."

"For real?" His eyes brightened. "Aight. You want to draw up the papers or should I?"

"My brother Wyatt will be more than happy to," I said evilly. "He'll get it to you by next week."

Kayvon held out his hand and we shook again.

"Alpha Barlow," said Alpha Quake as he joined us. "It feels wrong to say thank you to the man taking my mate's life. I know you really aren't, but still. So I'll just say, I am grateful you came here today."

"You're welcome." Jay was so much better at these soft skills, but I gave it my best shot. "It was my honor to help you."

As Kayvon wrapped his father up in a hug, I went over to the luna, put my left hand on the back of her head and my right on her chin. With a quick snap, I broke her neck. Without a wolf to heal her, that was enough to convince her body to give up. I eased her limp form back in the recliner and closed her eyes.

"It's done," I said over my shoulder.

"Thank you, alpha." Kayvon came over to stand at my side. "Ladies, is it okay to move my mom?"

"Yes. We're very sorry for your loss," Ariel said.

"Thank you." He carefully picked up his mother's body, then looked at his father. "Pops. I love you. I'm going to take care of Mom now."

"You do that, Von," Alpha Quake told him with wet eyes. "I love you, too, son."

Kayvon met my eyes and gave me a curt nod. We both knew what his father was going to ask, and I nodded back to let him know I'd take care of it.

"Thank you, Alpha Barlow."

As soon as he left the room, Alpha Quake grabbed my elbow and met my eyes with a steely glare.

"I request the same mercy you showed my luna, Alpha Barlow. I cannot live without her."

"Alpha Quake, you—"

"My wolf won't allow me to do it myself, so I'm begging you to spare my son the task."

Since I'd want the same thing, how could I refuse?

I gave him what he asked for, then we left the pack to its mourning and headed home.

#

*Ariel*

We were all quiet as the SUV ate up the highway miles.

Learning that poor luna had suffered for years had greatly disturbed Maria and me, and we knew Alpha Cole was affected by Alpha Quake's request to kill him. He'd made us leave the room while he did, but we felt his sorrow in the pack bond.

He was also exhausted from the long drive, and we had hours left before we got home. We both told him that we didn't mind driving if he needed a break, but he just shook his head and sank into silence.

*I think he just doesn't want us to drive his vehicle,* Maria linked me with a small smile, and I nodded.

*Tristan said he's possessive of it. If he starts going off the side of the road, though, we're going to make him stop.*

*Agreed.*

Thankfully, we made it home without incident. It was 5:30 p.m. when we pulled up to the alpha house and saw Tristan and Matthew waiting for us on the front porch.

Grinning at each other, Maria and I unbuckled and leapt out of the SUV as soon as Alpha Cole put it in park, then ran to our mates.

"I missed you!" I laughed as Tristan swung me around. "Even if it was only for a day!"

"I missed you, too, bluebird." He nuzzled his nose in my neck, making me shiver. "Let's head home."

"Okay. Alpha Cole?" I called and watched as he trudged up the walk with sleepy eyes. *Poor guy. Eight hours of driving in one day did him in.* "You have the container secured until Gelo can come to kill that thing, right?"

He gave me a thumbs up, and I turned back to my mate.

"Let me pop in and say hello to my luna, then we'll go," I told him and he nodded with a smile.

Maria had the same idea I did, so we linked arms and headed for the front door.

"We'll get your stuff out of Alpha Cole's SUV while you do," Matthew said.

"Thanks, puppy." Maria blew him a kiss and giggled when he made a show of catching it.

*Luna?* I linked. *Where are you? We want to chat for a minute before we head home.*

*You're back? I'm in the kitchen. Are you staying for dinner?*

*No. It was a long day with all that driving.*

*I bet it was. Come on in.*

We found her standing at the stove and stirring something that smelled absolutely divine.

"Did you have a good day, luna?" Maria asked, running over to hug her.

"Oh, yeah! Wait until you see how cute Reau and Spring are together!" She gave us a big grin. "But I'll tell you about it later. I can see how tired you are. Go home with your mates and we'll catch up tomorrow."

She and Maria pulled me into their hug, and we all giggled as we squeezed each other tightly. Just being around our luna lifted our spirits; hugging her and hearing her laugh made the world right again.

"Posy?" Alpha Cole called. "Come to the living room."

"Sounds like our cue to head out," I said. "See you later, luna."

"Bye bye. See you soon!"

We all hugged one more time, then Maria and I headed for the door.

## 15: New Wolf

*Ash*

I glanced over at my mate to find her sound asleep with her head against the window. The drive to Emerson's took about an hour if you weren't speeding like a maniac, and I knew she needed a good nap. We'd kept her up most of the night.

A little smirk tugged my lips as I turned my attention back to the road. If she didn't have a wolf, I doubted she'd be able to walk today. As it was, Wyatt had ended up carrying her down for breakfast this morning. She'd stayed curled up in a sleepy little ball on his lap and let him spoon cereal in her mouth, and only got awake enough to kiss Mase, Cole, and Jay goodbye before they left on their missions.

*Ashy wore mate out*, Sid snickered.

*Not just me,* I protested with a grin.

Last night, my brothers and I tried "sandwiches" for the first time. Since it was so successful with our wolves, we figured why not? Mase and Wyatt took her that way first, and she came *twice* before they finished. That encouraged me and Jay to try and we got the same results. Cole enjoyed a solo turn and, as usual, got a little rough. Also like usual, that excited her, and she jumped on Wyatt before he even finished asking her if she was up for a second round.

That led to more sandwiches and a third round and a fourth round...

Before I finally *had* to sleep, Jay convinced her to talk a bit about what she was and wasn't enjoying. That was always hard for her to do, but she eventually admitted that a dick in her ass was pleasurable, but it didn't make her come. A ball sack hitting her perineum, though, was a different story, especially if a second one of us was in her pussy or stroking her clit or playing with her tits at the same time.

Of course, she didn't use any of those words. Despite Wyatt's best efforts to corrupt her vocabulary, our proper, shy baby used softer terms and euphemisms, which we found adorable. She never made any sexual jokes, either, but her bright red face told us that she was picking up on more and more of our innuendos.

*I hope she'll still blush like that when she's eighty.*

We took her feedback seriously. Each time we mated, we noted every little thing that made her moan and writhe. We also kept a private tally of how many times each of us made her come. We couldn't help that we were competitive beasts, and she got nothing but pleasure from it, so what harm did it do? Right now, Mase held the record, but it was hardly fair. Before his first time, none of us knew that every thrust hit her g-spot when taking her from behind while she was on her hands and knees.

That was my second favorite position. Last night, my first became the top in a sandwich.

*Ashy has bum kink*, Sid teased me, and I shrugged.

I couldn't deny it. Her soft, smooth ass had the starring role in all of my fantasies. I loved to kiss it, touch it, knead it, bite it, squish it, and sink *all* the way into it. I loved her sweet, tight pussy, too, but her ass was fine as hell. Just watching it as she rode one of my brothers - or they rode her - made me hard.

*Which is happening right now, so stop thinking about it!* I growled at myself as my pants tightened. *Now is not the time!*

"Ash?" Posy yawned. "Almost there?"

"Yeah, princess. We're going up the driveway now."

"Sorry I conked out on you." She sat up and stretched, then rolled her neck.

"I understand why you did." I tried not to smirk, but couldn't stop myself. "You can take another nap later if you want."

" 'Kay. Tell me a bit about Spring."

"Well, he's one of the mature wolves. He's a lot like Garnet. Responsible. Straightforward. Dependable. He's a little more serious, though. I mean, he would *never* have gotten up at 4 a.m. to go play tag in the front yard. Of course, that was Spring before Ev's death. His personality could have changed."

"Serious will be good for Reau."

"I just hope they get along and this works," I admitted.

"Can you see Reau *not* getting along with something fluffy?" she chuckled. "If Spring can be patient, they'll be fine."

"Well, the moment of truth is fast approaching." I parked next to Emerson's vehicle. "We're here, and Spring and the therapist are due to arrive in a few minutes."

I hopped out of the SUV, ran around to her side, and opened her door.

"Can I carry you?" I asked with a big grin and held my arms out.

When she nodded, I scooped her up like a bride and kissed her before turning and bumping the door closed with my hip.

"I love you, Ash," she murmured as she laid her head against my collar bone.

She could say it 999,999 times, and my heart would still swell up with the millionth one.

"I love you, too, cupcake."

"Luna!" Thoreau shrieked as he flew off the porch.

Ignoring the walk, he ran in his bare feet across the grass. He didn't have a shirt on, either, just a pair of shorts, but he looked clean and his curly hair was groomed.

"Me! Me, alpha! Let me hold her!"

"Too loud, Reau," Emerson called as he came down the walk. "And you need to finish getting dressed. Alpha, is my little luna bunny okay?"

"Just tired," I told him and handed my precious bundle to the boy. "Don't drop her, Reau."

"Won't, alpha! I'm taking her to a special place!" Then he spun on his heel and sprinted off with her.

"You need to finish getting dressed," Emerson reminded him, but Thoreau kept running.

Emerson sighed.

"Where's he taking her?" I asked him as we did our bro-hug.

"Who knows?" He shrugged, but didn't seem concerned. "He discovered the garden yesterday, and he thinks it's amazing, so maybe there."

He sent me an image of an old wooden door with decorative iron hinges. It was set in an ivy-covered stone wall that was about six feet high and looked like something straight out of *The Secret Garden*. I could totally see how a kid like Thoreau would be eager to explore it.

"I'm happy he's in a better mood," he sighed. "At breakfast, he was anxious about meeting the therapist. I was lucky to get him showered and in shorts before you got here."

"Did you tell him about Spring?"

"Not yet. Didn't want to get him too excited when he was already stressed."

"Understandable." I ran my hand through my hair. "Posy so badly wants this to work."

"Angelo and I do, too. We want this to work for Reau *and* for Spring. Neither of them deserve what happened to their other halves."

"Facts, Em," I agreed. "Hopefully, the Moon Goddess thinks so, too."

#

*Thoreau*

After I showed the luna my secret fort, Bubba made me go into the house so I could put on a shirt and be ready to meet the guy who's going to fix me.

Bubba didn't *say* that's what he was here to do, but I knew it was. I really hoped he could, too. If he fixed me, maybe Mommy Daddy would love me. I didn't want to go back there, not ever, but if your mommy daddy can't love you, who can?

105

Bubba said he did. He told me every night when he tucked me into bed with Baby Tanner and turned on my star lamp. My heart believed him, but my head, well, that's what was broken, wasn't it? So of course it didn't want to listen.

I was really happy living with Bubba and Gelo and Leo, and now Poppy lived with us, too. I liked her so much! She gave good cuddles and went 'sploring with me last evening. That's how we found the secret fort!

*I can't wait to show Arch and Wayne.* I clapped my hands with excitement and almost fell off the kitchen stool.

Leo told me that stool could also mean poop, so now I wanted to find out if sitting on a stool made you go poop more than a regular chair. So far, I didn't notice a difference, but I just started my 'speriment two days ago when he said that.

"Reau," Bubba said as he sat down at the kitchen island next to me. "This is Dr. Alonzo York. Call him Dr. York. He's going to stay with us for a while. He wants to get to know you."

*He wants to fix me, is what Bubba means,* I thought. *Right, Tanner?*

Oh.

My shoulders slumped.

I forgot for a second.

Sighing, I looked at Dr. York as he sat across from me. He was *old.* Like older than Gelo! There was some gray in his hair above his ears! He must have gone to school for a long time to learn doctoring, so I guess it made sense that he was old.

I was going to school in the fall. Arch and Wayne said I'd be in their class, and that made me so happy! Not only would I finally get to go to school, but my two besties would be with me. We could eat lunch together and read books in the library and play sports. *And* they promised they'd make sure nobody messed with me!

"Reau, you're daydreaming," Bubba said with a sigh.

I straightened up and made myself pay attention. If Bubba got mad at me, he'd send me back to Mommy Daddy.

"I am Thoreau Ezra Jones, Dr. York." I held out my hand like Bubba had taught me. "I am happy you have come to fix— Get to know me."

He shook my hand with a little smile.

"It's nice to meet you, Thoreau. Your luna and Alpha Ash are arranging a surprise for you, so let's talk until they're ready. How does that sound?"

"A surprise?" My eyes widened. "For me?"

"Yep," Bubba said. "And if you talk nicely to Dr. York for a bit, you can have it before lunch."

"Okay!" I crowed and clapped my hands. "I'll be a good boy, Bubba!"

"Shh." Bubba held a finger to his lips, and I knew I'd been too loud.

"Sorry." I mumbled and slid my eyes to Dr. York, but he was smiling.

"Do you want your brother to stay here with us while we talk, Thoreau?" When I shrugged, not really caring, he said, "Well, if you want him to leave at any time, just tell us, okay?"

I nodded my head up and down really fast so he'd know I understood.

"You said I came to fix you. Do you think you need to be fixed, Thoreau?"

"No, I changed my words," I reminded him, "but yes, I need to be fixed. If you fix me, Mommy Daddy will love me, then other people will, too."

I watched as Dr. York looked at Bubba and Bubba looked at him.

"I'll tell the king and your alphas that I need my mate to join me. I'll be here for quite a while and I'm not living apart for so long," Dr. York said. "I'll also ask if we can stay in a guest house."

"You're not going to live with us? We got plenty of bedrooms. Bubba and Gelo have one and Leo and Poppy have one and I have one. That leaves, uh, eight minus three..."

I counted up my fingers, then did it again to make sure I was right. Leo was teaching me how numbers added and subtracted.

"Five more!" I told Dr. York, then dropped my voice to a whisper. "Although there are two ghosts in the attic and they make *a lot* of noise at night. We used to have just one ghost, but another one showed up last night. I asked Poppy if she brought it with her when she moved in yesterday, but she said no."

"Stop, Reau." Bubba's face was bright red. Was he mad? Did he want me to keep the ghosts a secret? "Angelo told you he'd take care of the ghosts, remember?"

"I 'member, Bubba." I stopped and tapped my chin as I thought. "Okay, Dr. York, you stay at the guest house. I don't want you or your mate to get scared by the ghosts."

"That's very kind of you." Dr. York grinned and looked like he wanted to laugh.

"Is your mate a girl or a boy?" I tilted my head and stared into his brown eyes.

"Uh, a boy."

"Like Bubba and Gelo? Okay. What's your mate's name? Is he nice? Will he like me? Will he play with me?"

107

"Reau, calm down, buddy." Bubba slung his arm around my neck and pulled me in for a noogie.

"No, Bubba! My curls!" I yelped and wiggled out of his hold. "Luna likes them looking nice. Don't mess them up!"

To get him back, I turned to Dr. York with an evil grin.

"You know, the other day, when Leo and I came in from playing basketball, Gelo and Bubba were on the living room floor. Leo put his hand over my eyes, but I saw them! They were kissy-kissy!" I burst out into giggles.

"Reau," Bubba groaned and covered his red face with his hands.

Dr. York laughed and gave me a high-five, and that's when I knew he was an okay guy.

Even if he was old.

#

*Emerson*

"Sorry if he overwhelmed or embarrassed you," I apologized.

I'd sent Thoreau upstairs to grab the sketchbook and pencils I'd bought him because Dr. York wanted to start with a few simple drawing activities. I knew it would take my brother a few minutes to find the supplies. I'd organized his desk for him when he failed to do it after four days, so he would have to hunt for them.

"What little routine we've been able to establish is disrupted," I explained. "We had a fight with dire wolves yesterday and he had to stay in the safe room for the first time. Then Leo met Poppy during the fight and she moved in. This morning, Angelo left for a mission before Reau was awake, then Alpha Mason picked up Leo and Poppy right after breakfast for *their* mission."

I scrubbed one hand over my face before looking back at Dr. York.

"So you asked to meet him without any background or preparation so you could form your own opinions. Do you want to know his history now, Dr. York, or work with him for a bit first?"

"Call me Alonzo," he offered. "Reau's a chatterbox and a rambler, isn't he? He'll eventually tell me everything himself, even things I don't need to know, like the ghosts in the attic."

My face burned at his knowing smirk, but Angelo was more than worth a little embarrassment.

"Yeah, we're doing some things to sound-deaden his room. Living with two newly mated couples, he's probably learning some things he shouldn't."

"He's learning what healthy love between mates looks like, which is not a bad thing for him to know when he finds his own."

108

Alonzo chuckled, then leaned back in his chair. "But, yes, you can tell me what you know about his life before he came to live with you. I always do my best to avoid triggering patients, but some front-loading will definitely help."

"All right. Once he's occupied with Spring, we'll talk. Thanks for doing this." I paused, then held out my hand for him to shake again, which he did. "I know Angelo said you owed him a favor, but since you'll be here longer than you originally planned, I want to pay you."

"I work for the king. He's footing the bill. Besides, Reau and Spring are both such fascinating creatures, I'd do this one for free." Alonzo chuckled again. "Don't tell King Julian I said that, though."

"Of course not." I grinned. "Let the king open *his* wallet. I'm sure it's way fatter than mine!"

"Exactly."

Thoreau came thundering down the stairs and I rolled my eyes. I must have told that kid a hundred times not to run up or down the stairs.

*Em?* Ash linked me before I could fuss at him. *We're ready for Reau to come outside now. Bring Dr. York, too, so he can study their first meeting.*

*We're on our way,* I let him know.

"Found it!" Thoreau shouted as he raced into the kitchen, holding the sketchbook up over his head.

"Inside voice, Reau," I reminded him. "Good job finding it. I think you earned your surprise."

"I did?" His beautiful eyes rounded. "For finding my sketchbook?"

"For behaving so nicely with Dr. York," I corrected while taking his supplies and laying them on the counter. "Alpha Ash said they're ready for us, so let's go."

Alonzo and I stood up while Thoreau bounced on his toes, looking too cute as he grinned and clapped his hands.

*Let's hope this goes well,* I muttered to Cove as I led them out the front door. *I don't want my baby brother to be hurt any more.*

*Spring will love our baby brother.* My wolf's tail wagged, excited to see his friend again. *Everyone does.*

*They do, don't they?* I smiled as I saw luna bunny and Alpha Ash sitting with Spring under the shade tree.

Thoreau stopped running ahead, spun around, and raced back to stand right in front of me.

"Bubba! My little eye spies a new wolf!"

"His name is Spring. He's been ... sick," I fudged, "which is why you haven't seen him around."

"Do you think he would be my friend? What's his human like? Is he my age or old—"

"Reau." I cupped his cheek in my palm and leaned down to kiss his forehead. "Go meet him and find out the answers to your questions yourself."

He blinked at me twice, then gave me an adorable smile before he took off again.

*I swear that kid doesn't know how to walk.*

\#

*Thoreau*

The new wolf was so cute!

His coat was shades of brown with some white, he had a black forehead and inner ears, and the way his chest hair curled looked like feathers!

My little eye was so distracted by his cuteness that I tripped, but just picked myself up and went on running to where he lay on the grass between luna and Alpha Ash.

"Can I pet you?" I squealed as I knelt down in front of him. "Please? Pretty please?"

The wolf raised its eyebrows, but nodded.

"Reau, this is Spring," Alpha Ash said. "Spring, this is Thoreau, Emerson's little brother. Everyone calls him Reau."

"It's a pleasure to meet you, Spring," I said politely to make Bubba happy. "You're so cute!"

*Thank you,* a rumbly voice sounded in my head. *You're cute, too.*

*Oh! You can link with me? You're in our pack?*

*Yes, little one. I was born in the Dark Woods pack.*

*This is Five Fangs.* I tilted my head and looked into Spring's amber eyes. *Are you mixed up?*

*No, little one. Did you not know that Five Fangs is made up of five packs, one of which is Dark Woods?*

*Huh-uh. You're cute* and *smart, wolfie!*

Grinning, I petted his fluffy chest, then rubbed my face in it, and Spring chuckled.

"I wish Tanner could have met you," I whispered.

*Who's Tanner, little one?*

"My wolf. Mommy Daddy killed him." I dropped my hands into my lap and sniffed. "I'm alone in my head and everything's scary without him."

"Hey, Reau, I'm here." Bubba sat down next to me and patted my back. "Luna and Alpha Ash are here, and now Dr. York is here. Angelo and Leo and Poppy will be home soon, too. We'll protect you."

110

"You can't protect me from my *brain,* dumb Bubba." I rolled my eyes at him. "That's where it's scary. It doesn't work right, 'member? That's why Mommy Daddy kept me locked up and hurt me and killed Tanner. My brain's retard—"

"What did I tell you about that word?" Bubba growled.

I flinched without meaning to, and he pulled me against him and hugged me hard.

"Sorry, honey. I just hate that they made you believe such bad things about yourself. Your brain is not broken, right, Dr. York?"

"No, Reau. Your brain is fine."

"But Mommy Daddy said—"

Luna reached over and held one of my hands, her little thumb rubbing over the back of my knuckles.

"They're not here, Reau. Do you know why you're here and they're not?" When I shook my head, she said, "Because they didn't deserve to know you. They were bad people for hurting a sweetheart like you. *They* were broken, not you. That's why the Goddess sent you to us. So you could grow and be free around people who love you."

It was a lot to think about. I hoped I remembered all the words she said because they made my heart warm. I wasn't so good at remembering, though. Tanner usually did that for me. Now I had to do it all by myself.

Spring, who had been watching me the whole time, suddenly got up and stood over me like I was his pup. Giggling, I poked my head out from under his chin to see everyone staring at us with wide eyes.

*He's my human now,* Spring told them.

"What does that mean? Where's your human?" I asked. "Won't he—"

*My human is dead. I am also alone in my head, and everything is scary without him.*

My mouth dropped open. I didn't think there was anyone in the world who felt like me, who understood what it was like to have an empty space inside you. I crawled out from under him to look into his pretty eyes, but just saw my face in them because they were so shiny.

*Will you be my human, little one?*

"Will you hurt me? Will you leave me?"

*No, little one. Never.*

"You say that now," I whispered, "but once you get to know me, you'll find out that I'm too much trouble. I'm not smart and I get grumpy and, oh, wait until you meet my two besties. They are *bad,* but I love them so much!"

Luna and Alpha Ash giggled for some reason, but I tuned them out because Spring was linking me again.

*I swear on the moon that I will never hurt you or leave you, Reau. Nothing about you can make me do either.*

That was a serious swear for a wolf. He could break it, but the Moon Goddess would punish him. I shivered. I didn't want to be punished ever again, and definitely not by the Moon Goddess! Spring must have really meant what he said, so I decided I would trust him.

*Yes, I will be your human,* I linked him because this was between us and no one else's ears needed to hear. *Will you be my wolf?*

*Yes, I will be your wolf.*

I wrapped my arms around his neck. My eyes were full of tears, but I was happy. How weird was that? I sighed, worried about all these emotions clogging up my chest and throat.

*We'll always be together now, right, Spring?*

He laid his chin on the top of my head and also sighed. Maybe he was all clogged up, too.

*That's right, little one. From now until forever, we'll always be together.*

"Hey, that rhymed!" I giggled. "Bubba, Bubba! I got a new wolf and he is so cute *and* super smart! I'm a lucky boy!"

*No, little one,* Spring disagreed. *I'm the one who's lucky.*

## 16: Betrayal

*Posy*

I fell asleep again on the drive home.

Ash didn't complain or tease me about it. In fact, he was humming happily to himself when I woke up as he opened my door.

"Can I carry you?" he asked with a grin and held out his arms, and a sense of *deju vu* made me shake my head.

"I think you'd carry me everywhere all the time," I yawned as I stretched.

"I would, cupcake. I should get one of those sling things like Mom has for the pups. I could tuck you right in against my chest or back and have you with me all the time."

I giggled at the idea, which made him giggle, too. He picked me up and sat me on his hip and carried me into our house.

"I'm going to pop in and check on Wyatt," he said as he put me on my feet in the kitchen. "Make sure he didn't get suffocated under a mountain of documents."

"Okay. I'll see what we have to make for dinner," I offered.

"We can always order something if you don't feel like cooking."

"No, I want to." I stopped and thought about it. "How about, if I don't find something I *want* to make, we'll order?"

"Okay, princess. Link us if you need us. Cole should be back soon."

"Yay!" I smiled as I opened the fridge. "And Mason said he'd be home later this evening, so I'll just be missing my dragon tonight."

"The rest of us will make sure you don't even notice he's gone," Ash teased.

Coming up behind me, he slid his hands under my waistband and inside my panties to squeeze my bare bum. I gasped as my insides tightened and my toes curled.

"This is mine again tonight," he rumbled roughly, "so take another nap if you need to after dinner."

"Why wait?" I whispered with more boldness than I could usually manage.

"Oh, I would, princess, but Wy knows we're home and he's demanding I help him. Besides, Tristan and Matthew are on their way to wait for their witches, and I don't want to be interrupted when I finally get to plow into your sweet ass."

"Ash," I moaned and leaned back against his chest. I clenched my thighs together to ease the instant ache in my core.

"Mmm. Does that turn my little cupcake on?" His long fingers kneaded my bum. "Hearing what I'm going to do to you? Will you come if I describe how I'm going to spread these soft cheeks and—"

*Ash!* Wyatt rumbled through the link. *You've been with our girl all day! Help me finish this so I can play with her, too!*

"Sorry, Posy." Ash removed his hands as he nuzzled my mate mark. "I'll be back."

"Ash!" I whined, wobbling a little as he stepped away from me.

He giggled as he ran out of the kitchen, and my eyes narrowed. That rat knew what he'd done.

*You know anything about revenge, waffle?* I linked him as I continued looking for something to cook.

*Um, what do you mean, dearest mate whom I love with all my heart?* he tittered nervously.

*I've always heard that revenge is a dish best served cold, but I never really understood that. Hmm. Maybe that means your part of the bed will be cold tonight?*

*Posy, my love, sweetheart, darling, I—*

And I closed the mate link.

*That right, girl,* Lark giggled. *Let him stew! Leaving you wet and needy! He deserve the blue balls you going to give him tonight.*

*Well, I probably won't be able to resist him for long,* I admitted, *but I can give him a good scare first, right?*

*Right!*

As I worked on dinner, Ariel and Maria linked me, and I heard the front door open. The smell of pine wafted into the kitchen, making me smile.

Cole was home!

Ariel and Maria visited me in the kitchen for a few minutes, then left when Cole called me into the living room. Snapping off the stove so dinner wouldn't burn, I washed my hands and dried them, then went to see my mate.

"Hi, Cole!" I grinned as I ran up to him. "I'm so glad you're back! I missed you."

Throwing my arms around his waist, I squeezed him, but then realized he was just standing there like a statue, not hugging me back. Confused, I dropped my arms and took a step away, tilting my head as I stared up at his blank face.

"Cole?"

"We need to talk."

His voice was surprisingly cold, and a bad feeling swept through me. Growing steadily more anxious, I looked around the living room.

114

Tristan stood with the front door hanging open behind him, and his eyes were fogged over as he linked someone. On the other side of the room, Ash and Wyatt sat shoulder to shoulder on the love seat. Their heads were down and their eyes fixed on their clasped hands.

*What's going on here?*

I tried to open my links with them, but they were all locked down tight. I checked Jayden's, then Mason's and found they were fine. In fact, they both responded immediately.

*Sorry, Posy, I can't talk long,* Jayden said. *Is it an emergency? We're literally attacking the prison right now.*

*Something's not right,* I told him, my uneasy feeling growing. *Give me a minute.*

*Are you in danger? Where are my brothers?* he demanded.

*I don't think so. And they're here. Focus on what you're doing.*

*Jay, I got it,* Mason told us both. *I'm just driving. We're about an hour from home.*

*All right. I love you, Posy,* Jayden said, then closed his link.

*What do you mean something's not right?* Mason asked.

*I don't know. I'll be back. I have to focus on what Cole's saying.*

*Posy? Don't close—*

I closed the link.

"This isn't working out. We don't want to be your mates anymore," Cole said. "We need a strong luna, not a useless runt."

Shock froze me in place. Even my heart stopped.

"What?" I whispered.

I heard Ash whine, but a wave of power brushed past me and he fell silent.

"Alpha Cole—"

Tristan spoke up, but Cole's fierce snarl cut him off. I felt another blast of power whip by me, and my beta whimpered.

Cole didn't take his eyes off of me, and I was shocked to see them glinting black. Something was very, very wrong. Topaz *never* talked to me in this tone or said such cruel things.

"You're pathetic," he continued. "You are worthless and weak. Even your *name* is weak."

Those were Alpha Briggs' words, but now they were coming out of my mate's mouth.

Trembling from head to toe, I looked at Wyatt and Ash, a spark of hope trying to stay alive in my heart.

"You don't want me, either?" I whispered.

They didn't move. They didn't even look at me. They kept their eyes fixed on their clenched hands.

Just like my brothers had each time their father hurt me.

115

I couldn't breathe. Pain ripped through me like claws, worse than any beating I'd ever taken.

*What did I do wrong? Why did they stop loving me?*

Matthew ran into the house and slid to a stop next to Tristan. His eyes swept the scene, then fixed on Cole.

*Is he in on this, too? Are all the betas? Does everyone here hate me? Was it all a dream?*

"Pack what you want and leave. *Now.*" Cole's face was carved from stone, and his glowing black eyes didn't blink once. "Don't you get it? We. Don't. Want. You."

My ears buzzed so loudly that I could hardly understand his words and something inside my chest swelled like an enormous bubble. It grew bigger and bigger until it exploded into every bond that connected me to Five Fangs, and shame washed over me. A luna's first job is to protect her pack, not wound it with her selfish grief and pain.

"Luna!" Matthew and Tristan both shouted, and Ash whined again.

Hearing a thump, I looked over to see Wyatt on his knees, his hands braced on the floor as his body shook.

I couldn't even go over to comfort him.

*Because it wouldn't help. Because it's my fault. Because I am everything Cole just said.*

Useless.

Runt.

Pathetic.

Worthless.

Weak.

Desperate to escape, I ran past Tristan and Matthew and out the front door, stumbling down the porch steps. Shaking with sobs, I wrapped my arms around my middle and tried to decide which way to go.

I could throw myself at the mercy of the royal pack, but the king and queen didn't need to be burdened with me. My brothers might take me back, but Green River was hundreds of miles away, and I had no way to get there. I didn't even consider taking one of my mates' cars. Even if I knew how to drive, nothing of theirs was mine.

Not anymore.

Maybe it never had been.

*Lark, we'll run into the wild.*

*We be dead in a day if we go alone,* she warned me.

*We're dead, anyway. The mate bond breaking will kill us. And if it doesn't, I'll do it myself.*

*No, Posy,* she begged. *No! Jayden and Mason still—*

*I'm done, Lark. I'm **done**. I don't want to do this anymore.*

116

Whimpering, she pulled into a tight ball in the back of my mind and wept.

It was clear that everything Alpha Briggs had said about me was right. I wasn't worthy of happiness or love. He'd tried to beat the knowledge into me, but some small part of me clung to the belief that he was wrong. It had taken my mates' rejection to open my eyes, but I finally accepted the truth.

"Luna! What happened?" Maria ran up to me, Ariel on her heels. "How can we help you?"

She went to hug me, but I held up my arms to keep her back, then began to toe off my sneakers so I could shift.

"Ask Alpha Cole," Matthew snapped as he and Tristan leapt down the porch stairs. "He just threw her out!"

"What?!" Ariel gasped.

"Something's wrong," Tristan said, "but we'll figure it out later. Luna is our priority now. Let's get her somewhere safe to calm down."

"Where's the parasite?" Maria asked in a panic. "Alpha Cole is guarding it until Gelo comes back."

"I don't know," Tristan told her, but kept his eyes on me.

I tuned them all out as I struggled to rein in the pain that radiated from me into the pack bonds. Several people - my other betas, Mom, Dad, Mama, Papa, Peri, Thoreau, even Gamma Reuben - nudged my pack link, their concern strong enough for me to feel even without opening it.

I was hurting everyone because I was stupid enough to think a runt was worthy to be a luna. That someone like me deserved mates and love and a family.

*I can't keep hurting everyone.*

From the house came a howl followed by the sounds of furniture being destroyed, then more wolves howling and snarling.

"We need to get her out of here!" Matthew barked. "It's not safe if the alphas are fighting!"

Tristan reached for me, but I dodged him. Giving up on my sneakers, I shifted, then fought my way out of my clothes. The four of them called out and tried to catch me, but my small brown wolf easily slipped away and streaked into the forest.

Then we ran.

## 17: Broken

*Posy*

Useless.
Runt.
Pathetic.
Worthless.
Weak.

The same words cycled through my mind, making me blind and deaf to the world around me. It was a good thing Lark was ascendant. If it were me in control, we would have hit a tree long ago.

She was getting tired and slowing down, though. Despite how strong I'd become over the last several weeks, I was still and always would be small and weak.

Useless.
Runt.
Pathetic—

*Stop it,* Lark gasped. *I need stop. And you need pay attention. We not alone.*

Had we run into a patrol? We were still in pack territory, so I knew it was unlikely to be rogues.

*The betas.* Lark slowed to a trot, then a walk. *Tristan and Matthew follow us since we left. Other three catching up.*

She wheezed with her head hanging low. I looked around and spotted a grassy clearing and pointed it out to her. She got us there, then collapsed on her side and panted heavily.

Matthew and Tristan joined us in an instant, still in their human forms.

*More proof of how weak I am. They didn't even need to shift to keep up with my wolf.*

Crew, Emerson, and Tyler ran into the clearing from different directions, all within a minute of each other.

"What happened?" Emerson demanded.

Matthew's eyes went glassy, and I knew he was showing them everything. I felt several nudges on the link again, but ignored them all. Once Matthew finished, anger lit Emerson's eyes and Tyler's face, and Crew looked upset.

"We need Alpha Mason to come home *now*," Emerson growled.

"He was already on his way home," Matthew told him. "Luna, he wants to know why you won't talk to him. What do you want me to tell him?"

I was too afraid to open any of my mate links.

*Does he know what happened?* I asked.

"No. I thought you would want to explain, but I can tell him if you'd prefer that."

*What if he says the same things? What if he doesn't want me anymore, either?*

Why did my mates stop loving me? Then a horrible new thought struck me. Did they *ever* love me? Was it all an act? But why? Why would they do that? What would they have gained from that other than humiliating me?

"No, my little luna bunny." Emerson reached over and stroked Lark's head. "I guarantee that's not the case."

I didn't respond, and Matthew came closer.

"Here, luna." He laid a stack of clothing next to me. "Good thing Lark is small. Your clothes survived the shift. You don't have to shift back if you don't want to, but at least you can if you do."

"I grabbed your Chucks, too." Tristan held up my sneakers, then sat them next to my clothes.

I nodded, but wasn't having much luck holding back the tears. They trickled into Lark's soft fur as I whimpered. Several people pushed on my pack link again, but I continued to ignore them.

"Don't cry, luna." Tyler knelt next to me and petted my ears. "We're going to figure this out. What happened with Alpha Cole wasn't real. I don't know what's going on, but I know for a fact that all five alphas love you with their whole hearts."

I didn't believe him, but nodded anyway.

*I'll shift if you don't mind putting my stuff behind a tree.*

"Of course not, luna." Crew grabbed it all before anyone else could and led the way to a giant oak. Laying my gear on the ground, he let out a heavy sigh and stroked Lark's head a couple times, then left.

After I shifted and dressed, I went back to the betas, dropped to the ground, and curled into a tight ball. They scooted as close to me as they could get.

"Alpha Mason is worried about you," Emerson said quietly. "If you don't talk to him soon, Garnet's going to take control, and he's one angry wolf right now. Considering he's driving at the moment, shifting wouldn't be a great idea, would it?"

Before I could answer, the betas froze and their eyes fogged over.

"What is it?" I asked.

"Alpha Cole is linking us," Tyler told me.

"Go," I whispered. "All of you should go. Just go."

"We aren't going to leave you, luna," Tristan said. "We're your guard, and the privilege to serve you takes precedence over all else."

119

"That's right. Not even all the alphas together could make us abandon you," Emerson added.

"You have new mates," I said.

"We've been linking them," Matthew told me. "In fact, all the witches fully support you, luna."

"Peri, too." Tyler rubbed the back of his neck. "She said she and her parents and Alpha Mason's parents have been trying to link you. None of them know what's going on, but Mom's ready to storm the alpha house to find out why you're so upset."

"Tell her not to do that," I said. "I don't want to cause a rift between her and Cole."

"You don't understand." Crew shook his head. "When the luna's not happy, no one in the pack's happy."

"I don't deserve happiness. It's the way I was born. It's why my step-father hated me. Why my brothers abandoned me. Why my mates are rejecting me. There's something about me that makes me unlovable."

The clearing filled with whines.

"That's not true," Matthew argued. "Never say or think that again!"

"It's only because I'm your luna." I shook my head and pressed my lips together to stop them from quivering. "The bond makes you feel this way. And I'm sorry for it. You shouldn't be tied to a weak, pathetic runt like me."

"We would kill for you!" Emerson growled. "We would die for you! You have our loyalty until we take our last breath!"

Tyler crouched in front of me and cupped my face in his palms.

"You will always be our luna. You want to leave the pack today? Then let's go, because we're coming with you. We're your betas until the end, and our wolves wouldn't have it any other way."

Trembling hard, I launched myself forward. He caught me, and I buried my face in his chest and sobbed.

"We're going to figure this out and fix it," he murmured as he held me, one hand holding the back of my head and the other hugging my waist. "Everything's going to be okay."

*I hope he right,* Lark fretted from the back of my mind.

*Don't hope too much.*

"Luna," Crew spoke up, "I know you're scared and upset and hurt, but please talk with Alpha Mason. Leo's linking us and... Well, it's not good. Alpha's going to burn the world down if he doesn't hear from you soon."

I bit my lip, but nodded. Still snuggled in Tyler's arms, I opened the mate link - and nearly collapsed under the weight of emotion on the other end.

*POSY!*

*Um, hi?*

*Do not close our link again. Do you hear me?*

*Yes, Mason.*

*Are you safe?*

*Yes. The betas are with me.*

*All right. Okay. Stay with them. Promise me, Posy.*

*I promise.*

*Now tell me everything, and I mean every little thing!*

I did and even sent the memory along for him to see. He didn't respond for several minutes, then a simple sentence broke the silence.

*I'm going to kill him.*

I waited and kept the link open since Mason said to, but heard nothing more.

"Uh-oh." Tristan said after a minute or two.

"What?" Crew asked.

"Alpha Mason wolfed out. Leo's driving now and Garnet's howling his head off and destroying the seats. Poppy's trying to calm him down, but not making any progress."

"Dang. Alpha loves that truck." Tyler shook his head. "He's going to be so pissed when he calms down."

"Hundred bucks says he makes Alpha Cole replace it," Emerson said with a smirk.

The other guys chuckled and, despite everything, I smiled a little, too. Mason really did love his truck.

*Hopefully, he still loves* me.

I was exhausted in every way there was to be exhausted and only half-listened as the betas continued to talk quietly. Curled up against Tyler, my eyelids grew heavier and heavier until they finally stayed closed.

"Something's wrong with Topaz, and whatever it is has affected Alpha Cole," I heard Matthew's voice from far away.

"I agree," Tristan said. "It seemed to me like Alpha Cole was controlling alphas Ash and Wyatt."

And that was the last I heard before I fell into the merciful arms of unconsciousness.

#

It felt like I'd only been asleep for five minutes when a roar like a sonic boom shook every tree surrounding the clearing, causing a few branches to snap and fall. I shot up as the rhythm of heavy thuds grew closer and closer. Glancing at the betas, I saw they realized the same thing I did.

Mason had arrived, and he was *beyond* angry.

His enormous black wolf barreled into the clearing and skidded to a stop, his thick claws ripping big grooves in the mossy ground. Showing his wickedly sharp teeth, he growled at the betas as fury flared in his eyes.

Smart guy that he was, Tyler slowly released me and backed away. The other betas, also being smart guys, followed suit, and all five of them moved to the outer edges of the clearing.

*Talk to Garnet,* Lark advised. *You the only one here he sure he not going to kill.*

Hoping she was right, I held my arms out.

"Will you please come here?" I asked, keeping my voice soft and low.

With one bounding leap, Garnet landed on his feet to stand over me. He carefully laid down and his soft chest fur tickled my face as he pushed me flat on my back and covered my whole body. When he stuffed his snout in my neck and sniffed me, I combed my fingers through his shaggy belly hair, inhaling his campfire scent.

*I don't want to lose this.*

*You're not going to lose me or Mason,* Garnet vowed. *Never. We belong to you and Lark forever.*

I wasn't convinced. If my other mates had turned against me, why wouldn't Mason and Jayden?

"Are you sure you don't want to get rid of me, too?"

*I should shift and* show *you how much I don't want to get rid of you!* Mason growled. *Let the betas watch me take their luna over and over, in as many ways as possible and as many times as it takes until you believe I love you and want you! You're my mate and I am never letting you go!* **Never!**

A hiccup slipped out before I could stop it, and tears followed. Garnet licked them from my cheeks with a soft whimper.

"What did I do wrong, Mason?" I sobbed and clung to Garnet.

*Nothing, baby. Not one thing. I don't know what that was about, but I know none of what Cole said is how he truly feels. I know it.*

"And Ash and Wyatt? Why don't they want me anymore?"

*They do. They want you, little flower,* he crooned.

"I thought marking you all tied you to me until I died. Why is this happening?"

*It does. I don't know, but I'm going to figure it out. I'll fix this, Posy, I swear.*

I cried for a long time, and neither of them lost their patience. While I hugged Garnet, Mason murmured soothing things and how much he loved me and wanted me.

"Excuse me, luna. I'm sorry to interrupt, but I have some clothes and shoes for the alpha," I heard a voice say from my left side.

Turning my head, I peeked out from under Garnet to see Poppy kneeling down next to me.

"Alpha Mason, you're probably going to want to shift." Leo came up and rested a hand on her shoulder. "Ariel and Maria will be here in a few minutes, and they have alphas Ash and Wyatt with them."

My eyes wide, I asked Garnet to let me up. He did, then sorted a pair of boxers out of the pile of fabric and disappeared behind a tree. I wiped at my face, feeling disgusting. My throat hurt, my eyes were raw and gritty, and my cheeks were sticky with tears and probably snot.

"Here, luna," Poppy murmured.

Blinking, I looked over and saw her holding out a wet piece of fabric. Her other hand held up a water bottle.

"Sorry. A strip off of Leo's shirt was the best I could do for a washcloth."

"Thank you," I whispered.

Taking it, I did my best to clean my face. She took the cloth and wet it again, then wiped my chin and neck. Dropping that piece, she handed me another strip of her mate's shirt.

"Blow your nose," she instructed.

I did what she said, then stuffed the makeshift hanky in my pocket.

"Sorry, Leo. I'll buy you a new shirt." I looked up at him.

"Luna, I am happy to sacrifice a t-shirt for your comfort."

Then Mason returned. He lifted me off the ground and crushed me against his chest as if I would disappear if he didn't hold me tightly enough. His face dove into the crook of my neck and he sighed.

"Alpha Cole's eyes!" Tyler yelped suddenly, and I jerked in Mason's arms.

"What about them?" Mason asked.

"Alpha Cole's eyes turned black, right, luna? But Topaz's eyes aren't black."

"They're silver!" I gasped. "But what happened to Topaz? Where is he? What would make Cole's eyes black?"

"I don't know, but he - or whatever it is - was definitely controlling Ash and Wyatt," Mason said. "Lark, see what you can find out. Garnet says all of Cole's and Topaz's links are locked down, but you should feel the mate bond at least. And can you reach Sid and Gran?"

123

*It there and strong as ever, but I no link with Sid or—* Lark interrupted herself with a sudden shriek. *Something hurting Cole! Topaz fighting it! He also healing Cole over and over. Taking all his energy. That why he silent.*

"Maria said they took a parasite out of the Cold Moon luna today," Matthew said slowly. "Do you think they missed one?"

"And it latched onto Alpha Cole?" Tristan added. "You think there's a parasite inside him?"

"If that's true, we need to get it out of him," Mason barked. "Poppy, how much damage could this thing do? And how quickly?"

She didn't know exactly without seeing the creature, but she had some theories. While she explained them, I spaced out, fear making the world around me spin in a blur.

One of my mates was in serious trouble. Even if he didn't want me anymore, I couldn't let Cole or Topaz die. They were exactly one-fifth of my heart.

I tuned back into the conversation as Mason asked Matthew and Tristan why they'd left Ariel and Maria behind at our house.

"We followed luna, as we should," Tristan told him. "Besides, they wanted to find the parasite Alpha Cole was guarding and try to determine why he was acting the way he was."

"You just left them there while Cole was acting aggressively?" Mason questioned them.

"They're *birds*, alpha." Matthew rolled his eyes. "When things get dicey, they shift and fly away."

"And they're witches," Poppy added. "They can more than take care of themselves, even against an angry alpha."

"Speaking of our mates, here they come," Tristan said and loped to the edge of the clearing.

Seconds later, Ariel and Maria walked out of the trees, leading Ash and Wyatt by the hand. My mates looked out of it, their pupils huge and their faces slack.

"We have a shield around their wolves," Maria explained as soon as we made eye contact. "The wolf has to answer to the alpha, but the man doesn't. It was the only thing we knew to try so we could get them away from Alpha Cole. It's not perfect, but it's working."

"We've had to shield their links, too, so that's why you haven't been able to reach them," Ariel added.

"They look high." Mason took my hand and led me over to them. "Ash? Wy? You good?"

"Good, Mase," Wyatt mumbled.

Ash nodded frantically, his curls bouncing, but said nothing.

"It's because they're separated from their wolves." Poppy tilted her head as she studied them. "The longer they go like this, I think the more they'd adapt and be able to function almost like normal, but let's not put it to the test."

"Is that why Reau is the way he is?" I asked her as I stared at Ash and Wyatt. "Because he lost his wolf?"

"No. He's a whole different little lollipop triple-dipped in issues." Poppy shook her head. "And the alphas' wolves aren't *dead*, just out of reach, which adds a level of frustration. Part of their brains feel numb, like when your hand falls asleep."

I *hated* when that happened and shuddered at the thought of my brain feeling like that.

*My poor mates! How they must be suffering!*

"Posy!" Ash shouted suddenly, making me jump. "Princess!"

He shoved Mason aside and threw his arms around my head and shoulders. Maria, who still had a death grip on his hand, was dragged around to my back.

"Alpha Ash, I told you we had to maintain skin contact!" she squealed.

Matthew growled to see his mate thrown around, but she shook her head at him.

"I love you, cupcake! Don't listen to him! Don't leave us!"

"Cutie?" Wyatt gasped, as if he too just realized I was there, even though I'd been standing right in front of him. "We wanted to stop him, but we couldn't move."

He stumbled over to me, too, dragging Ariel with him, and Tristan frowned as he trailed along to make sure his mate didn't get hurt.

Wyatt's arms went around my waist, and the two of them squeezed me, but not too tight.

"Why did he say those mean things?" Ash whispered. "It hurt my heart so bad."

"I don't know." I stroked his curls and kissed his cheek. "It hurt my heart, too."

Wyatt whined and buried his face in the side of my neck.

"I love you, Posy," he murmured in my ear. "To hell with Cole. He can have the pack if that's what he wants. We only want you."

"Uh, luna? Alphas?" I looked over my shoulder at Maria, who was tangled up in both of my mates' arms almost as much as I was. "Ariel and I know what happened. Alpha Cole isn't responsible for his actions right now."

"There was a ... miscommunication, I guess you could say," I heard Ariel's voice, but couldn't see her because she was behind Ash, clinging to Wyatt's hand. "He touched Luna Quake before we removed the parasite, and it spawned into him. It would have felt like a small sting, so he probably thought it was an insect bite."

125

"Why didn't the idiot wait until you'd cleared the victim?!" Poppy thundered. "Talk about a candidate for the Darwin Awards!"

"Easy, love." Leo laid his hands on her shoulders. "None of us are familiar with magic or how to work with witches, okay? It was a mistake. I doubt he did it on purpose."

"It *was* a mistake," Ariel explained. "On our half, too. As soon as we knew how we were going to solve the problem, we should have told him the steps we needed to take. Instead, when the family asked him to put the luna out of her misery, he carried on as he normally would."

"Okay. So, Cole's being controlled by a parasite?" Mason asked. "And he controlled Ash and Wyatt to make them go along with him?"

"In the simplest terms, yes," Maria said. "We'll tell you every little detail of what happened at Cold Moon, but let's get the parasite out of Alpha Cole first. Before it can do any more damage."

"For that, we need a plan." Mason nodded and rubbed his hands together. "Fortunately, I have one."

## 18: Too Much

*Posy*

Mason's plan went without a hitch. The witches called Cole outside, saying there was an emergency in the pack. As soon as he stepped off the porch, Mason locked him down with all the moon and alpha power he could pull from both Earthshine and Five Fangs. In the moment that Cole was frozen, Ariel and Maria released Ash and Wyatt from the shielding spell, and the two of them pushed out their own moon and alpha power from their packs.

And Mason was right - the three of them together were able to hold Cole so the witches could go to work.

Removing the parasite was disgusting to watch, but took less than a minute. Ariel drew the red-black leech out from Cole's nostril, Maria caught it in a glass jar that she sealed up quickly, and Poppy purified Cole and the area.

As soon as they called out that everything was good, Mason released Cole, who dropped to his knees, pitched over onto his side, and didn't move. Right away, Mason knelt next to him and checked his pulse.

"*COLE!*" I screamed.

Racing over, I fell next to his still body. Tears poured down my face as I grabbed his shoulders and shook him.

"Wake up!" I yelled.

He still didn't move, and my heart stalled.

"No, no, no! Don't you dare!" I screamed and shook him harder.

When he didn't respond, my lungs stopped and the world began to fade around the edges. Dimly, I was aware of arms gathering me against a big body that smelled of campfire.

"Breathe. In and out." A hand grabbed mine and pressed it to a hard chest. "Follow me. In. Now out. Come on, little flower, you can do it."

I tried. I opened my mouth and gulped in air, but it clogged in my throat and choked me.

Someone that smelled of vanilla dropped down next to me.

"He's alive, Posy." He took my other hand and held it over Cole's mouth and nose. "Feel that? He's breathing. You need to breathe, too. Come on, cutie. Calm down."

I could hear their words, but they made no sense.

Someone took my head, turned it gently, and laid my ear on Cole's chest.

"Listen! He isn't dead or dying!"

*Thump-thump. Thump-thump.*

What was that?

*Thump-thump. Thump-thump.*

A heartbeat?

*Thump-thump. Thump-thump.*

It was! A strong and steady heartbeat!

"Cole?" My mouth formed the word, but no sound came out.

"He's going to be fine. He just needs time to recover. He and Topaz fought a long, hard battle all alone."

"Wyatt?"

"Here, cutie." He brought Cole's hand up to my face and held it under my nose. "Smell."

Sipping the air, I groaned as the smell of pine went up my nose and pressed my whole face into Cole's palm.

"Keep breathing, princess. That's all you have to do right now."

"Ash?" I whispered.

"Shh. It's okay. Everything's okay, I promise."

I nodded, closed my eyes, and laid on Cole's chest as Mason, Wyatt, and Ash stroked my hair and back.

"Posy," a weak voice croaked, and I sat up, my mates' hands dropping away from me.

"Cole?" I stroked his long hair back from his face. "Open your eyes, Cole."

"Didn't mean ... what I said. Don't leave ... don't leave us. Love you."

"Cole, please open your eyes," I begged.

His eyelids fluttered, then slowly rose until I could see his fern-green eyes again. I let out a heavy sigh, almost convinced he was alive.

"Sorry. So ... sorry. Wasn't me ... talking, Posy. I swear ... by the moon."

"Is Topaz all right?" Neither Lark nor I couldn't reach him, and I worried that the parasite had eaten him like it had Luna Quake's wolf.

"Honey, ... I love you. I love you ... so damn much!"

He started to cough and tried to roll on his side. I helped him as best I could, but he *was* the size of a bear and almost as heavy, and Mason had to help me.

"Don't leave, Posy," Cole whispered, his pretty eyes latched onto my face.

"I won't. I'm here. How's Topaz?"

"Sleeping. Very tired. Fought the thing. Healed me over and over."

His voice was getting a little stronger, which encouraged me, although he still had to stop and take a breath after every choppy sentence. Closing my eyes, I pressed my lips to his forehead.

"Posy. I'm sorry." He grabbed my arm and pulled me against him and buried his face in my neck. "I'm so sorry ... those words came out of ... my mouth. You are none of those things. You are perfect, honey. I love you. Don't leave. Don't leave. Don't leave."

"Shh. Rest. I'm not going anywhere. I love you, Cole."

His tears ran down my skin and soaked my shirt, and I hugged him tightly as harsh sobs racked him.

"I had the witches check over everyone here," Mason told us, "to make sure there was no more spawn. We're all good."

"Why didn't it get Posy?" Ash asked. "She hugged Cole."

"Did you touch his skin?" Poppy asked, and I shook my head. "That's why, then. A parasite needs skin-to-skin contact to dump its spawn into a new host, which it will do only when it senses imminent death or danger because it risks killing itself to spawn."

Ariel and Maria joined us, and the betas formed an outer circle around our inner one. Ariel knelt near Cole's head and raised her hands, and soon a shimmer appeared in the air over him. After a minute, she finished and dropped her hands.

"He's going to be all right, luna," she said. "He's exhausted emotionally and mentally and needs a lot of rest, but his wolf has already healed the psychic damage. They need to sleep now. After that and a few good meals, they'll both be right as rain."

"Alphas, luna, I'm so sorry this happened," Maria choked out and my eyes flew to hers. It made me sad to see her cheeks stained with tears. "We should have prepped him better. We should have noticed that it spawned. We should have—"

"Maria, stop," I said. "It wasn't anyone's fault. Don't blame yourself. I don't, and I don't want you to, either."

"We're not used to working with anyone other than Gelo, and he would have known not to touch the infected host before we did our part." With a sigh, Ariel stood, and Tristan immediately gathered her into his arms. "We need to do some training with the alphas before we go on any more missions like that."

Cole's hold had slackened, so I sat up and speared each of my mates with a narrow-eyed glare. The sun had sunk below the horizon, but there was still enough light for them to see how serious I was right now.

"No more," I said fiercely. "No more missions. At least for a while. You are staying home and *none* of you are leaving my sight."

"Okay, honey." Cole reached up and cupped my face with hands that trembled, and I could hear the exhaustion in his voice. "Okay."

"We'll tell the king we're unavailable for the rest of the summer," Mason declared while nodding. "Like Ariel said, we need time to train with them. I don't want anything like this to happen again."

"Oh, yeah! We're on vacation for the next two months!" Wyatt crowed. "We'll take you on those dates we wanted to go on and to the queen's coronation and your mom's family reunion!"

"*And* to the beach!" Ash chimed in. "Then we can go shopping for your school supplies—"

"The beach?" I cut him off, that one word perking me up. "You promise?"

"I promise."

I smiled widely, flashing him my dimples, and he grinned.

"Sorry to interrupt," Crew said, "but Alpha Jay's team has returned. He dropped Sara off at Beatrix's. Emerson, Angelo's back at your place. Luna, with your consent, we'll leave you with your mates and go to ours."

"Of course. Thank you all so much." I stood up, wobbled a bit, and grabbed Mason's shoulder to steady myself. "I can't tell you how much it meant to me to have you by my side today."

"We will always be by your side," Tyler said and hugged me. Ducking down, he whispered in my ear. "Peri said you better call, text or link her soon, or she's going to raise hell until she finds out what's wrong."

Giggling a little, I told him I would contact her before I went to bed, but gave him permission to tell her and the parents what happened.

I hugged the rest of the betas and the witches and Leo, then they disappeared into the darkening evening.

Not too long after they left, I heard a vehicle was coming up the drive, but someone else would have to deal with whoever it was and whatever they wanted. I'd had enough for one day. All I wanted to do was curl up with my mates in our bed and sleep for a week.

"I'm sorry if I'm being selfish about wanting you to stay home," I told them, "and I know there are people who need help and I feel bad about that, but this was— This was just *too much*."

"I know, honey. I'm sorry I screwed up and—"

"No, Cole." I framed his face with my palms. "No blaming yourself. It happened and we got through it and that's what matters, but now I need a break. *All* of us do."

"You have to admit, it's been a crazy summer so far," Ash said. "Even for *us*, there's been a whole lot of weird shit going down."

"Language," Mason muttered, "but yeah, there has. My little baby is right. We need a nice, long break, and we're taking it together."

The lush smell of roses wafted under my nose, and I turned to see Jayden jogging up the walk. His dragon eyes went to me first, then swept over his brothers sprawled around me on the grass. With a frown, he kicked the bottom of Cole's shoe.

"What's wrong with you? What did I miss?"

"Aw, nothing much." Wyatt shrugged his shoulders and squinted up at him. "Cole touched another luna and caught a disease that made him yell mean things at Posy and fight me and Ash before the witches cured him."

Jayden's mouth opened, his face full of questions, but Cole raised his index finger and spoke first.

"For the record, I'd like to clarify that it was a parasite, not a *disease*."

"Same same." Wyatt shrugged again.

"Mase?" Jayden stared at his eldest brother.

"No, that pretty much summed it up. Lacked all details and skipped a few important bits, but accurate nonetheless."

"Yeah, I'm thinking I need to hear those details and important bits." Jayden sat down next to me and draped an arm around my shoulders. Drawing me against his side, he leaned down and kissed my forehead. "Missed you, sweetness. Are you okay?"

"I missed you, too." I rested against him with a sigh. "I didn't expect you back so soon, but I'm really glad you are."

"And are you okay?" He lifted my chin with two fingers so I'd look at him. "You've been crying."

Staring into his beautiful eyes, I felt too many things at once and couldn't untangle them enough to begin processing anything. Shaking my head, I held up a hand, silently asking for his patience. He nodded, caught my hand, and held it against his heart.

The rest of my mates crowded around me. Cole laid his head on my other shoulder and Mason, Ash, and Wyatt sat criss-cross applesauce in front of us, as close to me as so many knees would let them get.

As the final rays of light faded, I lifted my face to see the first of the evening stars twinkling in the velvet sky. Taking a deep breath, I started talking.

"I got knocked down pretty hard today. It wasn't anyone's fault, and it didn't help that my mind got so clouded by my past and low self-esteem that I focused only on the negatives and couldn't remember any positives."

I swallowed hard and looked around at my boys, meeting each of their eyes before I continued.

"I didn't want to tell you this, but I think you need to know. I thought about ending it all. When I ran from here, I told Lark that if this didn't kill us, I'd find a way to do it myself."

Five waves of anguish, solid and heavy, hit my mate bond. I acknowledged them with a small nod, but hoped they wouldn't interrupt me while I had the courage to speak.

"But I didn't." I lifted my chin. "I'm done crying, but I'm still working on getting up. I don't know how much time that will take, but when I do, I'll keep going. I won't give up. I'll keep going because—"

My voice choked up, and I stopped to take a few deep breaths until I could speak again.

"I'll keep going because I am stronger than anything that tries to keep me down."

Before the others could react, Ash unfolded his grasshopper legs, got to his knees, and leaned in to cup my face in his hands. His eyes met mine for several long seconds, then a brilliant grin stretched across his face.

"There she is. There's our amazing, beautiful, strong mate. She gets knocked down, she cries, she gets up, and she keeps going." His grin disappeared, and I saw dead seriousness in his chocolate eyes for the first time ever. "And you know what that makes you, princess?"

I shook my head, my cheeks warm from his praise.

"Yes, you do. You're our bad-ass bitch, baby."

"Damn right she is," the rest of my mates chorused.

And this terrible, horrible, no-good, very bad day finally ended with a round of laughter under a star-filled summer sky.

## 19: Consequences

*Lark*

As our humans fell asleep under the stars, my wolves and I talked about the many things - good and bad - that came out of today.

Of course, we started with the mission to Cold Moon, since it had the biggest impact. As Topaz slept, I shared everything I knew, and Garnet added in details that he'd seen. Granite and Sid didn't have too much to contribute, other than whining about how awful it was to be controlled by Cole, then shielded from their humans. Quartz asked a couple of questions, then decreed none of us would have anything to do with magic until we had a chance to learn about it and train with Angelo and the witches.

We were all on board with that.

Garnet talked a bit about what happened at Gray Shadows, but it didn't need much explanation. The king found Alpha Bellamy and Luna Ivana Jones guilty of killing an innocent wolf with illegal wolfsbane and abusing their pup. There was only one outcome for that, and Mason had taken care of it. End of story.

*Quartz, how it go at the prison?* I asked. *You save any shifters?*

I didn't ask about the human guards because I knew he wouldn't have allowed any to live.

*Seventeen alive. Most were very weak, in poor condition, dehydrated, and starved. We brought all but one back with us.*

*Why leave one?* I frowned.

*Two were wolf shifters. One from Bright Star and the other from White Pelt. Jayden contacted both their packs, and the Bright Star alpha himself came to pick up his wolf and thank us. As for the White Pelt, it will take some time for someone to retrieve her since that pack is in northern Canada. She is too weak and scared to go so far alone, not that I'd allow her to, anyway.*

*Then I happy you brought her home.* I gave him a smile. *If there only two wolves, what kind of other shifters?*

*They aren't* all *shifters, my love, but there were three jaguars from Brazil near the Amazon. A mated pair and their cub.*

*Cub?* Sid frowned.

*He will be fine. As I said, all the shifters are weak from hunger, but have no physical wounds.* Quartz blew an amused breath out of his nose. *Once we were far enough away, we stopped at a grocery store and bought out the meat section and several flats of water.*

*Bet that was fun to explain to cashier,* Granite snorted.

*No one asks Gelo too many questions when he has his work face on.* Quartz shrugged. *There was also a pair of chupacabras that Zayne killed, a gremlin that Zayden killed, a mated pair of coyote shifters, two thunderbirds, two pixies from the Woodland Realm, a black bear shifter, a peryton, and a dragon.*

Silence.

*A dragon?*

*Yep. The Goddess alone knows how a group of humans managed to drug and imprison* him. *Gelo says he's very young, though. He's not quite what we'd consider mating age.*

*Cool!* Sid chirped. *Even if only for a bit, I bet Five Fangs is only pack ever who can say a dragon lives there!*

*I meet him?* I asked Quartz.

*Sure. I don't see why not. He is pretty interesting.*

*What a peryton?* Sid asked.

I was glad he did. I had no clue what it was, but felt shy about asking. I didn't want my mates to think I was dumb.

*Deer with wings basically.* Quartz sent us an image of it. *Neither Jayden nor I knew what it was, either. Gelo had to tell us.*

*You said seventeen alive.* Garnet looked thoughtful. *Did some die in the fight, or you found them dead?*

*A trio of python shifters died before we could prevent it. The humans started slitting the prisoners' throats when they realized we were attacking.*

I shivered. I wasn't too fond of any kind of snake, but no one deserved to die at a human's hands for no reason.

*Were they the only deaths?* I asked, sensing they weren't, but not wanting to push Quartz if he didn't want to talk.

*A mermaid and a merman were dead in their tanks. The stupid humans hadn't kept the water fresh enough.* Quartz frowned. *It upset Jayden, but what could we do? They'd been dead for a couple of days before we got there.*

Quartz went on to explain that the king's inspectors arrived to clear out the office space and find clues as to who the human mastermind was behind the prison. King Julian wanted to shut down the whole operation - including the lab Poppy had heard mentioned - as soon as possible. He also wanted to know how the human leader had discovered shifters in the first place.

After that conversation, we were all tuckered out and drifted off, only waking up when we heard our humans complaining about being covered in dew at dawn.

Many, many people came by after breakfast to check on Posy The alphas, too, but mostly Posy. Everyone in the pack felt her pain through the bond yesterday and wanted to link or drop by to see that she was fine with their own eyes.

Cole took the day off and rested with her, although we all knew he needed more time than one day to get his head sorted out. He was so eaten up by guilt, it would probably take several visits with Dr. York for him to be okay again.

The whole family came over at dinner time and passed Posy around and around in hugs until she'd laughed and told them to stop before her mates got jealous. When the questions got too much, she changed the topic by asking about the prison survivors, wanting to make sure they had what they needed until they were ready to leave.

"Do they all have somewhere to go?" Peri asked the alphas.

"We'll find out," Wyatt told her and patted her on top of her head.

"Stop, doofus!" She swatted at his hand. "I'm a mated woman now, not a kid!"

"Mated or not, you're still a kid in my eyes, Periwinkle," he teased her. "You'll always be our baby sister."

"Until she has a baby," Posy giggled. "Then you get to be an uncle!"

"She ain't having a baby," Cole argued.

"Eventually, I want to be a mom." Peri rolled her eyes at him. "Ty and I want lots of pups!"

"No, you don't." He crossed his arms over his chest and narrowed his eyes at her. "You have to mate to have pups, and you're not ever mating with anyone."

"Well, I have news for you, big brother!"

"Uh, Peri? I don't want to die today," Tyler interrupted.

"Ty and I have already mated *plenty* of times and—"

His face and ears burning red, Tyler covered her mouth with his hand.

"Are you trying to get me killed?" he whisper-yelled.

"You've done *what?!*" Cole glared at Tyler, making Posy, Ash, Mom, and Mama giggle.

Throwing Peri over his shoulder, Tyler carried his mate to their car.

*"Tyler James!"* Cole roared.

Laughing, Posy wrapped her arms around him and distracted him with kisses, and Tyler and Peri made their getaway.

So it seemed like everything was back to normal at Five Fangs - except for one big problem that made itself known at bedtime that night.

Posy had a panic attack when her mates tried to touch her intimately.

135

I was confused, the alphas were shocked, and their wolves were heartbroken. She leapt out of bed, huddled in the corner, and shook like a leaf in a hurricane. It took the alphas more than an hour to calm her down and get her to sleep.

The next morning, they talked about it, and Posy couldn't explain why it happened. To be honest, I had an idea, but I kept my mouth shut to let her mates handle it. I mean, what did *I* know? I was just a wolf who'd been isolated from everyone for my entire existence except the last few months. Before our mates found us, I'd never even *talked* to another wolf except Agate and Slate, and then only before Alpha Briggs forbade me to talk to anyone.

When Posy panicked again the next night, we all realized the problem wasn't going to resolve itself on its own. She could hug and kiss and cuddle them and their wolves, but froze when things became passionate. The third night, despite the alphas telling her that they wanted to wait until they found the cause of her panic attacks, she insisted she wanted to try again and chose Ash.

Hesitantly, he agreed. He went slowly and kept checking in with her verbally, and we all relaxed a bit as things went along with no problem. Then I felt her begin to freeze up and told her to tell him to stop, but she forced herself through it until he slid her panties down. With a scream, she pushed him away, threw herself off the bed, and sobbed in the corner again.

Eventually, Mason was able to convince her to let him get close enough to pick her up. Wrapping her in a blanket, he cradled her in his big arms and rocked her until she fell asleep. The other alphas huddled around them, disturbed and upset, and the devastated look in Ash's eyes broke my heart.

The next morning, the alphas invited Dr. York to the house. They took him into the home office and talked to him for about an hour, then their wolves talked to him for another hour, although one of them - *cough*, Quartz, *cough* - wouldn't interact with him at all.

Finally, it was Posy's turn.

It took a good while before Dr. York earned enough of her trust, but once she opened up, he skillfully mined every last nugget of her past without her even realizing how much she was revealing.

Then he sat back, steepled his fingers in front of his face, and stared at the ceiling for a full five minutes.

"Luna," he said at last, "do you *want* to improve this situation with your mates, or are you content to continue your current platonic relationship?"

"What does platonic mean?" she asked. "I can make a guess, but I want to be sure."

"Friendly and loving, but no mating."

"I thought so. I want things to go back to the way they were. I—" She swallowed hard and her cheeks burned red. Keeping her eyes on her tangled fingers, she whispered, "I like being with them that way."

"Enjoying intimacy with your mates isn't anything to be embarrassed about or ashamed of," he told her gently. "It's normal and healthy. If you *didn't* enjoy it, this would be an entirely different conversation."

"I miss it," she admitted, still whispering, "and I'm afraid they're going to get impatient or think I'm punishing them or something. I don't want them to hate me."

"Oh, luna." Dr. York covered his mouth with his hand for a moment. "After meeting with your mates, I can tell you with absolute certainty that they love you. Even if you can never be intimate with them again, their feelings toward you will not change. Also, the marks you've given each other guarantee they will stay by your side forever just as you will theirs. Furthermore, they know you're not punishing them. They know you're dealing with something they can't understand."

*Of course they not understand,* I thought to myself with a huff. *They never locked in a dark room day after day until months blend into years. They never beaten by someone who supposed to love and protect them. They never silenced and not allowed to talk or link with anyone. Their wolves never tortured or drugged into a coma—*

"I don't understand why I'm panicking now, though," Posy's soft voice brought my attention back to the present.

"I have a theory, but it's just a theory." He shrugged. "The mind is a very fluid place where thoughts can be tricked and manipulated and opinions changed in a heartbeat. I could be wrong."

"I'd still like to hear your theory."

"When Alpha Cole said what he did while alphas Ash and Wyatt sat there without intervening, your mind connected that with Alpha Briggs and your brothers. Even though you knew they were two separate events, one in the past and one in the present, your mind melded them together and took you right back to that dark room you were kept in."

I nodded in agreement with Dr. York

*Now we getting to the heart of it. The lid got knocked off the box where my girl keep all those bad memories. Now she no can—* I stopped and remembered one of Garnet's lessons with me. *No, Garnet say use cannot. Now she* cannot *get it back on.*

"Alphas Mason and Jayden said you are usually extremely good at seeing each of your mates as individuals and not as mates collectively, which is amazing, to tell you the truth. I've worked with lunas before who struggled to divide their attention between twin or triplet mates, and you have five!"

He paused to see if she had anything to add or ask, but she only nodded for him to continue.

"But now, your mind sees them as a unit that, unfortunately, resembles your step-father. They're large men, powerful and dominant, and alphas. Attributes that usually are seen as positives for shifters, but for you, are warning signs of danger. Abuse. Pain. Isolation."

"I don't hate them. I'm not scared of them." Posy's eyes stung with tears.

"I know you don't hate them, but are you *sure* you're not scared of them?"

She opened her mouth, but only a whimper came out.

"Yeah." Dr. York nodded. "To be honest, with your history of such severe abuse, I'm surprised you were able to be intimate with them *before* the parasite incident. I bet it took you a while to "let" them touch you, and even longer before you *wanted* them to touch you, and even longer still before *you* wanted to touch *them*."

He didn't need her to respond. She and I both knew he was correct.

"As a runt, you are physically more fragile than most, and your mind is quite aware of how easy it would be for them to hurt you. They betrayed your trust once; how can you know they won't do that again? So, right now, a part of your mind sees mating as making yourself extremely vulnerable to five large, powerful, dominant alphas who could betray or hurt you at any moment."

"They didn't betray me," she mumbled. "I know what happened. I saw the witches take out the parasite, and I saw Maria's memory of how it infected Cole. And they wouldn't hurt me. Not ever."

"Your *rational* side knows the truth, yes. Your *irrational* side, though, doesn't agree."

She was quiet as she thought about what he said.

"So how do I get them to agree?" she asked after a moment.

"Well, I can give you some ideas to try, but, ultimately, you need to admit and accept what's wrong. Then you can begin to process it and heal."

*Posy, may I please speak with Dr. York?* I asked, unable to stay silent any longer.

*Oh. Yes. Of course. I forgot he also spoke to the boys' wolves. It's only fair that he speaks with you, too.*

*Do you mind if it private? It about me and my wolf mates.*

*Are you having trouble, too?* she asked, worried now.

*Some, but I think he might help me clear it up.*

*Is it with one wolf or all of them?* she wanted to know.

138

Grr. This girl always needed the whole story! Thinking quickly, I came up with something she'd buy.

*Just Sid.*

*Is this about Mr. Nibbles? Because I swear, I'm over that—*

*No, Posy. I worried about how he feeling after what happened between you and Ash.*

I felt her pain and grief in our bond. She was so very upset with herself for hurting Ash that way. I cursed at myself. I knew I should have said Quartz instead of Sid; she wouldn't have even questioned *him* as my problem.

*Oh, no! Is Sid depressed? Is he hurt? Is he—*

*Posy, you have enough with your mates. Please let me handle Sid, okay?*

*Okay. You're right.* She nodded. *He's your mate. I get it.*

"Dr. York, my wolf wants to talk to you in private," she told him. "Her name is Lark. I'm going to let her ascend while I think about all that you've said."

"Very well, luna."

Posy sank to the back of our mind and I blocked her out. I was far better at it than she was with me; she wouldn't hear a peep.

I didn't like to deceive or manipulate her, but I *had* to protect her. It was what I'd done all my life. I took the hits and pain for her when I could, healed her when I couldn't, tried to keep her hopes up by telling her we would escape and find our mate, and helped her maintain the good memories she had from her childhood. Not everyone would agree with some of my methods, such as tattling on her to the alphas, but I didn't always know how else to protect her.

Now she was once more trapped in a dark place, this time mentally instead of physically, and I would protect her again, even if it meant going behind her back.

"Hello, Lark," Dr. York said politely as he met my silver eyes.

"Hello, doctor. Now you and I is going to have a chat."

#

*Wyatt*

After our wolves' session with Dr. York, we took back control, turned the home office over to him and Posy, then headed to the living room.

None of us felt like talking. We didn't get a game out or even turn on TV. We just ... sat.

Finally, Dr. York came into the living room, but he was alone.

"Posy?" Cole asked.

"She went to take a nap. She said she'd be in her special room." He raised his eyebrow in question.

Jay explained it to him in a few quick sentences while I checked the mate link.

"She's already asleep, curled up with Mr. Nibbles," I said after Dr. York finished praising us for providing her with a safe place.

We knew he wouldn't have all the answers, and might need a few more sessions before he even had some suggestions, but we all hoped he had *something* for us today.

We were desperate to help our girl in any way we could. She was in so much pain, and we didn't even realize it until that first panic attack the next night after the parasite incident.

Talk about heartbreaking.

I ended up going wolfy for a couple of hours, and Mason found me passed out in the forest the next morning. When I questioned Granite, he assured me he'd only gone for a run.

*It was that or kill someone*, he shrugged, and I thanked him for being smart enough to choose the run.

"Well, doctor?" Mase broke the silence.

"Before we get to that, I'd like to request permission for my mate and I to join Five Fangs." Dr. York scrubbed his hands over his face and sank back in his chair.

"That bad, huh?" Cole grimaced.

"Between you five, your luna, Spring, and Thoreau Jones, I don't see my work ending here for years - and that's not taking into consideration any other member of your vast pack who may be in need of counseling or therapy."

"You want to leave a royal post to come here and work?" Ash asked incredulously.

"My mate and I are tired of shuffling through the kingdom every few months." He shrugged. "It was fine when we were younger, but I'm forty-three now. My mate is forty. We want a pack to settle down in, maybe adopt some pups who need a good home."

"What kind of work does your mate do?" I asked.

"He's a teacher. He's certified in middle and high school math. Everything from pre-algebra to trigonometry."

*Hey! Our first teacher for Posy's school,* Jay linked us, and we all smiled or nodded in agreement.

Dr. York was saying something more about moving here, but my ear caught the sound of footsteps pattering overhead.

*Posy's awake already?* I frowned. I wanted her to rest longer, seeing as she hadn't gotten much sleep the past few nights.

*One of you please help me?* Lark linked us.

*Sure, little wolf,* I answered before any of my brothers could. *What's up?*

*I stuck on stairs.*

*I got you.*

Standing up, I left the room and found Lark-in-Posy's-body frozen on the second step down, her fists clutching the railing, and I hustled up to her.

"I scared to go any further," she murmured. "I still clumsy in this body."

"It's okay, little wolf. I'll always help you." With a smile, I reached for her, then stopped. I couldn't watch her go through another panic attack. "Um, is it okay to pick you up?"

"Of course. Posy sleeping, and I no have same issue she does."

My lips pinched together in a grim line, but I nodded and scooped her up and took a calming inhale of her scent as I carried her down the stairs and into the living room.

"Ah, here she is." Dr. York grinned broadly. "The smart little wolf who has an idea that might help your mate."

My eyebrows climbed up my forehead as I sat down on the love seat, snuggling Lark on my lap.

"You have an idea, little wolf?" I murmured.

"To help Posy, yes."

"All right, sugar, we're all ears." Cole gave her a soft smile. "What's your idea?"

"Well," her cheeks flared red, "I mate with one of my wolves in this body and him in yours. My girl sees that there is no danger and feels safe."

"If you have not done this before, it may cause a deeper issue," Dr. York warned us.

All of our cheeks now matched Lark's as we remembered *that* afternoon.

*Sammiches*, I thought dreamily, and Granite purred with happiness.

"We have," Mase said bluntly. "You believe this is a good idea?"

"Yes. For the reasons Lark mentioned, but also because it will help luna begin to separate you individually from that collective you we discussed earlier, which will further distance her connection between you and her abuser."

"I'm game to try," I smirked.

"Well, it won't be with *Gran*." Mase gave me The Look. "No way would he be able to contain himself enough to do what we need."

"Remember, alphas, this is all theory. You are the first group of mates of this size I've ever heard of, so there are no cases to study for information or advice." Dr. York sighed and shook his head. "If you want to try this, which of your wolves can be the most gentle or even submissive to Lark?"

141

All our heads turned to Ash, who looked startled at the concentrated attention.

"What?" he asked.

"Sid," Mase, Cole, Jay and I said together.

"He'll be perfect," Jay clarified. "He was so tender and careful with Lark and responded well to guidance."

His eyes filling up, Ash covered his mouth with both hands and shook his head.

"I *can't*. I can't see her like that again because of me," he mumbled under his fingers.

"You can and you *will*," Cole declared. "It's about Posy, not you!"

"His feelings are valid, Alpha Cole," Dr. York interjected in a mild tone. "It's neither healthy nor kind to dismiss or belittle them."

Cole pouted at being chastised and crossed his arms over his chest.

*Doctor lucky not to eat Cole's fist*, Granite giggled, and I smirked.

"It will be Sid in control," Mase reminded Ash. "You'll just be along for the ride."

"And you *like* going for a ride, don't you?" I snickered.

"Shut up, douche!"

"I sorry. I no mean to upset anyone." Lark sounded like she might start to cry, and I held her closer.

"Shh. He didn't mean it like that," I whispered in her ear.

"No, no, no, little doll!" Ash dropped his hands from his face. "I'm not upset! Sid would love to be with you that way, but are you *sure* Posy won't panic?"

"She no panic," Lark said, "but if she do, I promise I tell you and Sid."

"All right. I'll do it. We'll do it." Ash scratched the back of his neck. "Who's going to tell Posy the plan?"

"Leave to me," Lark said with a smirk, which was the oddest thing ever to see on our sweet girl's face.

## 20: Wolf to Wolf

*Posy*

*Um, Posy?*
*Yeah, Lark?*
*I need to be with Sid tonight.*
I blinked a few times at her words.
*What do you mean,* be *with him?* I tilted my head. *You want to shift and play with him?*
*Not exactly.* Her eyes filled with tears, and I gasped.
*Oh, wolfie, don't cry! What's wrong? Is this related to your talk with Dr. York?*
*Sid and I* need *each other right now. I so sorry I no can—* she stopped and corrected herself. *I cannot mate with my wolves in my own body! I so sorry I is a burden to you! Especially when you having your own problems. But I just— I need him, Posy!*
It took me a minute to understand what she was trying to say, then my cheeks flushed with heat.
*Oh! Well, of course you want to mate with your wolves. I'm so sorry that I didn't realize you were struggling with this. And you aren't a burden, Lark! You're my wolfie, and I love you.*
*I know you scared of you mates right now—*
*I'm not scared of them!* I protested.
*Scared to mate with them, then. And I can wait if you—*
*No, wolfie. I want to mate with them. I do. I miss loving them every night.* I whimpered. *I hate this! I know they'd never hurt me, so why can't I—*
*You be scared if I use you body to mate with Sid tonight?* she interrupted. *You panic?*
*No, and maybe it will help me get over this mental block.*
*Yeah, maybe,* she agreed with a secret smile that I should have questioned, but was too upset with myself to bother. *So I can have him?*
*Sure. You'll be driving,* I grinned. *I'll just be along for the ride.*
She snorted, then giggled, which made me giggle, too.
*But if you scared,* she said, getting serious again, *we stop right away. If I no notice, promise you tell me.*
*I promise.*

#

*Sid*


I didn't know why Ashy had gotten so worked up. I'd mated with Lark before and no complaints. I'd pleasured her and made her come before me, and I hadn't hurt her. What was hard?

143

Well, besides *me*?

Now that I got to do it again, I shivered with excitement as Lark led us to our room. She giggled when I swung her up in my arms and carried her to the bed, carefully laying her down with a pillow under her head.

"Sid?"

She looked up at me with those big silver eyes, and I got even harder. I stood at the edge of the bed and felt my pants getting tighter and tighter.

"Yes, my darling?"

"I try something new?"

"I get to be inside you?"

"Oh, yes."

I grinned widely as I nodded. She grinned, too, and sat up on her knees. Reaching for me, she hooked her fingers in the drawstrings of my sweat shorts and tugged until they were undone. Then she slid my shorts down my legs and I kicked them off once she got them to my knees. My boxers didn't do *anything* to hide my hard-on, and she licked her lips.

"I need a little help with you shirt since you so *big*," she said in a husky voice that made me swallow hard to keep from coming right then and there.

Reaching over my head, I yanked my t-shirt up and off and dropped it to the floor. Her breathing picking up, she ran her delicate little fingers over my shoulders and pecs, then skimmed them up and down my abs a few times.

"My strong, big boy," she whispered before sucking one of my nipples into her warm, wet mouth.

The dancing sparks combined with her gentle sucking to make me so hard, my dick poked her belly button.

"I take your clothes off now?" I asked, also keeping my voice at a whisper.

I didn't know why we were whispering, but I wasn't going to mess up by not following her lead.

"Mm-hmm. My shirt off first, please."

Easy enough. It was actually Jay's shirt, so it was loose and long on her and slipped easily over her head. I let it drop to the floor on top of mine and stared at her lace-covered breasts.

"Now my shorts," she said and attacked my other nipple.

Opening the top button, I slid the zipper down, then slipped my hand inside to cup her pussy through her panties and was delighted to find she was already soaked. With my other hand, I slid her shorts down her bottom, smirking at Ashy's groan as I very gently squeezed one cheek.

144

Leaving her crotch, I put my hands on her waist and lifted her until she was on her feet. Even standing on the bed, she was shorter than me. I didn't even need to lean down to ease her panties and shorts to her ankles, making sure to touch as much of her silky legs as I could on the way down.

Moaning, she sank her fingers into my hair and gripped the curls, tugging just a little, and I growled as I laid an open-mouth kiss on her mate mark.

"Now my bra," she breathed in my ear, and my eyes rolled back in my head.

I couldn't figure out the clasp thing at the back, so I grabbed the fabric on either side and yanked until it came apart, then tossed it aside.

"Bad Sid," she scolded in a purr. "I liked that one. The lace so pretty."

"I buy you another just like it," I promised as her full breasts spilled into my greedy hands.

Ashy was an ass man, but I loved her pert titties with their hard nipples. Massaging the left one, I lowered my head and suckled her right, then tried to take as much of it into my mouth as I could.

"Sid," she moaned and leaned into me, tipping her head back so her long hair fell like a silk curtain down to her hips.

I slid one hand around to the small of her back and pulled her closer, and I couldn't stand the fabric between us any longer. Releasing her titty, I reached down and ripped my boxers getting them off. My dick flew up and rubbed against her soft belly, and I groaned.

I wanted inside her, and I wanted inside her *now*.

Wrapping my arms around her, I laid her back down on the bed and crawled over her, kissing any bit of glowing skin near my mouth.

"Sid, I going to try something new," she pouted.

"Oh. I forgot. What you want to try?"

"Can you lie on your back, please?"

"Anything for my darling."

I rolled over and watched her curiously as she eyed me up and down. When her gaze fixed on my groin, I wondered what she was up to.

Then her small hands were on me, stroking me up and down and massaging my ball sack, just the way Ashy had shown her to do with Wyatt.

This wasn't new, but I wasn't going to complain.

After a few strokes, she bent over and took me in her mouth, and I nearly jumped out of my skin in surprise.

*That* was definitely new.

Groaning again, I fisted my hands in the sheets and tipped my head back. Her hot mouth *devoured* me, sucking and licking, and her little hand wrapped around what didn't fit and stroked it up and down in time with her mouth.

I tangled my fingers in her hair as her head bobbed, gritting my teeth against the pleasure of it and trying to hold on as long as I could. Finally, I felt my balls draw up and caught her face in my hands.

"My darling, stop," I said hoarsely. "I not want to come in your mouth."

She raised her head slowly and released my dick with a wet *pop!* Giving me a beaming smile, she slithered her way up my body and rubbed as much of her skin against mine as she could.

"You like it?" she said against my lips.

"So much," I told her before I kissed her. "Now you tried new thing, we do the old thing?"

"Can we do old thing in different way?"

"What do you want to do?" I raised an eyebrow as mischief lit up her face.

"*You*, my big boy. I want to do *you*."

Confused but willing, I nodded, and was surprised again when she moved down to straddle my hips. Reaching between us, she grabbed my dick, making my eyes roll back again, then raised up on her knees to guide my tip to her pussy.

Finally, I got it.

She wanted to be on top, which was fine with me. So long as I got to be inside her, I didn't care what position she wanted to try. If she wanted to stand on her head, I'd—

My brain turned off as her warm, wet pussy slowly sank down on me. She bit her bottom lip when I was a little over halfway in, and I wondered if it was hurting her.

"Lark?" I whispered as I held her hips.

"So big," she whispered. "My big, *big* boy."

Her eyelids fluttered and she pushed down a little more.

"Darling, no hurt yourself," I begged, my hands holding her hips still.

"It not hurt, my love. It feel good. So, so good!"

And with that, she eased all the way down until I was completely inside her. Both of us let out a little moan at the same time.

Then she was moving, sliding back and forth, which I didn't expect. I thought she'd bounce up and down like she did with Quartz and Topaz, but this felt amazing, and I was glad she felt safe enough with me to try it.

I smoothed my hands up her sides to her titties and gently cupped them, stroking my thumbs over her nipples as she ground against me. The tight walls of her pussy closed around me, and I knew I wasn't going to last as long as I wanted to.

She slowly built up speed, sliding back and forth so her clit ground into me. Her glorious titties shook in my hands as she moved, and I raised my knees to force her forward so they were closer to my face.

"Sid!" she cried out and grabbed onto the headboard with both hands.

Then she rode me hard and fast. Lifting my head, I latched my mouth around one hard nipple and began to thrust upward with my hips, like I'd watched Quartz do.

*Now I know why, too*, I thought to myself with a chuckle.

Drawing her titty deeper into my mouth, I held her hips in my hand and met her every thrust with one of my own.

Panting, moaning, shivering, we gave and took from each other until we both came, her pussy tightening on my dick and pulsing over and over as it wrung every last drop from me.

She collapsed on my chest and I wrapped my arms around her neck and shoulders, my face digging into her throat.

"I love you, my darling," I whispered.

"I love you, too, my sweet Sid."

Sweating and breathing hard, she lay on me in a little ball, and I stroked her hair and kissed the top of her head. We cuddled like that for several long minutes before she spoke again.

"Sid?"

"Hmm?"

"Can I have Ash back?"

Raising my head, I saw pretty blue eyes instead of my darling's silver ones.

"Are you okay, Posy?" I asked, stroking my thumb along her cheekbone.

"Yes, my heart. I just want my turn."

She smiled, and I felt Ashy's panic.

*It okay,* I told him. *Lark right. See how happy and relaxed mate is?*

*Sid. I can't—*

*Yes, you can,* I said as I gave him back control. *Just let her boss you around like I did with Lark. It will work.*

*I hope you're right,* he sighed.

*I am, Ashy. I am!*

147

## 21: Right Where I Belong

*Posy*

"Are you sure?" Ash asked for the third time. "You don't have to do this, Posy."

"I know. I want to." I shrugged and smiled. "Now hush, waffle, before you kill the mood with your worrying."

"Are you bossing me around, princess?" His eyebrows flew up.

"Yes. Can we do what Sid and Lark did?"

"Which part?"

"Um, the me on top part." My cheeks burned. "I'm not sure about the mouth thing."

"That's fine. You do what you feel comfortable with."

"Why did Sid tell her to stop because he was going to, uh, climax?"

I was curious about that. I knew it wasn't because he was worried he wouldn't get hard again. No matter who was running the body, all of these boys were *very* quick to rise from the dead.

"Well, he thinks it's yucky," Ash admitted. "Lark would have had to either spit it out or swallow it. To spit it out, she would have tasted it. He didn't like that idea."

"Ew! Well, good thing then because, like we all agreed, we aren't ready for pups yet."

"What are you talking about?" He tilted his head like he was confused.

"Think about it! If pup-making juice gets in my belly, what's going to grow there?"

"Baby, we squirt it in you all the time and it doesn't make a pup."

"That's in my vagina or bum. Wyatt said a pup will grow in my *belly*."

He stared at me for a second, then laughed so hard, his face turned red and his eyes watered.

"Oh, my Goddess, cupcake! Okay, we're going to have an anatomy lesson later, but for now I'll just say that you can't get pregnant from swallowing semen. *Or* when you're not in heat. See? Either way, you're safe." Booping my nose with his index finger, he added, "Regardless, there's nothing wrong with spitting it out or swallowing, but Sid doesn't find it appealing."

"Oh. Good. Me, either." A funny memory came to my mind. "Do you know, I used to think that if you swallowed watermelon seeds, one would grow in your belly?"

148

"Ha ha ha! One time, Mom told us to spit them out so that wouldn't happen, and you know what Wyatt did?"

"Ate his to see if it was true?"

"Yeah!" Ash laughed and I giggled. "You tell Wy not to do something, he'll do it twice and take pictures."

As our amusement faded, I met Ash's smiling eyes.

"Are you sure you're okay with me bossing you around?"

"Yep!" Still flat on his back, he spread his arms wide and stared up at the ceiling. "Have at me, princess."

Unable to resist, I ever so slowly drew his bottom lip into my mouth, sucked it gently, and released it.

"Posy," he moaned and his hands bracketed my waist before I could move away.

"I had a little change I wanted to make." I hesitated for a second before I asked, "Do you mind sitting up? Like, against the headboard?"

"Not at all." He scooted there, then smiled and waited to see what was next.

"I don't get to strip you because we're already naked," I pouted, pushing my bottom lip out.

"You want me to get dressed again?" he teased with a smirk.

Shaking my head, I crawled up his body until I was sitting astride his hips and had the pleasure of watching his penis swell and stand up. Ignoring it for now, I ran my hands all over his stomach and chest.

"I know you like my bum," I whispered as I clutched his shoulders. "Will you grab it and squeeze it, please?"

"No, you need to say it like a command," he told me.

"I thought I was in charge?"

"You're *always* in charge, baby, but if you want to dominate me, you have to say it like a command, not ask me nicely."

"Dominate you?" I frowned. "I don't even know what that means, waffle. I just want to wear my bossy pants for a while."

He cracked up.

"Okay, Princess Bossy Pants," he managed to say through his giggles.

"Ash Loto Mitchell, grab my butt and squeeze it!" I grumbled.

He did, although his chest still shook with laughter. Rolling my eyes, I tangled my fingers in his mop of curls and pulled him down for a kiss. He smiled against my lips at first, then stopped teasing and let me in to explore. My tongue wrestled with his until we needed air.

By then, his stiff penis was digging into my belly, and I shifted my attention to it. My fingers skimmed over it to tease him, and his head fell back with a deep groan. Smiling to myself, I wrapped my

149

fingers around it and stroked him in the way I knew he liked until I ached to be filled with him.

Rising to my knees, I steadied myself by gripping his biceps. Like everything else about him, they were giant-sized and my fingers couldn't meet around them.

"Lift me up," I told him.

He raised his head and met my eyes, and I could tell he wanted to make sure I was okay and not going to panic, but he had nothing to worry about. Fear was the *last* thing I had on my mind at the moment.

"I said lift me up," I told him, my eyebrows drawn together and my lips pursed.

"How high, princess?"

"High enough that I can get you inside me."

"With pleasure," he purred, and a lazy grin stretched across his lips.

As he palmed my bum and lifted me, the solid muscles in his arms hardened under my hands, and I looked down to make sure we were lining up. Even inexperienced at this, I could see we needed a little help, so I guided him into place with one hand.

"Now down," I ordered. "Slowly."

The second his tip entered me, I shivered and moved my hand to his bicep again.

"Princess?" he whispered in my ear.

"Keep going," I whispered back.

My eyes closed on a moan as the delicious length of him inched into me.

"You like this, princess?" he murmured. "Does it give you pleasure?"

"Yes," I moaned again.

Soon, he was buried to the hilt and I stayed still for a few seconds, savoring the sensation of all of him inside me. I felt fine tremors in the arms I was clinging to and knew they weren't from my puny weight. I moved at a snail's pace and hoped I wasn't torturing him too much as I tried to figure everything out.

Watching Lark do it was not the same as doing it myself, and this wasn't the same angle as when we'd "made sandwiches," as Wyatt loved to call it.

Experimenting, I brought my knees up under Ash's arms and discovered that got me even closer to him. My breasts were pushed up to his collar bones, and I wrapped my arms around his head to draw his face into my neck. He took advantage of that and sucked my mate mark, shooting sparks all through me.

"Put one of your arms around my back. I like when you hold me close," I told him.

Humming, he clutched me to his chest and splayed his fingers over my ribs, and I loved how all my softness fit perfectly into the dips and planes of his muscles, leaving no space between us at all.

"Princess Bossy Pants, can I move us to the edge of the bed so I can bend my knees?" he whispered in my ear, and his hot breath raised goosebumps all over my neck and shoulders.

I nodded, and he swiveled on his bum and scooted us over. I wondered why he needed to bend his knees - were they hurting him or were his feet falling asleep? - but then he settled into place, and the feel of him so deep inside me overrode my curiosity.

Closing my eyes, I finally began to rock my hips, but slowly, so slowly that each thrust took an eternity. Our bodies were crushed together, and I felt like we were *breathing* each other in and out.

"I love you," he crooned as his lips grazed my skin with tender kisses. "You are my whole world."

I opened my mouth to reply, but the hand he had on my bum slipped between my cheeks, and all that made it past my lips was a long, low moan as his fingers rubbed up and down in sync with our super slow pace.

He pushed his face back into my throat and swirled his tongue over my mate mark, then sucked it gently. The fingers that were rubbing between my bum cheeks dipped further and found the wetness that flooded down my thighs and dripped onto his. Swirling his fingers in it, he pulled his hand back to find my bum hole again and used my own moisture to ease his thumb inside.

His other fingers caressed the area between my vagina and bum. Mason had told me what it was called, but I couldn't *speak*, let alone remember the term. He began to tap in time with our slow rhythm, and I realized he was mimicking the sensation of his scrotum banging into it.

My body reacted immediately. My thighs quivered, hot tears spilled down my cheeks, and the breath whooshed out of my lungs. Burying my face in his neck, I licked his mate mark with long, hard strokes that echoed our deep rocking. Then I grazed it lightly with my teeth, and his deep groan shook the whole bed.

"Princess!" he gasped. "Tell me I can come, baby!"

"Yes, yes! Come with me!"

I couldn't hold on any longer. I exploded, and my vagina clamped onto his penis and pulsed around it in steady waves. His big body went taut for several long seconds, then relaxed against me, and we clung to each other until the room stopped spinning.

Finally, I moved to look into his eyes.

"I love you," I whispered. "I love you so much, Ash."

"I love you, too, Posy." His fingertips brushed my jaw as his lips touched mine in a gentle, barely there kiss that curled my toes. "Our sweet, sweet girl."

Then he picked me up with him as he stood. Still dazed from such an intense release, I couldn't bring myself to care where he was taking me, but when I felt the bed under my back, I realized he was only laying me down. Chuckling, he fell down next to me.

"I'll be your bitch anytime, Princess Bossy Pants, so long as it ends like that."

Chuckling, I curled on my side and cuddled into him. He propped himself up on one elbow and ran his other hand up and down my back.

"And I am *so* glad you didn't panic."

"Me, too." I kissed all over his chest, then stretched up to kiss my mate mark on his neck.

He sucked in a sharp breath and the hand rubbing my back gave me a light spank on my bum, surprising me a little.

"Do that when we mate, cupcake, *not* after I'm spent," he smirked.

"Aw. Does that mean no round two?" I batted my eyelashes at him, and he chuckled.

"Actually, if you're okay with it, the others would like to join us. But only if you want to! And they don't all have to be here at once. You can ask for whoever you want, and I don't have to stay, either—"

I laid my fingertips over his mouth to stop his rambling.

"I want them here with me like usual, but I don't want to, um, what did you call it when I gave you commands?"

"Dominate," his lips moved under my fingers. "Like what Quartz and Garnet do with Lark."

"Yeah, I don't get that." Dropping my hand from his mouth, I frowned at him. "Why do they want her to call them Daddy? That seems ... odd."

"It's a kink— No." He stopped himself and shook his head. "I'm not explaining that right now. It's a way of playing in which the female is submissive and the male is all dominant and possessive."

I thought about it for a minute, then shook my head.

"*They* can play like that, but I'm not comfortable with calling any of you Daddy."

"That's okay. I don't think any of us are into that. Well," he corrected himself, "Wyatt maybe a little, but he's not going to ask you to call him Daddy."

"He *is* pretty bossy in bed!" I grinned.

152

"Do you like it?" Ash's eyes glimmered as he stared at me. "Do you like the things he says and the tone he uses?"

Heat flooded my whole face and spread down my neck to my collar bones.

"I guess I got my answer," he chuckled and stroked his fingers down my cheek. "There's nothing to be embarrassed about, baby. We're all still figuring out what we like and need. It's okay to experiment as long as everyone is open and honest about what they like and don't like."

"Experimenting like what we just did?" When he nodded, I admitted, "Ash, I really enjoyed it, but I'm not too sure I want to be Princess Bossy Pants again. Or at least, not very often. It's just not in me to be aggressive."

"Oh, baby girl, that was hardly aggressive." He rolled his eyes. "But I understand. I sure did like that position, though."

"Definitely," I agreed with a dimpled grin. "*And* the pace. Slow, but deep and powerful."

"Oh, yeah. I'll tell you what. If Princess Bossy Pants ever *does* want to come out to play again, I accept the position under her happily." Hovering over me, he leaned down to kiss me. "Eagerly." Another kiss. "And enthusiastically." Another kiss.

Bracing my hands on his chest, I giggled with each kiss, loving him so much that my heart felt like it would burst from it.

*Jayden? Mason? Cole? Wyatt?* I asked in the mate link. *Are you busy? Would you like to join us?*

Their responses were also happy, eager and enthusiastic.

*Hurry*, I whispered. *I miss my mates.*

"You shouldn't have said that." Ash shook his head and gave me a pitying look. "You've started a stampede of hungry alphas, and they're going to try to cram through that bedroom door any second now. I bet it won't be standing tomorrow."

"Let them come." Shrugging, I sank my hands into his curls and toyed with them.

"Oh, I know they will," he smirked. "Probably more than once tonight. I bet *you* won't be standing tomorrow, either, cupcake."

Finally understanding what I said and how he took it to a dirty place, I covered my bright red face with my hands and kicked his shin as he laughed and laughed.

I had to admit, though, that *all* of his predictions came true.

## 22: School

*Posy*

On Friday morning, I woke up alone, which confused me for a moment. I almost always woke up with Wyatt's face smooshed into my neck and his heavy arm curled around my boobs or stomach.

*Wyatt?* I linked.

*You finally awake, cutie?* he answered right away. *I'm in the kitchen. Mason made breakfast. Waffles and bacon. We saved some for you. Should I heat up your plate?*

*No! I'll do it when I'm ready,* I hurried to tell him.

I hadn't recovered yet from his attempt to boil spaghetti noodles a couple days ago. The kitchen still smelled faintly of smoke.

*Why am I waking up alone, fifth star?*

*We have a lot to do today, cutie, remember? We're going to get you registered for school, introduce you to the gammas, and begin self-defense lessons.*

*Oh, yeah!* I grinned, excited about school. *And you're already showered and dressed?*

*Yep! I'm here in the kitchen whenever you're ready.*

I frowned. Wyatt was not a morning person and rarely got out of bed voluntarily. Then I remembered my other four mates kissing a sleepy me goodbye at sunrise, and a smile spread across my face.

*Wonder which one of them dragged Wyatt out of bed so we wouldn't oversleep?* I giggled. *Ten bucks says it was Mason.*

Telling Wyatt I'd be down soon, I stretched, then rolled out of bed and headed for the bathroom, grateful that Ash had helped me put together an outfit last night. I wanted to look super-cute, and he'd made sure I would. All I needed to do now was shower, brush my teeth, and dry my hair, and I'd be ready to go.

Twenty minutes later, I went down the stairs and made a beeline for the kitchen. Wyatt sat on a bar stool by the window, writing in a book with a pencil.

"What're you doing?" I asked as I wrapped my arms around his waist and squeezed him.

"Just sketching." He put down his pencil and swiveled toward me. "Wow, cutie! You look gorgeous! Ash was right; those shoes are adorable on your tiny feet!"

"Thank you, my fifth star." I pecked his lips.

He pulled out his phone, told me to pose, and snapped a couple of photos while I clasped my hands in front of me and smiled.

"Um, what is sketching?" I asked after he put his phone away.

"Drawing, baby."

"Can I see your drawing?" I bounced up and down and clapped my hands. "Mason said you're awesome at drawing!"

"He did?" Wyatt's eyebrows flew up.

"Yeah. He said you designed his mechanical arm tattoo, which is amazing, by the way."

Wyatt looked happy as a clam to hear Mason had praised him, and I hid my smile.

"Well, I don't really like someone looking at it before it's finished," he hesitated, then grinned. "How about I show you some in my other sketchbooks?"

"You have more than one?"

"Yep! Three completely filled up." He stood and pulled me along with him toward the living room. "I used to just doodle on anything. Scraps of paper, napkins, the backs of envelopes. Then, for my sixteenth birthday, Papa gave me a real sketchbook. He was the first one to encourage me to take sketching seriously."

Every time I heard one of the boys say something good about Papa, conflict squeezed my heart. I didn't understand why Papa had been so cruel to Mason, but so kind and caring to the other boys.

Mama had told me how wild Papa was as a boy and that Mason's grandfather did what he had to do to curb that behavior before it got Papa killed or imprisoned. It may have worked for Papa, but I didn't know why he'd thought his son needed similar treatment when 'wild' was the last word anyone would *ever* use to describe Mason Price.

Pulling me out of my thoughts, Wyatt stopped at the bookshelf that held the family album Ash had shown me the other day. On the top shelf were three black-bound, hardcover books with dates hand-written on the spines in white. He pulled down one book and flipped through it as if he were looking for something specific while holding it up too high for me to see.

"Can I see all of the books?" I asked, greedy to learn about my mate through his art.

"Um, let me make sure the other two are ... clean."

"Huh? Clean?" I scrunched my face up as I stared at him.

"I took art in high school, and we studied human anatomy to learn how the body moves so we could draw it better."

"What's anatomy mean, anyway? Ash said I needed an anatomy lesson."

"He did?" Wyatt snorted. "Anatomy means the human body. Do I want to know *why* you need an anatomy lesson?"

"Never mind that," I muttered with a red face. Asking for more details about making pups was not a conversation I wanted to have with *Wyatt*, of all my mates. "So you drew a bunch of bodies in your sketchbook?"

"Yeah." His cheeks flushed, raising my curiosity.

For as much as he enjoyed embarrassing *me*, Wyatt himself did not get embarrassed easily.

*So what about drawing bodies would make him blush—*

"Oh!" Realization hit me, and I giggled. "The models were naky-naky?"

"Not completely, but my imagination filled in a lot of details," Wyatt giggled, too.

"I bet it did." I rolled my eyes, then took the sketchbook he held out to me and hugged it to my chest. "This one is clean?"

"Yep! I started that one last December and finished it a few days before we went to Tall Pines." He leaned down and kissed my forehead. "And now we need to get you some breakfast so we can leave. We're meeting Em, Gelo, and Reau at the school in half an hour."

"Yay! Some of my favorite people! After my mates, of course," I chirped as we walked back to the kitchen.

Wyatt chuckled and motioned toward the microwave.

"Okay, while you're eating your breakfast, I'm going to go pack a bag of workout gear for you."

I nodded, remembering the plan he'd told me yesterday. After we were done at the school, we were going to meet the gammas. There were showers and changing rooms at the training center, so I could switch my dress for shorts and a t-shirt and my sandals for sneakers before my first lesson in self-defense.

"Thanks, Wyatt." I gave him a dimpled smile and laid his sketchbook on the counter, reminding myself to grab it before we left so I could look through it as he drove.

"Of course." He turned to go upstairs, then spun back to face me. "Um. You *do* have your spandex under that dress, right?"

"Yep!" I flipped up the hem to show him the silky little shorts.

During our conversation about me going to school, the boys had asked me to wear them any time I had on a dress or skirt that came above my knees. They'd said it was in case some boy tried something stupid, like flipping my skirt up or trying to look up my dress when I was on the stairs. With worried eyes, I'd asked them how often that happened.

"Not often, but some boys do dumb things," Cole had said with a scowl. "It'll just give us peace of mind, honey, while we're not by your side."

Since I wanted to avoid any conflict, I'd agreed. Besides, wearing the little shorts would give me peace of mind, too.

"Don't flip your dress up to anyone else," Wyatt growled now as he pulled me in and kissed me breathless.

"Of course not, silly." I giggled, then sent him on his way so I could heat up my waffle.

#

A big hand covered the page I was studying, making me blink.

Looking up, then over at Wyatt, I realized he'd already parked in front of the school. I'd been so interested in his sketches, I hadn't even noticed we'd arrived. Reluctantly, I closed the sketchbook and laid it on my lap.

"Now, remember," he said, "Emerson and Reau are your brothers, and you all moved here last spring to escape your parents."

"I remember the story. I won't mess up," I assured him.

"I know you won't, cutie." He grabbed my hand, raised it to his mouth, and kissed my palm. "Em and Gelo prepped Reau as best they could, but I might have to alpha-command him if he begins rambling or revealing things he shouldn't."

I nodded to show I heard him.

I was a little nervous to meet the principal and guidance counselor, who were both humans and had no knowledge of the shifter world, but I wasn't *too* anxious because Wyatt said they were good people. It also helped that there weren't going to be many students around since it was July.

"They're here!" I clapped my hands as Angelo's truck pulled up next to our car.

Wyatt got out and came around to open my door, and a curly-haired whirlwind engulfed me in a hug as soon as I was on my feet.

"Luna! Alpha!" Thoreau shouted, then caught himself. "Oops! Sorry. Too loud."

"It's okay when we're outside," I told him. "Are you excited to go to school, *little brother?*"

"Yes, *big sister.*" He tried to wink at me, but ended up blinking both eyes, and I giggled.

"Wow, little luna bunny." Emerson stood in front of us, holding Angelo's hand. "You clean up good!"

"You look gorgeous, luna," Angelo echoed.

"Oh, yes, you do!" Thoreau's eyes went up and down me, then he squealed, "I love your shoes!"

"And pink diamonds look fantastic with your skin tone," Emerson added.

"Thanks." I smiled at each of them as my cheeks grew warm. I still didn't handle compliments well. Turning to Wyatt, I tilted my head. "This necklace has a real diamond?"

157

"*Three* real diamonds," he smirked.

"Wyatt," I swallowed hard. "I thought it was glass or something. It's too expensive to wear!"

"Cutie, what's the point of having good jewelry just to keep in a drawer?" He touched his finger to the heart-shaped pendant that lay just below my collar bones. "I knew as soon as I saw it that I had to get it for you. And Em's right. Pink diamonds are perfect for you."

"Now I feel way too dressed up for school," I mumbled.

"Well, I doubt many high school seniors around here wear diamonds and carry Louis Vuitton handbags," Emerson laughed, "but you look adorable, so don't worry about it."

"Louis who?" I blinked up at him.

"That $2,000 designer bag you're carrying," Angelo pointed to it with a chuckle.

"What?" I stared at the pink purse hanging from my elbow. "How much?"

"Baby, we don't buy cheap stuff." Wyatt chuckled now, too. "And we warned you that we were going to spoil you."

Biting my bottom lip, I took a deep breath in through my nose. I was more nervous being the guardian of such expensive items than I was about starting school!

Laughing, Wyatt tugged me along, and the others followed us into the school and down the hall to the main office.

"Well, as I live and breathe," chirped an older blonde woman at the counter. "Wyatt Black, and without a discipline referral in his hand."

"Hey, Mrs. Grizzard." Wyatt smiled at her and tugged me closer. "No referral, but a bride. This is my wife, Posy."

That's right. I was legally married to Wyatt in the human world.

Their laws didn't allow for more than two people in a marriage, or I would have married all of my mates. In the end, we decided Wyatt would be a good choice for a few reasons. Many people at school would remember him as the popular football and wrestling team captain, and he had a reputation for being someone you didn't want to mess with. The boys hoped that would add a layer of protection, just like my wedding rings and having pack members in all my classes.

*And* he won Rock-Paper-Scissors.

So the six of us dressed in our fancy clothes from the luna ceremony, went to the Justice of the Peace in the human town, signed some paperwork, and went out to lunch. Mason had the marriage certificate framed and hung in the home office next to the photo of all of us standing outside the courthouse.

158

So now we had our legal bases covered in the human world, although marriage meant little compared to marking and mating each other.

"Oh, my!" Mrs. Grizzard put her hands on her cheeks as her eyes widened. "Congratulations! It's lovely to meet you, dear. I got to know Wyatt quite well during his four years here."

"Thank you," I murmured. "And I'm sure he kept everyone on their toes."

"You have no idea," she laughed, "especially if Ash Mitchell was involved."

"Posy and her younger brother are enrolling here, Mrs. Grizzard." Wyatt tipped his head toward Thoreau. "We have an appointment with Mr. Varner and Ms. Terrell to get them set up and talk about their schedules."

"Yes, I have the small conference room ready for your meeting. Let's get you all settled there, then I'll fetch the others."

"Thank you, Mrs. Grizzard."

She was as good as her word, sitting us around a long table in comfy black chairs with wheels. Thoreau spun his around and around until Emerson made him stop, and just in time for Mrs. Grizzard to come back with two older adults.

"Wyatt Black." The man smiled and held out his hand. "I hear congratulations are in order?"

"That's right." Wyatt stood and shook his hand, his chest puffed out proudly as he turned to me. "This is my wife, Posy."

"Pleasure to meet you," I said quietly and kept my hands folded in my lap.

"Likewise, Mrs. Black. I'm Principal Edwin Varner."

He didn't look concerned that we were married. Unlike that clerk at the courthouse, who'd lectured us about being too young, Mr. Varner looked genuinely happy for us. That made me like him a little bit. When he turned toward Emerson and Angelo and didn't even blink at their clasped hands, I decided I liked him even more.

"I take it one of you is Posy's older brother?" he asked them.

"That's right." Emerson stood and shook the principal's hand. "I'm Emerson del Vecchio. This is my husband, Angelo, and my baby brother, Thoreau. He's fifteen, but we have no idea where he is academically because he hasn't been in school for several years now."

I was still getting used to hearing Emerson introduce himself that way, but he'd told me that he took Angelo's last name because he wanted no connection to his parents, and I couldn't blame him.

"Yes, when Wyatt made the appointment, he said there were unusual circumstances."

159

Mr. Varner introduced his companion, Mrs. Shanique Terrell, who was a guidance counselor that would be helping get our classes sorted out.

Wyatt and I left most of the talking up to Emerson, who explained that he'd managed to get us younger siblings out of the home of our abusive parents earlier this spring. We'd taken the summer to heal our injuries, move here, find a therapist, and begin rebuilding our mental and emotional health.

He also explained a bit about Thoreau, and Mrs. Terrell seemed to know what he was talking about. In fact, when Thoreau started to have a meltdown, she left the conference room for a few minutes and came back with a small bin of toys.

"Here, Reau," she said kindly. "Try playing with these and see if you like them."

He immediately reached in and grabbed two round metal balls that were shiny and reflective. I didn't understand what was so interesting about them, but he was fascinated for the rest of the meeting.

"We'll need to do a child study to have him formally identified and see what level he's on in reading and math," Mrs. Terrell said. "We need to have an official diagnosis, then we can assign a case manager who will create an IEP - an individualized education plan. This will include accommodations for in class, testing, and more."

"This is something you've seen and worked with before?" Emerson asked.

"Yes. I'm not a pediatrician or a psychologist. I can't and won't make any kind of diagnosis, but I have twenty-five years of experience working with students like Reau. I can tell some things just by observing and talking with him. You said he goes to a private psychologist?"

"Yes. Dr. Alonzo York," Angelo said. "He also moved to the area recently."

"I'm sure Dr. York can give you some advice on sensory toys like those reflective balls he's playing with right now, but his case manager will also have some information for you as he or she works up his plan. Does he struggle with anger or violent outbursts?"

"No. Not at all." Angelo shook his head. "He gets loud when he's excited, but does not like loud noises. He can also become quite fearful, which we believe stems from the abuse he suffered."

"He's a pretty happy kid most of the time, though," Emerson added, "and is usually content ticking along in his own little world. He has some quirks, but nothing I consider unmanageable."

Mrs. Terrell nodded, then said, "If you would prefer, your Dr. York can do the work up and that will save time. Otherwise, we can arrange for our school psychologist to meet and test him in a couple of months or so."

*"Months?"* Emerson's eyebrows shot up. "School will be started by then and he won't have a plan in place."

"I'm sorry." Mrs. Terrell gave him a gentle smile. "We have one psychologist for the entire district, and he had appointments and testing scheduled for well into December. That's one of the drawbacks of a public school, I'm afraid."

"Dr. York will do whatever needs to be done by the end of next week," Wyatt said, and reached into his pocket for his phone. "You can contact him directly to set it up. He also has years and years of experience, so he's probably done similar testing in the past. Do you have a piece of paper?"

She slid her notebook and pen over to him, and he copied Dr. York's number from his phone, then also listed his number, Emerson's number, and Angelo's number and labeled each.

"Now, let's talk about classes." Wyatt drew a line under the phone numbers. "Here is a list of people that I trust. So long as at least one of them is in each of Posy's classes, I'll be happy. As for Reau, he's great friends with my little brother, Wayne, and Cole's little brother, Archer Barlow. You remember Cole, right?"

"Oh, yes," Mr. Varner and Mrs. Terrell said in unison with an eye roll on the principal's part, making me giggle.

"Are you sure you want your little brother hanging out with Wayne and Archer?" Mrs. Terrell joked. "They're well-known pranksters around here!"

"Arch and Wayne are my besties!" Thoreau crowed, looking up from his toys for a moment. "Oops. Sorry! Inside voice."

"Make sure at least one of them is in Reau's classes, please," Emerson said. "They can help him if he goes off the rails."

"They have the same schedule, which I'm *sure* they planned, so that's easy to do," Mr. Varner said as he stared at his laptop screen. "I'm looking at their electives, though, and they signed up for Italian I, sculpture, and auto mechanics. Reau, are you interested in those things?"

" 'Talian?" Thoreau's curly head popped up again. "Gelo speaks 'Talian."

"Yeah, I can help him with it so that one's okay. I'm not sure about the other two, though." Angelo looked at Emerson.

"Auto mechanics is fine since they're always at Nathan Barlow's garage, but he's not going to like sculpture," Emerson said. "He got cookie dough on his hands the other day and that turned into major drama. I can't see him working with clay."

"What electives am *I* in?" I asked, looking up at Wyatt. "He could be with me. Or Tyler or Peri."

"Be—" Thoreau caught himself before saying beta. "Ty and Peri? Ooh! Ty is so handsome and Peri is so pretty!"

"Oh, dear, does someone have a little crush?" Mrs. Terrell teased with a sparkle in her eyes.

"Crush?" Thoreau's head tilted to the side. "Orange Crush? No, I like milk!"

"Ty and Peri are dating, and Reau is obsessed with how cute they look together," I told the guidance counselor. His head tilt had reminded me of something, and I brought it up before I forgot it again. "Reau has a service dog. Will he be allowed to come to school, too?"

"Of course." Mr. Varner nodded. "There was a girl here last year with a service dog, and his photo was even included in the yearbook. Do you remember, Wyatt?"

"Yes. Mesia was blind," he told me, "and her dog, Freddy, was a yellow lab. Freddy attended school every single day for four years, which is way better attendance than Ash and I can claim. Of course he deserved his picture in the yearbook."

"Spring can come to school with me?" Thoreau bounced up and down in his seat. "Thank you, thank you, thank you!"

"Sure thing, buddy." Mr. Varner chuckled, then motioned to his laptop. "Instead of sculpture, you and Posy could take photography together. Landry Benson is in that class."

*Who?* I linked Wyatt.

*Ash's gamma. You'll meet him today at your self-defense training.*

*Oh. Okay.*

"Sounds great. Reau?" I turned to him and waited until he met my eyes. Well, kind of. He always seemed to look at my forehead instead of making eye contact. "Would you like to take photos with me and Landry?"

"Yes, yes, yes!" He clapped his hands excitedly.

"Good." Mr. Varner nodded and referred to his computer again. "Posy, you can't earn enough credits to graduate this spring since you have no recent formal schooling. Do you think you'll continue working on your diploma after this year?"

"I want to experience high school, but I'm not sure I'm smart enough to pass a single class," I admitted, dropping my eyes to my twisting fingers.

"Oh, baby, you're plenty smart." Wyatt grabbed the arm of my chair and hauled me closer, then cupped my cheeks in his palms. "We'll help you go as far in school as you want, whether that's one year of high school or getting your doctorate."

"Thank you, Wyatt," I whispered with a little smile, then looked at Mr. Varner. "I'd like to see how this year goes before I decide anything."

Mason had explained what a GED was, and how I could work on it online from home. If regular high school was too much for me to handle, I could go that route if I wanted to later. I wasn't sure a diploma was all that important for a luna of a werewolf pack, but I wanted to be more educated.

I did not want to shame my mates.

"Very well." Mr. Varner nodded. "Let's focus on real-life skills and electives, then. How about Number Sense? It's a basic class, but will teach you real-world math skills that you'd actually use. I'd suggest the same thing for Reau. There's no way to tutor him enough in a few weeks to take algebra, which is the lowest math we have after Number Sense. Um, the only thing is, no one on your list is in that class, Wyatt."

"Can I see the rosters?" Wyatt asked. "I might have missed someone I can trust."

"There's only two sections, and this is the only one that would work to have Reau in it with Posy." Mr. Varner turned his laptop around, and Wyatt's eyes skimmed down the screen.

"Oh. Crew's little brother, Grey, is in there. Neither of you have met him yet," Wyatt looked at me, then Thoreau, "but he's a great kid. He's your age, Reau, and could be Crew's twin as far as personality goes. I think that will be all right, if you two are okay with it?"

"Sounds reasonable," I said, "and Reau and I will have each other."

"Cutie, I am not leaving the two of you unsupervised. Who knows what mischief you'd get into?" Wyatt grinned down at me, and I rolled my eyes.

"What else would you be interested in, Posy?" Mr. Varner asked.

"Jayden told me what social studies meant, and I'd like to take a few of those classes. And English because I want to be able to write and speak well so I don't sound dumb."

"Baby, stop calling yourself dumb!" Wyatt groaned.

Mr. Varner asked in a gentle way if I could read and write before we went any further with planning my schedule, and I assured him I could read and knew how to physically write, but not how to do essays or papers or anything. He asked what books I'd read and, when I listed the most recent, he asked if I understood them. We had a good conversation about *To Kill a Mockingbird,* and he nodded, satisfied that I could read well enough to do the work for social studies, even though I'd admitted there were some words I didn't know in the book.

"As far as writing, how about Introduction to Academic Writing?" Mrs. Terrell suggested. "That class focuses on grammar and how to compose essays, which helps improve how you organize your thoughts. You also present your essays to the class, so it helps with public speaking."

I said yes, then Mr. Varner listed off social studies classes that worked in the puzzle of schedules he was juggling. I chose Survey of World History, which I'd have with Tyler, and Geography, which I'd have with Peri.

"Now, for your other two classes, you could do home economics with Peri, keyboarding with Tyler, or, um, well, are you interested in weightlifting with Landry?"

"No, thank you, sir." I smiled a little. "What is keyboarding?"

"How to type on a computer."

Oh. That was disappointing. I wasn't good with computers, and that would probably help me get better, but it sounded boring!

"And home economics?" I asked more hopefully.

"How to run a house. Cooking, meal planning, doing laundry, cleaning."

"All the stuff you already know how to do," Wyatt interrupted with a chuckle. "You'd be bored, even though I know you want to be with Peri."

"There are a couple more options," Mr. Varner continued. "We could make your schedule work to do sculpture with Archer and Wayne and creative writing with Peri."

I could guess what sculpture was from Emerson talking about clay earlier, but I asked what creative writing was about. He explained that it included writing stories and poetry alone, with partners, and in small groups, and having the opportunity to compete in a bunch of different writing contests.

I asked for time to think about everything, so Mrs. Terrell explained the daily schedule and told Emerson and Angelo that Thoreau could have alternative areas to go for lunch if the cafeteria was too loud. By the time she was finished, I'd made my decisions.

"Mr. Varner, I'd like to take creative writing."

"Very good. I'll get that set up for you." He typed away on his laptop.

"So, let's recap." Mrs. Terrell smiled as she looked down at her notepad. "You filled out the registration forms online. I'll assign a case manager to Reau, who will organize everything related to his child study and be in touch with your private psychologist. Posy and Reau's schedules are set up, and I put an alert in their files about the list of their safe people that Wyatt provided. Did I miss anything?"

"Can Wayne and Archer bring them in to tour the school sometime before opening day?" Wyatt asked.

"Sure. Any time they want during regular school hours. Just stop and get badges from Mrs. Grizzard in the office first."

"And can you mark in their files that only people on Wyatt's list are allowed to sign them out and pick them up from school?" Emerson asked.

"Of course I can."

"Then I believe that's all." He turned to Thoreau. "You feel better about coming to school now, Reau?"

"Oh, yes, Bubba! Do we start tomorrow?" He blinked his stone-colored eyes up at his brother.

"No, honey. Not for a few more weeks."

"Aw." Thoreau's bottom lip poked out in a pout.

"We have to get ready, Reau," I told him. "We have to get our supplies first."

"Supplies? What are supplies?"

"A backpack. Pens and pencils and stuff like that." I reached over and petted his soft curls.

"Oh. *Shopping*." He made a disgusted face.

"Wayne and Archer will have to get their gear, too," Angelo reminded him. "What if we tag along with them?"

"And maybe get pizza and ice cream afterwards?" Emerson was not above a bribe, apparently.

Thoreau screeched with happiness and nodded really fast.

That settled that. We said goodbye to Mr. Varner and Mrs. Terrell and waved to Mrs. Grizzard, who was busy on the phone, but waved back with a smile.

We were on our way to the vehicles when Angelo asked what Wyatt and I were going to do now.

"Posy's starting self-defense lessons in," Wyatt paused to look at his watch, "about half an hour at the training center."

"Oh, Reau, you should come, too!" I clasped my hands under my chin. "You can learn with me!"

"Can I?" He looked at Emerson and Angelo with sparkling eyes.

"If that's okay with you, alpha?" Angelo looked at Wyatt.

"Pfft. If Posy asked, I have no say in it." Wyatt grinned when I elbowed him. "Hey, Gelo, maybe you and I could have a sparring session!"

He gave Angelo a wolfy grin in challenge, which Angelo returned, and I rolled my eyes.

"Alpha, if you're sparring, who's doing the training?" Emerson asked.

"The gammas."

"The gammas?" Emerson came to a dead stop right in front of Wyatt, crossed his arms, and frowned. "*All* of them?"

"Yeah. They're the best in the pack at fighting in human form against other human forms."

"And what if Landry hurts my luna bunny?"

"He would never." Wyatt shook his head and draped one arm around my shoulders. "A gamma is compelled to protect the pack, and a luna is the heart of a pack. He'll respect and protect her, whether he likes her or not."

"Well, he better not say so much as a mean word to my baby sister or I'll smash him," Emerson growled with Cove glinting in his eyes. "You and Gelo can spar away. *I'll* keep my eye on luna bunny."

"Why would Landry hurt me or say mean things to me?" I asked, confused. "Will he be mean to Reau, too?"

I was very nervous about meeting the gammas *and* trying to learn from them. They were going to have to get close to me or maybe even touch me, and I didn't know if I could handle that. Add in one of them being dangerous or mean, and I knew I'd just panic faster.

"No, baby," Wyatt said and kissed my temple. "Landry hates women, but he won't hurt either of you."

"Why does he hate women?" Angelo asked before I could.

"He found his mate a few months ago."

"And?" I asked, confused as to why that would make him hate women.

"She rejected him on the spot."

My hands flew up to cover my mouth.

I couldn't even begin to understand how much pain Landry was in, but I knew it had to be crippling.

As much as a shifter feared and worried about it, rejections rarely happened. Maybe once every four or five years, you heard of someone rejecting his or her mate.

It was a dangerous thing to do for several reasons. Unless they were the ones doing the rejecting, females usually didn't survive it, although males sometimes died, too, regardless of who was rejecting who.

Also, you only ever got one mate. There was no such thing as a second chance. You could take a chosen mate, but there were no sparks, no special scents, no unbreakable bonds to hold you together. Either of you could call it quits at any time and walk away.

*Maybe she rejected him because Landry is one of those types of males that Quartz warned me about? Who'd want to be mated to an abusive, controlling monster like my stepfather?* I stopped and frowned at my reasoning. *No, that can't be right. That would mean she was also a monster, because the Goddess pairs you with your perfect match.*

*No,* Lark spoke up for the first time today. *Your mates not allow someone like Kendall Briggs to **live**, let alone give him position of power in pack. Specially not gamma rank. Alphas trust him, and they not trust him if he a bad person.*

*True. So what reason would she have had for rejecting him?*

*Ask your mates,* she suggested before going back to sleep.

Frowning, I decided to do that, but later. I wanted to meet Landry first and see what I could see on my own.

I knew I couldn't show him pity, so I had to get my emotions under control before we got there. I also had to prepare myself for how he'd react to me, understanding that he could be anything from silent to aggressive.

*Be brave, Posy,* I told myself. *Even if he scares you, remember that he's broken and in pain.*

As his luna, I knew I could help him heal and find peace and, with each mile Wyatt drove, I became more and more determined to do so.

Whether he hated me or not.

## 23: A Little History

*Ash*

"Mate," Landry Benson murmured and his nostrils flared as his eyes scanned the cafeteria.

"Who is it? Who?" I demanded as I looked up from my sandwich. "*Who?!*"

"Dang, Ash, you sound like a freaking owl." Wyatt laughed and jabbed an elbow in my ribs.

Of course, I retaliated and punched his shoulder, which knocked him out of his seat. He got up and grinned in challenge, ready to wrestle, but Landry suddenly stood up and took off toward the doors at the front of the room, and we both turned our attention back to him.

We were almost as excited as he was for him to find his mate. I was going to be eighteen next week and Wyatt in April, and then my brothers and I could look for our special girl.

Sid squealed with delight at the thought, and I rolled my eyes.

As Landry jogged away, I used my height to peer over everyone's head and saw three girls standing by the doors. Two were humans happily talking to each other, but the third was Nia freaking Hashimoto, who strutted in by herself with a smirk on her lips.

*Oh, Moon Goddess, please let it be one of the human girls*, I begged. *Even as complicated as that can be, anyone is better than **her**.*

There weren't many good things to say about Nia Hashimoto. She got into a lot of trouble, then used her father's name to get out of it. Yuki Hashimoto had been Uncle Jay's beta, and a good one, too. His daughter, instead of living up to his respected name, dragged it through the mud.

She'd never had any boyfriend for longer than a week and even then cheated on him while they were together. Sure, lots of unmated shifters chose to play around until they found their mates, but wolves valued loyalty above all else, and that was what they expected from their partners. Needless to say, once the males of the pack caught on to her constant infidelity, they had little interest in anything she had to offer. Even the man whores, who went through girls like toilet paper, were faithful to the one they were with at the time.

Realizing the pack males were a lost cause, Nia targeted the human males at school. She broke up countless couples and even cost a teacher his job two years ago when she accused him of seducing her. Mase had investigated, found she was lying, and cleared Mr. Liberman's name, but his reputation in the community would never be the same. Mr. Liberman ended up moving to the other side of the country, and we'd paid for his moving expenses out of our own money.

Her offenses weren't all centered around her libido. She bilked an elder of the pack out of thousands with a fundraising scam, then stole a couple of credit cards from a human's wallet at Roger's Diner and maxed them out.

Mase ordered her to pay back every cent through community service, which resulted in even *more* drama. He assigned her to the orphanage because he thought she could handle working with kids. Sadly, she discovered that Tyler James, who was only fifteen at the time, lived there. On the last day of her sentence, she stayed after clocking out and snuck into his room. When he came home from football practice, he found her lying naked on his bed and was so upset and horrified, he ran away. Dad found him sleeping at the Busted Knuckle the next morning and made Ty tell him everything. Furious, Dad personally dragged Nia to the alpha offices for my brothers to issue consequences.

"Although disgusting and immoral, two-timing isn't a crime," Mase growled, "but having sex before you're an adult at eighteen *is*, according to werewolf law. After that debacle with Mr. Liberman, you were already treading on thin ice. Now you tried to seduce a fifteen-year-old kid!"

"We only gave you this many chances out of respect to your father and his years of service," Cole added. "But this is your last warning. Screw up again and you're gone, no matter who your daddy is."

As for Landry, he couldn't have been more opposite of Nia. Like me and my brothers, he had decided he wanted to wait for his Goddess-giving mate to experience all of his firsts with. He wouldn't have been upset if his mate hadn't waited for him, since that was a personal decision. However, your mate was supposed to be your perfect complement, so of course he hoped she saved some firsts only for him, and Nia Hashimoto had no firsts left to give anybody.

That issue aside, he was also going to have to overlook her stealing and other wrongdoings as well as what she'd done to him last fall.

Right before Thanksgiving, she decided she wanted him and harassed him day after day to go out with her. He was polite at first with his refusal, which was more than *I* would have been, but she became more and more aggressive as he continued to turn her down. When her "affection" turned to fury, she made his life miserable until Wyatt and I went against Landry's wishes and intervened. We told her to leave him alone or we'd tell Mase, Cole, and Jay some of the things they didn't know about yet, and that calmed her ass down.

And now Wyatt and I could only watch with dismay bubbling in our guts as Landry went right to Nia and came to a dead stop in front of her. He smiled down at her, and she smiled back.

*Really?* I sighed. *I mean, really?*

*Not good, Ashy,* Sid muttered.

*Well, hell,* Wyatt and Granite grunted in unison before Wyatt continued. *If it wouldn't be blasphemy, I'd say the Mood Goddess was drunk on this one.*

*We may not like her,* I told him, *but it looks like Landry's stuck with her, so we are, too.*

*But now we have to be nice to the bitch.*

*She could change for her mate,* I said without any real conviction.

*I hope so, for Landry's sake. There couldn't be a worse match—*

Nia's expression changed so quickly, Wyatt stopped talking mid-sentence. Her face twisted into a sneer and her hate-filled eyes glared at Landry.

Wyatt and I immediately legged it over there, instinctively understanding what was about to happen.

"You didn't want me for a girlfriend when I asked, so what makes you think I want you for a mate now?" she hissed, then raised her voice. "I, Nia Sakura Hashimoto, reject you, Landry King Benson."

At her words, Landry rocked back on his heels as if hit by a stiff wind, but stayed standing.

*What's wrong?* Mase demanded to know.

*Are you both okay?* Jay's calm voice had an undertone of panic.

*Is the school under attack?* Cole asked.

The parents, the betas, and the other gammas bombarded us, too, and that's when I realized Nia had flung open the whole pack link so everyone could witness her rejection. She knew doing that was only for extreme emergencies, like we were under attack or hunters were invading, and Mase was going to have her ass for it.

As Wyatt linked them back to explain, I stood by my gamma's side and kept my eyes on him. I couldn't understand his agony, but thought this was probably for the best. I was wise enough, however, to keep that opinion to myself.

Unfortunately, Nia wasn't done humiliating Landry.

"Aw. Did I break the poor gamma's heart?" she cooed in a baby voice. "Well, now you know how I felt last semester every time you said no when I asked you to be with me."

*Her rationale for rejecting him doesn't even make sense,* Jay linked all us brothers. *How can she equate having a temporary relationship with being life-long mates?*

*Nobody ever said the bitch was intelligent,* I smirked.

*Can we kill her now?* Wyatt whined.

*You know you can't,* Mase snapped. *Jay's on his way. He's going to escort her to the pack border and banish her.*

*Guess that'll have to do,* Wyatt pouted.

While Cole linked her to close the pack link or else, I watched Landry. Somehow, he kept his face blank, but his eyes told a horror story.

"All right, Nia. That's enough," I growled. "You had your monologue. Now exit the stage."

She didn't get the hint - or was too dumb to understand the metaphor.

"Good luck finding a girl to replace me, by the way," she purred. "No female will ever want a shifter who's so worthless that his Goddess-given mate rejected him."

Then she laughed.

The bitch *laughed.*

And I had heard enough. I couldn't remember ever being this angry in my entire life.

"Wy, get Landry out of here," I barked.

Grabbing Nia by her shirt collar, I dragged her out of the cafeteria and down the hall to the first empty classroom I came to, and let her drop to the floor. I slammed the door closed and locked it, then crossed my arms so I didn't strangle her.

"What do you think you're doing?!" she yelled as she scrambled to her feet. "You can't punish me for rejecting my mate, Ash! That is my right!"

"True, but you did it in front of humans! Some of them had their phones out recording, dumbass! We can't risk words like shifter, gamma, mate, and Goddess-given going viral on social media! You also opened the pack link just so everyone would hear you. You know that's forbidden unless it's a dire emergency."

"You're not alpha yet, asshole, so *you* can't do anything about anything!"

"*I* can't, but Mase, Cole, and Jay can. They warned you not to screw up again. You were on your last chance and you just blew it."

"Whatever." She rolled her eyes. "I don't need this pack, anyway."

"Good, because this pack doesn't need you, either. You're morally corrupt, and how you rejected Landry was unreasonably cruel."

171

"Again, nothing the alphas can punish me for!" she yelled and made a run for the door.

*Fool.*

Reaching out with one long arm, I grabbed a handful of her hair and anchored her in place. It wasn't nice, but I didn't want to touch her anywhere I might make skin contact. I'd need to go scrub with bleach if I did.

"I'm not finished yet," I snarled. "Setting aside the pack, our laws, and the right to reject your mate, you still hurt and humiliated my friend in front of the biggest audience you could. Why? Why'd you do it, Nia? Was it really because he turned you down last fall?"

"You're damned right it was!" she screeched. "How *dare* he say no to me!"

I shook my head in disbelief. Landry had had a lucky escape, if you asked me.

"You're a psychotic skank, and I'm overjoyed my friend won't spend his life tied to *you.*" I wished I could kill her right here and now, but I could bide my time. For now. "By the way, Jay is on his way to escort you to the border. After he banishes you, I suggest you run as far and fast as you can."

"Or what?" she sneered.

I yanked her head back and let Sid come out a bit as she met my eyes. She whined and trembled, which made me grin. Not too many people had ever seen this side of Ash Mitchell, and most of those who had, well, they weren't breathing anymore.

"You have until midnight," I smirked, "then I'm going on a rogue hunt. Might even bring Sid's buddies along. Quartz hasn't had a good chase in a while."

"You— You can't— " She swallowed and tears overflowed her wide, fearful eyes. "You can't *kill* me! I'll go lone wolf, not rogue!"

"Lone wolves are always so easy to confuse with rogues, aren't they? So hard to tell in the dark." I shrugged, then leaned closer and whispered, "So you'd better haul ass, hadn't you, bitch?"

Her breathing sped up and she shook harder. When the doorknob rattled, she yelped and struggled to get away. I wrapped her hair around my fist two more times, pulling it taut, and she grimaced and went still.

*I'm here,* Jay linked me.

Dragging her by her hair, I went over, unlocked the door, and opened it. With Quartz glittering in his eyes, Jay stared down at Nia, who whimpered and panted.

"Please," she begged in a whisper that we ignored.

"I see you've gathered up the trash for me to take out." Jay gave me a nod. "Thanks, brother."

His lip curling up with disgust, he tugged his coat sleeve down over his hand before grabbing her by the elbow. I unclenched my fist from her hair so he could haul her away.

"Oh, and Ash?" He stopped at the door and looked over his shoulder. "Make sure you wash your hands after touching this thing. Don't know what nasty diseases it might have, and I don't want you getting sick."

"Thanks for your concern, brother." I rolled my eyes.

"Well, you need to be healthy if we're going hunting tonight." He shot me a smirk, which I returned. "Quartz is hungry for a challenge."

Nia whimpered, then her eyes rolled back in her head and she crumbled to the floor like all her bones had melted.

Jay and I looked at her limp body, then each other, and I raised my hands and took a step back.

"Sorry, dude." I grinned. "You're the alpha, not me. I'm not even legally an adult yet, so suck it up, buttercup."

"Don't worry, sunshine, you have an unpleasant job to do, too," he taunted. "You get to comfort your gamma."

I groaned and jammed a hand through my hair, accidentally getting my pinky tangled in a curl and pulling it too hard.

"Owie!"

Jay burst out laughing at me, and Sid giggled.

Carefully untangling my finger, I glared at him and told my wolf to hush.

"Give me the damn bitch, Jay, and *you* go comfort Landry. You're way better at that shit than I am!"

"Stop swearing. Mase would have your ass for that language. Besides, *you* can't banish her, and *you're* Landry's alpha, not me. He needs you the most, so suck it up, buttercup, and stop scowling at me."

"I can't help what my face does when you speak, Jay, and your language is hardly better than mine, so shut up."

"Shut up? Really? That's your comeback, little bro?" He rolled his eyes. "You got any more amazing gifts for me like that today?"

The smug bastard always won when it came to a war of the words. Determined to crush him this time, I smirked and shouldered past him.

"Having me as your younger brother is gift enough," I said, then sprinted off before he could respond.

*Running away not a win, Ashy*, Sid snickered.

*It is in my book, buddy.*

## 24: Meeting the Gammas

*Posy*

Thanks to Wyatt's love of speed, we reached the training center before anyone else. That was okay, since we both had to change, anyway.

Wyatt led me back to the changing rooms and came inside with me, even though it was the girl's locker room.

"No one's here, cutie," he laughed when I looked at him with surprised eyes. "And even if there were, no one would say something to *me*."

"Don't be conceited, alpha." I shook my finger at him.

Grabbing it, he drew it between his soft pink lips and gently sucked on it. The heat in his eyes made my insides twist and tighten.

"Come on, baby," he whispered as he kissed the tip of my finger. "Get naked and let's have a quickie before the others get here."

"Wyatt!" I hissed, my face on fire, and pushed at his shoulders.

Of course, he didn't move. The guy was a tank, and my puny pushes didn't do anything. His wicked grin didn't budge, either.

"What? I'm just saying we have time—"

"Yo! Alpha!" a deep voice called. "You changing or what? We're here!"

"And you were saying?" Tipping my head to the side, I raised an eyebrow with a smug smile. "Now go change and leave me to do the same."

"But I want to watch," he whined, his hands gripping my hips and jerking me close enough to feel him growing hard. "I want to see you strip down to your bra and panties and—"

"Hmm." Stretching up on my tippy toes, I whispered in his ear, "If I promise to do that later, will you let me change in peace now?"

"All right, but you better make it up to me." He waggled his eyebrows up and down with a mischievous grin.

"Oh, I will. Ash picked out a super cute set that you're going to love. Sky blue, your favorite color, and silky with lace—"

His mouth caught the rest of my words and a deep groan vibrated out of the chest I was suddenly crushed against. We got lost in each other for several long minutes until a loud bang made me jump away from him.

"Luuunnnaaa! Where are youuuu?" I heard Thoreau call, his yodel echoing through the changing area - and probably the whole training center.

174

"Goddess, that kid," Wyatt grunted. "It's a good thing he's sweet and adorable. Otherwise, I'd get angry instead of amused."

Giggling, I pecked his chin, then grabbed my backpack from his hand and ran into one of the changing stalls.

I heard his chuckles growing fainter, and grinned to myself as I opened my bag to see what workout gear he'd packed for me. In addition to socks and sneakers, I discovered a pink and black sports bra and matching undies, a pair of close-fitting black shorts, and a black cropped tank top. Biting my lip, I stared at how revealing the top was before digging back in the bag, hoping against hope that I wouldn't have to wear it.

And, thankfully, folded up at the very bottom of the bag was a long-sleeved, v-neck shirt. Tearing up, I grabbed it and buried my face in the silky, dark pink fabric.

He remembered that I didn't like strangers seeing my scars.

After I got over my emotional moment, I changed quickly and bounced out the stall, then headed to the door to find him waiting for me.

"Looking good, cutie, even if all the best stuff is covered up." He ogled my boobs, which made my cheeks turn pink, then took my hand and led me out to where everyone waited for us.

Angelo, Emerson, and Thoreau had changed into workout gear, too, and I saw them talking with five big, scary-looking dudes.

*What is with these wolves that they all have to be giants?*

*At least you have Reau,* Lark teased. *He's a shorty, too.*

*He's four inches taller than me,* I grumbled as I rolled my eyes at her.

Wyatt took me over to one guy with black hair in short little braids. They weren't like Tristan's braids, which were tight against his skin. These hung loose and floppy all over his head. He was super cute with cornflower-blue eyes, a square jaw, and thick lips a little lighter than his dark skin.

"This is Rio Graves, Mase's gamma," Wyatt introduced us. "His mate is named Emmeline, and his wolf is Cedar."

"Hello. It's a pleasure to meet you," I said and bravely shook the hand he held out. "Maybe you can bring your mate to dinner one night."

"That would be an honor, luna," he said with a wide smile that showed strong, white teeth. "She would love to meet you. She's a human, so finding out about the werewolf world was a big shock to her."

"I'd love to hear the story of how you explained that to her without scaring her off or making her think you were crazy!" I grinned, and he laughed.

"Luna?" Thoreau tugged on my shirt sleeve. "I can come to dinner, too, right?"

"Reau, mind your manners," Emerson warned him in a stern tone but soft voice.

"Sure, sweetie. We'll arrange a dinner date," I told him. "In fact, I'm thinking about having the gammas and betas and their mates over for a cookout one evening. What do you think about that? Does that sound fun?"

"But I'm not a gamma or a beta." His bottom lip pooched out in a pout.

"You're Em and Gelo's baby, so of course you *have* to come with them."

"I'm your baby?" Thoreau looked up at his bubba and brother-in-law with wide, questioning eyes.

"Yes, you are," Angelo and Emerson said together, then smiled at him.

Thoreau looked absolutely delighted, and his happy little giggle made my heart hurt with how much I loved the little guy.

"Let's move on from the love fest." Wyatt rolled his eyes and turned to the next giant. "This is Nick Sylvestri."

"Hi!" Nick waved one hand and smiled. "I'm Alpha Cole's gamma. Birch is the name of my wolf."

He had almost black eyes, like Ash, and long black straight hair, like Cole, and high cheekbones like Poppy. His skin tone was similar to all of theirs, too.

I knew Ash's grandma was from Samoa, and Cole's mother was half Haida and half Maori - he'd had to explain who both were and where they were located - and Poppy had told me that she was Seneca, a tribe located in western New York. The fact that all three shared similar physical traits made me wonder if Nick also had indigenous people in his heritage.

I linked Wyatt, asking him about it, and was proud of myself for making the connection when he said yes.

*He's Crow. They're Native Americans located in Montana.*

"I'm glad to meet you, Nick," I told him with a tiny smile.

"Same, luna, and I'm looking forward to getting to know you better."

The next guy had a thick tuft of blazing white hair, which I would have thought was fake, except his eyebrows were also light, and his skin was super pale. Not like he was sick or anything, but like he'd burn before he tanned. He was very handsome and the tallest of the gammas, easily Mason's height, but lean like Jayden.

"I'm Alpha Jay's gamma, Adam," he said with a nice smile. "Adam Bishop. My wolf is Sequoia."

176

"Hello. Thank you for being here today."

"No worries, luna. It's my duty."

"Oh." I blinked. Was he forced to be here against his will?

"No, I didn't mean it like that." He covered his face with one of his palms. "Sorry. I'm lousy at talking to girls, even mated ones like you, luna. I'm an awkward nerd."

"He is," agreed my mate, Emerson, and the other gammas.

"You should have seen his clothes before we helped the brother out," Rio pretend-whispered with his hand cupping the side of his mouth. "All black t-shirts and jeans and old-man sneakers."

"And if it wasn't for us," Nick said, "he'd be camped out at the game shop playing Dungeons and Dragons or Magic every afternoon."

I didn't know what those games were, but I didn't like them making fun of him if he liked to play them. Crossing my arms over my chest, I glared at each of them.

"Are you bullying him?"

They stared at me with surprise in their eyes, except for Wyatt, who huffed out a laugh and pulled me into the shelter of his side.

"No, baby, they're not bullying him. They're teasing him. Adam, do you feel bullied?"

"Oh, no, alpha!" Adam raised his hands and met my eyes. "Luna, they *are* just teasing. They play D&D once a week, too, and I'm fully aware that I have no more dress sense than I've got game."

"I don't understand half of what you're saying, but as long as they're not bullying you, I guess that's okay." I uncrossed my arms and held out my hand to him.

He took it carefully in both of his, just like Beta Tristan had done, and bowed over it instead of shaking it. Rio's and Nick's eyes went from me to him and back to me, as if waiting for me to do or say something. Ignoring them, I gave him a full smile, dimples and all, and the pale skin of his cheeks blushed bright pink.

"My turn, now," said a voice I recognized. "I've met both of you before."

"Reuben Ford! Luna, he's Alpha Wyatt's gamma!" Thoreau crowed. "He bought me ice cream a couple of days ago!"

"Oh, that was so nice of him," I said.

"Yes, it was." Thoreau nodded his head rapidly. "His wolf, Larch, knows Spring. They gabbed like crazy while I ate my ice cream."

"It's good to see you again," I told Reuben, studying his face as I shook his hand.

He looked a lot healthier and happier than the last time I saw him, although I still saw shadows in his black eyes. He was just as scary as the others - tall and muscular with a bunch of tattoos, even one on his throat! - but Mom had trusted the guy to babysit Wesley and the heathens, and Tyler wouldn't have hung out with him if he were bad or mean.

That left the last gamma, who was easily the scariest. Even if I hadn't already learned the others' names, I would have known his just by the dead look in the aquamarine eyes that wouldn't meet mine.

And by the way Emerson tensed and Wyatt watched us.

"Landry Benson, Alpha Ash's gamma. My wolf's Oak," he said quickly and quietly, as if just wanting it over with.

I could relate to that.

He didn't hold out his hand. Neither did I, and I was sure we were both okay with that. I got the impression that he would respect me, and even obey me, as his luna, but that was all. He didn't like me, didn't *want* to like me, and had no intention of ever finding something about me to like.

*Kill him with kindness,* Lark advised.

*Well, I didn't plan to be unkind to him,* I said.

*You kind to everyone. It your default setting.*

*Thank you,* I told her, even though I knew she was laughing at me.

"It's nice to meet you, Landry. I appreciate you working with me today."

He nodded sharply once, and that was that.

"All right, Wyatt, shoo." I flapped my hand at him and pointed across the room to where Angelo was stretching. "Go do your thing so we can do ours."

"As you wish, cutie." He dropped a kiss on my cheek. "I'm right over there, okay? Say the word and I'll be here in a heartbeat."

"I know." I smiled up at him, gracing him with the dimples that he loved. "Thank you."

Pecking my lips, he swatted my bum, then ran away before I could retaliate.

*Only cowards run away,* I linked him with a scowl.

*And wise men make tactical retreats,* he replied, and I could hear his giggles all the way over here.

## 25: Self-Defense

*Posy*

"Luna, have a seat." Rio gestured to the edge of the thick mat.

I sat next to Thoreau with Emerson standing behind us, and the gammas arranged themselves on the mat, too.

"First, let's start with an explanation of why we react the way we do to threats." Adam sat criss-cross applesauce with his hands palm up on his knees. "Once your brain is triggered by a conditioned psychological fear, your body goes into flight-or-fight mode. It's very difficult to change your specific physiological reaction, since it's an automatic stress response."

Glancing at Thoreau, I knew he didn't understand anymore than I did what the gamma was talking about. Nick must have picked up our confusion because he rolled his eyes and cut Adam off.

"We ain't in a science class at school, dude," he laughed.

"What? I'm just explaining so they understand—"

"Understand? Do those blank faces look like they *understand*?"

Thoreau leaned closer to me.

"Is this what school is like?" he asked.

Making a face, I shrugged.

"Every time you got hurt in the past, your brain remembered it," Landry said, taking me by surprise. He didn't look at me at all, just kept his eyes on Thoreau. "When your brain thinks your body is going to get hurt like that again, it makes you react. Some people flee, or run away, and others fight. When you freeze, your brain can't decide which one to do and you're stuck."

"Nicely put, Lan," Reuben said. "With that being said, luna, Reau, we can show you how to flee and how to fight, but you still might freeze in a real situation. Hopefully, a lot of practice will help you not to, but nobody can predict how you'll react until you're in a bad situation."

"Makes sense," I agreed.

After weeks of my mates' love and support, I felt more confident than I ever had in my life. In the past, I froze every time Kendall Briggs beat me. Now, though, I hoped I was strong enough to do more than that. I didn't want to fight or hurt anyone, but I wanted to know how to keep myself safe.

"One thing we want you both to remember is that you need to do everything you can to protect yourself and get away," Rio chimed in next. "That means you have to overcome your fear of hurting the other person."

179

"That's going to be hard to do," I murmured, then bit my bottom lip.

"We'll only be practicing," he said with a little shrug, "not hurting each other for real. Now, sometimes, you might feel threatened even if there's no real danger, so we're going to start with some basics that don't involve physical contact. That way, if you misread the situation, you won't hurt yourself or the other person."

"All right," Thoreau and I said at the same time, which made us both giggle.

"But still, if you even feel uncomfortable, do something rather than nothing," Nick said. "Your gut instinct is usually right, and your wolf can sense if it's a real threat. Besides, being alive and safe is more important than having a red face because you were wrong and created drama for no reason."

"I don't have a wolf inside me," Thoreau told them with a pout, then turned to his big brother. "Bubba, can Spring come here? He might learn some things, too."

"They know you don't, honey," Emerson said, "and yes. I'll see if someone can drop him off."

Thoreau clapped his hands, and I smiled at his innocent happiness.

"Should we wait for Spring?" Adam asked, but Emerson shook his head.

"Okay, then," Nick started, "number one is be smart. Be aware of your surroundings. Don't let yourself get cornered. Know where the exits are. Stay around others instead of wandering off by yourself. And if you're uncomfortable, walk away or link one of the pack to join you."

I nodded. I did a lot of that already. Made sure I knew how to get out of a room and watched strange men's hands to make sure they didn't come flying toward my face.

"Number two is run," Rio said. "Try not to panic and run blindly, though. Head for a place where you know there will be people. Last thing you want is to end up trapped in an empty classroom. There's always someone in the main office, and the cafeteria is used as a study hall outside of breakfast and lunch."

"Finally, number three is scream," Reuben told us. "It startles your attacker, maybe even enough to scare him off. Plus, it lets everyone in the area know something's wrong. I know you both can link anyone, but screaming alerts humans, too, and most of them have good hearts and would help you."

"Can you remember those, Reau?" I asked him.

"Smart, run, scream."

"Good job!" I praised him.

"Give me head pats. Bubba gives me good job head pats."

180

"Oh, my bad." Biting back a smile, I reached up and patted his soft curls.

"Give me a good boy kiss, too."

"And who gives you those?" My brain was having trouble imagining Angelo or Leo pecking his forehead or cheek.

"I will let you be first." The way he blinked at me reminded me of Sid, Granite, and Topaz when they wanted belly rubs.

"If you do a good job until the end of the lessons, I'll give you a good boy kiss," I promised.

He jumped up and ran a lap around the entire center while the gammas chuckled at him and Emerson rolled his eyes. When he came back around, he plopped next to me, panting and red-cheeked.

"Now that good boy kisses have been sorted," Reuben smirked, "let's start with how to escape simple holds. I'll explain it, then act it out with one of the other gammas. After that, you can each try it. As I explain, I'm just going to say 'he' because statistics show males attack other people far more often than females, okay?"

"Okay," Thoreau said, and I nodded.

"So, first hold is a common one. If he grabs you by the wrist, don't try to jerk your arm back. That isn't ever going to work because your hand is bigger than the circle he's created around your wrist. You'll just pull him with you. What you do is turn your hand until your thumb lines up with his, then bend your elbow really fast at an angle. That works almost every time."

He had Rio stand in front of him and demonstrated what he'd just explained in super slow motion so we could see, then they repeated it at normal speed.

"Reau, do you want to try with me first?" Adam asked.

"Sure! Watch me, luna!" He leapt to his feet and met Adam in the middle of the mat. "You grab me or me grab you?"

"Whichever you want to try."

"Me grab you first, then the other way."

The two of them worked through the move a couple of times at slow speed and then twice more at normal speed. Thoreau's pretty stone-colored eyes widened each time it worked, making me chuckle. When they finished, they both sat down in their places again, but only after Thoreau had gone around and fist-bumped or high-fived all of the gammas and Emerson and I had patted the top of his head.

"Now, luna, who would you like to try this with?" Rio asked.

Swallowing hard, I pointed to Reuben only because he was more familiar to me than the others. I got to my feet and joined him on the mat, making sure to keep three feet between us.

"How about you try to grab and hold me first?" he offered with a kind smile.

Taking a deep breath, I nodded and slowly reached out to wrap my fingers around his wrist. It was so thick, my index finger and thumb didn't meet.

"Now I'm going to rotate my hand. Watch," he said and lined up his thumb with mine. "I'm going to bend my elbow, and it's going to pull my wrist out of your grip. Try hard to hold on to me, okay?"

I nodded and squeezed as tightly as I could, but his wrist easily pulled out of the weak spot made by my not-touching fingers.

"See how easy it is? Are you okay to try it? If so, it means I'm going to hold your wrist in my hand."

My eyes flew up to his as my lungs started to strain.

"Or not." He held up both hands. "You don't have to. You can have one of your mates try it with you later. Or even Reau."

"I'll try it," I said despite my rising heart rate.

"You don't have to, luna," he assured me quietly.

How much about my past had my mates shared with the gammas? I knew they'd told the betas some of it, and I'd confided a bit in a few others - Mom, Mama, and Peri - but I wondered if these guys knew what my stepfather had done to me. Was that why they were being so careful around me?

My thoughts must have slipped into the mate bond because Wyatt linked me.

*We only told them that you and Reau both came from abusive homes where you were locked up and away from everyone. They had to know, Posy, so they didn't say something dumb or trigger you accidentally.*

*I understand*, I told him, and I did.

"I want to," I said. "I want to be brave."

"You sure?" Reuben gave me one last chance to say no.

"Yes. Just, um, please let me go if I ask you to," I said in a shaky voice, "and, ah, move slowly."

"Of course, luna."

*You're strong. You're strong. You're strong*, I chanted to myself.

Keeping my eyes on his, I raised my arm and held it out to him. I knew I was trembling and everyone could see it, but there was nothing I could do about it.

"I'm going to hold your wrist now," he said, and I liked how he told me what he was going to do before he did it.

I nodded to let him know it was okay. Watching him closely, I saw his much bigger, stronger hand inch toward mine until his long fingers carefully and gently curled around my wrist.

At the touch of his skin on mine, I whimpered almost soundlessly, just a breath of distress really, and felt everyone around me tense.

*You're okay, cutie,* Wyatt linked me immediately. *He would never, ever hurt you.*

*Breathe, luna bunny,* Emerson murmured. *I'm right here, little sister.*

"Luna, don't be scared!" Thoreau called out. "Gamma Rube is nice. He bought me ice cream!"

Despite my distress, a tiny giggle slipped out. I didn't know how Reuben buying Thoreau ice cream was supposed to make me not scared, but at least it eased some of my nerves.

"Are you ready to try to break free?" Reuben asked.

He kept his fingers loose around my wrist, so loose that I probably could just slip my hand out of the circle of his fingers without needing to do the move he was teaching us.

"Tighten your hold so I can practice properly," I said.

Nodding, he did, not enough to make me panic, but enough that I'd have to use the move to escape. Turning my hand like he had, I got our thumbs aligned, then bent my elbow and jerked my hand to the side and out of his hold.

"You did it!" he chirped with a grin.

"Yay, luna!" Thoreau cheered. "Do you want good job pats?"

"No, thanks. I'm good," I murmured, my cheeks hot. "Let's try again, Reuben, but faster, please."

We did and, although my heart and lungs were running a little harder than normal, I managed to break out of his grip at normal speed two times before I stepped back.

"I got it now. Thank you."

"You did great, luna," he praised me, and my face heated up again.

Nodding once, I went back and sat next to Thoreau, and it was like everyone in the room took a big breath for the first time since I stood up. Thoreau bundled me up in a hug, bouncing us up and down as he giggled with glee, and I smiled as he patted my head.

"I'm going to need to go drinking after this," Nick muttered and pretended to wipe sweat from his forehead.

"You and me both," Rio said out of the side of his mouth.

After we explained to Thoreau that they weren't thirsty and didn't need him to go refill their water bottles, Nick got up and stood in the center of the mat.

"This next technique is for when you get grabbed from behind," he said. "You have three options. Punch or grab his balls, kick your heel into his knee, or grab his pinky finger and bend it the wrong way. That last one doesn't sound like much, but it's painful as hell and should distract him enough for you to scream and run."

183

I went through the three options in my head, picturing each one and wondering if I could manage *any* of them.

"Reau, want to go first again?" Nick asked.

"Yep-yep! Watch me, luna!"

I giggled, sensing that was going to be his line every time now.

Thoreau and Nick moved into position in front of us, and Nick slowly put his arms around Thoreau's upper body.

"Which do you want to try to target? Groin, knee—"

Gamma Nick's sudden yelp made me jump, and I couldn't understand why he was rolling around on the mat while Thoreau stood over him with a puzzled look.

"Did I do it wrong, Gamma Nick?"

Frowning, I looked at the other gammas. Reuben and Rio were smirking and Adam grimacing. Landry's face was as blank as it had been since I met him.

"Wait. What happened?" I asked.

"Reau! You have to *pretend*!" Emerson scolded. "You can't do it for real! You hurt him."

"Oh, I am so sorry!" Thoreau dropped to his knees next to the curled-up gamma and patted his head and shoulders fretfully. "Gamma Nick, are you okay? Do you need cuddles?"

"He needs an ice pack," Rio snickered.

"I will get one!" Thoreau hopped up and took off.

"Did Reau hit him in the—"

"Yep!" Reuben interrupted me with a laugh. "Just like Nick told him to."

"His wolf will heal him in a minute," Adam said with a wince, "but damn! He got him good."

When Thoreau came back with an ice pack, he helped Nick to the edge of the mat, but Nick shooed him away when he went to put the ice pack where he'd punched the gamma. For some reason, the moment made me think of Topaz, Granite, and Sid's obsession with each other's boy parts, and I covered my mouth with my hand to hold back a grin.

## 26: Surprise Attack

*Posy*

Rio was brave enough to volunteer to trying again with Thoreau, so the two squared up in the middle of the mat. This time, Thoreau was the attacker, and Rio demonstrated how to escape the hold, which was a little difficult because Thoreau was eight inches shorter than Rio.

"Okay, time to switch," Rio announced. "I'll grab you this time, Reau, but remember: Don't really hit me in the balls. I need them for later tonight."

"What are you doing with them later tonight?" Thoreau cocked his head to the side and blinked up at Rio.

Reuben burst out laughing, Adam's face turned pink, and even Landry smirked.

"Ask your housemate Leo what he does with his at night when he and Poppy go to bed. He can tell you *all* about it."

"Rio! He's only fifteen!" Emerson growled, and Rio jumped.

"Just kidding, Reau." Rio cleared his throat. "I think you're good with that attack, anyway. Try to kick my knee - just pretending, remember - or bend back my little finger."

"I will try both," Thoreau said with a nod. "I will pretend and not hurt you."

He was as good as his word and performed both escapes at slow speed, then normal speed. I clapped for him, then patted his head again when he came over to sit down again.

"Luna, your turn. Would you feel more comfortable trying this with Emerson?" Rio asked. "It's okay if you do. We understand. It's a much more vulnerable position, and you may want someone you trust more than five guys you just met."

"Show her how to block being picked up first," Landry grumbled before I could answer.

"Right! Good idea, Lan," he admitted. "Luna, because you're so small, a guy will most likely just grab you and take off. You have to stop him from getting you off your feet because once he has you over his shoulder, it's game over. There's no getting out of that for someone your size. Not on your own or unless you have a weapon."

So Rio had Landry stand up and showed me how to lock my foot behind an attacker's leg by wrapping my foot around his calf, preferably just below his knee. The attacker wouldn't be able to pick me up and his groin was left open for attacks. Rio recommended that I use open-palm strikes, which basically meant slapping him as hard as I could 'down there.'

185

I twisted my fingers together, unsure I could actually hurt someone like that, even if they were trying to kidnap me or whatever. Still, like the gammas had said earlier, until I was in the situation for real, I couldn't predict how I'd react.

And, unlike in my past, I had something worth living and fighting for now. When Kendall Briggs beat me to a bloody pulp, I didn't have a single reason to get up, yet I did. Over and over. So how much more determined to get up would I be with *five* reasons?

"Luna?" Reuben crouched in front of me, careful to keep a couple of feet between us. "You okay?"

"Yes, thank you, but I don't think I can try this one today," I admitted and dropped my eyes to my knotted fingers. "I'm sorry. I don't mean to waste your time—"

"Hey, hey, you're not wasting our time. You're learning just by watching us and Reau. Like Rio said, this hold puts you in a very vulnerable position, so it's completely understandable that it makes you uncomfortable. We'll build up to it until you can try it, okay?"

I nodded, but still didn't raise my eyes. I could tell he was upset that I wasn't looking at him, and kind of thought he was linking someone. When he stood and Emerson took his place, I knew I was right.

Emerson put one big paw under my chin and lifted my face, and I met his concerned eyes.

"You don't have to do everything all at once, little luna bunny," he whispered. "We can do this every day or once a week or however often you want. And no more worries about wasting their time. This is their job. Waste as much as you want. Work them to death."

"Emerson!" I gasped and swatted his hand away.

His mouth unfurled in a wide grin, and I huffed at him.

"Are you okay with just a couple more things," he asked after a minute, "or do you want to be done for today?"

"Can I just watch if I don't want to try something?"

"Of course."

With a tiny smile, I nodded.

"We good to go on?" Adam asked as Emerson stood up.

"Yep," he said and moved back to stand where he had been.

"Reau, you should be able to do these next two. Luna, you're tiny." Why did Adam also feel the need to harp on my size? "Which makes them harder for you, but try to stab your finger into the guy's eyes or slap your palms over his ears *hard*. Those are both very effective ways to stun him long enough for you to get away."

Adam beckoned Thoreau forward with two fingers, and Thoreau scrambled to his feet with excitement in his eyes. Emerson grabbed his shoulder before he got too far, though, and waited until Thoreau made eye contact before he spoke.

"Listen carefully, Reau. Do *not* really put your fingers in Adam's eyes or slap his ears hard. Just pretend."

"Pretend on me first, Bubba."

"Okay. Here." Emerson brought one sausage-like finger up close to Thoreau's eye. "Poke."

Next, he held his hands on either side of Thoreau's head and brought them to his ears in super slow motion.

"Of course, you'd do it faster and harder if you were in real danger, okay, honey?"

"Yes, Bubba."

Then he raced over to Adam and they went through the routine: Two practice rounds at slow speed and two at normal speed.

"Luna," he shouted when they were done and I'd clapped for him, "come pretend on me!"

"Sure." It was easy enough. I wouldn't even be touching him.

I stood and joined the pair of them, and Adam monitored us to make sure I was doing it right. When my eyes moved from Thoreau's face to Adam's, I could see what he meant about it being hard for me.

"Yeah," I nodded. "I don't think it would be as effective for me if I have to jump to poke out his eye or ask him to wait until I find a step stool to deafen him."

Adam laughed and Nick, fully recovered now, came over and joined us.

"Now, if things go south and you get desperate," he said, "kick, bite and scratch any part you can reach. Kick a guy in the nuts or the knee. Let your wolf ascend and use your fangs and claws, even if it's against a human. If necessary, the alphas can work out some kind of story as to how you caused so much damage. It's more important that you're alive and safe."

"That doesn't seem like something we can practice," I hedged, hiding my hands in my long sleeves.

"No, that's something you can't practice," he agreed. "It's a fight-for-your-life moment that adrenaline and your wolf will control."

From the corner of my eye, I saw Landry stand up. He walked over to us, but never looked at me. He kept his eyes fixed on Thoreau.

"Last lesson for today," Landry said. "If your hands are free, strike your assailant in the nose, throat, or solar plexus. The heel of your palm works good for any of those three targets, but you can also use your fist. Just keep your thumb on the outside or you'll break it, which could slow you down or prevent you from getting a second hit in if your wolf can't heal it in time."

"What is solar plexus?" Thoreau asked, and I let out a breath, glad I wasn't the only one who didn't know.

Landry took his shirt off and pointed to the center of his chest above his defined abs and below his heavy pecs.

*A she-wolf turn down all that?* Lark slobbered and pretended to fan herself. *Goddess, she a dummy!*

*Lark!* I scolded. *You have five mates!*

*Just looking and appreciating,* she giggled.

"Watch me, luna!" Thoreau called out for what I hoped was the last time today.

I dutifully watched as he touched the heel of his hand to Landry's nose, then his throat, then his solar plexus. Landry didn't react, except to nod when he finished the first round to acknowledge he'd done it right. Thoreau did it once more at slow speed, then twice at a faster speed, and Landry nodded again.

"Yay!" I cheered for him and patted him on the head when he turned to me with expectation in his pretty eyes.

"Now you, luna." He nodded his head toward Landry. "You saw how easy I did it. You can, too."

"Um." I bit my lip and looked at Landry's face. His eyes showed nothing in them, not even the hate I'd expected.

"Go ahead," Nick said.

"Yeah, luna, you can do it," Adam encouraged me. "I think you can even hit his nose without jumping."

"I might die of laughter if you keep being so funny." I narrowed my eyes at him.

"I wasn't being funny." He frowned and seemed offended that I thought he was.

"All right, Landry," I said. "Here I go. Hold still for a minute, please. I'll just try the slow version."

Swallowing hard, I pretended to ram the heel of my hand first into his nose, then the Adam's apple prominent in his throat. I knew I'd have to put a lot more force and intent to harm behind a real strike against an attacker, but I had a good idea of what I was doing now.

Wanting to get this done, I drew my arm back for the third time and struck forward, the fat pad of my hand lightly bumping Landry's chest, and he dropped to the ground, screaming in agony.

"Whoa! What happened?" Adam shouted.

"What the hell?" Nick barked at the same time.

As Thoreau backed away with scared eyes, the other four gammas dropped to their knees next to Landry, who had one hand gripping his chest where I touched it while his other dug into the mat, his wolf's claws extending and tearing up the thick foam.

"I didn't—" Tears clogged my throat and stung my eyes. "I didn't mean to! I don't know what I did! I'm sorry!"

"Shh. We'll figure it out." Emerson wrapped an arm around me and tucked me against his side.

"Lan? Can you hear me?" Adam shouted over the screams. "What hurts?"

"Oak, can you heal him?" Reuben spoke directly to Landry's wolf. "Can you tell what's wrong?"

Nick was cursing up a storm as Rio tried to pull Landry's hand away from his chest, but it wasn't budging. Gasping, I clung to Emerson's shirt and tried to bury myself in his side.

"What did I do? I did the exact same thing Reau did. Why did it hurt him?" I sobbed.

"Luna bunny, you didn't do anything. I was watching. This isn't anything you did," he tried to comfort me.

By then, Wyatt and Angelo had sprinted over. Angelo grabbed Thoreau, who was crying silently with his hands over his mouth, and Wyatt helped Rio pry Landry's hand away. When they did and I got a good look at his chest, I felt my stomach churn and bile filled my mouth.

Right where my hand had made contact with his chest was a round reddish-purple bruise that grew bigger and darker as we watched.

"Gelo, get the witches here!" Wyatt roared, and I sensed him linking his brothers.

"Oh my Goddess!" Rio gasped and fell back on his butt, and my eyes darted to Landry's chest again.

Thick veins the color of eggplant had popped out of the center of the bruise and were slowly spreading outward. The bruise grew darker and pushed oily ink into the veins, each of which pulsed and twisted like snakes.

Angelo nestled Thoreau under Emerson's other arm and the two of us clung to the giant beta and sobbed.

"I'm going to pour healing into him," Angelo said, crouching next to Wyatt. "See if it combats this."

"Should I, too? I ain't *never* seen shit like this!"

"None of us have, alpha," Angelo muttered. "For now, keep your healing in reserve in case I run dry and he needs it."

"By the moon, what *is* this?" Adam clenched his fists, tears streaming down his face. "We can't even help him fight it because we don't know what it is!"

"Ariel's almost here." Angelo laid his hands on Landry's shoulders and gold glittered around his fingers. "She and Tristan were bringing Spring. They're two minutes out."

Two minutes! Two minutes was a lifetime. Two minutes might be two minutes too late.

*Please, Goddess*, I prayed. *Help him!*

And all the while, Landry screamed and screamed and screamed.

## 27: Heart of Darkness

*Gamma Reuben Ford*

Beta Tristan Harrington and his witch mate ran into the training center and right over where we were gathered. Spring sprinted to Thoreau, who fell to the floor and buried his wet face in the wolf's fur.

Shooing Alpha Wyatt and the rest of us back, Ariel dropped to her knees next to Landry's jerking body and went to lay her hands on his shoulders.

"Don't touch him!" I yelled.

She ignored me and held her hands a couple of inches above Landry's skin, making the air shimmer between them, and Beta Tristan glared at me for hollering at his mate.

"Sorry," I said to both of them, "but that's what started this. Luna touched his chest right where the center of *that* is."

"Did anyone else touch him there?" Ariel asked.

"Reau. Nothing happened," Alpha Wyatt said. "Rube, play the memory."

So I did, and included everyone in the room in the link so they could all add anything I didn't see. Meanwhile, alpha got to his feet and hustled over to luna, who Emerson had managed to calm enough to stop her crying.

"Posy! Are you okay?" Alpha yanked her away from the beta and buried her in his arms. "Did any of it get into you? Do you hurt anywhere?"

"I'm fine, fifth star," she murmured. "Stop panicking."

"I can't help it. After that scare with the parasite, all I could think of is some of it spreading into you."

"I'm fine," she repeated.

After he kissed all over her face a dozen times, he finally released her with a huge sigh. With one last kiss on her forehead, he tucked her under his arm and looked at Ariel as she worked.

"Have you seen anything like this before?" he asked her.

"Maybe."

Landry suddenly went still and silent. The pulsating black veins shrunk back into the bruise as quickly as earthworms diving into their holes when a flashlight is shined on them. The bruise faded to raisin, then scarlet, and then was gone.

"Okay." Ariel blinked, dropped her hands, and sank back on her heels.

"You cured him just like that?" Rio stared at her with wide, incredulous eyes.

191

"I did nothing." The witch shook her head. "I was running a check for evil, magic, and infernal elements when it withdrew all by itself. Is this the first time this has happened to him?"

"To the best of our knowledge," Nick said.

"Angelo, did your healing power seem to have an effect?"

"No, *piccola uccella azzurra* (little bluebird)." He shook his head and got to his feet and walked over to Beta Emerson, who draped an arm around his lower back. "It did nothing, not even ease his suffering."

"Tell me about him. All I know is his name." Ariel looked at me, probably because I was right next to her.

"Nothing out of the ordinary about him, except one thing." I scrubbed my hand over the back of my neck, hating to even say it out loud. "His mate rejected him."

"When?"

"On his eighteenth birthday in January." I looked at alpha, who had his fingers tangled in luna's hair. "Should you play the memory for her? Maybe she'll see something."

He nodded, then broadcast that horrible day right up until Alpha Ash dragged the bitch out of the cafeteria while Alpha Wyatt led Landry to the parking lot, where Landry passed out. Alpha Wyatt hauled him up in a fireman's carry, settled him into his precious Jag, and drove him home to Landry's older sister, Olivia, who was one of our pack's best unranked warriors.

"Hmm." Her witch-ness stared into the distance and tapped her index finger on her chin.

"Hmm what?" Rio demanded with a frown. "What did you see that we didn't?"

"I'll get back to that in a minute. So this ... whatever it is ... never happened when anyone else touched Landry?" Ariel looked around at each of us.

"Again, not to our knowledge, and it would be pretty hard to miss this reaction," I said.

"Try to touch him, Ariel," alpha said.

We all swiveled toward him, and luna stared up at him with wide, worried eyes.

"No," she whispered. "It'll hurt him again."

"We don't know that. Let's experiment for a second. He's out of it, anyway." Alpha shrugged.

"Wyatt!" Luna slapped him on the chest with one tiny hand. "That's mean!"

"We need to know, baby."

"Okay," Adam nodded. "To do an experiment, you need a control. Touch him through his shirt first and see what happens, then touch his skin."

"Should I touch the same place luna did?" Ariel asked. "Science was never my best subject."

"Let's start with somewhere safe like his arm," Adam suggested, "then try his chest."

She did as directed, laying Landry's abandoned t-shirt over his forearm and touching him, then removing it and hesitantly laying her fingers against his skin.

Nothing happened.

"Okay, now do the same where luna touched him. The solar plexus."

She did the whole process over, and again nothing happened.

"Hmm."

"Stop with the hmm, witch, and tell us what you think!" Nick grouched.

"Careful, gamma," Tristan growled.

"Calm down the testosterone, boys," Ariel murmured. "I know tensions are high right now, but we're all friends here, Tris."

"Hmphf." Beta Tristan crossed his arms over his chest and glared at Nick, who glared back.

Rolling her eyes, Ariel turned to alpha.

"Pretty sure it's a curse, and I think I might know which one. How it got here, I couldn't tell you, but I highly suspect it involved that bitchy mate of his. What was her name again?"

"Nia," alpha spat out.

"She really was mean, wasn't she?" Luna's bottom lip quivered and her big blue eyes watched Landry's face. "Why was she so cruel? Turning someone down for a date was his right, yet she acted like it was a sin and insult against her."

"Who can understand how a psycho thinks?" I shrugged.

"It's a curse involving his heart, isn't it?" Adam asked.

"Yeah. I could be wrong, but I believe it's Warm Hands, Cold Heart."

"And what is that?" Rio asked.

"The warm part means he's acting normal for the most part, but the cold part means someone put a shard of ice in his heart."

"Um, I'm assuming you mean that figuratively?" Adam asked as we all stared at her.

"Wait. What is a shard, and what is figur— Whatever you said?" luna asked.

"A shard is a piece of something, usually with sharp edges," alpha told her.

"And figuratively is a way of saying something is a symbol of something else," Emerson explained. "There's more meaning than just the actual item."

"Have you used this spell before?" Nick asked Ariel.

"Hell, no! Are you stupid?" She pressed a hand to her own heart, breathing a little faster than normal.

"Whoa! Sorry, Miss Witch," he apologized. " I don't know anything about magic in the real world."

"Sorry, too. I didn't mean to snap. It's just, what goes around comes around," she said. "Even dark witches hesitate to do anything that affects the heart. Whoever did this to Gamma Landry froze his heart, and that means serious karma is going to catch up to the caster. No witch of the light would ever do this."

"Oh, I know this story!" Thoreau pulled his face from Spring's ruff and nodded really fast, making me smile at his cuteness. He started singing, " 'Strike for love and strike for fear. There's beauty and there's danger here. Split the ice apart. Beware the frozen heart.' "

"Reau, you know this spell?" she looked at him with consternation. "You know magic?"

"No, but like Grand Pappie says, 'The heart is not so easily changed, but the head can be persuaded.' "

"I don't know who he is," she admitted, "but that's true. And how did you know that little rhyme? It sounded like a chant you'd use in a spell."

"Grand Pappie is a character from *Frozen*," Angelo chuckled, "and those were just the words to the opening song of the movie."

All our eyes went to the Angel of Death.

"What?" he scowled. "Reau likes us to watch Disney with him in the evenings. We've watched that one a hundred times."

"Fourteen," Thoreau corrected him with his own scowl.

"*Anyway*," Ariel brought us back on track, "was Gamma Landry's mate a witch?"

"No. Absolutely not." Alpha shook his head emphatically. "There was never any evidence of that, and, at the very least, Ty would have smelled her."

"With all due respect to Tyler's olfactory skills, she could have shielded herself."

"He smelled *you* under a shield," he argued. "That day you led the Tall Pines wolves to our border, he said he smelled a witch before any of you even came out of the treeline."

"He did?" Her eyebrows flew up in surprise. "I had a really solid shield up."

"He did, and Matthew told him he was imagining it. The rest of us didn't clue into your witchiness until that lead wolf knocked you unconscious and disrupted your spellwork."

Beta Tristan's low growl rolled around the room, and his face twisted with anger.

"Then I'll trust Ty's nose," she said, squeezing her mate's hand to soothe him. "That leaves only a couple of possibilities."

"She bought a spell-storing item from a dark witch or else paid one to cast a curse for her," Adam spoke up, "or this isn't magic-based at all."

"Exactly."

"Dude." Rio elbowed him. "How did you know that?"

"I read." Adam cocked up an eyebrow. "You should try it sometime. It's amazing what you can learn and how it can help you think more logically."

"And you've seen similar things in a *Dungeons & Dragons* campaign, haven't you?" Rio snorted.

"Maybe," Adam admitted.

"If we could keep our focus on the problem?" Ariel scolded them. "Do you have any idea where the girl is now? You could interrogate her to find out—"

"Um, remember what you were saying about what goes around comes around?" Alpha Wyatt scratched the back of his neck. "Yeah, so, after she rejected our boy here, karma *did* catch up to her."

"Karma named Quartz and Sid," Emerson smirked.

"What about her wolf? Do you remember anything about her wolf? Anything odd?"

"Lorikeet always seemed very quiet." Alpha frowned as he thought about it. "Didn't interact much with other wolves. I can't remember me *or* Gran ever really talking to her, to be honest, but I'll ask my brothers."

"She *was* quiet," Nick agreed. "Birch says he talked with her once or twice. Very shy and timid."

"The opposite of her human half, then," Rio grunted.

"Some are," I murmured. "Like Alpha Jayden and Quartz. Or Beta Tyler and River."

"Well, I guess we'll have to figure out what this is on our own." Ariel frowned and looked at Landry's chest again. "I need the rest of my coven here."

"Wyatt, whoever and whatever she needs, you get it for her *right now*," luna demanded.

"Your word is our law, cutie," he murmured before his eyes fogged over.

"But why is it just the luna's touch that gets the reaction?" I asked as I thought about it. "At first, I believed maybe it was a gender thing. It never happened with any of *us*, and his mate rejecting him could have left some kind of impact we don't know about concerning females. But he didn't do that when Ariel touched him, so it's only luna's touch doing it."

"Maybe it's not a bad thing," Beta Emerson suggested, making us all wheel around to stare at him. "We can ask Ty, since the kid practically lives in the alpha research library, but who's ever heard of a luna's touch causing harm to a pack mate? No one. That's because everyone knows that her touch is a healing one. What if that's what's happening here?"

"He caught the curse, however that happened, and luna was drawing it out of him like poison?" Adam asked.

"Just a thought." He shrugged. "That black stuff came out of him after she touched him, then disappeared back into him shortly afterwards."

"Let's do a test!" I suggested, only for the alpha and both betas to snarl at me. Raising my hands in surrender, I turned to Ariel. "You know we need to do it."

"Luna, you said you were not affected in any negative way, right?" Ariel asked while alpha shook his head with a fierce scowl.

"Right. Wyatt, I want to do it." She tried to unpeel alpha's arms from around her body. "If it helps Gamma Landry, I *need* to do it."

"NO!" he growled. "I won't let you—"

"There's no *let* me." She looked at him with raised eyebrows. "I don't need your permission to help a pack mate, Wyatt, any more than you need mine."

I smirked a little. Our tiny luna might look like a fragile butterfly, but she had wings of diamond and steel.

Alpha obviously didn't like it, but how could he argue? Releasing her, he walked her over to Landry's prone figure and knelt with her, holding tightly to her hand as she followed the same process Ariel did.

She got no reaction from touching the t-shirt on his arm, his bare arm, or the t-shirt over his solar plexus. The second her fingertips met the skin of his chest, though, the bruise reappeared and began to darken.

"Posy! Are you okay?" Alpha demanded, looking ready to pull her back at any second.

"I'm fine."

"Then why are tears streaming down your face?" he barked.

"I don't like hurting him."

196

He huffed in irritation, but didn't interfere.

"Luna, don't break contact, but slide your hand up a little toward his heart," Ariel requested.

She did, and the whole bruise and squirmy black veins thing happened much faster this time.

"Yep. Warm Hands, Cold Heart." Ariel nodded, looking pleased with herself for figuring it out.

"So what does she need to do?" Alpha demanded gruffly.

"Just what she's doing. Luna, his body will probably start shaking here in a minute, but keep your hand on him. Every time you let go, the curse will sink back into him."

"I'll hold on. I won't let go," she vowed, her wet eyes locked on Landry's flinching face.

The other alphas suddenly burst into the training center, tripping over each other in their haste to reach luna's side and shouting at Alpha Wyatt and the rest of us for letting her get involved. Luna dropped her mate's hand to put her other fingers on Landry, and Alpha Wyatt stood up to continue arguing with his brothers.

My boys and I traded glances, worried about Landry, but also knowing how volatile our alphas could be when they were all upset. The last thing anyone needed was for a fight to break out here and now.

Betas Crew and Matthew showed up with their two mates, shortly followed by the Maxwell twins with theirs. The witches and Angelo made a circle around Landry and the luna, and I was pretty sure it was to keep the alphas from interfering until it was done.

The betas and the twins kept an eye on the five brothers, ready to intervene if it looked like things were headed toward a throw down, and me and my boys watched Landry.

The longer the luna held her fingers to his chest, the darker and fuller the veins became under his skin. She looked lost in her own world, clearly concentrating on her task, and I for one was so proud to have a luna like her for our pack.

*The Goddess blessed us*, I linked my boys, and they all nodded, catching on immediately to what I meant.

"Now, luna," Sara said, "I believe the vein-like things will begin to rupture soon. When that happens, there will be a quiet noise, then a small puff of air and a vile smell. Can you continue through that until they all rupture?"

"Rupture means pop?"

"Yes, luna."

"I can continue. I won't let him down. I won't fail."

"I know you won't," Sara assured her with a gentle smile.

"Wait! Won't it get into her?" Alpha Cole shouted in a panic. "When they rupture, won't the curse latch onto her?"

"No, alpha," the witches all said at once, then Maria went on to explain, "It's a once and done spell targeted to one specific person. As soon as it leaves his body, it's neutralized."

After that, the alphas watched in utter silence, so many emotions swirling in their eyes that I had to stop looking at them. Finally, the first vein blew exactly as Sara described, and a whiff of evil hit our noses.

"Nasty shit," Tristan whispered, and we all nodded, waving our hands under our noses.

Five minutes passed as vein after vein burst, each one sending a foul odor into the air, until nothing was left except for the bruise. Despite being so much closer to the horrible stench than the rest of us, the luna held on, true to her word, until the dark circle faded to red, then pink, then nothing.

*Oak?* I called. *You there?*

*Tired, Rube.*

*You can sleep in a minute. How are you feeling otherwise?*

*Good. Healthy. Happy. Light and free.* Oak sighed. *It was heavy, Rube. So heavy.*

*Rest now, friend. We'll talk later.*

I shared that conversation with the others, and the witches all nodded.

"I bet it *was* heavy, carrying a revolting curse like that one." Beatrix scowled and her hair began to rise on an invisible wave of heat. "I wish I had that little slut here! Too bad you killed her, alphas. I would have liked to purify the evil from her, and nothing purifies so well as fire."

"Our little pyro." Zayne draped his arms across her shoulders while Zayden did the same around her waist. "Such a bloodthirsty girl."

"You love it and you know it," she snorted, but I noticed she calmed down and it didn't feel like an oven door had opened behind me anymore.

Watching Landry's face, I saw the lines of pain had disappeared, although the dark shadows persisted under his eyes, and he seemed to be sleeping peacefully.

In unison, the witches hunkered down and raised their hands above him for a second, then nodded at each other.

"It's all gone now, luna," Maria said. "You can let go."

That was all the alphas needed to hear to descend on their girl. She was swept up in Alpha Ash's arms before she could get off her knees. He kissed her fiercely before passing her to the next alpha, and each of them kissed the poor luna senseless.

Finally, Alpha Jayden set her on her feet, put his hands on her shoulders, and made her look into his eyes, which burned with worry.

She smiled up at him, her dimples on full display, and *her* eyes sparkled with something, but I couldn't tell what.

"Jayden! Did you see what I did?" she squeaked.

"I did, sweetness. You saved him. That was so brave of you, but are you *sure* you're okay? I've never been so scared in my life!"

She nodded and opened her mouth to reply, but Quartz's furious roar overrode anything she might have said.

*Damn, damn, damn!* Larch muttered, and I one-hundred percent agreed with my wolf.

Quartz in a temper was never a fun time, and someone always got hurt.

As if the sound of his fury had opened a dam, the other four alphas began to yell. Even *Alpha Mason* lost his cool, which wasn't something I had ever witnessed before, and I'd once seen the man with his arm nearly torn off after breaking up two young hotheads at fighter practice.

"I can't believe you did that, Posy! You could have been hurt! You could have been *killed*!"

"You put your life in danger!" Alpha Cole shouted. "How could you do that? Do you know what would happen if we lost you?"

"What were you thinking?! Why would you do something so stupid?" Alpha Ash, the most laid-back of the five, was red-faced with anger.

"You should have waited until we could research it more!" Alpha Wyatt hollered. "There had to have been a solution that didn't put you at risk!"

And under the weight of their shouting, our luna reached her breaking point.

Hands clenched in fists at her sides, face red, tears streaming down her cheeks, she opened her mouth and screamed two words that turned all of us into statues.

*"SHUT UP!"*

## 28: Fury

*Posy*

For the second time in my life, I lost my temper.

"I know you're scared and angry because I was in danger, but you have no right to yell at me like this or call me stupid. You think I don't get scared or worried when you leave the house every morning to do *your* job? Or when you go on missions for the king to a pack that's in so much trouble, its own alpha can't handle it?"

I held up my hand when Ash and Wyatt opened their mouths, and thank the Goddess they closed them again or I might have done something violent.

"But I don't hold you back. I don't complain or cry or scream at you and say mean things. Sure, I asked you to stay home for a little while after the parasite incident, because I think we all deserved and needed a break, but I would never try to stop you from being who you are. Being *what* you are. Strong, brave, powerful alphas that people look to for help. And you need to do the same for me."

"Posy—"

"No, Cole! You be quiet and listen to me for once! *I* helped Landry. *Me.* Nobody else here could do anything for him, only *me*, because I'm his luna. And do you know how that made me feel? Proud. I was *proud* of myself! For the first time since I was a pup, I was proud of something I accomplished on my own. I finally felt like the luna of this pack - *and you took that away from me!"*

"Sweetness—"

"Jayden, none of what I'm saying is meant for you. Quartz, on the other hand, is a different story."

Shaking my head, I crossed my arms and narrowed my eyes at my other mates.

"Topaz, Garnet, Granite, Sid, take control and shift. *Now!* Jayden, if you shift, can you control Quartz so he doesn't ascend?"

"Yes, sweetness." He raised an eyebrow, clearly puzzled, but nodded. "You want me to shift now, too?"

"Please." Even angry, I wanted to be polite to the one who *hadn't* hurt me.

Nodding again, he tugged off his t-shirt and knelt to untie his shoes, and I looked at the rest of my mates. Their wolves glittered in their eyes, but they remained in their human forms.

Just like that, my anger exploded into fury - something I'd *never* experienced before - and I nearly staggered at its intensity. It was terrifyingly powerful. I felt like I could slap the Devil off his throne and rule Hell myself.

*Whoa. No wonder Quartz is so dangerous when he's furious!*

Thinking of him, something he told me during a snuggle session came back to me.

My mates were each the alphas of their own pack as well as Five Fangs, but I was luna of all six of them. Me. Posy Anne Everleigh. *I* was the only person, male or female, in the whole world with access to that much power.

Which meant these wolves were going to listen to me.

Getting Lark to help, I reached deep into all five mate bonds until I found the immense well of moon power behind each alpha. I called it all to me and boomed it out with one word.

**"*SHIFT!*"**

The sounds of shredding fabric made me spin around, and I held in a groan at what was happening behind me. I hadn't thought to direct all that power only at my mates, and now everyone in the training center was shifting, except Angelo and Thoreau, who had nothing to shift into, and Landry, who was still unconscious.

*Oh, well*, Lark snickered. *Nothing you can do about it now. 'Sides, after this, they* all *need run. Need blow off steam. Just roll with it, girl.*

Shaking my head, I turned back to my mates.

"Now, go run. As far and as long as you need to until both man and wolf are calm and sensible again. Only then can you come home and not a second before."

*I asked Ty to come here,* Jayden linked me. *He's on his way. I know Gelo and Reau are here, but Ty is your friend as well as your beta. I thought he could—*

*It's fine, dragon,* I told him and sent him a wave of love that he immediately returned.

Looking around, I saw seventeen wolves and four songbirds sitting and staring at me, but not moving, so I drew in a deep breath and marched over to the door. Flinging it open, I gathered up all that moon power again and threw it at them one more time.

**"*GO!*"**

I pointed my index finger outside, and a colorful herd of furry bodies ran past me at high speed, the witches following on fluttering wings, and I was left with a smirking Angelo, a jaw-dropped Thoreau, and a knocked-out Landry.

Sighing, I took a second to close my eyes and rub the skin between my eyebrows with the tips of my fingers.

"I'm proud of you, luna," Angelo said softly as he and Thoreau padded over to me. "You did good."

My heart still hurt, but as the adrenaline faded, fear and worry hounded me.

"Was I too harsh?" I asked and bit my bottom lip.

"I don't know how you held back as long and as much as you did," he grunted. "Arrogant dumbasses."

"Bad word, Gelo!" Thoreau shook his finger at him, then hugged me.

"Sorry, Reau. Luna, I would have done the same thing. Your mates should have followed Alpha Jayden's example and praised you, not scolded you."

"Yeah, they deserved it," Thoreau agreed with wide, serious eyes. "They were being meanies, and no one is allowed to hurt luna, not even her alphas."

Then he surprised me by dropping a tiny kiss on each of my cheeks.

"Good girl kisses for luna."

"Thank you, Reau."

"Don't forget my good boy kiss, though," he whispered.

"Never, sweetie." Despite everything, I smiled. "Come down again."

He did, and I pecked his forehead.

"My first good boy kiss!" he crowed, his cheeks pink and his eyes glimmering. "Wait til I tell Wayne and Arch!"

"Won't they be jealous?" Angelo teased, but Thoreau, as usual, took him seriously.

"No. They get good boy kisses all the time from Mom and Dad. I never got *any* kind of kisses from Mommy Daddy, and now I don't have any mommy daddy, so no kisses ever."

We'd all noticed that he lumped both parents together in one title, and Emerson had tried to correct him, but Thoreau stubbornly resisted. Dr. York told him to leave it alone, saying Thoreau understood the concept of individual parents and gender terms, but his tormentors were one inseparable unit in his mind.

"Reau, Emerson's your mommy now." Angelo pulled him for a hug. "You're our baby, remember?"

"Bubba will be my mommy? I don't want a mommy again. Mommies are mean." Thoreau shook his head so fast, his curls flopped all over. "Bubba will be Mama. Will Gelo be Papa?"

*Oh, my heart! This kid's eyes should be illegal!* I linked Angelo.

*I know. We can't be strict with him for anything when he uses them.* He chuckled. *His mate is going to be in so much trouble.*

Snickering, I watched as Angelo pecked Thoreau's forehead.

"Yeah, *piccolo cucciolo* (little puppy). I am your papa. Em is your mama, but you can still call him Bubba if you want, okay?"

"Okay, Gelo. Wait! I mean, Papa!"

202

Throwing his arms around Angelo's waist, Thoreau squeezed him hard, burying his face in Angelo's chest for a second, then looked up and smiled the most adorable smile.

"I love you, Papa."

And the fearsome and feared Angelo of Death had to wipe tears from his eyes before he responded in a voice that cracked.

"I love you, too, Reau."

"Hey!" Landry called out. "Can someone tell me what's going on? What happened to me? Why is Oak exhausted? Why am *I* exhausted? Why am I laying on the floor? And who left an elephant dance on my chest?!"

"Lelofant!" Thoreau screeched and raced over to Landry. "I want to see an lelofant! Where's the lelofant? They are so cute with their trunks! Baby lelofants use their trunks to hold their mommy's tails. Isn't that so sweet?"

He stopped and made a sound of disappointment, then scowled and kicked the bottom of Landry's sneaker, causing Landry to stare up at him in a confused sort of fascination - a state I could totally relate to when it came to Thoreau.

"Bad Gamma! Papa Gelo! Gamma Landry is lying! There are no lelofants here."

Thoreau plopped on the mat next to Landry and rambled on and on about getting Mama Bubba and Papa Gelo to take him to the zoo to meet some 'lelofants.' Landry nodded from time to time, obviously too drained to contribute much, not that Thoreau needed *any* help carrying the conversation.

My eyes met Angelo's, and we both burst into laughter, and I couldn't have asked for a better way to get the last of the anger and stress out of my system.

"Alpha Jayden never would have left if it wasn't for Quartz," he said after we quieted down.

"I know." I sucked my lips between my teeth. "How long do you think they'll be gone?"

"My dear girl, they were ready to come back, tails tucked between their legs, five minutes ago," he chuckled, "but don't worry. They know they need a plan to get back into your good graces. I'd expect some fancy gifts, if I were you. Make them crawl on their bellies before you forgive them."

"They don't need a plan, and I can't be bribed with gifts, and I won't shame them. I just want them to apologize and tell me they know that I'm the luna, not just their mate."

"They *do* know that, but I understand why you need to hear it from them." He grinned and tapped my nose with his index finger. "Listen, sweetheart, let them make fools of themselves for you once in a while. It does them good to have their egos knocked down a peg or two every once in a while, yeah?"

"Well, you are a man, so I guess you know better than me about that part," I smiled. "All right. I'll let them eat a bit of humble pie."

"It's what's best for them, after all."

"Then I guess I can tolerate a little groveling."

"Only a little," he agreed and held out his fist.

"For their own good."

And I gently knocked my knuckles against his.

## 29: We're in Trouble

*Mason*

As per their luna's orders, our wolves stayed in control until we'd all calmed down, which had only taken a few minutes and a couple of miles. We continued to run in wolf form, though, long after the others had wheeled off to return home. We were hoping to wear off some of the anger we had for ourselves.

Besides, Quartz was far from calm. We could all hear his enraged bellows, and I winced in sympathy for Jay.

*Dude did the right thing and is still being punished. He was the only one of us who reacted like we* all *should have.*

We were about forty miles into Dark Woods, where no one ever really went except for border patrols, when Ash pointed out the obvious.

*We're going to need help,* he muttered in the alpha link. *I don't know about you all, but I have no clue how to get her to forgive us. An apology ain't enough this time.*

*Nor should it be,* Cole grumbled. *We screwed up beyond saying sorry.*

*And who's going to help us?* Wyatt snorted. *Mama would give us a lecture on how disappointed she is, and Mom would slap us upside the head and yell.*

*Papa would probably tell us to figure it out ourselves and close the door in our faces,* Ash picked up. *I can just hear him saying, "You got yourselves into this mess; you can get yourselves out of it."*

I smirked; that was actually a pretty good imitation of him, and one of his more common phrases.

*Dad would laugh, then say he never screwed up this badly to know how to advise us,* Cole said. *And the betas are no good. They already want to tear our lungs out for hurting their luna.*

*The gammas wouldn't be of any use, either,* Ash added. *They're all single except for Rio, and his human mate is still learning about our world. I mean, Emmeline might have some ideas for us, but she wouldn't understand the nuances of the situation.*

*What do you think, Mase?* Wyatt asked.

*I think you all know there's only one person who will help us,* I admitted against my will. *For her own entertainment, if nothing else.*

*You can't be serious,* Cole groaned.

*Got a better idea?* I challenged him.

He hung his head and shook it, so I ignored Jay's snicker and my other brothers' whining and led them to the place none of us wanted to go.

*Peri*

Tyler wasn't happy about it, but I let the five long faces into our house.

While my mate was comforting Posy, it looked like I was stuck helping my stupid big brothers figure out how to un-wreck their lives.

Mase bravely opened his mouth first, and I held up one hand.

"I already know everything. Come into the dining room."

It was the only room with enough furniture to seat us all, but I didn't want them to know that. They'd order half a furniture store and have it delivered before dark if they did.

Once they were seated like naughty children around the rectangular table, I stood in front of them with my hands on my hips and glared.

"All right, here's what you're going to do. You're each going to make her an apology card. Over the next couple of days, each of you will take her on a special date and give it to her, then all of you will take her on a group date to somewhere she really wants to go."

"Apology card?" Ash and Wyatt said together.

*That's all they got out of it?* marveled Dove, my wolf.

"I like the special date idea, but I don't know how to *make* a card. Can't we just buy one?" Cole scowled at me.

"Oh, that's the easy part." I waved one hand. "I have all kinds of craft supplies you can use. You take a blank card, decorate the front, and write a letter inside."

"What do you mean, decorate the front?" Ash said.

"Well, you can draw or paint something, use stickers or stencils, or glue flowers or something on it. I'll show you some examples."

"And the letter?" Wyatt raised his eyebrows. "We need to write a letter? I don't know what goes in a letter."

"Think of it like a long text or link. Just start with Dear Posy, add in some forgive mes and I'm sorrys, and end with Love, Wyatt."

"So I have to think of something to write." Ash crossed his arms over his chest. "I'm not good with words, Peri, and I can't draw for shit."

Taking a deep breath, I stood up and went into the kitchen. It took me a few minutes to find what I was looking for, but I finally did and carried it out to the dining room. Plunking it on the table, I gave Ash a hard glare.

"Two dollars, please." I gestured toward the plastic container shaped like a bear that once held animal crackers.

"Oh my Goddess. How did you get the swear jar away from Mom?" Ash groaned as he reached into his wallet, pulled out two ones, and dropped them in.

"It's mine," I smiled smugly. "The babies polished off the animal crackers last week, so Mom said I could have it for my own swear jar."

"Ty doesn't have a potty mouth," Jay said, but his eyes held the question.

"Not for him," I muttered. When they laughed, I added, "Well, after growing up with *you* guys, what did you expect from me? But I'm trying to break the habit because Mom will kill me if her grandpup's first word is dammit. Oh, dammit! Argh! See?!"

Slapping my hand against my forehead, I went over to my purse, grabbed four singles, and put them in the swear jar.

"And don't forget the f-bomb is a ten dollar fine," I reminded them as I dropped back on my chair.

"I'm going to run out of cash," Wyatt complained. "I can tell already."

"What are you going to do with the money? You going to donate it like Mom does?" Cole asked.

"Probably to the O," I nodded.

"All right, we can do the card-making and letter writing here and now if you don't mind us using your supplies," Mase said. "We'll pay you back, of course."

"Don't worry about it, Mase. It's some paper and glue. The important part is what you'll write inside your card." I gave him a gentle smile. "Your words to her are priceless and far more meaningful than any card you could buy at a store."

"Let's talk about the date part before making the cards, though, because we're going to need something ASAP. No way is she sleeping angry, upset, and alone for even one night."

"I would advise against that as well," I agreed with him. "She may be pissed at you, but not going home to her tonight is the worst mistake you could ever make."

"I could take her to the county fair tonight," he suggested with bright eyes, but they quickly dulled. "Oh. It's Friday *and* opening night. It would be crowded, and that would make her uncomfortable."

"Yeah, let's think of something else for tonight."

"Well, it won't work for tonight," Cole said slowly, "but I want to take her to the zoo."

"Aw! I want to do that with her, too," Wyatt whined.

"Me, too," Ash pouted.

"*I* wanted to go to the fair with her, but you didn't hear me complaining when Mase called dibs on it, did you?" Cole grumbled.

"Let's agree to save things like the fair and the zoo and amusement parks for group dates," I said. "For now, come up with activities you like that Posy would enjoy, too, and we'll see if one works for tonight. Wyatt, let's start with you. What's something that you like to do and want to share with Posy?"

"Mess around with cars, although she wouldn't be interested in that." He tilted his head as he thought. "Drag races, but again, not something our girl would enjoy since she doesn't like loud noises and crowds. Sports, but would she like going to the batting cages? That's not much of a date. Argh! I don't know!"

"Art," Mase suggested. "Take her on a date involving art. You said she loved looking at your sketchbooks, right?"

"How do you make that into a date?" He ran his fingers through his fluffy hair with a frustrated scowl.

"You could do a couple of different things," Jay said before I could. "You could take a painting class in the city, or go through some of the galleries and the art museum, then hit up a nice place for dinner."

"Or you could pack some supplies and a picnic lunch and take her to the lake." Ash smiled, obviously proud of himself. "You'd have privacy there, too, in case things get heated afterward."

"I see no problem with mating in a public place," Wyatt told him with one raised eyebrow. "The museum has one of those family bathrooms that we could lock ourselves in and—"

"TMI! TMI!" I slammed my hands over my ears.

"What?" He gave me a mocking look. "You're a mated woman now. You and Ty have mated *plenty* of times, remember?"

"Yes, we have, but I don't need to hear about my brother's scandalous sex life. Now, unless you like the lake idea, Google some art-related activities nearby while I help these other knuckleheads."

"Thanks, Per." Cole rolled his eyes at me.

"Let's take her to the fair together after we have our individual dates with her," Ash said. "If we each spend a day with her, that would be Wednesday night. I know she wants to go to the beach, but we can't pull that together before Wednesday. Or can we?"

"The fair is only in town until next weekend," Cole reminded him, "so let's save the beach for later. It can be a big surprise. Maybe we can go after the queen's coronation at the end of the month and before her family reunion at the beginning of August."

"Make those two events bookends on a beach trip?" Mase nodded. "I like it."

"Perfect!" I smiled. "Okay, so who's going first tonight into tomorrow?"

"Me," Mase said quickly. "I'll take her out to dinner at Roger's because she asked if we could go there a couple of days ago. Then I'll get a room for tonight. I don't think she's ever stayed in a hotel."

"And you'd have nothing but privacy if things get—"

"Ash, let's just assume that things *will* get heated for all of your dates," I rolled my eyes, "and plan accordingly, hmm?"

"Which hotel? You better get to booking somewhere if it's for tonight," Wyatt spoke up.

With a nod, Mase took out his phone, apparently to look for vacancies.

"What will you do tomorrow?" I asked him.

"Go to the Saturday flea market. That's why I wanted to go first. I'll encourage her to pick some stuff for her special room. Then lunch somewhere nice before I hand her off for her next date."

"Sweet!" Ash stood up and high-fived him. "Not only is it a great date, it gives the rest of us time to put something together."

"Take her to that little tea shop next to Stella's for lunch," Jay told him. "She'll definitely love that."

"Perfect! Thanks, man."

"And I'll meet you there to pick her up for *my* date," Wyatt said. "We're going to the art museum first, then dinner, then doing a painting class for the rest of the evening. Who am I handing her off to on Sunday after lunch?"

"Wait, where are you sleeping?" I asked.

"I rented a place," he said simply, which concerned me.

"Does it have a bathroom? A shower? What about a change of clothes for her?"

"Yes, it has a bathroom! Stop worrying. I know what I'm doing." He flapped a hand at me. "And we can each bring her a bag of clothes and stuff when we meet up. Which reminds me. Someone remember to put Mr. Nibbles in her overnight bag tonight. Just in case."

"I'll go next," Jay said before any of us could interrogate Wyatt further about the 'place' he rented.

I hoped that didn't come back to bite us in the butt. Still, it was Wyatt. There was only so much damage control we could do.

"What are you going to do, Jay?" Cole asked. "I can tell you already have something planned."

"I'm not telling you."

"What?!" Ash and Wyatt screeched and Cole said, "You can't keep it a secret from us!"

"Yes, I can." Jay crossed his arms and narrowed his eyes at his brothers. "You'll only make fun of me, so no, you don't need to know. It's nothing any of *you* would ever do, anyway, so what does it matter?"

"It matters because we want to know!" Wyatt yammered.

"It matters because you're our brother," Cole corrected, "and we support you. And we're nosy as hell."

"Two dollars, brother," I murmured and pointed to the swear jar.

"One of us needs to make a run to the ATM," he griped, but paid his fine.

"Come on, Jay!" Ash whined. "Just tell us!"

"No. You'll hassle me and make fun of it."

"You're taking her to the alpha library?" Of course, Mase got there before the rest of us.

Jay's lips pressed together in a white line as he waited for the explosion of laughter and teasing from our brothers.

*Goddess help me, I will* end *you if you laugh at him*, I warned Ash, Wyatt, and Cole. *It's a great idea. She's been asking to go for a while now, and it's his special place. Do. Not. Ruin. It. For. Him!*

"Yeah, man," Cole nodded and patted Jay's shoulder. "She'll love that. I know she's been wanting to go since Ty mentioned it."

"And you can set up a cute nook under a canopy and fill it full of pillows and blankets and string up fairy lights." Ash grew more excited with each idea he threw out. "And you have to put flowers *everywhere*. You know she loves flowers. Oh, my goodness! Rose petals! Rose petals on the floor! Dude, I am *so* helping you set it up! It's going to look like a scene from a movie!"

He stood up and shimmied in a happy dance, and I rolled my eyes.

"Dude!" He froze mid-wiggle and whisper yelled, "Take your guitar, dude! Oh my word, she would just *die* if you sang to her in your little love nest!"

Jay's cheeks flushed bright pink, making us giggle at him, but the happiness in his eyes at the idea was clear as day.

When Ash wasn't being obnoxious, he was a very sweet guy.

"And for dinner," Wyatt chimed in, "you can order in a bunch of different food she hasn't tried yet. Like explore your world or something. That goes with a library theme, doesn't it?"

"Good idea," I praised him.

*Wow. That's more thoughtful than I ever expected from Wyatt*, I linked Mase. *He's really changed since you guys met Posy.*

*He has, but not* that *much. Just wait for it*, he warned me with a resigned sigh. *He's never* not *going to throw shade at his brothers.*

"I know it is, Periwinkle. Jay needs to show her there's more to him than being a nerd." Wyatt said it with a straight face, too.

Reaching over, Mase slapped Wyatt upside the head.

"Don't tease him," he rumbled.

"I wasn't *teasing* him!" Wyatt protested. "I was *describing* him! We all know he's a nerd."

"Thanks for calling me smart." Jay flipped him off.

"Go to hell, asshole."

"With you here, it feels like I'm already there."

"Boys, boys!" I threw my hands up and raised my eyes to the ceiling, begging the Moon Goddess for patience. "How do you guys get any work done at the office? And the finger still counts as an f-bomb, Jay, so pay up. You, too, Wyatt. Now, can we *please* move on?"

As they put their money in the swear jar, I took a deep breath to compose myself. I'd forgotten what it was like to deal with all five of them at once.

*Goddess bless you, Posy Everleigh.*

"Where are you getting lunch, Wyatt?" I asked. "Jay can pick her up there afterwards."

"The hibachi on North Broad Street. I want her to experience the cook making the food at the table and see her face when he does the onion volcano. I bet she totally catches the shrimp he flicks at her!"

"Nice," we all agreed.

"Now we're down to Cole and Ash." I looked from one to the other. "I can give you ideas, or do you have your own?"

"Well, I was looking on Pinterest," Ash started - and that's all he had to say to get the yapping started again.

"*Pinterest*?" Cole guffawed. "I didn't know there was an old lady hiding inside your giant body."

"I'm not going to lower myself to your level of ignorance. You'd just beat me down with your years of experience."

"Let me guess. You found that shitty comeback on *Pinterest*," Cole sneered.

"Enough!" Mason barked. "Pay your fine and quit teasing, Cole! Where were you thinking of taking our girl, Ash?"

"On *Pinterest*," he emphasized with a glare at Cole, "I saw a Choose Your Own Adventure date, but I'm going to modify it a bit. I'm going to write some ideas on cards and let her choose which one to do first, then next, and so on. I could do the same with dinner: Write a bunch of restaurants on a different color of cards and let her draw one from the hat. What do you think?"

"I think she will really get excited about that," Jay told him with a broad grin. "As long as you give her good choices, it's going to be a lot of fun."

"What activities did you have in mind?" Mase asked him.

"Mini golf, old-school arcade, Bounce, roller skating, ice skating, bowling. Stuff like that." He shrugged.

*Mostly physical, wear-you-out stuff,* Dove said, amused.

*Are you surprised that Mr. ADHD came up with that list?* I replied, then giggled. *I don't think she's going to have the energy for things to become 'heated' later.*

"I'll help you make the cards," Jay said, which gave me a sense of relief. He'd make sure there were some low-key activities, too.

"Sweet! Thanks!" Ash fist-bumped him.

"Maybe add a nap in the park as one," Mase suggested, obviously on my wavelength. "She might get worn out if you're running from one thing to the next all day."

"Good idea."

"And for Tuesday?" I asked him. "More of the same?"

"Nope! I already linked Spero Bel Aire about taking her horseback riding, and his daughter's going to get us all set up at their farm for a beginner lesson and a short trail ride. Then we'll grab lunch from wherever she wants and come home because she'll want to shower after being on a horse."

"Where are you sleeping on Monday night?" Wyatt asked.

"Oh, I forgot. The guest house at Bel Aire's. Think she'll like that? We should get an awesome view of the stars if the weather's nice."

"She'll love it," Cole said. "It's a pretty little place. Find a stargazing app on your phone, though, so you can at least sound intelligent about the constellations."

"*Sound* intelligent? I *am* intelligent."

"Keep telling yourself that," Cole muttered.

"So what did *you* come up with, big brother?" I asked to prevent another war of the words. "After you pick her up at the alpha house, where are you taking her?"

"To the cabin," he declared. "There's a ton of stuff to do. Canoeing, swimming, hiking, fishing, whatever makes her happy. I just need to figure out dinner. Then we'll eat lunch and come home to clean up and get ready to go to the fair with you guys."

"I think the cabin's a great idea, especially after Ash's busy date," Mase told him. "It'll give her a chance to relax before we hit the fair, too."

"Keep dinner simple, like the rest of your date," Wyatt suggested. "Roast hot dogs and marshmallows over the fire pit."

Looking at each other from the corner of our eyes, Mase and I began to count down.

*Five, four, three, two—*

"Of course, after putting up with your craptastic personality all day, she'll probably want to roast *you* over the fire pit."

And Cole's hot temper, all ready on edge after today's events, sparked.

212

"I swear, if you don't shut your mouth, the next thing coming out of it will be teeth!"

And as usual, Wyatt didn't get the hint that Cole was done playing.

"Chill, dude! What, are you manstruating? Sheesh. Next time Posy wants to give you a nickname, just tell her to call you Oscar, you old grouchy butt."

With a roar, Cole leaped over the table and launched himself at Wyatt, smashing the chair to splinters as they both crashed to the floor.

*Thank the Goddess I only spent three dollars per chair at the thrift shop.*

"They never change, do they?" I smirked at Jay as Mason dove in to break them up and Ash laughed so hard, he fell on the floor.

"I have to live with this." He closed his eyes and scrubbed his hands over his face. "All day, every day. For the rest of my life."

"They're not this bad around Posy, are they?" I asked, suddenly concerned.

I couldn't see my sweet friend liking the fact that her mates wrecked each other on the regular, and I doubted she'd see their guy banter as playing.

*Well*, I admitted, *it's 'playing' right up until it turns into WrestleMania in the middle of the dining room.*

Jay dropped his hands in time to dodge as a tooth did, indeed, go flying past his face.

"Dammit, Wyatt!" Cole roared. "That was a canine! It'll take all night to grow back!"

"It helps that Posy's like a tranquilizer for us," Jay answered me without missing a beat. "The fact that she's, one, not here and, two, mad at them is fraying their tempers. Not to mention how mad they are at themselves right now. They're spoiling for a fight, even Mr. Ice."

*He's not really Mr. Ice, though, is he? He just pretends to be.*

I kept the thought to myself. Jay was as aware as I was of how much Mase hid under his mask, and saying something wouldn't help anyone right now.

"And Quartz is, too, isn't he?" I asked gently.

"Yeah, but I can't risk giving him control."

"What if you stayed in human form and went to the gym so he could take out some anger on a punching bag or two?" I suggested.

"I don't know if I could keep him from shifting, and if he gets out in wolf form while he's this angry, someone will die - probably several someones - and I'm not chancing that."

*Poor Jay. He's always stuck between a rock and a hard place.*

"Can I ask you something without him hearing?" After he nodded, I asked, "Would you trade him? If you could, would you swap him for a different wolf?"

His eyes went far away, and he was quiet as Mase got Cole and Wyatt separated. I didn't think he was going to answer, but as our brothers cleaned up the broken chair and Ash picked himself up off the floor, Jay looked at me and smiled brightly.

"Six years ago, I would have said yes in a second. Now? No. I respect Quartz, and I admire him. He has a lot of good qualities that other shifters would never notice, let alone acknowledge. A softer, less mature wolf would have gotten me killed or walked all over, although it took me a long time to recognize that, and even longer to appreciate it. I needed my opposite in a wolf as much as he needed his opposite in a human. I wouldn't trade him for any other wolf, even if he is a pain in the ass more often than not."

"Aww." I went over and hugged him tightly. "You're a good man, Jay Carson. And that's two dollars in the swear jar, please."

He hugged me back while chuckling.

Meanwhile, Mase brought another wooden chair in from the kitchen and pushed a smirking Wyatt in it, sat a sullen Cole down between me and Jay, and took the seat next to Wyatt.

"Now that our dates are sorted, let's do the apology cards," he said, his normally unperturbed expression now perturbed. "If you're still willing to help us, Peri.

"Of course!" I chirped brightly and stopped hugging Jay. "Would you come with me to carry the supplies down? We can work here at the dining room table."

There weren't many furnishings in the rest of the house, other than our bedroom, and that's only because Mom and Dad gifted us with a whole bedroom suite as a mating gift.

Mase agreed and followed me up the stairs. As we headed toward what would become my craft room, he touched my shoulder and I stopped walking to look up at him.

"We'd buy you anything you wanted or needed, yet your new house is nearly bare," he said softly. "Is it your pride or Ty's standing in the way?"

"Neither. We want to furnish it in our own time with our own money." Seeing him scowl, I patted his cheek. "We're not being rude or proud, but we don't want any handouts. We have a plan for our future and we want to build it with our own hands. Ty has a good-paying job and I'm going to start waitressing at Roger's in the afternoons once school starts."

He opened his mouth, and I knew he was going to protest that, but I laid my fingers over his lips.

"Mase, you of all people understand the need to stand on your own two feet," I told him. "Plus, it will give me something to do while he's at football practice so I'm not home alone and can't get roped into free babysitting for Mom."

He smiled at that for a second, but a frown wiped it away pretty fast.

"You have enough food and toiletries and stuff, though, right? I swear, Peri, if you hide something like that from us, we will be so angry with you. And this state of affairs isn't going to continue for long. I'm going to make it my mission to grow Ty's investment portfolio exponentially, since you won't take any help from us."

"We have plenty of everything we need. Mama and Papa gave each of us money for our birthdays, and your mate also offered us any amount we needed to set up house. We told her we'd let her know and now I'm telling you the same. If we get in trouble, we'll tell you, but we're happy and taken care of, Mase. I promise you."

I could see he was surprised to know Posy had offered us money, but he shouldn't have been. She was the sweetest, most generous and practical person I'd ever met.

*The perfect mate for our brothers*, Dove chortled with glee. *Especially now that she's not afraid to put them in their place!*

*Agreed*, I grinned.

## 30: Crafting with My Bros

*Peri*

Mason and I carried down all the card-making supplies I had and spread them out on the table. I showed the boys the different papers they could use, and Wyatt immediately grabbed the watercolor paper and asked if I had the paints, too. Fortunately, I did, and I passed them over to him with the few brushes I had.

"Will they work?" I asked hopefully, knowing how fussy he was about his art supplies.

"Yes, these will be fine. I'm going to get water and some paper towels."

And he was off to the kitchen.

"Don't use my good glasses!" I called. "Grab the mismatched coffee mugs. They're only fifty cents each at the thrift store!"

"Thrift store?" Ash's head whipped up and his eyes narrowed at me. "Why are you shopping at a thrift store?"

"Don't, Ash," I said softly. "Leave it for now. Please? There's been enough drama for today. Plus, I have Ty in my ear snarling about how his luna is crying because she's worried that her mates won't ever come home since she was mean to them."

"She's crying?" His dark eyes filled up with tears.

"She really thinks we won't come home?" Mase's mouth pulled into a taut line.

"She thought *that* was being mean to us?" Wyatt shook his head with a frown. "We deserved a lot more."

"Let's get these cards done so you can go home and begin to make up with her," I said with forced enthusiasm.

"You're going to have to walk us through it," Cole said.

"No problem! First, think of a design for the front."

I explained some different things they could do and showed them a couple of cards I'd made for upcoming birthdays so they could see the finished product.

"That's the easy part," I warned them. "The hard part is deciding what you'll write on the inside."

"Okay, so what do you say in an apology?" Ash asked with dead serious eyes.

"Um, what?" I tilted my head. Was he *really* asking me how to apologize?

"What do you put in an apology?" Wyatt spoke up this time. "Like, specifically?"

"Well, first, say what you're sorry for and ask for forgiveness. Add some love words and promises, and that's it."

While Jay - who didn't even *need* to make a sorry card - went right to work, the other four sat there and stared at me.

"Uh, can you get us started?" Cole asked, tapping a pencil on a piece of scrap paper. "An outline or something?"

"Dear Posy," I said in a dry monotone, "I'm sorry I hurt your feelings. Please forgive me. I'll try my best not to do it again, but since I'm a dumbass, I probably will. Have patience with me. I'm almost sure I'm worth it. Love, your name."

They'd been nodding along with me until I hit the 'dumbass' part, then their earnest faces screwed up into scowls.

"Thanks, sister," Wyatt grumbled. "Two dollars in the swear jar."

"You're welcome, brother, and it's worth it."

It took a good thirty minutes before they all had drafted what they wanted on scrap paper before copying it inside their cards. Since I figured it would be the hardest part for them, I wanted that done before I let them decorate the front, which should be simple with all the stickers I had.

And if they screwed up the front too badly, we could always cut their words out and paste them inside a new card, but I knew if they had to keep redoing the words inside because the front turned out bad, their patience wouldn't hold.

"Peri, read this," Cole said and held out his piece of scrap paper.

I took it and looked it over, corrected the spelling on two words, and handed it back.

"Very good," I told him, and he smiled at me before he began copying it into his card.

*I can't believe how well this is going,* Dove remarked, eyes wide with amazement. *I thought for sure there'd be chaos—*

"Dammit, Ash!" Wyatt shouted as he jumped up and whaled his card at his brother. "I was almost done!"

"What did I do?" Ash's eyes were wide with bewilderment.

"You bumped the damn table with your freaking knee right as I was filling in the last leaf! You ruined it, shit head!"

"Hey, dude, I'm sorry! I didn't mean to, honest!" Ash picked up Wyatt's card and looked at it. "I mean, you could paint over it or something, right?"

"No, I can't *paint over it!* This shit is watercolors!"

"Language!" Mase snapped and pointed to the swear jar.

"Take a breath and start again, Wyatt." Jay calmly plucked Wyatt's out of Ash's hand and looked it over. "It's a beautiful design and I know you want it to be perfect for our girl, so take your time. We'll be careful not to bump the table anymore, right, brothers?"

217

"Right," they all said.

"Don't read what I wrote inside." Wyatt lunged across the table, grabbed the card from Jay, and tore it up into little pieces. "Peri, can I have another piece of watercolor paper?"

"You bet."

I handed it to him and he immediately started again, his head bent and all his concentration on his painting.

He was always so cute when he did his artwork.

Looking over at the others, I saw Cole and Mason were making the most of my sticker collection, and Jay had picked a piece of paper that was its own design, making it easy for him. Ash, on the other hand—

"What are you doing?" I asked.

"Using this shiny shiiii— Um, stuff to decorate my card. Why?"

"Honey bunny, you have to use glue with glitter. Just dumping glitter on paper won't make it stick."

"Oh. Okay. You got glue?"

"Of course." I handed him a tube of liquid paste and a stick of solid. "Pick your poison."

He grabbed the liquid paste and began squirting it *on top* of the glitter pile he'd made on his card.

"Whoa! Stop that!" I jumped up and tore the glue tube out of his hand.

"What? You said you needed to use glue with it."

"You put the glue *first* in the shape you want, then sprinkle - not *dump* - the glitter on the glue. That way you don't waste the whole container of glitter. When the glue dries, you shake the extra glitter off," I explained, not understanding how he thought what he did was going to work.

"Well, what am I supposed to do with this mess?"

"Take a deep breath and start again," Wyatt mocked, not looking up from his work.

Ash gave him the bird, but he was too focused on his art to notice.

Looking in my paper pile for another piece of what Ash had picked out, I asked him to take his card over to the trash can.

"Ash, I'm done with my card," Jay said. "I'll get this for you so you can work on yours."

"Thanks, bro. I owe you one."

I watched as Jay carefully picked up the card, folded it so the glitter was more securely contained, and slowly began his trek around the table to get to the garbage can.

*Maybe I should get him to bring the can over here rather than carry the card over there—*

I didn't get any further with the thought before Mase turned his head and sneezed right as Jay walked by him.

"Oh. My. God. Dess." Ash whispered in amazement as glitter flew up in a cloud, then shrieked, "Do it again! Glitter bomb! Do it again! Again!"

"Uh-oh." Cole realized the *true* problem before the rest of us. "Duck and cover, everyone."

"AAAAHHH!"

Wyatt's angry scream made me cringe and cover my ears, especially as it went on and on. My eyes went right to his card and saw the issue. While the worst of the glitter had splattered up the front of Jay's t-shirt or hit the floor, the line of wet glue landed like a sparkly snake right across Wyatt's perfectly painted pansies.

"You bastards are doing it on purpose now! The flowers were just dry enough for me to start adding the fine details! Now I have to re-write that damn letter for the third time!"

"It was an accident, I swear," Jay told him.

"It was my fault," Mase said at the same time.

Wyatt clearly wasn't listening to either of them. As he stood with clenched fists and steam billowing from his nose and ears, I left to fetch the vacuum from the hall closet. Some might call it cowardice, but I wasn't getting paid to risk my life to calm that monster down.

I wasn't getting paid, period, and not only was I providing all the supplies and intelligence for this project, I now had an almighty mess to clean up. So I took my sweet time to get there, grab the thing, and tow it back.

*Good thing Ty talked us into waiting to get a new area rug for under the table,* Dove murmured, and I nodded in agreement.

When I walked into the dead-silent dining room, I saw Wyatt calmly seated in glorious solitude at the kitchen island, his paints and water cups around him, while his brothers sat at one end of the table, as far away from him - and the glitter mess - as they could get.

I raised an eyebrow at Cole when he met my eyes, and he shook his head, so I kept my mouth closed, plugged in the vacuum, and got to work. Most of the glitter came right up, then I went to Jay and ran the attachment over him. I would have offered him one of Ty's shirts to wear, but the vacuum did a great job sucking it up, so I left it alone.

As I cleaned up as much of the glitter as I could, Jay helped Ash make a new card, and Mase and Cole finished theirs. Wyatt's was dry by the time I came back from putting the vacuum away, and they proudly displayed their cards on the table for me to admire and praise them. Good sister that I was, I did so and they fist-bumped each other.

*Now for the hard part*, I told Dove, who wished me good luck.

"So, listen, we have one more person who needs to write his apology, then you guys can go home to your mate and send mine back to me." Turning toward Jay, I quietly and calmly asked, "Quartz, are you ready to come out and make your card?"

*I abso-fucking-lutely am **not** making a fucking card! And I'm not writing a motherfucking letter, either. I'm a fucking alpha wolf! Miss me with this human bullshit, bitches! And another thing—*

As Quartz continued his diatribe, Jay took out his wallet and dropped bill after bill into the swear jar. One hundred and forty-eight dollars later, Q ran out of profanities, and Jay had one ten left. He held it over the jar for a second, but his wolf stayed silent. He had just sat down and put the bill back in his wallet when Quartz let out a strangled howl.

*Give me a piece of white paper, Peri, and a box of markers! Jayden, do I have your permission to come out long enough to make this fucker?*

Standing up again, Jay dropped his last bill in the swear jar while I gathered up what Q had asked for.

"All right, boys, I'm letting him out," he told his brothers when he sat down. "And in case you can't tell, he's a wee bit irritated."

Wyatt snorted and Ash snickered, then we all went still and silent as Jay's eyes turned to gold. For ten tense minutes, the only sound was the squeak of markers as Quartz-in-Jay's-body drew a gray rabbit on the front of the card, and the only movement came when he held it out to me.

"Peri, you write what I say word for word," he demanded, "and don't make one damned mistake because I ain't drawing that shit over."

"Why don't you do it yourself?" Mase's tone was extra mild. "I know you can write, and it will mean more to Posy that way."

"Because my handwriting looks like a fucking toddler's!" He hurled the gray marker he'd been using across the room. "Damn it! This fucking sucks! Why should I—"

"The handwriting won't matter, I promise," I dared to interrupt, hoping to keep him from going off on another rant. Giving him a sweet smile, I added, "She loves you so much, Q. Will you please do this one little thing for her?"

"Fine," he muttered, laid the card on the table, and held out his hand. "Black pen."

I gave him one, and he grabbed it and went back to work. One laboriously written letter at a time, he composed his apology, and only the Goddess and Jay knew what he said in it, but he did it all by himself and that was what mattered.

Finally, he slammed back in his chair, threw the pen in the center of the table, and gave the reins to Jay without even being asked to. Jay was so startled by the abrupt changeover, he could only sit and blink for a minute.

"Sorry, Jay," I murmured. "I didn't know it would be so much."

"No, it's not your fault. Quartz is just Quartz and—"

"Oh, no, dear brother," I grinned, "I meant, you owe the swear jar another twenty-six dollars."

## 31: Can't Go Wrong with Flowers

*Jayden*

While Peri put our cards in envelopes, I linked Angelo to drive my SUV over. I chose to link *him* because he was already at our house, the betas weren't too happy with us at the moment, and the gammas and the witches were busy interrogating Landry at Matthew and Maria's house.

And no way was I bringing the parents into this if I didn't have to. I knew they'd hear about it sooner or later, but I preferred later.

*Sure, alpha,* Angelo linked right back. *Do you mind if I bring Reau along? He's getting antsy.*

*Yeah. And if you don't mind, can you go into our bedroom closet and grab the gray duffel bag on the right side? It's sitting on the floor just inside the door.*

*Okay?*

Hearing the question in his voice, I explained how the betas each kept a saddlebag of our clothes. The bags were designed especially for their wolves to carry in case we had an emergency. Since we'd shown up at Peri's in wolf form, she'd given us the shorts and t-shirts out of River's bag to wear.

*The gray duffel is full of replacement gear she can use to repack it,* I finished.

*Hey, that's a smart idea, especially for alphas Mason and Cole with their special needs in size,* he commented, then chuckled. *Just like my darling. Doing his laundry opened my eyes to how much bigger his pants are than mine.*

*Gelo, I don't need to know that his is bigger than yours,* I told him with a smirk.

*Why not? I'm secure enough in my own size to brag about his,* he laughed. *Anyway, Reau and I got the bag and we're in the car now. See you in ten.*

We helped Peri clean up and carry her supplies back where they belonged, and Wyatt washed the cups he'd used without even being asked to, and he *hated* washing dishes.

Soon, we heard a vehicle pull in the driveway followed by running footsteps, and Peri opened the front door before Thoreau could knock.

"Well, hello, sweetie!" she cooed. "Did you come to see me?"

"*Somebody* said you had a surprise for me!" He corrected his volume when she winced. "Oops! Sorry, pretty. Inside voice."

That's right. He called Peri pretty. He'd heard Ty call her sunshine and started to copy him, then Emerson had to explain that sunshine was Ty's special name for Peri. Thoreau then decided *he* needed to come up with one for her, too, and pretty was it.

He also called Ty gorgeous, but he couldn't pronounce it right and it came out as george-us, which made the beta blush, scowl, and laugh all at the same time. The first time we witnessed it, Wyatt nearly wet himself giggling, and Ash and I fell on the floor in tears.

*This boy is a gift of light to all of us,* Mase linked me and our brothers, then added darkly, *I should have killed his parents slower and more painfully for abusing and neglecting this precious soul.*

*What's done is done,* I told him, *and he's happy and safe with us now. That's what matters.*

"Oh, that's right!" Peri drew our attention as she grabbed Thoreau's hand. "Come on. I'll show you what we found."

As they skipped off, Angelo came into the house, dropped the duffel bag inside the door, and handed me my keys. When I asked if he wanted a ride home, he shook his head with a smile.

"Em ran in wolf form to the training center to get my truck. He's going to pick us up and take us home from here. Our baby says he's starving and needs his peabutter sammiches before he falls down and *dies*."

"Thanks for staying with Posy and helping us out," I said and shook his hand.

"You're welcome." He shook all our hands and only smirked a little. "Good luck, alphas."

"They're going to need it," Peri chimed in as she and Thoreau came back into the room.

Thoreau, holding a big plastic jar full of sticks and leaves, slowly and carefully walked up to Angelo.

*I think this is the first time I haven't seen Reau running*, Cole linked us, making us all chuckle.

"Papa, Papa, look!" he squealed. "Pretty and george-us said I can have it for the secret fort!"

*Papa?!* my brothers and I all linked at once.

*Yeah,* Angelo chuckled, *and just wait until you hear Mama Bubba come out of his mouth. Em didn't know whether to laugh or scold him or just accept it.*

"What do you have there, Reau?" Ash, of course, had to know.

"No, alpha. You were a bad boy. You don't get to see the praying mantis."

"Aw, but I like interesting bugs!" Ash's bottom lip popped out in a sad pout. "I *am* sorry, Reau, and I'm going to apologize to Posy as soon as we get home."

223

"Then that's a good boy. You want good boy pats or kisses?" Thoreau tilted his head, his beautiful eyes wide and innocent as he stared up at Ash.

"What's a good boy pat?" Wyatt asked me out of the side of his mouth.

I shrugged.

"I pat the top of your head," Thoreau said in a *duh* tone.

"I'm good, bud," Ash told him. "Your curls are looking great, by the way. You been taking care of them like I told you?"

A couple of days ago, Angelo had linked us in a panic. He was the only one at home and had been trying to brush Thoreau's hair, but it kept getting frizzier and frizzier. Ash carefully explained how curly hair was different and couldn't be brushed like straight hair.

"Yep! Wash once or twice a week with conditioner, then finger comb and air dry," Thoreau repeated. "Never brush, never blow dry."

"Good job." Angelo gave him 'good boy pats' and Thoreau beamed before going back to his bug. "Thanks again for the lesson, Alpha Ash. I would have ruined his hair otherwise."

"Well, when you're ready to get it cut, I'll take him to my barber. He knows how to do it."

"It has to be cut in a special way?"

Ash only nodded because Thoreau had relented and was now showing him the praying mantis, and Ash was as engrossed by it as the boy was.

"Yes," Peri answered for him. "One time, Mom tried to cut it like she does all the boys, and it was a disaster. You have to cut it the way the curl wants to go, not just across like you do with straight hair."

"Ah! I'll remember that." Angelo nodded.

"All right. Time to go," Wyatt grumbled. "Thanks, Periwinkle. We owe you one."

"Damn right you do, doofus." She reached up and patted his cheek.

"Two dollars in the swear jar, baby sister," he smirked as he went out the door.

"Thanks, Peri. We appreciate your help today. Let us know if you need *anything*." Mason gave her a meaningful look, and I made a mental note to ask him about that later.

"Yeah." Cole kissed the top of her head. "Thanks, sissy."

As I hugged her, I whispered in her ear to use the swear jar money for something she and Ty needed, then Ash grabbed her up in a bear hug and swung her around, making her giggle.

As we finally got on our way, Wyatt asked what we should do when we got home.

"I mean, we forgot to ask Peri, and I sure don't know. Do we all go in together or one at a time?"

"I'd say all together," Mase answered. "We all screwed up together."

"And when do we give her these cards?" Ash asked.

"On your date," I said. "Wait until you feel it's the right time and give it to her."

"You really think *I'm* going to know the right time?" Ash asked incredulously. "Dude, no. Just tell me when to give it to her."

"All right, if nothing else, give it to her when she first wakes up in the morning."

"Pull over, Jay!" Wyatt shouted suddenly.

"What? Why?" I slowed down and looked around to see if there was a problem.

"Flower shop! Flower shop!" Wyatt crowed and pointed to the shopping center on our right.

"Good call, Wy," Cole said, and Ash gave him a high-five.

So I put on the turn signal and wheeled into the lot. Once we were parked, we piled out and hustled our butts inside, anxious to get home to our girl.

#

*Ash*

"What should we get?" I asked as we walked towards the shop. "Each of us pick a bouquet or each of us pick individual flowers to make up one bouquet?"

"She deserves a whole bouquet from each of us," Wyatt said, pulling open the door and waving us ahead of him. "And grab a vase if yours doesn't come with one because I think we only have one at home."

We didn't dawdle with our selections, but we also took our time to think about what we were choosing and why. Jay got a mix of pink, white, and red roses. No brainer there.

Cole picked out an arrangement of sunflowers that he thought suited our girl's normally sunny disposition.

Mase cheated and Googled flowers that represented purity and innocence. Once he had a list of options, he went with pink and white lilies.

Wyatt hemmed and hawed before going with a mix of purple and white flowers since purple was her favorite color.

As for me, I'd seen what I wanted the second I walked in the shop.

There was a special display set up that featured little animals made out of carnations and set in a variety of charming containers. I

225

grinned as I reached for a little white doggy perched on a metal garden cart.

"I think you want that more for yourself," Wyatt teased.

"What? It's so cute!" I squealed. "She'll love it!"

Then I walked toward the register only to stop when I realized Jay was staring off into space with a heavy frown.

*Brother?* I linked him directly.

*Quartz does and doesn't want to get her flowers, too,* he explained in a dry tone. *You know how he is. If he can't kill a problem, he's lost with how to solve it, and he won't bow his head to anyone, except our mate.*

*Would it help if I gave him an alpha command?* I winced as soon as I said it. Quartz became even angrier and more stubborn when someone gave him orders. *Better idea! I could tell him **not** to get flowers. Use a little reverse psychology?*

*Hmm. We haven't tried that before, although Posy did to get him to the pet store. It worked for her, so let's try, but don't use your alpha voice. Not when he's this aggressive already and we're around humans.*

"Jay, what's taking so long? We're ready to check out," I said aloud.

"Q is still deciding."

"Quartz," I barked, "why don't you leave the flower-buying to humans? It's too hard for a wolf to figure out, and we don't need any more screw-ups today."

The growl that rumbled out of Jay's chest made the hair stand up on the back of my neck, and our brothers yipped and linked to ask what was wrong.

*Should have warned them, Ashy,* Sid snickered.

*Naw, makes it more believable for Q. I'm surprised he hasn't questioned why I'm acting out of character.*

*Too upset at himself to notice,* Sid suggested, and I nodded in agreement.

***I will pick flowers for my little mate!*** Quartz thundered.

*At least he didn't curse,* Jay said with a shrug.

Which was a good sign that he was calming down. For a brutal bastard, he was normally a very well-spoken wolf, but his language deteriorated with his temper.

"Fine!" I muttered, holding back a grin of triumph, and motioned for the others to head to the check-out.

We paid and headed back to Jay's SUV, where he handed off his purchases so he could drive. In addition to their own arrangements, Mase took charge of Jay's roses while Cole held a little terracotta pot of pansies.

I looked at it and snorted.

*Don't be jealous that mine's the best,* Quartz taunted with a smug smirk.

"What?!" I held up my doggy flower cart. "Mine's the most adorable thing ever! I mean, look at it!"

*Mine is her favorite flower, and it's alive, unlike all of yours. She'll still have mine next year this time while yours will be in the garbage can next week.*

"Oh, shut up!" I groaned.

*Your pouting only proves you know I'm right,* he chuckled darkly. *Now tell me how flower-buying is too difficult for a wolf.*

#

*Wyatt*

Tyler met us at our front door with a stony look on his face and River ablaze in his eyes.

"Where's our girl?" I asked. "Is she okay?"

"She fell asleep on the couch about twenty minutes ago."

"Ty—" Ash began, but he shook his head slowly, and Ash shut up.

"You are my alphas, my brothers-in-law, and my friends, so all I'm going to say is, fix this and fix it fast."

He narrowed his eyes at each of us as his wolf snarled with rage.

"And with the greatest respect, don't *ever* hurt my luna like this again."

To anyone who didn't know him, it probably looked ridiculous to see one young beta squaring up against five alphas, but Tyler had the heart of a lion. Hard as nails and twice as tough in a fight, he didn't go down easily, and he kept getting back up if he did. There was no quit in him, and that was *without* River in the equation. Once that wolf exploded, he was as brutal as Quartz.

*Maybe even more,* Granite said. *Q straight up kills. Riv likes to play with his victims.*

*Facts,* I agreed.

"Thank you for staying with her, Ty," Mase said simply.

Acknowledging him with a nod, Tyler shouldered his way past us and went out the door.

*Well, that went better than I expected,* I thought.

*And River didn't come out,* Granite agreed, *so that's good.*

*Very good.*

"Okay, what now?" Ash asked, tapping his vase of flowers with impatient fingers.

"Let's surround her with our bouquets," I suggested, "so she sees them as soon as she wakes up."

They all liked that idea, and we headed to the living room, where we came to a dead stop and stared at our sleeping beauty. Her eyes were a little puffy and the tip of her nose was red, and my heart clenched painfully.

I hated seeing the evidence of her crying. Not a single tear should ever fall from her beautiful blue eyes.

Mase, Cole, and Jay arranged their vases in a row on the side table behind the couch where she slept. Ash and I put ours on the coffee table in front of her, and Jay set Quartz's pot of pansies next to Ash's flower puppy.

*Did Quartz tell you to put it there?* I linked with a smirk. *He does realize this isn't a competition, doesn't he?*

***You** can ask that? You, for whom everything is a competition?* Jay shook his head. *You know he did.*

"Let's make sure to put our cards in our overnight bags so we don't forget or lose them," Mase said quietly. "I'll go pack mine and Posy's bags now while she's asleep, but link me as soon as she wakes up."

"Don't forget Mr. Nibbles," the rest of us whispered in sync, then grinned at each other.

"And a sun hat for her for tomorrow," Jay added. "Probably sun block, too, since some of the flea market is outside."

"Good idea." He nodded and trotted off upstairs while the rest of us kept watch over our angel.

"Which do you think is more likely to happen when she wakes up? Yelling or crying?" I muttered.

"What kind of question is that?" Cole hissed.

"I need to prepare myself if it's crying," I hissed back.

*Link so you don't wake her,* Jay told us, and we all nodded.

*Yelling bothers me more,* Ash admitted with a shiver. *I don't like getting yelled at.*

*Aw, I'm used to getting yelled at.* I shrugged. *Sure, it hurts coming from Posy, but it's just yelling. Tears, though? They kill me. I can't stand to see her cry.*

*None of us can,* Cole said, and we all nodded.

Silence fell between us, and we settled around her to wait for those big blue eyes to open - and hoped they wouldn't be filled with tears.

## 32: Making Up is Hard to Do

*Cole*

Our little mate began to stir, and her small fists stretched over her head.

"Mmm. Pine," she whispered with a smile and snuggled into her pillow more.

Shocked that she'd call *me* out over the others, I took a second to respond, and Ash wasn't having it.

"That's you, dude!" he said in a hushed yell, which was as close as he ever got to whispering. "Talk to her! Touch her!"

Shooting him an irritated look, I touched her jaw with my fingertips. She hummed in approval and leaned into my hand, and I cupped the whole side of her face in my palm.

"Posy?" I murmured. "Are you okay?"

Her eyes blinked a few times before they stayed open.

"Cole? You're really here?" She looked around and saw my brothers hovering anxiously around her. "You're all really here? You came back?"

"Of course we did, honey. We will always come home to you." With a soft smile, I stroked my thumb over her cheekbone. "You know why? Because you *are* our home."

"I'm sorry I got mad and yelled at you." She lowered her eyes. "I only ever lost my temper like that once before. It didn't end well then, either. I should have stayed calm and talked to you. Instead, I screamed at you and sent you away. I'm sorry."

"Oh, no, little flower." Mase grabbed her hands and pulled her into a sitting position. Then he took her chin in his hand and made her look up. "*You* don't apologize. We messed up. We deserved everything you said because you were right. In fact, there was a lot more truth you should have yelled at us."

"For example, you should have told us to trust you," Wyatt said next. "You knew what you were doing, and had Ariel there in case something went wrong. I even saw for myself that you were fine and in control. I shouldn't have doubted you."

"You also should have yelled at us for embarrassing you in front of the gammas and betas." Ash's sigh seemed to come from the depths of his soul. "That had to hurt, and we were wrong to do it."

"We are sorry about so many things that happened in that tiny span of time," I finished. "Everything fell apart so quickly, and it was entirely our fault. We're going to do our best to make it up to you and earn your forgiveness. We're also going to celebrate your achievement with a ton of surprises."

"I don't need—"

"We *want* to, sweetness." Jay sat down next to her and laid his hand on her knee. "And we're going to. Even if you can't forgive us right now, we want to do some things to give you back your happiness. It hurts our hearts so much to know we robbed you of that today."

"Let us pamper and spoil you a bit, little flower," Mase added. "We're not trying to buy your forgiveness. We want to give you our time and attention to show how much we love you. That's what Cole meant by surprises."

She looked around at all our faces with wide eyes, but remained silent. Had we missed something, or was she waiting to make sure we were done?

"We're okay again, right?" she said at last. "You're not mad at me for getting mad at you?"

She bit her bottom lip before continuing, making me moan silently. *I* should be the one doing that.

"Because I don't like this ... this upset between us. It makes me so sad and anxious, I feel sick. I don't want to do this again."

"Oh, baby," I said, laying my head in her lap, "we don't, either. This last hour or so has been absolutely horrible."

"I'm sorry!" She sank her hands in my hair and massaged my scalp. "It's my fault for making you feel that way. I—"

And she stopped herself. I felt her body tense under me and raised my head to look at her, but all I saw in her eyes was curiosity.

"What is it, cutie?" Wyatt asked, and I knew my brothers also recognized something had happened in her thought process.

"Ty explained the fawning response that some trauma survivors have after stress," she said slowly, "and I'm doing that right now. Huh. It's so ... odd to think about the way you're thinking, isn't it?"

We looked at each other, then slowly shook our heads.

"We know what the word fawning means, sweetness, but we've never heard of the fawning response you're talking about. Will you explain it?" Jay asked for all of us.

"Basically, to keep from being hurt again, trauma survivors like me and Ty will say or do anything to please the other person, usually agreeing with them even if we really disagree or know it's wrong. He said it starts as children because our caretaker is also our abuser, so we learn to try to please them to avoid pain."

When she paused for breath, I linked the boys that we needed to bring this up during our next session with Dr. York. They all agreed, then we listened in fascination as she continued.

"He also said it can lead to big problems later in life because we'll give up boundaries that we shouldn't. That's why he said to try to notice if I'm doing it and to stop myself if I can. I'm going to talk to Dr.

York about it next time. Oh, and I also want you to set up an appointment for Ty with him. Ty's worked hard to educate himself about his mental health, but I think now that he has a mate, he would be thankful to get some professional support."

"Oh, my love," Wyatt whispered, his eyes full of anguish. "Can I hold you?"

She looked at him as a gentle smile tilted her lips up.

"Yes, please!"

We moved aside a little so he could gather her up in his arms, and he held her like a baby as he walked back and forth, his face buried in her neck near her mate mark.

After a few minutes, when his sniffling stopped, he wiped his face with the front of his t-shirt, then linked us to ask who would like to hold her next.

We sorted out an order and passed her around with her consent, each of us hugging her and whispering in her ear, until finally she caught sight of the flowers and gasped.

"Are these all for *me*?"

"Yes, honey." I was the last one to hold her, and I was making the most of it. I wasn't going to put her down until she asked me to. "Do you want us to tell you who picked which, or do you want to try to guess?"

She clapped her hands and her eyes once more sparkled with happiness.

"Guess, of course!" she laughed. "What do I get if I'm right?"

"The same thing you'll get if you're wrong," Wyatt said with a wolfy grin. "Long, lingering kisses that usually end in a tangle of sweaty limbs, but we have a surprise planned for you, so you'll have to wait for that until tonight, cutie."

Sighing, Mase reached over and smacked his head, but not nearly as hard as usual. Probably because it was true.

Posy's pretty pink blush told us she caught his meaning, and her shy smile and demurely lowered eyes told us she wasn't opposed.

*Pressure's on you, Mase*, Wyatt linked with a waggle of his eyebrows. *Better rise to the occasion so you don't disappoint her.*

Mase shot him the bird behind Posy's back.

"What is it? What's my surprise?" she asked.

"If we told you, it wouldn't be a surprise, now would it?" Ash teased her. "Now try to guess which flowers are from who."

She got all of them right and made a big fuss over each bouquet, thanking us profusely with hugs and kisses, even though we told her that she didn't need to thank us for getting her make-up flowers after we screwed up.

After smelling Jay's roses, she told him he shouldn't have bought her any since he had nothing to apologize for. He just shrugged and told her he wanted to.

Then she asked who the pansies were from.

"Did you just buy an extra?"

"No, sweetness, there's one more person who wants to apologize."

Jay gave us a look, and we all nodded silently to show that we understood he was letting Quartz out for a minute.

"Posy," Quartz said in a grave, formal tone that made us hide our grins, "I owe you my deepest apologies. If I hadn't lost my temper, these idiots wouldn't have, either."

"Oh, Quartz," she mumbled before throwing herself in his arms, the lucky dog. "I forgive you."

After he released her and gave control back to Jay, she looked at each of us with a happy smile.

"I forgive all of you."

With sighs of relief, we passed her around again, this time with solemn thank yous and delicious little kisses. She ended up in Mase's arms, and he smiled down at her.

"And now, sweet little flower, you need to freshen up and put on one of your favorite outfits," he told her. "I've taken care of everything else."

"Why? What's going on?" She tilted her head, looking more adorable than Ash's flower puppy - and that thing was damn cute.

"I'm taking you on a date, baby," Mase said with the biggest grin I'd seen on his face in a long while.

The way her eyes widened and sparkled as rosy pink flushed her cheeks made us realize just how remiss we were to not follow up on our promises to take her out. In our defense, a lot of things had been going on this summer that we had no control over.

*But now it's time to fix that*, Topaz said with a wiggle, happy to see our mate happy. *I hope she likes* our *date, boss!*

*Oh, she will*, I grinned. *I'll make sure of that.*

Dear children,

If you are reading this, I died before I could explain anything to you, and for that I am sorry. A sad story poorly told on notebook paper will have to be explanation enough now.

Kendall Briggs was not my Goddess-given mate. We met at an alpha conference when I tagged along with my father, William Swift. At thirty, I was one of the oldest unmated females there, and Kendall the oldest unmated male at thirty-four. We chatted and found some common ground we thought we could build on, so we made an arrangement. We would be chosen mates with the understanding that we'd separate amicably if ever one of us found our true mate.

Kendall did not stand by that agreement. When James was four and Aiden three, emissaries from the king arrived at Green River, and among them was my true mate. Logan Everleigh wasn't an alpha or a beta, not a gamma or even a delta. He was a regular wolf, as he liked to call himself, but to me, he was everything I ever wanted in a mate.

When the emissaries left to return to the royal pack, I went with my mate and brought you boys along. I should have known then that Kendall was plotting something. If I hadn't been blinded by bliss, I would have realized that he'd never let his heirs leave Green River.

For three months, my mate and I lived in happiness and peace, visiting often with my family. Every day shone brighter, and I dared to dream we had the rest of our lives to spend together as a happy family. Logan loved you both, James and Aiden, as if you were his own sons. Posy, you would have been the apple of his eye, his little princess, if only he had lived to know you.

Unfortunately, Kendall destroyed everything. Before I was even sure that Posy slept under my heart, Kendall found us and killed Logan. He killed my mate in front of my eyes while James and Aiden were at school. He reported to King Magnus that he'd found the man who'd 'kidnapped' us, but was too late to save me from Logan's 'madness.' He faked my death so that my family wouldn't know to save me, then spun a tale for his pack to think I'd been taken by rogues.

In his ignorance of the truth, the king praised Kendall for his unrelenting dedication to finding us and offered him compensation for the 'atrocious crimes' committed by a member of the royal pack.

How ironic that Kendall was paid handsomely for killing my innocent mate and dragging us all back to Green River - or should I say, dragging us back to hell?

Children, I promise you, if I'd known what awaited us there, I would have slit all of our throats that very night. Ever since our return to this alpha house, I have tried to escape or at least contact my family for help, but every attempt has been punished with torture, starvation, and rape.

I don't know how much more my body can stand. I am only sorry to leave you behind, darlings. I'd stay and shield you until he beats the last breath from my body if I could, but I fear the sickness will end me before he can.

By now, I pray that you are free from the monster known as Kendall Briggs. If you are not, keep trying, my darlings. Try and try until you escape this wretched hell. If you cross the borders of his territory, head for my father's pack, Crystal Caverns. He and my family will protect you.

My loves, I am sorrier than words can say that I ruined your lives and caused you such suffering at the hands of that monster. I pray he meets an appropriate end for his atrocious crimes. Learn from your mother's mistakes, children, and wait for your true mate no matter how long it takes. It may be painful or embarrassing at times, but trust in the Goddess and await her gift.

I hope that all three of you know how very much I love you. May your futures be as bright or brighter than the one I dreamed for each of you.

Your loving mother

## *Family Trees*

### THE ALPHAS' SIDE

**Royal and Julia Price** AKA Papa and Mama
Former alpha and luna of Earthshine pack
<u>Children</u> (twins):
- Mason Andre, 21
- Willow Diane (deceased)

**Nathan Barlow** AKA Dad
Former alpha of Great Rocks pack
<u>Children</u> with Goddess-given mate and luna Kelly (deceased):
- Cole Nathaniel, 20
- Peri Eloise, 17
- Archer Graham, 15
<u>Children</u> with chosen mate Genevieve Black:
- William Paul, 5
- Winston Jack, 3

**Jay and Denise Carson** (both deceased)
Former alpha and luna of Moonset pack
<u>Children</u>:
- Jayden Ellis, 19
- Ash Loto Mitchell (adopted; Jay's nephew), 18

**Gabriel and Kristy Mitchell** (both deceased)
Former alpha and luna of Dark Woods pack
<u>Child</u>:
- Ash Loto, 18

**Genevieve Black** AKA Mom
Former luna of River Rapids pack
<u>Children</u> with Goddess-given mate and alpha Shawn (deceased):
- Wyatt Shawn, 18
- Wayne Andrew, 15
- Wade Vincent, 12
- Wesley Alec, 9
<u>Children</u> with chosen mate Nathan Barlow:
- William Paul, 5
- Winston Jack, 3

**POSY'S SIDE**
**(as known to date)**

**William Swift**
Former alpha of Crystal Caverns with luna Zora (deceased)
Children:
- Isaac (deceased)
- Aaron (deceased)
- Naomi (deceased)

  Isaac and Ginger Swift (deceased)
  Children:
    - Liam, 23
    - Camille, 19

    Liam and Leyly Swift
    Alpha and luna of Crystal Caverns
    Child:
      - Gage, 6 months

  Naomi
  Children with chosen mate Kendall Briggs, alpha of Green River (deceased):
    - James, 23
    - Aiden, 21
  Child with Goddess-given mate Logan Everleigh (deceased):
    - Posy, 18

End of Book Three

Printed in Great Britain
by Amazon

25797214R00135